KU-175-059

6 3

LAKE WOBEGON DAYS

Garrison Keillor is the bestselling author of *Lake Wobegon Days*, *Happy to be Here*, *Leaving Home*, *We Are Still Married*, *Radio Romance*, *The Book of Guys* and *Wobegon Boy*. He is the host of 'A Prairie Home Companion' on American public radio and a contributor to *Time* magazine. He lives in Wisconsin and New York City.

by the same author

HAPPY TO BE HERE
LEAVING HOME
WE ARE STILL MARRIED
RADIO ROMANCE
THE BOOK OF GUYS
WOBEGON BOY

for children

CAT, YOU BETTER COME HOME
THE OLD MAN WHO LOVED CHEESE
THE SANDY BOTTOM ORCHESTRA
(co-written with Jenny Lind Nilsson)

LAKE WOBEGON DAYS

GARRISON KEILLOR

faber and faber

LONDON · BOSTON

First published in the USA in 1985
by Viking Penguin Inc. New York
and simultaneously in Canada
by Penguin Books Canada Limited, Ontario

First published in Great Britain in 1986
by Faber and Faber Limited
3 Queen Square London WCIN 3AU
Paperback edition first published in 1989
This paperback edition first published in 1998

Photoset by Intype Ltd, London
Printed and bound in Great Britain by
Mackays of Chatham PLC, Chatham, Kent

All rights reserved

© Garrison Keillor, 1985
Portions of this book originally appeared in the *Atlantic Monthly*

Garrison Keillor is hereby identified as author of this
work in accordance with Section 77 of the Copyright,
Designs and Patents Act 1988

*This book is sold subject to the condition that it shall not,
by way of trade or otherwise, be lent, resold, hired out or
otherwise circulated without the publisher's prior consent in
any form of binding or cover other than that in which it is
published and without a similar condition including this
condition being imposed on the subsequent purchaser*

A CIP record for this book
is available from the British Library

ISBN 0–571–19417–6

2 4 6 8 10 9 7 5 3 1

PREFACE

In the spring of 1974, I got $6000 from the *New
Yorker* for writing a piece about the Grand Ole Opry,
the most money I had ever seen, and so my wife and
small son and I left home in St. Paul and got on the
Empire Builder and headed for San Francisco to visit
our friends, not knowing that this windfall would be
most of my earnings for the year. I had never been
west beyond Idaho, where I went to Bible conferences
in my youth. We got a Pullman compartment and
left Minneapolis late at night, awoke west of Fargo,
watched the prairie roll by as we ate a good breakfast
and lunch, and as the train headed into the northern

Rockies, I sat in the bar car and took out a couple of stories from my briefcase and worked on them, a successful American author who provided good things for his family. In Sand Point, Idaho, late the second night, close to where the Bible conferences took place, we derailed coming through a freight yard. The train had slowed to a crawl so none of us were hurt—our Pullman car simply screeched and swayed and bumped along the ties a little way—and we packed our suitcase and climbed out. We stood around a long time in the dark and got on an old bus that smelled of engine fumes, and headed for Portland, where we could catch the southbound Coast Starlight for San Francisco. My wife dozed next to me, the little boy lay across our laps and slept, and I sat and thought about the extravagance of this trip, the foolishness—one stroke of good luck, the Opry story, and I was blowing a big wad of the proceeds on what? *False luxury*, which was now derailed. The motive was good, to try to put a little life and color into a disappearing marriage, but I thought about the expense as we chugged across Washington, and the magnificence of the Columbia valley was lost on me, and reaching Portland at last, I made up my mind to finish up the new stories right away and sell both of them to the *New Yorker* and cut my losses. An hour later, I lost them both in the Portland train station.

I took my son to the men's room and set the briefcase down while we peed and washed our hands, and then we went to the cafeteria for breakfast. A few bites into the scrambled eggs I remembered the briefcase, went to get it and it was gone. We had an hour before the southbound arrived. We spent it looking in every trash basket in the station, outside the station, and for several blocks around. I was sure that the thief, finding nothing but manuscripts in the brief-case, would chuck it, and I kept telling him to, but he didn't chuck it where I could see it, and then our time was up and we climbed on the train. I felt so bad I didn't want to look out the window. I looked straight at the wall of our compartment, and as we rode south the two lost stories seemed funnier and funnier to me, the best work I had ever done in my life; I wept for them, and my misery somehow erased them from mind so that when I got out a pad of paper a couple hundred miles later, I couldn't re-create even a faint outline.

To make me feel better, we trooped up to the dining car and ordered steaks all around and Man-hattans for the grownups, which only made me worry about extravagance again, which now I was even less in a position to afford. By the time we got to San Francisco, the two stories loomed as two lost landmarks of American comic prose, a loss to the entire nation, and I was ready to go home.

Our California friends were sympathetic and encouraging, and so were my friends in Minnesota when we got home two weeks later. People always are encouraging about a terrible loss, so that some-times the loser would like to strangle them. People tell you about other writers who lost stories, Heming-way, Carlyle, great men who triumphed over misfor-tune—"You'll go on and write something even better," they say, not knowing how good those stories were. I still have the two three-by-five file cards on which, bumping along on the train, I wrote everything I could remember about the stories: one is entitled "Lucky Man" and the notes describe a man who feels fortunate despite terrible things that happen to him. Even now, looking at it, I faintly recall what a fine work it was. The other is entitled "Lake Wobegon Memoir," and the notes are sparse: "Clarence and Arlene Bunsen," "the runaway car," "Wednesday night prayer meeting," and "Legion club dance" are the extent of it. The lost story shone so brilliantly in dim memory that every new attempt at it looked pale and impoverished before I got to the first sentence.

I started a radio show in July, "A Prairie Home Companion," a live musical-variety show like the Opry. I struggled on as a writer, started a novel that stumbled along for a thousand pages and then tipped over dead. My wife and I split up in 1976. Somehow the radio show kept going, perhaps because I had no illusion that I was good at it, and I brought in Lake Wobegon as the home of a weekly monologue, hoping that one Saturday night, standing on stage, I would look into the lights and my lost story would come down the beam and land in my head. Eleven years later, I am still waiting for it.

It has been a good run and I'm a very lucky man, I think. One pretty good idea for gainful employment eleven years ago is still my livelihood, thanks to my longtime colleagues, Margaret Moos, William H. Kling, Lynne Cruise, and Richard ("Butch")

Thompson, all patrons of the lost cause of live radio, and other friends in and out of the business who gave me so much good advice. I am indebted to Kathryn Court, the editor of this book, and to my agent, Ellen Levine, and to a parade of others going back to my teachers George Hage, John Rogers, Deloyd Hochstetter, Fern Moehlenbrock, and Estelle Shaver. I'm grateful to them. All the same, I wish I hadn't lost that story in the Portland lavatory, and I am still waiting for it to come back. I believe it was a story given to me as in a dream, that if found and people heard it they might discover something they too were looking for all these years, and I foolishly forgot it while washing my hands and don't know what to do to get it back. Sometimes, standing in the wings, I feel that story brush against my face and think I'll remember it—maybe if I closed my eyes it would land on my shoulder like one of the Performing Gospel Birds. This book, while not nearly so fine, will have to suffice until it returns.

Dogs don't lie, and why should I?
Strangers come, they growl and bark.
They know their loved ones in the dark.
Now let me, by night or day,
Be just as full of truth as they.

HOME

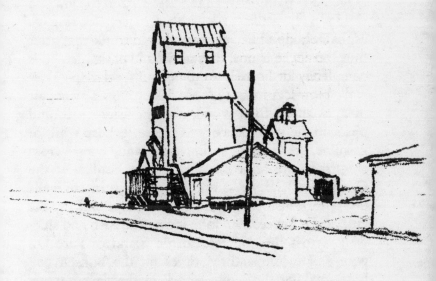

The town of Lake Wobegon, Minnesota,* lies on the shore against Adams Hill, looking east across the blue-green water to the dark woods. From the south, the highway aims for the lake, bends hard left by the magnificent concrete Grecian grain silos, and eases

---

*"Right on this road 0.7 *m.* to OLD WHITE BARN, then right 1.2 *m.* to LAKE WOBEGON (1418 alt., 942 pop.), named for the body of water that it borders. Bleakly typical of the prairie, Lake Wobegon has its origins in the utopian vision of nineteenth-century New England Transcendentalists but now is populated mainly by Norwegians and Ger-

over a leg of the hill past the SLOW CHILDREN sign, bringing the traveler in on Main Street toward the town's one traffic light, which is almost always green. A few surviving elms shade the street. Along the ragged dirt path between the asphalt and the grass, a child slowly walks to Ralph's Grocery, kicking an asphalt chunk ahead of him. It is a chunk that after four blocks he is now mesmerized by, to which he is completely dedicated. At Bunsen Motors, the sidewalk begins. A breeze off the lake brings a sweet air of mud and rotting wood, a slight fishy smell, and picks up the sweetness of old grease, a sharp whiff of gasoline, fresh tires, spring dust, and, from across the street, the faint essence of tuna hotdish at the Chatterbox Cafe. A stout figure in green coveralls disappears inside. The boy kicks the chunk at the curb, once, twice, then lofts it over the curb and sidewalk across the concrete to the island of Pure Oil pumps. He jumps three times on the Bunsen bell hose, making three dings back in the dark garage. The mayor of Lake Wobegon, Clint Bunsen, peers

---

mans who attend LAKE WOBEGON LUTHERAN CHURCH (left at BANK .1 *m*.) and OUR LADY OF PERPETUAL RESPONSIBILITY CHURCH (right at CHURCH .08 *m*.), neither of which are remarkable. The lake itself, blue-green and brightly sparkling in the brassy summer sun and neighbored by the warm-colored marsh grasses of a wildlife-teeming slough, is the town's main attraction, though the view is spoiled somewhat by a large GRAIN ELEVATOR by the railroad track.

North of town .3 *m*. is the junction with an oiled road."

—*Minnesota*, Federal Writers' Project (2nd edition, 1939)

out from the grease pit, under a black Ford pickup. His brother Clarence, wiping the showroom glass (BUNSEN MOTORS — FORD — NEW & USED — SALES & SERVICE) with an old blue shirt, knocks on the window. The showroom is empty. The boy follows the chunk a few doors north to Ralph's window, which displays a mournful cardboard pig, his body marked with the names of cuts. An old man sits on Ralph's bench, white hair as fine as spun glass poking out under his green feed cap, his grizzled chin on his skinny chest, snoozing, the afternoon sun now reaching under the faded brown canvas awning up to his belt. He is not Ralph. Ralph is the thin man in the white apron who has stepped out the back door of the store, away from the meat counter, to get a breath of fresh, meatless air. He stands on a rickety porch that looks across the lake, a stone's throw away. The beach there is stony; the sandy beach is two blocks to the north. A girl, perhaps one of his, stands on the diving dock, plugs her nose, and executes a perfect cannonball, and he hears the dull *thunsh*. A quarter-mile away, a silver boat sits off the weeds in Sunfish Bay, a man in a bright blue jacket waves his pole; the line is hooked on weeds.* The sun makes a trail of shimmering lights across the water. It would make quite a picture if you had the right lens, which nobody in this town has got.

---

*It is Dr. Nute, retired after forty odd years of dentistry, now free to ply the waters in the *Molar II* and drop a line where the fighting sunfish lie in wait. "Open wide," he says. "This may sting a little bit. Okay. Now bite down."

The lake is 678.2 acres, a little more than a section, fed by cold springs and drained from the southeast by a creek, the Lake Wobegon River, which flows to the Sauk which joins the Mississippi. In 1836, an Italian count waded up the creek, towing his canoe, and camped on the lake shore, where he imagined for a moment that he was the hero who had found the true headwaters of the Mississippi. Then something about the place made him decide he was wrong. He was right, we're not the headwaters, but what made him jump to that conclusion? What has made so many others look at us and think, *It doesn't start here!*?

The woods are red oak, maple, some spruce and pine, birch, alder, and thick brush, except where cows have been put, which is like a park. The municipal boundaries take in quite a bit of pasture and cropland, including wheat, corn, oats, and alfalfa, and also the homes of some nine hundred souls, most of them small white frame houses sitting forward on their lots and boasting large tidy vegetable gardens and modest lawns, many featuring cast-iron deer, small windmills, clothespoles and clotheslines, various plaster animals such as squirrels and lambs and small elephants, white painted rocks at the end of the driveway, a nice bed of petunias planted within a white tire, and some with a shrine in the rock garden, the Blessed Virgin standing, demure, her eyes averted, arms slightly extended, above the peonies and marigolds. In the garden behind the nunnery next door to Our Lady of Perpetual Responsibility, she stands on a brick pedestal, and her eyes meet yours with an expression of deep sympathy for the sufferings of the world, including this little town.

It is a quiet town, where much of the day you could stand in the middle of Main Street and not be in anyone's way—not forever, but for as long as a person would want to stand in the middle of a street. It's a wide street; the early Yankee promoters thought they would need it wide to handle the crush of traffic. The double white stripe is for show, as are the two parking meters. Two was all they could afford. They meant to buy more meters with the revenue, but nobody puts nickels in them because parking nearby is free. Parking is diagonal.

Merchants call it "downtown"; other people say "up town," two words, as in "I'm going up town to get me some socks."

On Main between Elm and McKinley stand four two-story brick buildings on the north side, six on the south, and the Central Building, three storys, which has sandstone blocks with carved scallops above the third-floor windows.* Buildings include the "Ingqvist

---

*The stone plaque on the facade fell off one hot July afternoon, the plaque that reads CENTRAL BLDG. 1913, and crashed on the sidewalk, almost hitting Bud Mueller, who had just stopped and turned to walk the other way. If he hadn't, he would have been killed. He didn't know why he had turned. "It was like something spoke to me right then," he said. Others realized then that *they* had been on the verge of walking by the Central Building moments before and something had spoken to them. "You know, I was thinking, 'Maybe I will go to Skoglund's and purchase a pencil,' but then something said, 'No, you wait on that,' so

5

Block," "Union Block," "Security Block," "Farmers Block," and "Oleson Block," their names carved in sandstone or granite tablets set in the fancy brickwork at the top. Latticed brickwork, brickwork meant to suggest battlements, and brick towers meant to look palatial. In 1889, they hung a man from a tower for stealing. He took it rather well. They were tired of him sneaking around lifting hardware off buggies, so they tied a rope to his belt and, hoisted him up where they could keep an eye on him.

Most men wear their belts low here, there being so many outstanding bellies, some big enough to have names of their own and be formally introduced. Those men don't suck them in or hide them in loose shirts; they let them hang free, they pat them, they stroke them as they stand around and talk. How could a man be so vain as to ignore this old friend who's been with him at the great moments of his life?

The buildings are quite proud in their false fronts, trying to be everything that two stories can be and a little bit more. The first stories have newer fronts of aluminum and fake marble and stucco and fiberglass stonework, meant to make them modern. A child might have cut them off a cornflakes box and fastened them with two tabs, A and B, and added the ladies leaving the Chatterbox Cafe from their tuna

---

I didn't go. If I had gone, it would've killed me," Mr. Berge said. He was one of many whose lives had been spared by a narrow margin. The plaque broke into five pieces, which Carl Krebsbach glued together, and it was remounted on the facade with a protective mesh to keep it in place.

sandwich lunch: three old ladies with wispy white hair, in sensible black shoes and long print dresses with the waist up under the bosom, and the fourth in a deep purple pant suit and purple pumps, wearing a jet-black wig. She too is seventy but looks like a thirty-four-year-old who led a very hard life. She is Carl Krebsbach's mother, Myrtle, who, they say, enjoys two pink Daiquiris every Friday night and between the first and second hums "Tiptoe Through the Tulips" and does a turn that won her First Prize in a Knights of Columbus talent show in 1936 at the Alhambra Ballroom. It burned to the ground in 1955. "Myrtle has a natural talent, you know," people have always told her, she says. "She had a chance to go on to Minneapolis." Perhaps she is still considering the offer.

Her husband Florian pulls his '66 Chevy into a space between two pickups in front of the Clinic. To look at his car, you'd think it was 1966 now, not 1985; it's so new, especially the backseat, which looks as if nobody ever sat there unless they were gift-wrapped. He is coming to see Dr. DeHaven about stomach pains that he thinks could be cancer, which he believes he has a tendency toward. Still, though he may be dying, he takes a minute to get a clean rag out of the trunk, soak it with gasoline, lift the hood, and wipe off the engine. He says she runs cooler when she's clean, and it's better if you don't let the dirt get baked on. Nineteen years old, she has only 42,000 miles on her, as he will tell you if you admire how new she looks. "Got her in '66. Just 42,000 miles on her." It may be odd that a man should be so proud of having not gone far, but not so odd in this town. Under his Trojan Seed Corn cap pulled down tight on his head is the face of a boy, and when he talks his voice breaks, as if he hasn't talked enough to get over adolescence completely. He has lived here all his life, time hardly exists for him, and when he looks at this street and when he sees his wife, he sees them brand-new, like this car. Later, driving the four blocks home at about trolling speed, having forgotten the misery of a rectal examination, he will notice a slight arrhythmic imperfection when the car idles, which he will spend an hour happily correcting.

In school we sang

> Hail to thee, Lake Wobegon, the cradle of our
> youth.
> We shall uphold the blue and gold in honor and in
> truth.
> Holding high our lamps, we will be thy champs,
> and will vanquish far and near
> For W.H.S., the beacon of the west, the school we
> love so dear.

And also

> We're going to fight, fight, fight for Wobegon
> And be strong and resolute,
> And our mighty foes will fall down in rows
> When we poke 'em in the snoot! (Rah! Rah!)

But those were only for show. In our hearts, our

loyalties to home have always been more modest, along the lines of the motto on the town crest— "*Sumus quod sumus*" (We are what we are)—and the annual Christmas toast of the Sons of Knute, "There's no place like home when you're not feeling well," first uttered by a long-ago Knute who missed the annual dinner dance due to a case of the trots, and even Mr. Diener's observation, "When you're around it all the time, you don't notice it so much." He said this after he tore out the wall between his living room and dining room, which he had not done before for fear that it was there for a reason. In the wall, he found the remains of a cat who had been missing for more than a year. The Dieners had not been getting full use of the dining room and had been silently blaming each other. "It's good to know that it wasn't us," he said.

In school and in church, we were called to high ideals such as truth and honor by someone perched on truth and hollering for us to come on up, but the truth was that we always fell short.* Every spring, the Thanatopsis Society sponsored a lecture in

---

*I grew up among slow talkers, men in particular, who dropped words a few at a time like beans in a hill, and when I got to Minneapolis, where people took a Lake Wobegon comma to mean the end of the story, I couldn't speak a whole sentence in company and was considered not too bright, so I enrolled in a speech course taught by Orville Sand, the founder of reflexive relaxology, a self-hypnotic technique that enabled a person to speak up to three hundred words per minute. He believed that slow speech deprives us of a great deal of thought by slowing down the

keeping with the will of the late Mrs. Bjornson, who founded the society as a *literary* society, and though they had long since evolved into a conversational society, the Thanatopsians were bound by the terms of her bequest to hire a lecturer once a year and listen. One year it was World Federalism (including a demonstration of conversational Esperanto), and then it was the benefits of a unicameral legislature, and in 1955, a man from the University came and gave us "The World of 1980" with slides of bubble-top houses, picture-phones, autogyro copter-cars, and floating factories harvesting tasty plankton from the sea. We sat and listened and clapped, but when the chairlady called for questions from the audience, what most of us wanted to know we didn't dare ask: "How much are you getting paid for this?"

Left to our own devices, we Wobegonians go straight for the small potatoes. Majestic doesn't appeal to us; we like the Grand Canyon better with Clarence and Arlene parked in front of it, smiling. We feel uneasy at momentous events.

---

mental processes to one's word rate. He believed that the mind has unlimited powers if only a person could learn to release them and eliminate the backup caused by slow discharge. I *believe* that's what he said—it was hard to understand him. He'd be rattling on about relaxology one moment and then he was into photography, his father, the Baltimore Orioles, wheat germ, birth and death, central heating, the orgasm—which was satisfying for him, but which left me in the dust, so I quit, having only gotten up to about eighty-five. And after a few weeks, I was back to about ten or eleven.

Home

Lake Wobegon babies are born in a hospital thirty-some miles away and held at the glass by a nurse named Betty who has worked there for three hundred years—then it's a long drive home for the new father in the small morning hours, and when he arrives, he is full of thought. His life has taken a permanent turn toward rectitude and sobriety and a decent regard for the sanctity of life; having seen his flesh in a layette, he wants to talk about some deep truths he has discovered in the past few hours to his own parents, who have sat up in their pajamas, waiting for word about the baby's name and weight. Then they want to go to bed.

Lake Wobegon people die in those hospitals, unless they are quick about it, and their relations drive to sit with them. When Grandma died, she had been unconscious for three days. She was baking bread at Aunt Flo's and felt tired, then lay down for a nap and didn't wake up. An ambulance took her to the hospital. She lay asleep, so pale, so thin. It was August. We held cool washcloths to her forehead and moistened her lips with ice cubes. A nun leaned over and said in her ear, "Do you love Jesus?" We thought this might lead to something Catholic, involving incense and candles; we told her that, yes, she did love Jesus. Eight of us sat around the bed that first afternoon, taking turns holding Grandma's hand so that if she had any sensation, it would be one of love. Four more came that evening. We talked in whispers, but didn't talk much; it was hard to know what to say. "Mother always said she wanted to go in her sleep," my mother said. "She didn't want to linger." I felt that we should be saying profound things about Grandma's life and what it had meant to each of us, but I didn't know how to say that we should. My uncles were uneasy. The women saw to Grandma and wept a little now and then, a few friendly tears; the men only sat and crossed and uncrossed their legs, slowly perishing of profound truth, until they began to whisper among themselves—I heard gas mileage mentioned, and a new combine—and then they resumed their normal voices. "I wouldn't drive a Fairlane if you give it to me for nothing," Uncle Frank said. "They are nothing but grief." At the time (twenty), I thought they were crude and heartless, but now that I know myself a little better, I can forgive them for wanting to get back onto familiar ground. *Sumus quod sumus*. She was eighty-two. Her life was in all of us in the room. Nobody needed to be told that, except me, and now I've told myself.

Incorporated under the laws of Minnesota but omitted from the map due to the incompetence of surveyors, first named "New Albion" by New Englanders who thought it would become the Boston of the west, taking its ultimate name from an Indian phrase that means either "Here we are!" or "we sat all day in the rain waiting for [you]," Lake Wobegon is the seat of tiny Mist County, the "phantom county in the heart of the heartland" (Dibbley, *My Minnesota*), founded by Unitarian missionaries and Yankee promoters, then found by Norwegian Lutherans who straggled in from the west, having headed first to Lake Agassiz in what is now North Dakota, a lake that turned out to be prehistoric, and by German Catholics, who, bound for Clay County, had stopped a little short, having misread their map, but refused to admit it.

A town with few scenic wonders such as towering pines or high mountains but with some fine people of whom some are over six feet tall, its highest point is the gold ball on the flagpole atop the Norge Co-op grain elevator south of town on the Great Northern spur, from which Mr. Tollefson can see all of Mist County when he climbs up to raise the flag on national holidays, including Norwegian Independence Day, when the blue cross of Norway is flown. (No flag of Germany has appeared in public since 1917). Next highest is the water tower, then the boulder on the hill, followed by the cross on the spire of Our Lady, then the spire of Lake Wobegon Lutheran (Christian Synod), the Central Building (three stories), the high school flagpole, the high school, the top row of bleachers at Wally ("Old Hard Hands") Bunsen Memorial Field, the First Ingqvist State Bank, Bunsen Motors, the Hjalmar Ingqvist home, etc.

I've been to the top only once, in 1958, when six of us boys broke into the Co-op one July night to take turns riding the bucket to the tiny window at the peak of the elevator. It was pitch-black in there and stifling hot, I was choking on grain dust, the motor whined and the rope groaned, and up I rode, terrified and hanging onto the bucket for dear life—it was shallow, like a wheelbarrow, and pitched back and forth so I knew I'd fall into the black and break my neck. All the way up I promised God that if He would bring me safely back to the floor, I would never touch alcohol—then suddenly I was at the window and could see faintly through the dusty glass some lights below that I knew were Lake Wobegon. The bucket swayed, I reached out for the wall to steady it, but the wall wasn't where it should have been and the bucket swung back and I fell forward in one sickening moment; out of my mouth came an animal shriek that almost tore my face off, then I felt the cable in my left hand and the bucket swung back to level, then they released the brake and the bucket fell twenty or fifty or a hundred feet before they threw the brake back on, which almost broke my back, then they cranked me down the rest of the way and lifted me out and I threw up. Nobody cared, they were all crying. Jim put his arms around me and I staggered out into the night, which smelled so good. We went to someone's house and lay on the grass, looked at the stars, and drank beer. I drank four bottles.

Right then I guess was when I loved Lake Wobegon the most, the night I didn't quite die. I turned sixteen the next week and never told my parents what a miraculous birthday it was. I looked around the table and imagined them eating this pork roast and potato salad with me gone to the graveyard, imagined the darkness in the tight box and the tufted satin quilt on my cold face, and almost burst into tears of sheer gratitude, but took another helping of pork instead. Our family always was known for its great reserve.

We climbed the water tower, of course, but spent

more time on the third highest point, Adams Hill, which rose behind the school and commanded a panoramic view of town and lake from the clearing at the crest. As a small boy who listened carefully and came to his own conclusions, I assumed that the hill was where God created our first parents, the man from the dust in the hole where we built fires, the lady from his rib. They lived there for many years in a log cabin like Lincoln's and ate blueberries and sweet corn from the Tolleruds' field. Adam fished for sunnies off the point, and their kids fooled around like we did, Eve sometimes poking her head out the door and telling them to pipe down.

There was no apple tree on Adams Hill, but that didn't weaken my faith; there were snakes. Here, above the school, God created the world.

When I was four, I told my sister about the Creation, and she laughed in my face. She was eight. She gave me a choice between going back on Scripture truth as I knew it or eating dirt, and I ate a pinch of dirt. "Chew it," she said, and I did so she could hear it crunch.

There, for years, to the peak of Paradise, we resorted every day, the old gang. Nobody said, "Let's go"; we just went. Lance was the captain. Rotting trees that lay in the clearing were our barricades, and we propped up limbs for cannons. The boulder was the command post. We sat in the weeds, decked out in commando wear—neckerchiefs and extra belts slung over our shoulders for ammo and Lance even had a canteen in a khaki cover and a khaki satchel marked *U.S.A.*—and we looked down the slope to the roofs of town, which sometimes were German landing boats pulled up on the beach, and other times were houses of despicable white settlers who had violated the Sacred Hunting Ground of us Chippewa. We sent volleys of flaming arrows down on them and burned them to the ground many times, or we pounded the boats with tons of deadly shells, some of us dying briefly in the hot sun. "Aiiiiieeee!" we cried when it was time to die, and pitched forward, holding our throats. There were no last words. We were killed instantly.

Near the clearing was a giant tree we called the Pee Tree; a long rope hung from a lower branch, which when you swung hard on it took you out over the edge and showed you your real death. You could let go at the end of the arc and fall to the rocks and die if you wanted to.

Jim said, "It's not that far—it wouldn't kill you." He was bucking for captain. Lance said, "So jump then. I dare you." That settled it. It would kill you, all right. It would break every bone in your body, just like Richard. He was twelve and drove his dad's tractor and fell off and it ran over him and killed him. He was one boy who died when I was a boy, and the other was Paulie who drowned in the lake. Both were now in heaven with God where they were happy. It was God's will that it would happen.

"It was an accident, God didn't make it happen, God doesn't go around murdering people," Jim said. I explained that, maybe so, but God *knows* everything that will happen. He has known every single thing since time began, and everything that happens is part of God's plan.

"Does He know that I'm just about to hit you?" Jim said.

"Everything."

"What if I changed my mind at the last minute and didn't?"

"He knows everything."

Jim believed that God sort of generally watched over the world but didn't try to oversee every single detail. He said that, for example, when you're born, you could be born American *or* Chinese or Russian or African, depending. In heaven are millions of souls lined up waiting to be born, and when it's your turn, you go down the chute like a gumball to whoever put the penny in the slot. You were born to your parents because, right at that moment when they Did It, you were next in line. Two seconds later and you could have been a feeb. Or a Communist. "It's just pure luck we're Americans," he said.

When it was hot, we all lay around in the grass and talked about stuff. At least, if you were older, you could talk. Little kids had to shut up because they didn't know anything. Jim leaned on one elbow and tore off tufts of grass and threw them at my face. I told him twice to quit it. He said, "Tell God to make me quit it. It's God's plan. He knew that I was going to do it. It's not my fault." He said, "If you think God planned you, then He made a big mistake, because you're the dumbest person I know."

I was on top of him before he could blink and pounded him twice before he wriggled out and got

me in an armlock and shoved my face into the dirt.
Then Lance broke us up. We sat and glared at each
other. We fought once more, and went home to
supper.

I lived in a white house with Mother, Dad, Rudy,
Phyllis, and we raised vegetables in the garden and
ate certain things on the correct nights (macaroni
hotdish on Thursday, liver on Friday, beans and
wieners on Saturday, pot roast on Sunday) and sang
as we washed dishes:

> Because God made the stars to shine,
> Because God made the ivy twine,
> Because God made the sky so blue.
> Because God made you, that's why I love you.

God created the world and ordained everything to
be right and perfect, then man sinned against God's
Will, but God still knew *everything*. Before the world
was made, when it was only darkness and mist and
waters, God was well aware of Lake Wobegon, my
family, our house, and He had me all sketched out
down to what size my feet would be (big), which bike
I would ride (a Schwinn), and the five ears of corn I'd
eat for supper that night. He had meant me to be
there; it was His Will, which it was up to me to
discover the rest of and obey, but the first part—
being me, in Lake Wobegon—He had brought about
as He had hung the stars and decided on blue for the
sky.

The crisis came years later when Dad mentioned
that in 1938 he and Mother had almost moved to
Brooklyn Park, north of Minneapolis, but didn't

because Grandpa offered them our house in Lake Wobegon, which was Aunt Becky's until she died and left it to Grandpa, and Dad got a job with the post office as a rural mail carrier. I was fourteen when I got this devastating news: that I was me and had my friends and lived in my house only on account of a pretty casual decision about real estate, otherwise I'd have been a Brooklyn Park kid where I didn't know a soul. I imagined Dad and Mother talking it over in 1938—"Oh, I don't care, it's up to you, either one is okay with me"—as my life hung in the balance. Thank goodness God was at work, I thought, because you sure couldn't trust your parents to do the right thing.

Until it became a suburb, Brooklyn Park was some of the best farmland in Minnesota, but Lake Wobegon is mostly poor sandy soil, and every spring the earth heaves up a new crop of rocks.* Piles of rock ten feet high in the corners of fields, picked by generations of us, monuments to our industry. Our ancestors chose the place, tired from their long journey,

---

*Though unpromising for agriculture, the Lake Wobegon area is beloved among geologists for the diversity of its topography, lying within the Bowlus Moraine left by the retreat of the Western Lobe of the Superior Glacier and including the St. John's Drumlin Field of pale brown sandy till featuring numerous Precambrian rocks and pebbles that come to the surface in the spring. Certain plutonic rocks, mainly granite, appear in outcroppings, while some metamorphic minerals such as garnet and anchorite crystals have been found, but not enough to make much difference. Had the Superior Glacier moved slower twenty thousand

sad for having left the motherland behind, and this place reminded them of there, so they settled here, forgetting that they had left there because the land wasn't so good. So the new life turned out to be a lot like the old, except the winters are worse.

Since arriving in the New World, the good people of Lake Wobegon have been skeptical of progress. When the first automobile chugged into town, driven by the Ingqvist twins, the crowd's interest was muted, less whole-hearted than if there had been a good fire. When the first strains of music wafted from a radio, people said, "I don't know." Of course, the skeptics gave in and got one themselves. But the truth is, we still don't know.

For this reason, it's a hard place to live in from the age of fourteen on up to whenever you recover. At that age, you're no skeptic but a true believer starting with belief in yourself as a natural phenomenon never before seen on this earth and therefore incomprehensible to all the others. You believe that if God were to make you a millionaire and an idol whose views on the world were eagerly sought by millions, that it would be no more than what you deserved. This belief is not encouraged there.

---

years ago, permitting the Moorhead Glacier to race eastward with its valuable load of shale-rich soil, Lake Wobegon's history would be much brighter than it is. Adding insult to injury, geologists now point out that the town lies in a major fault zone, where deep-seated forces may one day with no warning send us running in terror from our beds.

Home

Sister Brunnhilde was coaching a Krebsbach on his catechism one morning in Our Lady lunchroom and suddenly asked a question out of order. "Why did God make you?" she said sharply, as if it were an accusation. The boy opened his mouth, wavered, then looked at a spot on the linoleum and put his breakfast there. He ran to the lavatory, and Sister, after a moment's thought, strolled down the hall to the fifth-grade classroom. "Who wants to be a nurse when she grows up?" she asked. Six girls raised their hands, and she picked Betty Diener. "Nurses help sick people in many different ways," she told Betty as they walked to the lunchroom. "They have many different jobs to do. Now here is one of them. The mop is in the kitchen. Be sure to use plenty of Pine-Sol."

So most of Lake Wobegon's children leave, as I did, to realize themselves as finer persons than they were allowed to be at home.

When I was a child, I figured out that I was

1 person, the son of
2 parents and was the
3rd child, born
4 years after my sister and
5 years after my brother, in
1942 (four and two are 6), on the
7th day of the
8th month, and the year before
had been 9 years old and
was now 10.

To me, it spelled Destiny.

When I was twelve, I had myself crowned King of Altrusia and took the royal rubber-tipped baton and was pulled by my Altrusian people in a red wagon to the royal woods and was adored all afternoon, though it was a hot one—they didn't complain or think the honor should have gone to them. They hesitated a moment when I got in the wagon, but then I said, "Forward!" and they saw there can be only one Vincent the First and that it was me. And when I stood on the royal stump and blessed them in the sacred Altrusian tongue, "Aroo-aroo halama rama domino, shadrach meshach abednego," and Duane laughed, and I told him to die, he did. And when I turned and marched away, I knew they were following me.

When I was fourteen, something happened and they didn't adore me so much.

I ran a constant low fever waiting for my ride to come and take me away to something finer. I lay in bed at night, watching the red beacon on top of the water tower, a clear signal to me of the beauty and mystery of a life that waited for me far away, and thought of Housman's poem,

> Loveliest of trees, the cherry now
> Is hung with bloom along the bough.
> It stands among the woodland ride,
> Wearing white for Eastertide.
> Now, of my three-score years and ten,
> Twenty will not come again. . . .

and would have run away to where people would appreciate me, had I known of such a place, had I thought my parents would understand. But if I had said, "Along the woodland I must go to see the cherry hung with snow," they would have said, "Oh, no, you don't. You're going to stay right here and finish up what I told you to do three hours ago. Besides, those aren't cherry trees, those are crab apples."

Now I lie in bed in St. Paul and look at the moon, which reminds me of the one over Lake Wobegon.

I'm forty-three years old. I haven't lived there for twenty-five years. I've lived in a series of eleven apartments and three houses, most within a few miles of each other in St. Paul and Minneapolis. Every couple years the urge strikes, to pack the books and unscrew the table legs and haul off to a new site. The mail is forwarded, sometimes from a house several stops back down the lines, the front of the envelope covered with addresses, but friends are lost—more all the time, it's sad to think about it. All those long conversations in vanished kitchens when for an evening we achieved a perfect understanding that, no matter what happened, we were true comrades and our affection would endure, and now our friendship is gone to pieces and I can't account for it. *Why don't I see you anymore? Did I disappoint you? Did you call me one night to say you were in trouble and hear a tone in my voice that made you say you were just fine?*

When I left Lake Wobegon, Donna Bunsen and I promised each other we'd read the same books that summer as a token of our love, which we sealed with a kiss in her basement. She wore white shorts and a blue blouse with white stars. She poured a cup of Clorox bleach in the washing machine, and then we kissed. In books, men and women "embraced passionately," but I didn't know how much passion to use, so I put my arms around her and held my lips to hers and rubbed her lovely back, under the wings. Our reading list was ten books, five picked by her and five by me, and we made a reading schedule so that, although apart, we would have the same things on our minds at the same time and would think of each other. We each picked the loftiest books we knew of, such as Plato's *Republic, War and Peace, The Imitation of Christ*, the *Bhagavad-Gita, The Art of Loving*, to have great thoughts to share all summer as we read, but I didn't get far; my copy of Plato sat in my suitcase, and I fished it out only to feel guilty for letting her down so badly. I wrote her a letter about love, studded with Plato quotes picked out of Bartlett's, but didn't mail it, it was so shameless and false. She sent me two postcards from the Black Hills, and in the second she asked, "Do you still love me?" I did, but evidently not enough to read those books and become someone worthy of love, so I didn't reply. Two years later she married a guy who sold steel supermarket shelving, and they moved to San Diego. I think of her lovingly every time I use Clorox. Half a cup is enough to bring it all back.

When I left Lake Wobegon, I packed a box of books, two boxes of clothes, and two grocery sacks of miscellaneous, climbed in my 1956 Ford, and then, when my old black dog Buster came limping out from under the porch, I opened the door and boosted him into the back seat. He had arthritic hips and was almost blind, and as Dad said, it would be better to leave him die at home, but he loved to go for rides and I couldn't see making the long trip to Minneapolis alone. I had no prospects there except a spare bed in the basement of my dad's old Army buddy Bob's house. Buster was company, at least.

Bob had two dogs of his own, a bulldog named Max and a purebred Irish setter who owned the upstairs and the yard, so Buster spent his declining months on a blanket in Bob's rec room, by my bed. Bob kept telling me that Buster should be put out of his misery, but I had too much misery of my own to take care of his. Instead of shooting him, I wrote poems about him.

Old dog, old dog, come and lay your old head
On my knee.
Dear God, dear God, let this poor creature go
And live in peace.

Bob kept telling me to forget about college and he would line me up with a friend of his in the plumbers' union. "Why be so odd?" he said. "Plumbers get good money." His son Dallas was in the Air Force, stationed in Nevada, and he liked it a lot. "Why not the Air Force?" Bob asked. One day, he said, "You know what your problem is?" I said I didn't. "You don't get along with other people. You don't make an effort to get along." How could I explain the duty I felt to keep a dying dog company? A dog who had been so close to me since I was a little kid and who understood me better than anyone. I had to leave him alone when I went looking for work, and then while I was working at the Longfellow Hotel as a dishwasher, so when I got back to Bob's, I liked to give Buster some attention.

Bob remembered the war fondly and had many photographs from his days with my dad at Camp Lee and then in a linen-supply unit of the Quartermaster Corps, stationed at Governor's Island in New York City, which he showed me after supper when I was trapped at the table. "People were swell to us, they invited us into their homes, they fed us meals, they treated us like heroes," he said. "Of course, the real heroes were the guys in Europe, but it could've been us instead of them, so it was okay. You wore the uniform, people looked up to you. Those were different times. There were a lot of pride then, a lot of pride."

Clearly I was a sign of how far the country had gone downhill: an eighteen-year-old kid with no future, sleeping in the basement with a dying dog. Bob left Air Force brochures on the breakfast table, hoping I'd read them and something would click. One August morning, when a postcard arrived from the University saying I'd been accepted for fall quarter, he warned me against certain people I would find there, atheists and lefties and the sort of men who like to put their arms around young guys. "I'm not saying you have those tendencies," he said, "but it's been my experience that guys like you, who think you're better than other people, have a lot of weaknesses that you don't find out about until it's too late. I just wish you'd listen, that's all. But you're going to have to find out the hard way, I guess."

Buster died in his sleep a few days later. He was cold in the morning. I packed him in an apple crate and snuck him out to my car and buried him in the woods by the Mississippi in Lilydale, which was like the woods he had known in his youth.

I felt as bad that night as I've ever felt, I think. I lay on the army cot and stared at the joists and let the tears run off my face like rain. Bob sent his wife, Luanne, down with some supper. "Oh, for crying out loud," she said. "Why don't you grow up?"

"Okay," I said, "I will." I moved out, into a rooming house on the West Bank. I lived in a 12 × 12 room with three bunkbeds and five roommates and started school. School was okay, but I missed that old dog a lot. He was a good dog to know. He was steadfast, of course, as all dogs are, and let nothing come between us or dim his foolish affection for me. Even after his arthritis got bad, he still struggled to his feet when I came home and staggered toward me, his rear end swung halfway forward, tail waving, as he had done since I was six. I seemed to fulfill his life in some way, and even more so in his dotage than in bygone days when he could chase rabbits. He was so excited to see me, and I missed that; I certainly didn't excite anyone else.

More than his pure affection, however, I missed mine for him, which now had nowhere to go. I made the rounds of classes and did my time in the library every day, planted myself in oak chairs and turned pages, and sorely missed having someone to put my arms around, some other flesh, some hair to touch other than my own. And I missed his call to fidelity. My old black mutt reminded me of a whole long string of allegiances and loyalties, which school seemed to be trying to jiggle me free of. My humanities instructor, for example, who sounded to be from someplace east of the East, had a talent for saying "Minnesota" as if it were "moose turds," and we all snickered when he did. You don't pull that sort of crap around a dog. Dogs have a way of bringing you back to earth. Their affection shames pretense. They are guileless.

I needed Buster to be true to and thus be true by implication to much more, to the very principle of loyalty itself, which I was losing rapidly in Minneapolis. Once I saw Ronald Eichen in Gray's Drug near campus, my old classmate who twice lent me his '48 Ford now sweeping Gray's floor, and because our friendship no longer fit into my plans, I ducked down behind the paperbacks and snuck out. I was redesigning myself and didn't care to be the person he knew.

I couldn't afford to buy new clothes at Al Johnson, Men's Clothier, so I tried out a Continental accent on strange girls at Bridgeman's lunch counter: "Gud morrning. Mind eef I seat next to you? Ahh! ze greel shees! I zink I hef that and ze shicken soup. Ah, *pardon*—my name ees Ramon. Ramon Day-Bwah." This puzzled most of the girls I talked to, who wondered where I was from. "Fransh? *Non*. My muthaire she vas Fransh but my fathaire come from Eetaly, so? How do you say? I am *internationale*." I

explained that my fathaire wass a deeplo*mat* and we
traffled efferyvhere, which didn't satisfy them either,
but then my purpose was to satisfy myself and that
was easy. I was *foreign*. I didn't care when I was from
so long as it was someplace else.

A faint English accent was easier to manage, at
least on Mondays, Wednesdays, and Fridays. My
composition instructor, Mr. Staples, was English,
and an hour in the morning listening to him primed
the pump and I could talk like him the rest of the day.
Englishness, however, didn't free my spirit so well as
being truly foreign did. Mr. Staples smelled musty,
walked flat-footed, had dry thin hair, and went in for
understatement to the point of blending in with his
desk. European was a better deal. If I could be European, I'd be right where I wanted to be as a person.

I invented new people for the ones I knew, trying
to make them more interesting. At various times, my
father was a bank robber, a college professor, the
President of the United States, and sometimes I
imagined that we weren't really from Minnesota, we
were only using it as a cover, disguising ourselves as
quiet modest people until we could reveal our true
identity as Italians. One day, my mother would put
the wieners on the table and suddenly my father
would jump up and say, "Hey! I'ma sicka this
stuffa!" She'd yell, "No! No! Chonny! Please-a! The
children!" But the cat was out of the bag. We weren't
who we thought we were, we were The Keillorinis!
Presto! Prestone! My father rushed to the closet and
hauled out giant oil paintings of fat ladies, statues of
saints, bottles of wine, and in rushed the relatives,

hollering and carrying platters of spicy spaghetti, and my father would turn to me and say, "Eduardo! Eduardo, my son!" and throw his arms around me and plant big wet smackers on my cheeks. *Caramba!* Then we would dance, hands over our heads. *Aye-yi-yi-yi-yi!* Dancing, so long forbidden to us by grim theology of tight-lipped English Puritans—dancing, the language of our souls—*Mamma mia!* Now that's *amore! Viva, viva!* Do the Motorola!

I went home for Christmas and gave books for presents, Mother got *Walden*, Dad got Dostoevsky. I smoked a cigarette in my bedroom, exhaling into an electric fan in the open window. I smoked another at the Chatterbox. I wore a corduroy sportcoat with leather patches on the elbows. Mr. Thorvaldson sat down by me. "So. What is it they teach you down there?" he said. I ticked off the courses I took that fall. "No, I mean what are you learning?" he said. "Now, 'Humanities in the Modern World,' for example? What's that about?" I said, "Well, it covers a lot of ground, I don't think I could explain it in a couple of minutes." "That's okay," he said, "I got all afternoon."

I told him about work instead. My job at the Longfellow was washing dishes for the three hundred young women who lived there, who were the age of my older sister who used to jump up from dinner and clear the table as we boys sat and discussed dessert. The three hundred jumped up and shoved their trays through a hole in the wall where I, in the scullery, worked like a slave. I grabbed up plates, saucers, bowls, cups, silverware, glasses, passed them under a hot rinse, the garbage disposal grinding away, and slammed them into racks that I heaved onto the conveyor that bore them slowly, sedately, through the curtain of rubber ribbons to their bath. Clouds of steam from the dishwasher filled the room when the going got heavy. Every rack that emerged released a billow of steam, and I heaved the racks onto a steel counter to dry for a minute, then yanked the hot china and stacked it on a cloth for the servers to haul to the steam table. We had less china than customers, and since they all wanted to eat breakfast at seven o'clock, there was a pinch in the china flow about seven-fifteen, when I had to work magic and run china from trays to racks to steam table in about sixty seconds, then make a pass through the dining room grabbing up empty juice glasses because the glass pinch was next, and then the lull when I mopped up and waited for the dawdlers, and finally my own rush to nine o'clock class, American Government.

The soap powder was pungent pink stuff; it burned my nostrils when I poured it in the machine, but it made glittering white suds that smelled, as the whole scullery smelled, powerfully *clean*. The air was so hot and pure, it made me giddy to breathe it, and also the puffs of sweet food smells that wafted up from the disposal, cream and eggs and, in the evening, lime sherbet. (I saved up melted sherbet by the gallon, to dump it into the disposal fan and breathe in a burst of sugar.) I worked hard but in that steambath felt so slick and loose and graceful—it was so hot that even the hottest weeks of August, I felt cool for the rest of the day—and felt *clean*: breathed clean steam, sweated pure clean sweat, and even sang about purity as I worked—all the jazzy revival songs I knew, "Power in the Blood" and "The Old Account Was Settled Long Ago" and "O Happy Day That Fixed My Choice" and

Have you *come to Jesus* for the *cleansing power*,
Are you *washed* in the *blood* of the *Lamb? (Slam. Bang.)*

When Lucy of composition class, who let me have half her sandwich one day, asked me if I had a job and I told her I was a dishwasher, she made a face as if I said I worked in the sewer. She said it must be awful, and of course when I told her it was terrific, she thought I was being ironic. Composition class was local headquarters of irony; we supplied the five-county area. The more plainly I tried to say I liked dishwashing, the more ironic she thought I was, until I flipped a gob of mayo at her as a rhetorical device to show *un*subtlety and sincerity, and then she thought I was a jerk.

I didn't venture to write about dishwashing for composition and certainly not about the old home town. Mr. Staples told us to write from personal experience, of course, but he said it with a smirk, suggesting that we didn't have much, so instead I wrote the sort of dreary, clever essays I imagined I'd appreciate if I were him.

Lake Wobegon, whatever its faults, is not dreary. Back for a visit in August, I saw Wayne "Warning Track" Tommerdahl stroke the five-thousandth long fly ball of his Whippet career. "You move that fence forty feet in, and Wayne could be in the majors," said Uncle Al, seeing greatness where it had not so far appeared. Toast 'n Jelly Days was over but the Mist County Fair had begun and I paid my quarter to plunge twenty-five feet at the Hay Jump, landing in the stack a few feet from Mrs. Carl Krebsbach, who asked, "What brings you back?" A good question and one that several dogs in town had brought up since I arrived. Talking to Fr. Emil outside the Chatterbox Cafe, I made a simple mistake: pointed north in reference to Daryl Tollerud's farm where the gravel pit was, where the naked man fell out the back door of the camper when his wife popped the clutch, and of course Daryl's farm is *west*, and I corrected myself right away, but Father gave me a funny look as if to say, *Aren't you from here then?* Yes, I am. I crossed Main Street toward Ralph's and stopped, hearing a sound from childhood in the distance. The faint mutter of ancient combines. Norwegian bachelor farmers combining in their antique McCormacks, the old six-footers. New combines cut a twenty-foot swath, but those guys aren't interested in getting done sooner, it would only mean a longer wait until bedtime. I stood and listened. My eyes got blurry. Of course, thanks to hay fever, wheat has always put me in an emotional state, and then the clatter brings back memories of old days of glory in the field when I was a boy among giants. My uncle lifted me up and put me on the seat so I could ride alongside him. The harness jingled on Brownie and Pete and Queenie and Scout, and we bumped along in the racket, row by row. Now all the giants are gone; everyone's about my size or smaller. Few people could lift me up, and I don't know that I'm even interested. It's sad to be so old. I postponed it as long as I could, but when I weep at the sound of a combine, I know I'm there. A young man wouldn't have the background for it.

That uncle is dead now, one of three who went down like dominoes, of bad tickers, when they reached seventy. I know more and more people in the cemetery, including Miss Heinemann, my English teacher. She was old (my age now) when I had her. A massive lady with chalk dust on her blue wool dress, whose hair was hacked short, who ran us like a platoon, who wept when I recited the sonnet she assigned me to memorize. Each of us got one, and I was hoping for "Shall I compare thee to a summer's day?" or "Let me not to the marriage of true minds," which might be *useful* in some situations, but was given Number 73, "That time of year thou mayst in me behold," which I recited briskly, three quatrains hand over fist, and nailed on the couplet at the end. The next year I did "When in disgrace with fortune and men's eyes."

Listening to combines on a dry day that is leaning toward fall, I still remember—

That time of year thou mayst in me behold
When yellow leaves, or none, or few, do hang
Upon those boughs which shake against the cold,
Bare ruined choirs where late the sweet birds
   sang. . . .

Learned at sixteen in a classroom that smelled of

Home

Wildroot hair oil and Nesbitt's orange pop on my
breath, it cheers me up, even "the twilight of such
day/As after sunset fadeth in the west" and "the ashes
of his youth."

This thou perceiv'st, which makes thy love more
strong,
To love that well which thou must leave ere long.

NEW ALBION

The first white person to set foot in Lake Wobegon and claim credit for it was either Father Pierre Plaisir in 1835 or Count Carlo Pallavicini the following year, depending on whether Father Plaisir set foot here or much farther to the west. According to his own calculations, he was near Lake Wobegon (or Lac Malheur, as the voyageurs called it), but the terrain he describes in his memoir, *Le Monde* (1841), seems to be to the west, perhaps as far as Montana. The mountains he says he saw were not any of ours.

He and his six *amis* had come to the New World to gain *gloire* and *bonneur* through *nouveaux exploits* despite *les dangers*, but instead got lost and spent June and July looking for the route back to where they had come from, the Northeast Passage. When they made camp at Lac Malheur, if that is where they were, their confusion was complete and their leader was suffering from *abominable abdominale*. He was *misérable* even before he lay down to sleep in the grass and the *muskitos* attacked him.

He had observed in his journal that "these are big vicious *muskitos*, not like our French insects," but that was before they got serious. A cloud of them descended after dark, and he lay and suffered for a while, then yelled, *"J'expire! Je quitte!"* and tore into the underbrush. His friends shouted, *"Courage, mon père!"* and ran after him. Their footsteps made him think his *ennemis* were coming, and he dashed west in *terreur* for some distance until he was captured by the Ojibway. They looked on it as protective custody, but when Father Plaisir returned to France and wrote his book, he described them as savages and said the country was a wildnerness and he would never go back. He forgot that he had never been invited.

Count Carlo, who took one look and decided Lake Wobegon was *not* the headwaters of the Mississippi but was not far from it, was happier there. *"Mio contento,"* he sighed as he stripped away his count's clothing and waded into the cool waters after a hard morning of exploring. He is said to have eaten a cheese sandwich and written a poem ("La Porta" or "The Door") before continuing. He did not know that Henry Schoolcraft had discovered the headwaters four years before and far to the north. He thought of Lake Wobegon as the gateway to his great destiny.

The first white folk known to have spent time in the Wobegon area were Unitarian missionaries from Boston, led by Prudence Alcott, a distant and wealthy relative of the famous Alcotts of Concord, a woman who sent a stereopticon and a crate of boysenberry jam to Henry Thoreau at his cabin by the pond, although he never mentioned her in his book.

On June 14, 1850, at two-forty P.M., according to her meticulous journal, while crossing Boylston Street on her way to reflect in the pond of Boston's Public Garden, she had a vision of a man in hairy clothing who told her to go west and convert the Indians to Christianity by the means of interpretive dance.

Having witnessed an Algonquin Rain Dance at the Lyceum [the] previous night, the Expressive Beauty of their Spirits convinced me that the worship of the Supreme Being in our English Language is dry, tasteless, & insufficient to the present Need, & then amid a scene of such confusion & Commerce & bustling Traffic, it was shown to me that All is One under Heaven, All are Children of God & I must preach to our savage Brethren, using the language of Dance. I proceeded to my beloved Pond filled with Certainty and Rejoicing.

Selecting three of her friends to be her followers, Prudence made plans to entrain immediately for the territories, taking only enough cash to see them to the Mississippi whence they would cast themselves upon Providence, but their departure was delayed by the enthusiasm of local servants who subjected them to an exhausting round of parties, lectures, and receptions, so they did not leave Boston until September 21 and arrived in Minnesota just as the weather was turning ugly. Staying only one night at Fort Snelling, the Unitarians pushed north, traveling upriver with a band of Ojibway merchants for ten days until, rounding a bend in the river and seeing a pine in the shape of a V, Prudence shouted "Here!" and there they were dropped: Prudence, her cousin Elizabeth Sewell, a seminary student named George Moore, and a poet, Henry Francis Watt, who was interested in native speech rhythms.

A hike of three days brought them to the site of the present Lake Wobegon, where they built a lean-to of alder branches and settled in to await the leading of the Spirit, and where two days later they looked out in the morning to see a foot of new-fallen snow. Prudence's certainty and rejoicing were just about all used up.

Lay awake all night hearing cries of wild beasts, hoots, screams &c. Elizabeth sleeps easily but our diet of nuts & berries does not sit well & makes me restless & agitated & also Henry & George snort & grunt in their sleep & throw their arms & legs about & disgust me [with] their gross sensuality & brute appetites. This is a desolate & God-forsaken land & I do not see that any civilized society could find comfort and nurture here. Would that I had brought warm clothing!!

By Thanksgiving Day, Prudence had said her prayers, laid down, crossed her arms, and hoped to die, when crashing was heard in the underbrush and into the clearing rode an immense swarthy man wrapped in bearskins who dismounted from his spotted pony, threw back his huge hairy head, and laughed out loud: "Haw! Haw! Haw!"

"He was covered with sweat & filth & phlegm ran down his face unchecked & he gave off the aroma of one for whom bathing is as unwelcome a prospect as a broken leg," wrote Prudence, but he was also, she learned, Basile Fonteneau, a French trapper, who knew his way around those parts, and when he offered to lead them to his hut at the other end of the lake and put them up for the winter, she did not say no. She was cold and hungry and wasn't sure that Providence would make a better offer.

In a few weeks, her spirits lifted somewhat. "M. Fonteneau delights in half-cooked bear meat which he eats *sans* utensil & sleeps in a heap with his four brutish dogs & sings bawdy ballads in a coarse voice & relieves himself in the open & engages in other lewd practices, but I am satisfied that Providence has led us here in order to test us with fire & I am happy to be proved & strengthened in my Faith," she wrote.

By the spring thaw, she had found in her heart some fondness for Basile and written two sonnets on the letters of his name. One of them began:

Base metals may to pure gold changèd be,
As, too, base mortals angelic may become,
Silver-winged, gold-tongued, by fiery alchemy,
Ill-bred their parts but O the glorious sum. . . .

By May her thoughts were centered on him. She gazed on him as he slept, and his face seemed to possess nobility of purpose and a spiritual demeanor she had not noticed during the cold months. "Compared to Basile—his strength, his native cunning, his constant good humor—Henry & George seem pale & slender stems of some weaker strain of plant. They while away the hours perched on rocks above the Lake & dispute theology & amuse themselves with their own wit & in their placid ignorance never take note that there is wood to be got. Each day I invent new reasons why we cannot press on with our Mission and must remain here a little longer, but there is no need to convince them—they would be content to sit until fall."

One evening as the sun set and a warm breeze carried the thought of spring flowers, Basile asked Prudence to walk with him to a peninsula to pick lady-slippers. As they walked, she found herself talking about her Mission to the Indians and her feeling that dance, not oratory, is the basis of true religion. As she talked, she began to dance for him. He ran after her as she danced on and on until, exhausted, she fell in a heap and he picked her up and carried her to the water's edge and threw her in. He stripped off his clothing and jumped in after her.

"I was astonished to see that he is actually quite a

young man," she wrote in her journal that night. "It was only his husk that was old & smelly & degraded & corpulent & when he shed it he appeared quite slender & muscular & all in all a very comely individual. We swam & sported in the cool waters & my petticoats were so cumbersome I dispensed with them &c. 'You must not look upon me!' I cried &c. He spoke to me in French, which I took to mean that he felt it was his Duty to look on me or else I might drown & he then took my hand & guided me to deeper water for modesty's sake & showed me to swim &c. We returned to camp very damp & much refreshed & when I saw the others, reclining where I had left them & murmuring about the Spirit of Truth, I determined to send them back East & remain with Basile."

There her journal ended. She and Basile were maried in St. Anthony in July by a Fr. Sevier, who also had come west to convert the Indians, and settled in St. Paul, where Basile built a hotel called The World, and they prospered and had seven children. The first account of Lake Wobegon to reach the East was Henry's, in his poem "Phileopolis: A Western Rhapsody," which begins

> I lie upon the vacant shore,
> Fleecy banners flying o'er,
> And look beyond this desolate place,
> To yon bright city turn my face:
> Phileopolis.
>
> Turn from this weedy tepid slough
> To yonder vision fair and true,

From land of toil, care and grief
To richer soil of my belief:
Phileopolis.

The poem, all 648 lines of it, was never published
in the East, where Henry hoped it would make his
reputation and lead to something, perhaps an introduction to Longfellow. The short and insistent meter,
the sheer length (which, by line 182, is already leading to such rhymes as "sibylline/porcupine" and
"cereal/immaterial"), and the burden of the poem—
the emptiness and spiritual languor of the frontier
and the comfort of civilization as found in dreams of
Greece—left even Henry's friends a little sleepy after
a few pages, and the poem was eventually returned
by James Russell Lowell at *The Atlantic* with a note:
"We are grateful for having had the chance to see
this and trust you will understand that, whatever the
qualities of the poem, it does not meet our particular
requirements at this time. (In the future, please
enclose postage with your submissions."*

---

*The manuscript, subtitled "Thoughts, Composed A Short
Distance Above Lake Wobegon," was discovered in the
Boston Library by Johanna Quist in 1916, who actually
was searching for material on Manichaeanism for a class
oration and had looked under "Mechanism" by mistake.
She copied the poem out by hand and mailed it to her aunt
Mary Quist, secretary of the Lake Wobegon Thanatopsis
Society. The poem Henry wrote in loathing as he beat off
mosquitos and dreamed of renown back East received its
first publication, in Lake Wobegon, by the Thanatopsians
(1921), who hailed Henry as "Our First Poet" and placed a

Henry Francis was not easily discouraged. Back in Boston by September of '51, he tried the lecture circuit and spoke in several towns and made a good impression on some people, including a handsome young woman in Amherst who became his wife and also a wealthy Boston coffee broker who was a partner in the Albion Land Company which, as it so happened, was looking to the Minnesota territory with an eye toward speculation.

Henry's lecture was entitled "Descriptions of Innocence & Independence in the West." He had changed his mind. He had grown fond of "this desolate place" after a few months in the East, had come to imagine it as his true spiritual home. He wanted to leave Boston, which was crowded with poets and philosophers, and return to the lake and woods where he was the sole proprietor of serious thought. In "Descriptions," he gave such a fine account of his thoughts, feelings, etc., as a poet in the West, and

---

picture of him, looking weary indeed, in the library. Five hundred copies of "Phileopolis" were printed, of which fifty remain wrapped in waxed paper in the library basement. For years, students of the senior class were required to read it and answer questions about its meaning, etc. Teachers were not required to do so, but simply marked according to the correct answers supplied by Miss Quist, including: (1) To extend the benefits of civilization and religion to all peoples, (2) No, (3) Plato, and (4) A wilderness cannot satisfy the hunger for beauty and learning, once awakened. The test was the same from year to year, and once the seniors found the answers and passed them on to the juniors, nobody read "Phileopolis" any more.

rose to such flights of imagination that he himself could not believe he had left such a paradise for "the stale, tedious, over-traveled roads of transcendentalism."

"Saw Emerson at a dinner," he wrote in his journal. "How tired he looks! If that is what fame leads to, I would as soon be a simple schoolteacher in the wilderness!"

A portrait of Henry and his new young wife shows a plump, somewhat damp young man with a faint aura of beard, seated, gazing far beyond the camera, with a sturdy woman in black silk standing at his side. She smiles modestly, her hand on his shoulder. On her fingers are three rings bearing large stones. His mother opposed the match. "My dear Son," she wrote from Cambridge, "do you really *know* Elizabeth as a man should know his intended wife? Have you looked into her history, her family, etc.? Do not be enchanted by the flutter of talk & the whisper of feminine dress & the thin veil of youthful romance, but gather the plain facts as you would if you were entering into any other enterprise. Elizabeth impresses me as a peasant woman, quite possibly one of gypsy blood, who is unsuitable for a man of your sensitive health. This is sound advice from your mother. Ignore it at your peril."

Henry didn't care about her history. It was enough for him that his wife looked on him as her teacher, her truest friend and her one sure guide. Nobody had ever trusted him so much. Far from questioning his dream of returning west, she encouraged it. "I wish to begin life anew in a new country," she wrote, "and I pray God it will be with you, my friend."

His dream was simple. He would return to Minnesota and found a college, a city of learning on a hill, and would give his life to it. Harvard had turned him down as a teacher, so had Yale. Everywhere he encountered failure. Even "Descriptions" got him only five bookings in three months, and of those, three refused to pay the agreed amount after the performance and insisted on a much smaller fee, which he was forced to accept. The inheritance from his father's furniture shop was small.

So his meeting with the coffee broker was pure godsend. The man, whose name was Bayfield, was coarse, untutored, favored garish clothing, and had an unpleasant habit of chewing coffee beans and letting the brown juice run down his chin, but Henry swallowed his pride and cultivated him, regaling him with pictures of the distinguished institution they two would together create, until at last Bayfield agreed. In the spring, Henry would travel to St. Paul, join a wagon train of the Albion Land Company, accompany them to a site, and begin construction of a town named New Albion and a college. Henry argued for stone; surely there must be a good supply of granite somewhere close by, and granite would speak for the permanence of New Albion in such a way as to encourage settlement; but Bayfield said no, it would be brick.

Henry described the beautiful spot by the lake where so much poetry had come to him. He pleaded with Bayfield to build his town there. "Fortune is drawing me to that spot," he said. He didn't know that Bayfield already owned it.*

In late August 1852, a train of heavy wagons

---

*In the spring of 1851, as the Ojibway near Lac Malheur were preparing to cede vast tracts to the government, several chiefs who smelled the deal coming had decided to sell out early to Bayfield's group of Yankee investors who they met two years before on a buffalo deal. The chiefs didn't like the looks of the federal agents who came to parley. They were big hearty men who clapped the Ojibway on the shoulders and told them how they, the agents, considered themselves deep down to be really Indians at heart and, when questioned about the value of the paper they offered in exchange for land, were hurt. "We are your friends," they told the Ojibway, tears welling up in their eyes. "We go back to Washington and defend you to the Great Father and make the very best treaty that we possibly can for you—and now you question our honesty! We are deeply offended. Very deeply offended."

Most of the chiefs much preferred Bayfield who never claimed to be interested in anything but making a pile and who came to meet them in an immense canoe paddled by fourteen French-Canadians, and offered three times the agents' best price plus a large gift for signing, a walnut dresser with three drawers and an oval mirror, brand new. In the fall, three Ojibway chiefs signed with his New Albion Land Company, for the sale of almost five hundred square miles, including the present site of Lake Wobegon. The sale was opposed by the agents, who felt it could lead to a bidding war, with wealthy Eastern oligarchs tempting the Ojibway with large sums and purchasing vast lands for the pleasure and profit of the few. Minnesota should be opened

47

rumbled north on the Winnipeg Trail, drawn by octets of oxen, the drovers walking alongside, followed by a coach carrying seven bricklayers and a carriage driven by Mr. Bayfield with Henry and Elizabeth aboard, drawn by two high-stepping grays who tossed their handsome heads, upset at the slow pace. Twenty miles a day the caravan moved, along what is now U.S. 10, from St. Paul (formerly called Pig's Eye) to the lumbering camp of Anoka and through the Benedictine mission of St. Cloud, then struck out cross-country to the Albion site north-northwest. In six days, they met up with only one southbound traveler: a man named Moon, on foot, who stood in their path and inquired for news. "You are the first I've seen all summer!" he cried.

He was wrapped in rags tied with leather thongs and wore a good beaver hat and carried a sack on his

---

up to the common man, they said, and should be settled on the basis of equal opportunity, not on the ability to pay. So the deal with Bayfield was cancelled by a squad of soldiers from Fort Snelling, the Ojibway received the standard 3¢/ acre from the government for the Albion tract, which the government gave in 1852 to the Albion Land Company. The Indians didn't hold a grudge against the Yankees for making the best deal they could, though, and during the "Sioux Uprising" of 1862, when Little Crow's band was eliminating white settlers wherever they could be found, in New Albion the Indians only took thirty-four hostages and redeemed them later for cash. Bayfield's son James bargained hard for the hostages, which included his two young daughters and several elderly aunts, finally talking the Indians down to $35 per head, $20 for children under sixteen.

back that jingled when he set it down. "Tools of the trade," he said. "Tinkering, preaching, and doctoring. Man and beast."

"You're far from any settlement to practice trades like those," Bayfield said. "I know that now!" the man replied. He clutched at Bayfield's sleeve and looked deep into Bayfield's eyes—"The war with Mexico! Tell me how the battle goes!" he cried. "Has General Taylor yet taken Santa Anna?"

"The war is won, I'm pleased to tell you, and General Taylor has been rewarded with election to the Presidency three years ago, but now that Mexico has surrendered, the country is under attack from the north."

"The north?"

"Sir, let us speak privately so as not to alarm the lady—" and Bayfield led him away from the wagons, Henry following, to a low sandy hill under a small oak tree—"war with Canada is coming as sure as I stand here. The East is all ablaze with it. Villainy, sir! Unspeakable things! Crimes that no God-fearing man would care to contemplate! Yes, sir, the vicious Canuck will not rest until the Republic is lying in its own blood and gore! And where will they strike next, sir? Why, right here, in the most defenseless regions! That is why we are headed north, sir. And that is why you must continue south—to warn the citizens of St. Paul that the Canucks are moving! They are coming overland, they are moving by the rivers. And what is more heinous—their armies are infested with small-pox! Yes! Great swarthy brutes with rheumy eyes and fevered brows, open red sores on their bodies and green pestilence running down their legs! Go, sir! To St. Paul! And trust no man who denies the truth of it! Their agents are thick in the countryside. Spread the word! Go! Godspeed!"

The poor man looked at them in horror and ran away south, his bag jangling at his side. Henry watched in disbelief. "The frontier is for the strong," Bayfield said. "Let rumours of war and disease keep the weak at home so the strong can flourish."

"Lies," Henry whispered. He sank to the ground. "Lies. You shouldn't tell so many lies."

"Courage!" Bayfield grabbed his hand and hauled him up. "A little courage, sir. We've come to build a city, a great, rich, populous city, and before we build, we must believe in it. Is that a lie? Is this a lie?" He reached into his coat and pulled out a sheet of paper which he unfolded and thrust at Henry.

It was a printed poster entitled NEW ALBION, THE BOSTON OF THE WEST, and under the title, a perfect picture of a town with great buildings, stately homes under broad trees, avenues thronged with traffic. "Home of New Albion College, World Revered Seat of Learning Set in This Mecca of Commerce and Agriculture. Dr. Henry Francis Watt, Ph.D., Litt. D., D.D., President. Choice Lots Remain For Purchase, $100."

"Mr. Bayfield," Henry gasped. "You take me for a much better man than I am!"

"Mr. Watt," Bayfield replied, "you will do just fine, sir. You will accomplish the purpose admirably, I have every reason to believe it."

"But *Doctor!* You have me a doctor of philosophy,

literature, divinity—great God! I'll be found out! There will be scandal! Outrage! People will never forgive it!"

Bayfield put his arm around the young man's shoulders. "You seem to be ignorant of the true nature of doctors," he said. "My boy, the first and foremost work of a doctor is to inspire confidence in his being one. So long as the public has faith in him, then any man can be a doctor, and if the public hasn't faith, then the greatest doctor in the world will have no effect on them."

"But the degrees. I have no degrees," Henry pleaded.

"First, we shall get the college on its feet. Then the college will grant you every degree that is needed."

"I will get my degrees from my own college? Me, the president of that college? Do you think it is right, Mr. Bayfield?"

"This is the West, Mr. Watt. Here, men are not so dependent on the opinions of others. Here, it matters less what others think than what a man himself says he is. Look around you, sir, and you will see men who were mere mechanics, workingmen, even foreigners, become masters of great affairs and vast estates. That is why we have come here. So as not to be held back by requirements!"

"I wish I had your confidence," Henry said.

"Begin to have confidence. Let yourself have confidence in small things, and soon you will believe in great things. Take a word of advice, Mr. Watt. Begin with your wife."

"My wife?"

"You let her be too familiar. Tell the good woman that henceforth she must address you as Dr. Watt. Enforce a little respect in your home, and the world will follow suit, and you will be Dr. Watt wherever you go. But be Henry to her, and the world will sense the weakness, and you will never be any more than a Henry, and, sir, this college cannot be founded by such a man. It requires a doctor."

This conversation had almost exhausted Henry. Beyond the ruts of the trail, he saw no sign of settlement, no sign that humankind had ever come this way, only woods and, to the west, the river. I should turn back now, he thought. It would be more honourable. But he didn't know where he was. Dark was coming on. Elizabeth had weak ankles. To do the right thing: go straight to the wagons, take the trunk from the carriage, and turn back for St. Paul—he was too tired. And the trunk—he had packed a small library in there, it weighed two hundred pounds. All those books, should he just dump them in the woods?

"Can I trust you?" he asked Bayfield.

"I hope that you will. I know that you can."

"Then I do," Henry said, and they returned to the wagons.

Late that evening they arrived at the site. They wrapped themselves in blankets and lay down, exhausted, on the ground and fell asleep. When they awoke, they were in their new home.

A thick mist lay on the lake, giving it a look of vastness. Bayfield was gone. The drovers made a fire and put on a pot of coffee and began frying up pancakes and slabs of pork. Bayfield returned from the lake with three good-sized fish. "Everything looks better in the morning," he said. Elizabeth went down to the lake to bathe. Henry sat on a rock and waited for breakfast. "All my life, my one great talent has been resignation," he wrote. "I have been prepared for defeat, have welcomed failure, and have quietly walked away from every enterprise that engaged me. Now, God give me strength. Now this place is home, and here I make my stand. This is our new life, beginning today. There is nowhere to go to from here." He wrote "New Albion College" and under it listed a dozen subjects, including Philosophy and Oratory but also Manual Arts and Husbandry.

Three years later, in 1855, a Mr. Wm. Stinson, eighteen, observed the same lake on a misty fall morning, and rushed off for pencil and paper to write the New Albion College hymn.

> New England's wealthy store
> Would draw us ever near.
> Its mighty factories roar.
> We cannot linger here.
>
> All through the night we steer
> Across the ocean deep.
> Our hearts shall have no fear.
> God watches whilst we sleep.
>
> Though mighty tempests rage,
> The western sky is clear.

The dawn of a new age
Awakes the pioneer.

On deck we pilgrims stand,
United all the more,
Looking out for land,
The Minnesota shore.

Seven boys comprised the choir, they being the entire student body: Mr Stinson and his cousin B. Maxwell; two Baxters, Jn. and Jas.; P. Herman; Robt. Powell; and a seventh whose name is only a blue pool on the ledger due to water damage. This hardy band of scholars descended on a village half-housed in tents and shanties, a college that was no more than a long pine table and Dr. Watt standing at the head of it and reading from Hunt's *Second Latin Primer*; a college that bore no more resemblance to the advertisement than a pine cone to an oak tree, but they were true scholars and didn't question such a discrepancy. Years later, Mr. Stinson, then of Stinson & Maxwell wheat brokers, recalled New Albion as the happiest years of his life. "Pioneering! That glorious word is one the boy of today, alas, will never know," he wrote in 1880, "the delicious pleasure of studious pursuits in a world that remains to be made—to be pupil *and* carpenter—to pore over the copybook at a desk built with one's own hands! It speaks a beauty to my soul that is now departed, I am afraid, from our institutions of learning."

In 1855, New Albion College moved from its handsome little edifice on Van Buren Street (now owned by Bunsen Motors and used for storage) to a campus at the other end of the lake. Bayfield had left, gone to Wisconsin to buy up land and become a timber baron and lay waste to three counties. Without his mentor on hand to remind him from whence the *Dr.* had come, Henry grew into his title and even added a new one, *Reverend*, and became ever more stately, grandiloquent, and obese. "Reverend Watt occupied the pulpit for almost two hours," the St. Paul *Democrat* reported of his preaching debut in that city, "and his strength did not wane nor his voice abate but continued with full force to the very end."

New Albion in 1855 was a settlement of some two hundred souls, mostly New Englanders, who had built from memory a few substantial buildings, including a Lyceum for the College and a white frame church, its great needle of a spire rising high above the oaks, and also a large collection of houses, most of them small and considered temporary until the inhabitants should prosper and build themselves the great homes they aspired to, the ones pictured on the prospectus.

"Mr. Bayfield's advertisement is a noble vision of what shall be," Mr. Horace Shaw wrote home to Connecticut; he had joined Mr. Thomas Getchell in Shaw & Getchell Transfer Company, which hauled a load of lumber to New Albion, arriving in May 1855. Half the lumber was used for traction, the streets, though laid out at right angles as in Bayfield's plan, being almost impassable whenever it rained and during the spring thaw.

They had known mud in New England, of course, but there was no mud like what they found in Minnesota. The town sat in a swamp from April until June, and then again in July, and often in August, too, while September brought some more, and one October, three days of rain made them a lake that promptly froze over for six months, a spacious icecap, though that was an unusually cold winter— often, January brought a false thaw and a week or two of mud.

In the mud season, men drove their teams through yards to avoid the streets, until the whole town was churned up. Sanitation being informal, houses sitting in a sea of mud and manure strewn with scrap lumber and odds and ends of every sort of trash, a man could stand on the backstep, look at the yard, and with a clear conscience throw out a bucketful of slops and the contents of the thunderjug: what was wrong with a little bit more when there was so much already?

The names on the 1854 tax roll included: Ames, Hinkley, Putnam, Giddings, Cutter, Bellville, Branch, Crandall, Getchell, Stewart, Brown, Knox, Varney, Porter, Sutton, Beatty, Hatch, Frost, Fairbanks, Lane, Court, Robbins, West, Sellers, McKinney, Smith, Woodbury, Twitchell, Lindsay, Hines, Burns, many of whom formed the "Fifty-fourers" club in 1860.

Fifty-nine votes were cast on April 7, 1854, electing the town board, Mr. Getchell being the leading vote-getter with seven, four others receiving six apiece.

A flour mill was completed about Mar 1, located

on the creek. There was hardly enough wheat to keep it running, but a mill had been in Bayfield's plan so it was built, howbeit much smaller than pictured. In 1855, when the wheat harvest was more abundant, the mill broke under the load, having been poorly designed by Mr. Robbins from an article in *The National Husbandman*, which omitted several small parts having to do with lubrication.

One store had been opened, McKinney's and Branch's, to be joined by a second, the Mercantile, which then began a newspaper, *The New Albion Star*, to promote its goods, which rivaled that of "any emporium west of Chicago" for "dry goods, groceries, clothing and provisions." The Albion House, a "large and commodious" hotel, was kept by Mr. A. M. Varney, and "in the thoroughness of its appointments has secured a reputation second to none in the territory and would do no discredit to any town in the Northwest, even St. Paul."

"Fifty-one buildings, including dwellings &c., now enliven the western shore of Lake Wobegon,* a con-

---

*Thus the name "Lake Wobegon" was introduced into public print. In Bayfield's promotions, "Lake Victoria" was used, though the lake was more commonly referred to as "Mud Lake" or "Green Lake," particularly after a bolt of lightning disturbed the lake bottom and half the water drained out, a situation that only gradually remedied itself. "Lake Victoria" no longer seemed appropriate for what was left, a brackish puddle surrounded by mud flats that for months stank of dead fish. "Lake Wobegon" apparently was an attempt to be accurate while still putting the best face on things. To scholars of the Ojibway tongue,

siderable work in a town of scarcely sixteen months
age, especially for persons of refinement," wrote the
Star. The term "persons of refinement" had been
used by Bayfield in the circulars he mailed east, and
apparently it was they who made the arduous journey to his settlement, expecting to find persons of
similar refinement when they arrived. New Englanders all and Congregationalists, they brought with
them a love of music and pictures, not to mention
back-breaking loads of books. They built first the
College—a one-story frame cottage with two Greek
columns slightly taller than itself, then the handsome
brick edifice—and some time later built a grammar
school, the students having been housed in the train
depot, the railroad having not yet arrived. Of the
fifty-one buildings, of which the "&c." included
some woodsheds and privies, one of the first was an
Opera House, a long shed where every Saturday
night those who could sing did and the others
observed, and where, in 1856, an opera was performed, Mrs. Groat's *Song of Hiawatha* for "5 singers, violin, cornet, harmonium, and tom-tom" and
featuring the town's own Madame Juliet Putnam,
whose composer-husband James Nelson Putnam
penned, upon his arrival, the town's first song:

> O blessed Muse grant us ere long
> The gift of glorious word and song

"Wobegon" or "Wa-be-gan-tan-han" means "the place
where [we] waited all day in the rain," but some translated
the word as simply "patience" and it was used by the *Star*
in that sense.

That we may sing, ere breath is gone,
The praises of New Albion.

And, the very next day, his petition answered, he brought forth

What dazzling sights mine eyes behold,
So beauteous, bountiful and bold,
Where blessings are made thousandfold—
Our noble home, New Albion.

"The city of New Albion was owned and laid out by a company of energetic men from Boston, principally Mr. Benjamin Bayfield, who has now turned his energies to the lumbering business elsewhere," Mr. Gretchell wrote home to his brother in Milford, Maine. "It is a thriving and very refined community where King Alcohol has yet to rear his terrible head, and growing like a house afire. Every day newcomers arrive and the next day they have established an address—that is pioneering: move your family and belongings onto the ground and build the walls around them. I am very pleasantly situated in my house made of logs hewed, two storys high, with a parlor in front and kitchen back and all the rooms papered and carpeted, in which parlor the City Council meets once a month, of which I have been elected the president. The state of things is prosperous at present—indeed, all are getting rich at a rapid rate and think nothing of doubling their prosperity once in five or six weeks. The price of farm land rises by leaps and bounds and town lots too, of which I have purchased seven at $500 each for the small sum of

$70, which is the first year's interest on the mortgage and which I hope to sell within six months and become a creditor myself. Meantimes, I must find a livelihood, however, as I don't have ready cash on hand and am considering using two of the lots as security to purchase a half-interest in the newspaper."

The town's main industry appears to have been speculation, judging from feverish articles in the *Star* that predicted the imminent arrival of the St. Paul & Manitoba railroad and great fortunes for all. The town was mortgaged to the hilt; by 1856, six thousand lots were owned by two hundred forty-seven persons, most of whom, while practicing a trade temporarily, were really in the business of waiting—waiting for the railroad to appear on the horizon and buy right-of-way (along the obvious practical route from the south, lots were going for up to $1000), and deliver carloads of innocents to drive up the value of land. (Unbeknownst to them, the first-comer, Mr. Bayfield, already had sold off the New Albion Land Company, after first issuing three thousand new shares, and by 1856, his sole interest in town was a four-room house, empty except for a spinet in the parlor, still in its crate.)

"This is a strange place," wrote Mr. Getchell's brother, who spent two months in New Albion in the spring of 1856, to his wife in Milford.

Tom will hear of nothing but future prosperity, but one's view of the future depends on how deeply one is in debt—to him, who holds a ream of paper elegantly engraved in gold and giving him title to acres of mud and weeds, New Albion is at the verge of triumph, and to myself who am free and clear, it is not so much a City as a trance, a whimsey built on a swamp, a steeple waiting for its church, a naked man in a fine silk hat. In the public room of the Albion House, such men spend their afternoons in languid conversation about this and that, the Republican Party, the Kansas question, the writings of Whittier and Mrs. Stowe and Howell's 'Prometheus,' Unitarianism, and the Individuality of Experience and the Nature of the Soul and the Moons of Neptune, and what work is accomplished is done by, at most, a dozen hands, and that not always of an enduring nature—for example, a board-walk laid yesterday and today capsized in the mud. It is a 'City' of leaning fences and mishung doors, of buildings begun and then forgot, of handsome unpainted houses, of timid little shops huddling behind magnificent facades. Scenes of squalor so long associated with drunkards, you will find here, the population being intoxicated by dreams of easy income. No common labor for them! No thrift—they are 'financially embarrassed' but do not blush! To them, what is is not but is what shall be, a seat of wealth and influence and themselves sitting squarely in the middle of it.

In this Parnassus of the prairie, the Rev. Dr. Watt was the leading citizen of his day, a cleric, scholar, poet, orator, and a man who, as someone said, "woke up each day and wrapped greatness like a cloak around him. On his daily constitutionals, Dr. Watt is impeded by neither mud nor livestock. Morning and evening, he sets forth on his accustomed round, prepared for magnificent and learned discourse. At the sight of an audience, even a solitary soul leaning against a fence or heading toward a privy, Dr. Watt will cross any street however miry and challenge oncoming horses or herds of swine in order to engage his fellow man in scholarly exposition on the ideas of the day. Many are the citizens who have been thus engaged and, with little effort or expense on their part, profitably educated, for the Doctor is as unsparing of his wisdom as he is generous with his time."

Profound as he was in public, Henry in his journal often gave way to bitter complaints against conditions in town, the mud in particular:

14 Apr. The 4th day of rain and we are up to our knees in mire and a man can't cross the street but he may have to abandon his boots halfway across—this western soil, so highly advertised as an agricultural *paradiso*, is clay and loam in the exact proportion needed to make thick soup with only a little water needed—a day of dismal rain, mixed well by horse and wagon traffic, and a man is a prisoner in his house, surrounded by impassable swamp. An apt illustration of our spiritual condition here: hemmed in by despond & despair, life churned up by mere commerce and society—rode last week to the end of the lake. A magnificent

site. High ground, well drained. *Firm*, even when wet. Natural clearing on hill, view of water & distant village. I am to speak to trustees again Wed. & must make a clear & strong argument. Perhaps my resignation will carry the day.

Henry had offered his resignation so many times, the trustees of the college had come to expect it; it was the first order of business at their meetings and was easily disposed of, since the price of his happiness was low. A little praise from them and a little money for a bell for the college belfry, a few dozen books, a professor of rhetoric, and the letter of resignation disappeared into his pocket. What sold them on the new campus that spring was the wonderful effect it would have on the value of land nearby. All conceivable lots had been sold at the townsite, and now, with the college moving to the eastern end of the lake, the land around the new campus could be divided into lots and put on the market. Their delay in approving the plan was to gain time to buy up surrounding property; then they voted 5–2 to purchase a hundred acres from themselves for the college. The two opposed were gentlemen with no money to invest.

So anxious was Henry to move the college to the country, he had completed a dedicatory ode before construction began, and on May 24, 1855, in the morning, the faculty (four) and students (now swelled to twenty-five) assembled in front of the lyceum, where the bell was placed on a wagon and, led by a small brass band and accompanied by half the citizenry, proceeded out the old Pender Road a mile and a half through what was then dense woods to its new abode on the hill. An account in the Minnesota *Forward* of June 16 included this description:

> The rain of the night before had left the air cool and sweet, and the cheerful singing of choirs of birds mingled pleasantly with the strains of drum and bugle, as our long caravan wound up hill and down, o'ertowered by stands of oak through whose branches the sun shone as a blessing. One could not but feel the College had embarked on a venture of such magnificence that Nature herself rejoiced to see it. Soon a chorus of shouts was heard from the vanguard as it entered the clearing, and the lovely blue lake lay before us beyond the brow of the hill. The bell was gently lifted to the place of honor on the sturdy platform constructed for the day's ceremonies. The first building will be raised on this spot. . . . Following the dedicatory ode of Dr. Watt, the college hymn was sung as the bell was softly tapped with a mallet.

In September, thirty-six students enrolled at Albion, arriving for fall term to find the main building completed except for the interior work—an imposing brick edifice nevertheless. The first floor was given over to a large chapel and a gallery for paintings and sculpture, the second to the college offices, a lecture hall, and two spacious classrooms. Unfortunately, a large sum of money that had been promised by an Eastern benefactor did not materialize, and so there was no dormitory or dining hall.

Meals were taken in the gallery, which were simple meals pending the arrival of a cookstove, and the student body spent the first three weeks of the term constructing two log bunkhouses near the lake; meanwhile they slept in tents.

Mr. F. B. Reithman, professor of moral psychology, supervised the project, while writing to his brother in Philadelphia:

Our president is occupied with making great plans for us, and we are busy making a place to sleep before winter comes on. The morale of the students is very fine and would be even better were it not for daily chapel, which lasts upward of an hour. With little by way of tools, they are accomplishing heroic things worthy of Napoleon's army. Finished a cabin of four rooms for Dr. and Mrs. Watt last week, and now we are engaged on a structure sixty by twenty feet, one of two that will be student quarters, God willing, if our hands don't peel off. Send gloves, if you can, and some salve.

The faculty, consisting of Mr. Reithman, Mr. Waite, and Mr. Coutts, bedded down in the attic of Main, and by the middle of October, the most urgent construction completed (that the two bunkhouses, named Emerson House and Carlyle House), they set about teaching. The course of studies comprised Classics, Theology, and Commercial: under Classics appeared Latin, Greek, Rhetoric, Poetry, and Oratory; under Theology were Moral Psychology, Old and New Testaments, Ecclesiastical History, and Science; and under Commercial, Arithmetic,

Penmanship, Bookkeeping, and Hygienics. Mrs.
Watt offered lessons in music, and manual training
and was available anywhere on the campus. The fee
was $18 per term for tuition and board, plus twenty
hours of labor per week—in the afternoons and on
Saturdays, the students threw themselves upon the
immense unfinished tasks of the college, including:

Felling four acres of timber and hauling the logs to
town to be milled.

Clearing two acres of tree stumps so a garden
could be planted in the spring. Planting fifty apple
trees. Digging a well. Digging deep pits and building privies. Cutting and splitting fifty cords of
firewood. Raising a flagpole. Raising a cross.
Building a cookshed behind Main. Laying a
wooden walk from the Watts' cabin.

The work was interrupted by a tragedy October 11
when Frank Sutton was struck down and crushed by
a tree. Apparently, he had cut it, then lost his footing
on the slope as he attempted to run. He was alone in
the woods when this happened, and his body lay for
several hours before it was discovered by the science
class; meanwhile a wild beast had chewed off one
arm and carried it away. The body was returned to
Minar's Grove for interment, and a memorial service
held at the college the Sunday following.

Dr. Watt inspected the work daily. He devoted his
chapel sermons to the topic of building, comparing
the students to the children of Israel who were delivered out of captivity in Egypt and came into the
promised land of Canaan, comparing the work to the

building of the temple under Solomon, leaving the students to figure out who was Solomon in the analogy. In his journal, he complained of shortness of breath and dizziness, and noted, "I am too heavy," but the rapid progress of the college excited him:

We are working a miracle here! Every day shows us some new success as our vision takes form—a wall rises, then four, doors and windows appear, a roof rises, a handsome building stands where once was only leaf and shadow—this amazes & inspires me to watch it! I walk around & am filled with new visions, dreams, ideas &c. of a great University that shall someday stand on this hill to rival any of the planet. I dare not speak these dreams to any person—any *sensible* man would laugh uproariously at such a notion! but then no "sensible" man could have accomplished here what we have done. This College is the one great work of my life. May God grant me a humble spirit to give all thanks to Him for bringing me to this place.

He decided to hold another grand occasion to celebrate the great work that had been brought so far, and once the thought struck him, he went into a fever and spent two days shut in his office writing an address. He called it Founders Day, October 30, and invited everyone he could think of, of whom some two hundred attended, including Mr. Bayfield, who was in the area foreclosing. The *Forward* wrote:

Approaching New Albion College from the east, the writer gained the crest of a hill crowned with blazing oak and gaudy maple and, upon glimpsing the distant campus through the trees, stopped the team so as to impress the agreeable vista on his memory, for against Nature's dying ostentation, New Albion unfolds a seemly tableau of such simple unaffected grandeur as to appear imagined, an apparition of Academe in the desolate forest, with its trim and handsome cottages, the well-laid walks and promenades, the orderly plantings of ornamental trees, and, bestriding all, the majestic spire of Main itself like an upraised finger calling all to stand in hushed wonder at what Providence had wrought. . . . Notable citizens from as far distant as St. Paul were in attendance to gaze upon the marvel for themselves, and those who admire the art of oratory found it in abundant supply.

Two-thirty P.M., October 30, was perhaps the high-water mark of Henry's life, for which the previous thirty-eight years had been rehearsal, when Mr. Bayfield spoke a few words of introduction to the crowd and Henry arose in his voluminous black gown, took his place before the fresh oak lectern on the porch of Main, placed his right hand in the gown between the third and fourth buttons and stretched out his left in the hortatory position, glanced down at his two-pound address, and lobbed the first sentence out toward the woods. Underfoot he felt solid white pine planks, behind him was solid brick rising to a spire from which a bell would toll when he sat down, and before him lay a yard something like he had known at Harvard, with grass and little trees trimmed to make perfect globes. And his audience, too, of course: two rows of solemn faculty, trustees, and dignitaries, including Governor Alexander Ramsey, Honorable Thaddeus Browne, the steamboat titan, Honorable Charles F. Peabody and Honorable Horatio Parker of the New Albion Land Company, Honorable Aldrich Bryant, Honorable Emerson Fremont, Honorable James Knox, Bishop Upton of the Methodist Church, and behind them, students and New Albion citizens in solid ranks, leaning forward to catch his voice. For several nights running Henry had had bad dreams, dutifully recorded in his journal ("Night sweats . . . lost in woods, running, terrible darkness & sounds of crashing & tearing . . . figures rising up from behind rocks & my own voice weeping & pleading . . . awoke exhausted & lay awake until dawn"), which he attributed to nervousness, but he was himself now as he warmed up to his address—a true physical feat, speaking outdoors, it demanded a stout man to sustain the force and trajectory to carry the vowels in full cry to the farthest listener, and he was not helped by a breeze off the water, but Mr. Reithman, writing home, reported, "I crept away into the woods after an hour and his voice followed me there. I walked over the first hill and stood in a rocky ravine and put my arm around a tree and still Dr. Watt was there; the very rocks seemed to ring, and even the tree trembled to our president's peroration."

The address itself was lost in the turmoil of the following winter, and we have only a half-page of

notes taken by a student, R. Williams, who perhaps
thought he would be examined on the subject:

a.   Gratitude. Much accmp. Much rmns.
         1. Orpheus. Made nature sing.
         2.
B.   How puny comp. to Works of God. Moon,
      stars &c.
         1. But He leads us to work His Will.
I.   Divine Will
      A. The Creation.
         1. power of idea
II.
III. Word in state of sin (Chaos) must be made
      obed. to Will
      A. America
      Laws of nature, laws of God
         1. Based on Ideals, not material
            "To believe your own thought is true for
            all men, that is genius." RW Emerson.
         2. Ideals Come from above, not below
            "The history of the world is the biography
            of great men." Carlyle
         3. Education
            1. guardian of ideals
      Western frontier.
      Testing
      I Cor 15

                    Elizabeth Peabody
                    Elizabeth Peabody
                    Elizabeth Peabody
                    Elizabeth Peabody

Henry spoke for two hours, and at the end, the people "rose to their feet with one accord and pressed forward to grasp him," except Mr. Reithman, who "fell asleep in a pile of leaves and I did not awake until dark when I lay and admired the vast canopy of stars, a million million, and wondered at what mysterious fate had brought me to New Albion." He then saw flames from the college and ran to investigate. It was the flames of four bonfires burning on the shore, one for each class, the students racing to fetch wood to make their fire burn the brightest.

Bitter weather set in on November 14, a heavy wet snow in the morning, driven by a stiff wind that grew stronger all day until Main could not be seen from the Watts' cabin or from the bunkhouses by the lake. The blizzard did not abate all night, and by morning the bunkhouses, both Emerson and Carlyle, were buried, sheets of snow sweeping across the lake to make six-foot drifts, and so were some students, the snow having blown through the cracks and drifted onto the blankets. Emerson suffered two broken windows and was half full of snow and so cold that the residents emigrated to Carlyle during a lull in the storm and spent the next night there, two and three boys to a bed.

They had no food the first day and didn't dare venture up the hill in that blinding white, so dazzling that four feet from the door they saw nothing. "We're going to die," said one boy. The others told him that help would arrive soon, and then they decided to play dead when help did come. They posted a lookout and practiced being dead, lying in grotesque poses as they imagined death might seize them, sprawled on backs across beds with heads hanging and mouths open, sprawled on the floor and one arm reaching toward the door, curled in a ball, crumpled and broken, as if death had flung them against the wall, seated and slumped forward and a hand grasping a pencil and a few lines of farewell letter ending with a long descending stroke as the writer perished. They practiced so they could do a good death scene in three seconds after the lookout's "Go!" and imagined Mr. Reithman's reaction when he shoved the door open and looked upon this carnage of the storm. The tragedy! The poor boys, innocent boys, the fragile flame of life snuffed out suddenly and so much candle left! Then, of course, they would all jump up and yell at him, but some boys let their imagination skip over that and go on to the next part: the long trip home in a box, the weeping family, the funeral where so many would shed bitter tears of remorse for not having done better by him, that cold still form of their former brother and friend.

"The stove! We have to let the fire go out! He'll know it's a joke if he opens the door and the cabin's warm!" Some argued that, no, you *can* die in a warm room, suffocate from poison gases given off by stoves, but of course *he* might not think of that, so they let the fire go out, and then as the chill quickly came over them and an hour passed and no Reithman came, they gave up the idea and started up the fire. It was dark now. The boys whose idea death had been were now talking about sending a messenger to the College.

After some debate, on the afternoon of the second day, they voted to send Weiss. He was the only volunteer. They gave him one end of a ball on twine and out he went, the wind so strong he could hardly stand. He fought his way uphill, missed the path and he had to struggle through deep drifts and thick brush, where the end of the string tore from his mitted hand, and he panicked, broke into a gallop, ran into the gale so fierce he couldn't hear himself scream, ran, fell, ran again, hit a tree, and finally ran full tilt into the porch of Main, which caught him at the knees, and dragged himself to the door and crawled in.

He lay on the floor, too tired to move. He noticed the strange light in the cold chapel, as if he were underwater, a luminous predawn light, and saw a faint corona around the window above the pulpit. And then he heard breathing that was not his own, and stood up, and saw the bear sitting in the doorway to the gallery, and he turned away and fouled his pants and sat down.

The bear made no movement toward him and made no sound except for its breathing, which was rough like the rasp of sandpaper. Spit fell from its mouth and froze into a pale milky beard. Its eyes were dim green coals. It was an immense bear, or seemed so to him who had never seen a bear, and staring at it, he could not move where he sat, not even to scratch his nose. The bear seemed to hold him in the power of its evil gaze and in the musky odour of bear. He sat, thinking no thought but that his death was close at hand.

In Carlyle, when the twine went slack, the students knew he was lost and would die. Some started to go after him and had to be held back by classmates; others stood a few feet outside the door and shouted and shouted his name, "Weiss! Weiss!" The wind was so strong they couldn't see their hands in front of their faces. Still, they took turns calling to him and whistling and clapping and beating on the eaves with a board, and others knelt in the long dark hall and wept and prayed for him, even after night fell and after they had crawled into beds together to keep warm, they prayed, and one would open the door and shout, long into the night.

The morning of the third day, they woke up and saw the storm had blown itself out. They wasted no time; all piled out the door and climbed single-file up the path through drifts five and six feet high and broke into the chapel and found him under the pulpit, wrapped in a drape he had torn off the wall, half-frozen, wide-awake, and he told them about the bear. When they didn't believe him, he showed them his pants.

On December 10, the question of foreign immigration was debated by members of the Phileopolis club, the affirmative team winning 12–7, nineteen students being all who remained, the others having left. The bear in the chapel had frightened everybody, and then the bear didn't go away even after they set off rockets and blew a bugle and banged on a drum. Its tracks were found outside Dr. Watt's house, then on the lawn by Main, then in a circle around Emerson, and then students began to withdraw from the College, one by one, two by two, hauling their trunks to the road to hail a ride to Little Falls and the daily coach to St. Paul. Even Dr. Watt could not stop them. After the first visitation, after paths had been shoveled and the supply of firewood replenished, Dr. Watt spoke at morning chapel a marathon sermon that left his congregation as weak as if they had spent the time struggling through snowdrifts. "His opening prayer consumed twenty-six minutes," Mr. Reithman noted, "and touched on many points of Old Testament history."

Though they didn't know it, it was a desperate Henry who faced them. His wife had announced at the height of the storm her intention to return to Boston. She had announced this several times before and in better weather, and now she announced it finally and asked him for five hundred dollars. She had suffered, she said, from his neglect. He was silent around her; he sat reading Bible commentaries and writing his sermons and staring into the fire. Outside their home, she said, he was voluble and manly and kept a cheerful disposition, but once in the door, he collapsed into a dark and impenetrable mood, and whenever she spoke, he didn't respond. He did not respond to her affections, he did not appear to recognize her. "How can you be so generous with others, even utter strangers, and here in your house with your own wife be so cold, so removed?" she wondered. "Your better nature you show to the world, and your dark nature you show to me and to me alone! All I see is darkness and brooding and silence. Have you no love left for me?" She stood over him as she spoke, and he couldn't look at her. He said nothing. She wept, she knelt and touched his knee, then her voice turned quiet and resolute and she demanded the money—all this without a word from Henry.

Dr. Watt's sermon began with Christ's suffering on the cross, and it proceeded to other suffering of those faithful to Him, of Stephen and other apostles and martyrs, and it went back to the prophets and their foreknowledge of that suffering, and to the Psalmist and the Children of Israel and to Job, and here Dr. Watt himself was exhausted but he beat on and began to talk about the bear as a messenger of God. God uses animals to work His Will, sometimes happily as with the dove of Noah and the birds who fed Elijah and the lions who proved Daniel's faith and the swine who received the demons cast out, but also as instruments of judgment as in the case of the bear who came out of the woods to devour the children who mocked God's servant Elisha for his baldness. As he delved into Elisha's career, it became terribly evident to all that the President, now freed from his text and moving away from the pulpit and into the aisle and bracing himself with one hand against pew after pew and speaking thunderously, considered himself to be Elisha and was searching the chapel for those children who had mocked him in their hearts, to whom God had sent the bear as punishment. He couldn't stop himself. He recited his many efforts in their behalf, his dedication, his hard work, and their offenses, their indolence, their unworthiness."Why?" he shouted. "Why? Why has thou forsaken me?" Nobody made an attempt to stop him. Everyone in the room was making his own plan for escape.

Five boys left immediately after chapel with the father of one of them, who had come in a wagon with clean laundry. Dr. Watt didn't come out to say good-bye.

That afternoon, fresh tracks were found by two students returning from cutting wood, and a band of five led by Mr. Reithman with a rifle marched off to find the beast's den and to kill it. The bear was large and black, judging from the footprints and the tufts of hair found in bushes, and their long trek only determined that he had been circling the College, approaching as near as a hundred feet to Carlyle and Emerson, and that he had been joined by a second bear and perhaps a third. That night, a guard was posted in the belfry. "A sleepless night for all," wrote Mr. Reithman, "due in some part to choruses of ursine snorts and growls which the wakeful addressed to those who slept, some of whom awoke to find tufts of bear fur on their pillows."

Mrs. Watt left on the 13th to spend Christmas with friends in St. Paul, four boys leaving with her. Dr. Watt explained to Mr. Reithman that she was nervous and preoccupied due to lack of feminine company, and he was sending her away lest she lose her senses. Mrs. Watt handed Mr. Reithman a note as he helped her into the sleigh. The note begged him to pray for her and to put food out for the bear. Instead, a trap baited with jelly and syrup was rigged close to the fresher circumference of tracks. It was found licked clean but unsprung on the morning of the 14th. A nearby tree showed deep claw marks to the height of ten feet.

On the 15th, Dr. Watt announced in chapel that Christmas vacation would be spent at the College in academic pursuits. Six boys left on foot in the afternoon, leaving baggage behind and a student body of four souls: Borden, Smith, Godfrey, and Weiss. The four "are in a desperate state, afraid to disobey, afraid to remain," wrote Mr. Reithman in his journal. "They enrolled here expecting much and are reluctant to abandon ship, though I have argued with them. I believe they trust me too much and think that matters will improve so long as I remain. God help me. I must go and take them with me. Our President is crazed."

He told Dr. Watt that the College must be closed. Dr. Watt replied that he would sooner kill himself. "It is no time to be giving in to fear," he cried. "This institution is the only one! It stands alone, friendless, far from any sympathetic soul! If we retreat now, sir, we permit ignorance to stand unchallenged for years to come!"

On the afternoon of the 18th, shots were heard from the woods and shouts—a Mr. Slocum from town ran out from the trees and yelled to the lookout, "I have killed him!" They followed him back the way he had come and found the bear humped in a pile as if he had tried to gather himself for one last leap. His blood lay steaming on the snow, bright red, a great burst of it.

Mr. Slocum took the skin for himself and four big steaks. He hacked off the head and said he would come back for it. Four boys and Mr. Reithman put the rest of the meat on a sled and hauled it to Main, and that night they ate a good part of it themselves— Dr. Watt said he had no stomach for bear—roasting it over an open fire, a feast that got livelier as it lasted on into the night. They ate with their fingers half-cooked bear meat and sang song after song, and piled more wood on the fire, until the flames nearly reached the treetops. They piled every stick of wood they could find on the fire and went off for more, and evidently that was when the second bear attacked.

Two boys, Emmett Borden and Alton Smith, had found a fallen birch and were carrying it back toward the bonfire when they heard crashing behind them and dropped their load and ran. The bear pursued and caught them just short of the fire, where a third boy, Miles Godfrey, watched in horror. Emmett was bit in the throat and perished on the spot. Alton, a brilliant student who later embarked on a distinguished career in public life, suffered gashes on the chest and shoulders from the animal's trying to drag him away, and bore scars to the day of his death in 1908. Miles Godfrey was thrown to the ground and his foot nearly chewed to the bone, but recovered, and eventually made his fortune in the grain trade in Minneapolis and Chicago. Mr. Reithman hurled chunks of ice at the beast and drove it away. Mr. Weiss was not present, having gone to bed. Mr. Reithman obtained a new position at Carleton College in Northfield and taught there for fifteen more years until his untimely death in a boating accident. Mr. Weiss remained at Albion College until the spring, his mind unhinged, and had to be removed to the state asylum at St. Peter, where he lived until his decease, the date of which is not known.

———————

The winter of the bears ushered in the Panic of 1857, when Minnesota Life Insurance & Trust Company gravely and gracefully crashed and banks in St. Paul stopped dealing in legal tender; when the investors of the New Albion Land Company opened the treasurer's strongbox and found dried grass, some gravel, and a few feathers; and when every piece of paper held by New Albion speculators became a piece of paper. Deflation was followed by a plague of dysentery. The grasshoppers came in August, from the west, a black funnel cloud of them on the 7th, the sky turning black with bugs on the 12th. Those who had scorned speculation in favor of honest labor now found their crops destroyed by the infestation.

That August, the poet Putnam wrote:

> Were I a bird, a wingèd bird,
> And sped the airy regions through,
> I would fly to the east where comes the light,
> Land of the Pilgrims' godly might,
> Land of the good and true,
> Far from this prairie vast and dry
> Where clouds of locusts from on high
> Blacken the dreary land and sky.

No song we hear, no sun we see
For clamor of insect gluttony—
Blasting our crops and fields beneath
The whining onslaught of their teeth,
Blasting our hopes and pleasures, too,
This darkest hour of the night.
O had I wings on which to flee,
I'd bid the wretched west Adieu,
Fly Bostonward—O blessed sight!
Were I a wingèd bird.

He and Madame Juliet were among the escapees, many of whom went to California, to a town named Albion City in the mountains east of Sacramento, where there was said to be quite a lot of gold remaining in certain abandoned sites that a brother of Mr. Halliwell knew about. The Putnams went south to St. Louis, where she had friends in the theater.

About half of the residents had left New Albion by 1858, the year that Minnesota achieved statehood, including Dr. Watt. His last act as President was a letter to a Mr. Waters who had applied to him for a teaching job.

New Albion, Minn.
Jan. 18, 1858

Mr. W. H. Waters
St. Paul, Minn.

Dear Sir: Your favor of 2nd ints. was duly received, requesting information concerning your obtaining a position with New Albion College as an instructor of moral theology. It was good of you to recall so pleasantly our lecture on "American Poets" of ten years ago at the Philolectian Club in your city, of which we are pleased to have a fair copy and send to you with warmest recollections of that evening.

We are only sorry to report that the College has suspended classes after some skulduggery hereabouts by wild bears struck terror into our ranks and emasculated our numbers, hence we are unable to offer employment. Of course, we intend to persevere and triumph over the present trouble, to which end we depart Wednesday next for Boston where we hope to secure support, both financial and moral, of a nature and amount more generous than could be found in this sparsely populated county, and when we return, we trust that we will have better news for you. With best wishes for success and prosperity.

Very truly yours,

Henry Francis Watt, *Ph.D.*

Evidently, Dr. Watt did make the trip to Boston, because it was there that he died in April, of a seizure, in a hotel room, following a dinner with prospective backers. When he failed to return to New Albion, the trustees of the College voted to suspend operations until the fall, and in the fall, when no students appeared (they had heard the College had closed), the College closed for good, and the property was put up for sale; a few years later, after a fire destroyed the Main building, the land was bought by a Mr. Moore who built a barn on the old foundations and used the remaining structures for storage. The great bell had fallen in the fire and Mr. Moore was able to raise it just enough to turn it upside down to where it could be used to water livestock.

"The year 1857 will be remembered as the year when all false hope was lost," wrote Mr. Getchell sadly to his brother in Maine. "So much is gone that once we could not live without, and yet we do live somehow and even sometimes think hopefully of tomorrow."

———

The railroad took its sweet time arriving. The Northern Pacific reached St. Cloud and continued north along the Mississippi to Little Falls, and the Great Northern swung west through St. Joseph, Avon, Albany, and Freeport, while the Soo Line ran northeast from Albany to just south of Little Falls, the three lines making a triangle and each missing the town by miles. Bribes were paid to railroad officials, of course, but other towns paid bigger ones. The handsome depot built to lure the lines sat empty and its platform opened onto a field of alfalfa where a tiny sign on a pole stood, which said "W." The town board sent monthly petitions to St. Paul, and a delegation attended every grand opening of new track for miles around, of which there were many. Each of the major railroads had a ceremonial train known as a "jacker" with a flatcar for a band, two or three coaches for the guests, and a palatial parlor car to haul the dignitaries, and when the line reached a town or a spot where the railroad intended to promote a town, the special train was run out for the day for speeches, music, and the driving of a special spike, usually brass. The Albion delegation lobbied hard at these occasions, carrying a satin banner emblazoned "New Albion—Gateway To Central Minnesota," not knowing that the dignitaries on hand were men of great dignity but little influence who had time on their hands and enjoyed sitting on platforms for a small per diem.

Years later, Jonson Ingqvist visited the abandoned Great Northern building on Market Street in St. Paul, looking for a good used desk, and found in a pile of rubbish on the fourth floor a file marked "Albion" containing letters from the town promoting itself as a rail center. The file was marked: "Error—no such appears on map—must mean Albany." Albany, to the south of New Albion, was on the main G.N. line.

The ultimate connection of the town, in 1885, with the so-called "Lake Wobegon spur," was a mistake on the railroad's part, a siding that took a sharp angle due to misplaced surveyors' stakes and that kept going for sixteen miles in an attempt to find its way back to the main line. When the track crew reached New Albion, which was not on their map and which at any rate was now called Lake Wobegon, they simply stopped and returned to St. Cloud by horse-drawn wagon, leaving the track where it is today, a quarter-mile south of town, ending in thick brush by the depot. (The depot was moved south on skids to reach the end of the line.) A district superintendent was fired for his negligence; the spur appears on G.N. maps as a dotted line marked "See Code," but there is no code. The company nonetheless began regular shipping over the spur that year, which continued until 1965. Passenger service was always by petition, fifty names being required due to the inconvenience of the stop (trains have to back in the full distance), and so was mostly limited to great occasions such as the Norwegian Tricentennial, the inauguration of Governor Burnquist, and Dan Patch's running at the State Fair.

In 1922, the westbound Empire Builder entered the spur by mistake on June 4, shortly before midnight, and raced toward Lake Wobegon carrying 432 passengers, including Rita Melitta, The Cream of Wheat Quartet, The Laughing Waters Orchestra, and Douglas Byron Rochester, author of *The Boy Brigade* series. The great train swept on towards its doom, its bar car blazing with light as the merrymakers danced in the aisle, until, a quarter-mile short of sure death, their lives were saved by a Holstein belonging to a farmer named Brown, which strolled onto the tracks. The engineer applied his brakes too late to save the cow but just in time to stop the train at the station, where he noticed a few yards ahead, the two rails end. The passengers disembarked for a few minutes while a trainman ran to find out where they were. No lights appeared in town, everyone had turned in. "Who would want to live in a burg as dead as this?" remarked Rita Melitta, not knowing that Mr. Lundberg the undertaker had nearly received her business that night.

A few months later, the train carrying the Sorbasol

All-Star barnstorming team backed into town, carrying Babe Ruth, Walter Johnson, Long George Kelly, and Wild Man Ringsak, and departed in the evening on the long end of a 17–5 score.

———

The first primary school in Mist County (aside from the singing school run by Madame Putnam) was taught by Miss Emily Chase (later Mrs. Getchell) the winter of 1853–54, a private school kept in a boarding house run by a Mr. Charles Church which later was discovered to be a tavern. The next winter there was no school, and in the summer of 1855 Mr. Bayfield's empty house was pressed into service, twenty-six pupils attending, run by Miss Ida J. Packard who was all of sixteen and was hard put to keep order. Early in November 1856, a regular schoolhouse was built on Van Buren (now McKinley) next to the Albion Shoe Company, and some forty-five pupils enrolled under Mr. Sewell W. Smiley, whose brother Newell was in the shoe business. Miscreants were sent to him and put to work scraping cowhide in the cellar, where, it was said, the vapors from the curing vats were strong enough to destroy human hair and where, some older children said, Mr Newell Smiley had once made four pairs of ladies' boots from a 14-year-old boy. The school year passed without incident.

The first county superintendent of schools appears to have been Dr. Tuttle, who served from 1860 until his death in 1874. A four-room schoolhouse was built in 1866 on Maple, and the Van Buren school was moved to Taylor Street, where it was used for storage by Shaw & Getchell—or else the new school was built on Taylor and the Van Buren school was moved to Maple, in which case *it* is the building that burned in 1871—no one is quite certain on this point. Some tend to believe the latter, since Shaw & Getchell were out of business by then, though Mr. Shaw himself still operated a couple wagons for hire and might have needed storage facilities—and yet, if the Van Buren school was moved to Taylor, how does one explain the building in the 1870 photograph labeled "Old School," which stood next to the Congregational Church and which, judging from the children hanging out of the windows, was used for a purpose other than storage? On the other hand, the structure on Maple that burned the following year is described in some accounts as "abandoned"? Is it possible that the "Van Buren" school was actually built on *Taylor* and then *moved* to Van Buren (where the Congregational Church stood) after the Maple school was built and before the fire destroyed the Shaw & Getchell warehouse (abandoned because they had gone out of business)? Or—and I lean toward this theory—was there a *third* schoolhouse involved, one that was known as "Old School" and which was not adjacent to the church (a thin white line appears between the two in the photograph) but which remained on Van Buren (on the corner with Maple)? That would leave two other buildings, one to be a warehouse and the other to burn. In any case, the abandoned New Albion College (the building in town) was taken over by the school district in 1882 (the year after a fire damaged but did not destroy it). It stands today on McKinley (formerly Van Buren) and is used as a warehouse.

The first person to be killed by a white man in the New Albion area was the French-Canadian voyageur named Tourtelotte, struck on the head with a paddle by Boule Simmcon in 1742 as they entered the lake after a long day going upstream on the Malheur River and saw they had followed the wrong branch of the Sauk. Authorities at the Hudson's Bay Company headquarters in Grand Portage ruled that the homicide was justifiable—Tourtelotte was known as a man who always took the bow position in the canoe and used a sweep-stroke that achieved little propulsion while splashing the man in the stern—and anyway Simmcon had suffered enough from the victim's company. "M. Tourtelotte knew but two Voyageur's Songs and of those only the Choruses," said the inquest report, "and made of them such a Constant Clangour as to propagate Dread and affect a Shew of Force."

A man was shot in New Albion on election day in 1860, but recovered. He had not made his loyalty evident and might have been a Republican, but the Republican who shot him was taking no chances. He was held in the town jail but was released to join the Army, which he did, and died at Antietam.

In April 1861, Robert Wise, visiting his uncle, Mr.

Tripp, was killed by a trapper named Bowers who thought the young man had stolen his furs and who was wrong about that and felt remorse and hung himself in his cell; he was acquitted by the jury on account of his death.

On December 24, 1868, at a dance at the New Albion House, a man was stabbed and killed who was not the man the assailant intended to kill, the man who had given an expensive brooch to a woman nearby, but the man standing next to him. The murderer served several years at the penitentiary in Stillwater. The woman had been betrothed to the murderer. She married the man who gave her the gift and they removed to Minneapolis.

In June 1875, Mr. Herman Daly was shot and killed in his field by a neighbor, Azariah Frost, whose son David had married Mr. Daly's daughter Maud two years before; Frost then returned home and killed himself.

On a Sunday evening in May 1880, persons came to the window of the Shaw residence while members of the family were eating supper and fired a Winchester rifle and a shotgun loaded with buckshot, killing Mr. Horace Shaw and his young son, Charles, while severely injuring Mrs. Shaw who was pierced by several bullets but survived in a crippled condition. Two daughters, Mary and Agnes Shaw, fifteen and seventeen years of age, had gone to the kitchen to cut a blueberry pie and were uninjured. A detective from St. Paul was called in on the case and, following up various clues, he put the finger on two men from

St. Cloud who had been seen in the company of the Shaw girls at a dance only a week before the murders. The girls admitted to authorities that they had agreed with the young men to marry them if they killed their parents so the girls would inherit the house. Reprehensible as the crime was, the girls were put on a train to Minneapolis to live with an aunt. The young men were tried for murder and found not guilty by the jury, which felt that the girls were equally culpable, whereupon a man named Conway shot and killed a juryman. He was never apprehended.

The following August, a newborn child was found in a privy, and in October, the decomposed body of what appeared to be a young woman of wealth was found in a field during plowing. A string of pearls was around her neck, and the bones of her right hand clutched a Bible. That winter, a man was stabbed and left to die in a ditch north of town. Nobody could identify the body. Mr. Thorvaldson offered a gravesite and a stone. The body was buried under the name "Oscar Thorvaldson," though the deceased was no relation to him.

Doctors came and went. Four had hung up their shingles in five years and then left, taking the shingles with them. One of them was all right if you believed in that sort of thing (roots, mainly, and leaves), one was a drunk, one peddled snake oil, and the other didn't get much business, so there was no telling about him. A fifth man, Dr. Thompson, was good and left after the diphtheria epidemic of 1866, his own health shattered.

When Dr. Louis Holter, E.D.D., set up shop in 1872, the town had lost faith in the current office-holder, a Dr. Pfeiffer, who dispensed white powders and brown liquids that put his patients in a stupor. Once, after a massive outbreak of dysentery, he dosed them with a combination of the two, and half of New Albion lay flat on its back, seeing faces in the wallpaper.

Dr. Holter brought the most advanced equipment of the day: an electrical chair, solid oak, with a crank in back that the physician turned to create magnetic energy that entered the body through wires and straps and achieved a more perfect balance of forces within the corporal field. The electrical chair, he instructed them, was no *interventive measure* to be called on when illness struck but rather a *preventive* and *restorative* device, meant to be employed on a weekly basis. The patient would notice the benefits only after a serious and sustained program of treatment.

The electrical chair produced a pleasant tingly sensation. One could actually feel things happening in the legs and up the spine, as negative power came into balance with positive, and the flow of positivity was redirected *to* and *from* the cranial extremity, making vibrations in the peepers and leading to tremendous benefits that one was already beginning to imagine.

Word-of-mouth built Dr. Holter's trade, and he took over the Albion House, which became the

Holter Sanitarium. Three more electrical chairs were brought in and two trained magneticists to crank them, and by 1874, upwards of a hundred persons were taking weekly sittings. The treatment was especially popular among the New Englanders, Dr. Holter being a Maine man. The Germans and Norwegians, having recently arrived, couldn't afford him, and so their health was not affected.

For the regular customer, the dosage of magnetism needed to make one feel things happen soon got to be quite a jolt, and then one noticed other things happening, such as headaches and fatigue. The doctor's supporters grew pale and listless. One magneticist left and then another as trade declined, and finally Dr. Holter retired to Wyoming. Mr. Getchell was his last patient that day. He sat in the electrical chair, bound with straps and wound with wires, as the doctor cranked away, and for a moment, Mr. Getchell sensed that he was on the verge of feeling good again, and then he felt a numbness at the top of his head and briefly forgot his own name. When he stood up, he almost fainted. When he walked out the door, the town seemed dim, insubstantial, and filled with an ominous low hum. On the streets were strange people who spoke a foreign language.

New Albion became Lake Wobegone in 1880, a change voted by the City Council to celebrate the fact that Norwegians had gained a 4–3 majority. Then the City Council voted to become the Town Council.

The New Englanders bitterly opposed both changes, arguing—even shouting – that they were undignified, unprogressive, and would make the town a laughing-stock. "Woebegone means dismal, unhappy, dilapidated, bedraggled!" they said. "You can't do this!" The Norwegians just sat and smiled. To them, Wobegone was the name of the lake they loved and nothing more. They liked the sound of it.

In 1882, Lake Woebegone became New Albion again, Mr. Fjelde having lost his seat to Mr. Weeks by two votes. Mr. Fjelde got back on the Council two years later, and then it was Lake Wobegone again. State statute permits four name changes, after which a name is considered permanent and can be changed only by the legislature, so the Council changed it one more time, from Lake Wobegone to Lake Wobegon. Mr. Getchell resigned in protest and was replaced by Mr. Oskar Tollefson. Businessmen didn't order new stationery right away, however, not even those who favored the change, but used all their New Albion stock until it ran out.

FOREBEARS

The oldest living Wobegonian, Mr. Henry Anderson, eighty-nine, is in a state of decline, and his memory of town history now includes such things as President Warren G. Harding living at the Sons of Knute temple and elephants in the woods and people running down the street after the Great Earthquake, so the oldest reliable memory may be Hjalmar Ingqvist's, of his grandfather standing with an arm around an elm tree on a summer night singing *"Til Norge In Sogn Or Rein"* ("To Norway in Sun or Rain") with tears running down his cheeks. He was sixty years away from Norway, still he sang—

> *O Norway, your rugged mountains and towering*
> *pines call to me though I have crossed the*
> *ocean never to return.*
> *O bird in the sky, fly quickly and tell all of my*
> *dear ones that my heart is filled with*
> *unspeakable love and sorrow.*

Homesickness hit the old-timers hard, even after so many years, and it was not unusual, Hjalmar says, to see old people weep openly for Norway or hear about old men so sad they took a bottle of whiskey up to the cemetery and lay down on the family grave and talked to the dead about home, the home in Norway, heavenly Norway.

America was the land where they were old and sick, Norway where they were young and full of hopes—and much smarter, for you are never so smart again in a language learned in middle age nor so romantic or brave or kind. All the best of you is in the old tongue, but when you speak your best in America you become a yokel, a dumb Norskie, and when you speak English, an idiot. No wonder the old-timers loved the places where the mother tongue was spoken, the Evangelical Lutheran Church, the Sons of Knute lodge, the tavern, where they could talk and cry and sing to their hearts' content.

> *O Norway, land of my childish fancies, thy dark*
> *green forest is where my soul goes to seek*
> *comfort.*
> *O bird in the sky, tell me—do they remember me*
> *in the old home or am I a stranger wherever I*
> *roam?*

Hjalmar was ten years old, the president of the fifth grade, and when his grandfather cried, Hjalmar got up and left the room.

His father heard the old man out and said, "Well, Father, if you're unhappy here, I will be happy to pay your fare back." The old man sighed. He remembered the trip over. Fourteen days across the North Atlantic in heavy weather. Men, women, and children packed into dark rooms that stank like a stable. The room rolling, rising and falling. Everyone lay on wooden pallets. A girl from near his village in Trondheim fell ill the first day at sea. An old woman took one look and said, *Mother*, but the girl cried, No! And died four days later in childbirth. The baby died too. They were buried at sea.

That was the voyage over, and in the old man's mind that would be the voyage back. In America where he lived, he was dying, and the ship back to his true life in Norway was the ship of death. He would take that ship eventually. He was not ready to go just yet.

Hjalmar's father owned the majority interest in the Farmers' Grain Elevator and Flour Mill, traveled regularly on business to Chicago, once spoke to William Howard Taft (on the train, in English), and was a considerable man, not the sort to suddenly burst into tears for another country. He spoke Norwegian only when spoken to. At seventeen, he had gone to work for Mr. Weeks who owned the elevator and mill, a gentleman who avoided the office whenever possible, preferring to stay home and read Emerson, and Jonson Ingqvist, left to his own, learned the business quickly. He was glad to run it and, in 1908, after three years of poor crops, when Mr. Weeks panicked, Jonson was glad to take it off his hands for a modest price, no cash in advance. There were rumors that Jonson had juggled the books. He said only, "Mr. Weeks read too much. He wasn't so bad off as he thought." Jonson outsmarted him in the English language, and he was proud of it. Mr. Weeks was foolish and lacked faith in the land and the farmers, and Jonson had faith, but he also had very good English and spoke it with little trace of an accent.

He campaigned for English in the Lutheran church. "When we preach in Norwegian, we preach only to ourselves and to fewer and fewer of us," he said. "This is no preaching, this is speaking in tongues!" He believed that since they were in America, they should be Americans. ("Of course, America had been good to him," says Clarence Bunsen. "The rich can afford to be progressive. Poor people have reason to be afraid of the future." Clarence's grandfather worked for the Ingqvists, filling flour sacks.)

When Birgit Tollefson, Hjalmar's sister, moved back to Honolulu in 1964 after her husband died, she plunged into service for the Mist County Historical Society, gathering up old letters, papers, and other artifacts, doubling the Society's collection in a year's time, much to the displeasure of Mrs. Halvorson, who, before Birgit showed up, had *been* the Society. "We don't have room for all that junk!" Mrs. Halvorson complained to anyone who would listen to her.

97

"She's hauling in everybody's attic! I looked in one of those boxes and found ten pairs of ladies' underwear! *Underwear*, mind you! Are we going to have a display of *underwear*? Get a big glass case and fill it up with *underwear*? Why not enema bottles and thunder jugs? Why don't we collect all the *outhouses*? We could have forty or fifty of them, all in good working order!"

There wasn't room for both of them in the Society, so Birgit founded the Daughters of the Pioneers, membership limited to descendants of Norwegian families who settled in Lake Wobegon by 1895, which neatly cut out Mrs. Halvorson, whose grandfather had come in 1896.

After Honolulu, Birgit's Norwegian heritage appeared wonderful and exotic to her. "Marvelous," she cried, holding up some old *rosemaling* painting that had been on someone's kitchen wall for fifty years. "Marvelous! Incredible!" Anything Norwegian held fascination for her: any antique that had been in Norwegian hands, old Norwegian newspapers that she could not read, old family pictures held her spellbound for minutes, even pictures of families she had never known—they were Norwegian and that was all that mattered.

For *Syttende Mai* of 1965, the Daughters planned a procession to the cemetery, and the question arose: who should carry the flag? The committee voted for an honor guard of seven Daughters whose ancestors had arrived first, and the club archivist, Darlene Tollerud, set about looking through old letters and church records to see whose ancestors would be the winners.

In a chest that Birgit had gotten from Luther Rognes, Darlene found a packet of letters written by Magnus Oleson to his family in Norway, which the family brought when they joined Magnus in the New World, and what was clearer than day in the letters was the fact that Magnus was not only the first arrival, he was also a deserter from General George McClellan's army. Magnus, on reaching New York in 1861, had accepted $200 from a man named West to take his place in the Army which Magnus understood would be for only a few weeks, and when he found that army life was brutal, the food was not fit for animals, the camp was full of sickness, the officers were cruel, and he, who scarcely spoke English, was being put in places where people shot at him, he decided it was no war for a Norwegian. His only good words were for General McClellan who did not push the army too hard to go into battle. That was fine with Magnus. He had written to Lincoln, explaining the odd circumstances that had brought him into a war that he wanted no part of, and got no reply. "He does not care, he is a butcher and a barbarian," Magnus wrote to his family.

A few days later, he wrote again. He had stolen an officer's horse and was in Kentucky. He went from there to Wisconsin and then to Minnesota, putting as much distance as possible between himself and the fighting. He arrived in Lake Wobegon on the stolen horse in the summer of 1863, about the time his regiment was being destroyed in the battle of Gettysburg.

He bought land north of town where he lived all his life, dying in 1911. He fathered eight children, two of whom died in infancy. The six others bore children of their own, and one way and another, the name of Magnus Oleson was in the family tree of almost every Norwegian in town.

The idea of the honor guard was quietly put aside. A baton twirler carried the flag. The Daughters marched together in a group.

Clarence Bunsen told his wife Arlene, a Daughter, "I don't see how you can hold it against your ancestor for not getting himself killed. If all of us had heroes for ancestors, then where would that leave us?" She said it was a shock, that was all, and people would get over it in time.

When Magnus arrived in 1863 from the bloody campaigns of the Union army, the town was still New Albion, the citizens were New Englanders, whom he called Woodmen—from the name of their lodge. The Mystical and Enlightened Order of Woodmen, and also from their appearance; their faces looked like lumber. Nobody greeted him in Norwegian. He knew only enough English to ask for what he wanted. He got a job in the New Albion Mill shelling corn, which was done by walking horses over it, and boarded with a family named Watson, which treated him like a young and not very bright child. In a photograph of townspeople gathered at the church after hearing of the assassination of President Lincoln, a short figure in a white shirt whose face is blurred appears to the far right of the crowd of black suits; it is assumed to be him. He appears to have only stopped in passing and then not to have stood still enough; certainly his loyalty to Lincoln's cause was very slight. He wrote home to Norway:

> Men will walk ten miles for a scrap of news about the war and then walk back and discuss it late into the evening. A newspaper from St. Paul or Chicago is a feast to them although it is full of lies. They are all strong for the Union here, having never fought for it or seen the bodies stacked like firewood. I lie in my bed and listen to them. Their voices sound like woodsaws!

Three veterans returned to New Albion of the twelve young men who left, including Albert Watson, who asked Magnus questions about his whereabouts the past few years. "It is a great advantage at times not to understand English," he wrote, "and at times I find it better to understand less than I do." One night Albert arrived home late from a lyceum at which a Horatio Stevens had spoken on "The American Republic as a Movement Of Regeneration" and seized the young millhand by his leg and hauled him out of bed, but Albert was too weak to beat him. He sank to the floor exhausted. He was flushed and feverish. He was coming down with diphtheria.

The diphtheria epidemic swept through New Albion in three horrible weeks of October 1865, and devastated many families, killing thirty-seven children, eleven women, and four men, including Albert. Dr. Thompson drove himself to exhaustion, riding for miles into the country from bedside to bedside late into the night, dozing off in the buggy when his horse finally headed for home, awakening a few hours later with a new call for help, a new case, another frantic father at his door. There was little that a doctor could do. The only treatment was to offer hot raw alcohol to try to keep the throat open: at first by the spoonful, and then, if the patient got worse, by the cup, until the poor person began to choke and gasp for the last few gulps of breath; then the doctor could only hold them as they struggled.

All that month and for weeks after, New Albion was practically a ghost town. People were terrified of contagion and avoided any contact with their neighbors. What with his daily contact with the sick, Dr. Thompson was shunned by the well. His own wife and children left for St. Cloud, and when people there learned where they had come from, the family was told to move on to St. Paul. School was closed, of course, and church. Those merchants who still could stand retreated to a back room when customers came in. Any communication was shouted from a distance. Out in the country, men on their way to town stopped their teams fifty yards from an infected house and shouted, "Do you need anything?" and if the inhabitants were strong enough to shout back what they wanted, their neighbors brought it—flour and pork, beans, coffee, maybe brandy, liniment, Dr. Clarke's Oil of Arnica—and left it on a stump, but if the passerby heard nothing, he went on. Days passed before someone came out and looked in the house.

That someone was often Magnus, who was untouched by the disease, having encountered it in the army, and who devoted himself to burying the dead. He was offered money for this and after giving it thought he accepted it. The work was hard, and he was the only one who seemed up for it.

The word came at night—a farmer stopped and shouted up at my window, and in the morning I hitched up the horse and drove out six miles across the fields where corn rots for lack of able bodies to pick it, arriving at the silent little house about ten o'clock. I knocked and heard a very slight scraping inside, the door opened slowly and a man who looked almost dead himself looked out the crack and then withdrew. A moment later he reappeared and with great difficulty opened the door wider and passed out to me the sad little bundle of his dead son wrapped in a piece of blanket. He did not weep for he was too sick, and I did not weep either for I have done this so many times. I carried the precious cargo to a grove of trees about thirty feet away where I had already dug the hole and placed the child in it and set to work. I prayed as I shoveled. There was not even time for a hymn! I did not pray for the child's soul, for of that I had no doubt that it was with the angels, but rather prayed that God would give me many children of my own. I would like to have twenty or thirty!

It was not until 1867 that the woman arrived from St. Paul to become his wife, and while he waited for her, he began to prosper a little. During the epidemic he did the work of six men, and when the town recovered, he was promoted to foreman of the mill, the old foreman having left in a panic, and he bought a house in the woods about a half-mile from town for $30, the former inhabitant having died of the disease. He carried all the furniture out of the house, piled it in the field, doused it with kerosene, and burned it: a featherbed and bedstead and black walnut dresser, a rocking chair, a fine oak table and two chairs, a sideboard, a divan, and much more—the deceased, a young man by the name of Ward, having been prosperous, though Magnus had never seen him work a day. He left behind a closetful of fine suits and white shirts, which Magnus also put to the torch. Only the two stoves remained.

The house gave him fresh hope that the life he had longed for was soon to arrive. He walked through the rooms, a kitchen and front room and bedroom downstairs and two little bedrooms up under the eaves, and imagined them filled with his family. That winter he bought himself a large bed. "It is not so beautiful to some perhaps," he wrote to his cousin Bjorne, "but to me it is like a temple. Here someday my lonely existence will be filled with laughter. I hope that she is young and beautiful and all the children are loud and strong."

On May 15, 1867, sitting in the shade of a stone abutment at the mill, eating his lunch, he saw a party of four wagons and some men on horseback ride slowly down the hill into town. Even at a distance, something about them caught his eye, and he got up and walked in their direction, and then a word of Norwegian flew like a bird on the wind, and he began to run. He tore down the dusty street past the church to the square and leaped at the youth on the first horse and pulled him down and got him on the ground and hugged him. It was Oskar Tollefson, 16, leading thirteen of his countrymen back from the desolate Dakota Territory where they had migrated in hopes of resuming their livelihood as fishermen. Magnus went from one to the other, touching their faces, kissing the women, embracing the men, hoisting the three little children high in the air, and seeing how happy he was, not realizing it was on their account, they assumed this must be a fine home for Norwegians and fell to their knees and thanked God for bringing them here. Then he took them to his house and all of them lived there for a few weeks, during which he stopped talking only long enough to sleep and work. At last he could speak intelligently and with feeling! About anything under the sun!

The Tollefson party's misbegotten journey to Dakota was due to their own lack of English when they arrived in St. Paul in October aboard a train from New York. They managed to recover four pieces of baggage that had been marked for points west and got rooms for the night at a hotel and even bargained with a livery for wagons and horses, but when they asked about a great lake, nobody knew what they were talking about.

"I stood in the street in front of our lodging and watched for a kind and patient face, and when a man came along, I said, 'Please help me,' and then tried to indicate by gesture what it was we were seeking," Oskar wrote years later. "I indicated a very large lake such as we had heard about from Norwegians in New York. I indicated a fishing boat with two sets of oars and a small mainsail and indicated the nets and big fish in the nets and myself pulling them in, and then sailing home and the great happiness that awaited us on shore, and cleaning the fish, and eating them."

Evidently Oskar indicated a great *calm* lake, for the man who saw the pantomime assumed that the youth was looking for open prairie. He led him to the end of the street and pointed up the hill to a train of Red River oxcarts just making their way over the crest, where the Cathedral of St. Paul stands today, and indicated that he should follow them a great distance. The man also indicated that the carters were drunks and wild men, and that Oskar should keep his money on his person at all times.

The trip north and west to Dakota took three weeks. The cart drivers weren't drunks; they drank every drop of their whiskey the first night out and after that were cold sober. They weren't wild men, despite the brilliant sashes and beads they wore, and their impenetrable language, a mixture of French, Ojibway, and Gaelic, and the wrestling matches they put on at night, the singing and dancing, the coffee they drank that dropped Oskar to his knees. When it came to pressing forward, they were all business. The trail followed woodlines and rivers and led them through sloughs that looked impassable, but the carts plunged right in and the wagons followed, linked to each other by long leather straps. One day thick fog set in and the train never paused: the screeching of wooden cartwheels on ungreased wooden axles could be heard for miles, and nobody got lost. From settled country where little homestead shanties were planted three and four to the mile across the undulating prairie, they slowly moved into another country, not only unsettled but unsettling: absolutely flat, unbroken by a tree, flat as a table, straight to the horizon, like a dream, the earth stripped of scenery, of every feature by which one finds his way.

Day after day the Norwegians searched the horizon for the mountains that must engirdle the great lake, and saw nothing ahead, this country went on forever, until one morning beyond Fort Abercrombie, the leader of the train approached them as they squatted around the breakfast fire drinking coffee, and said, "C'est la wiki wanki, laddies," indicating with a sweep of his arm that they had come to the place where they wanted to go.

It wasn't the place at all! They studied it as the carts pulled north and before the screeching had faded away, the Tollefson party turned their wagons around and headed back. "We did not know what would become of us in land so flat," Oskar wrote. "We would become like dumb animals, oxen, or go crazy, and probably both. It was so far from where anyone else lived, and would anyone else ever come live there? We certainly doubted it." They reached the Fort and kept on, not seeing any land that looked quite right, feeling ashamed of themselves—pioneers who turned back!—until they reached the little town where the man rushed toward them, shouting "*Ar du Norsk?*" They were glad to say "*Ja!*"

Besides Oskar, the members of the party were: his father and mother, Jens and Solveig, and brothers Thorstein and Jacob and little sister Nina; Mrs. Tollefson's brother, Olaf Tollerud, wife Drude, and son Paul; a Mr. Hans Ager and a Mr. Waldemar Jaeger; Mr. Jaeger's sister and her husband, Luth and Eva Fjelde; and an old man, J. S. Bjork, who died six months later.

Glad as he was to have them, generous as he was and quick to share anything he had and ready to help them settle, delighted as he was to unfold in Norwegian some thoughts he had kept to himself so long, nevertheless Magnus noted immediately that the party included no marriageable woman, and after asking if by any chance more Norwegians were just behind them and being told no, not that they knew of, he mailed an ad to the St. Paul paper with 35¢ wrapped in tissue and waited.

> *HE IS HONEST, hard-working, clean, in good health, has his own house and money in bank, and sincerely seeks a good woman for the purpose of matrimony. Norwegian pref. Magnus Oleson, New Albion.*

She rode the St. Paul & Pacific to St. Cloud where he met her, holding a placard with his name on it, and they went straight to a judge and then drove the long miles home in silence, arriving around sunup. The first thing she did was fix him a good breakfast. Her name was Katherine Shroeder, and he didn't know much more than that. She was tall, strong, wide in the hips, had black hair that, unbraided, came to her waist, and looked to be about twenty. When she got off the train and spotted him, she put her hands over her face and wept, she was so afraid he'd be angry with her. They had exchanged letters, and hers were written by her brother. She spoke no Norwegian and very little English. She spoke excellent German.

"He ate his breakfast in silence, her watching his every bite, and tried to think what to do next, it had all happened so fast," says Clarence Bunsen, a great-great-grandson. "She tried to look pleasant for his benefit but she was terrified because back in Germany the punishment for deceiving a suitor was pretty stiff, and she couldn't tell him, of course, that it had been her brother's doing. She must've felt like a convicted criminal. He felt sorry for her but he also felt that it was God's will that she came and it was up to him to take the next step, so what he did was get up from the table, clear it, and over her protest he washed the dishes. She'd never seen a married man do that. It was his way of telling her how much he cared about her, being unable to say it. And then presumably they went up to bed."

The first Norwegians emigrated from Stavanger on the west coast, later ones from Telemark and Hallingdal, and almost none came from Christiania (Oslo). They were country folk who were squeezed by virtue of living in a small country with large mountains that left only so much land to farm, not nearly enough. Crops were poor, and then one fall, the fishing boats returned to Stavanger, riding high in the water. The herring had disappeared.

The people went straight to church and prayed God to send them an answer. No herring! It was as if the sun had vanished.

They were honest and proud people who had always worked hard, and poverty was no shame to them—a comical trait to the sophisticates of Oslo who flocked to the popular operetta *Stavanger! O Ja!*, in which the westerners were portrayed as dolts who played fiddles and ate *lutefisk* and talked funny and who felt flush if they had a kroner in their pocket—but this calamity shook them to the innermost for, without fish, they were faced with death by starvation.

They were certain of one thing, though: they would not migrate to the city, as others had done. Years of fervent preaching had taught them that Oslo was a sinkhole of Swedish depravity and Danish corruption, where honest people quickly descended to atheism and indolence and a taste for worldly display. They had seen young men depart for Oslo with a promise to remain pure on their lips, only to return a few years later, decked out in silken European waistcoats and feathered hats and prissy satin slippers, talking with the fashionable Oslovian stammer, the sophisticated Oslovian lisp, and making fun of their own families, not with the hearty Stavanger laugh (*hor-hor*) but with the despicable Oslovian nose-laugh (*hhnn-hhnn*).

To maintain their honest rural way of life, they decided they must leave the homeland, and America loomed large in their imagination as a country with plenty of country in which to settle and prosper and hold to all they kept closest to their hearts. Some friends had gone to America already and sent back glowing letters that were posted in the churches and copied and passed from hand to hand.

My dear Christian [wrote Gunder Muus, in Wisconsin, to his Stavanger cousin in 1867], you will scarcely believe my good fortune in the six short months I have been in America. I was warmly received in New York from whence I travelled by train to Chicago and thence to here in Muskego where I found a fine situation with a merchant. He is from Norway as are most citizens here, so one feels quite at home instantly but without the deprivation and worry. The air is sweet, the land is good, timber is plentiful, and the fishing is excellent. In the lake near town, two Sundays ago, I caught ten pounds of fish in only an hour—real fighters, both of them, but I hooked them, using only worms for bait, and hauled them onto the shore after an exhilarating duel. This is quite ordinary here. Everyone catches fish! Not like back home where the few good spots are reserved for landowners. Perhaps someday you yourself will come to America, and then I promise you a good time at the lake.

The next year, Muus had relocated in Goodhue County, Minnesota, where he settled down to try his hand at farming, but fishing was uppermost in his mind.

My dear Christian, I have many thoughts of home, most of them sad and full of longing, but when I feel most dissatisfied and lonely, I can always improve my disposition with a few hours on Lake Roscoe or the Zumbrota River. Truly America is a great country where a poor Norwegian immigrant can drop his humble line and bring in great fish. Only string do I use and a hook! No aristocratic contraption for me! And yet with a little patience and industry and some cunning, the ordinary man can lure five-pound fish, as many as he likes, where others much wealthier may not get a single nibble. Thus do we prosper here, and I pray that you will soon be here with us, cousin, and enjoy the bounty of America.

Muus lost all in the Panic of 1873 and had to move to Minneapolis and take a job as a stockboy in a grocery store, a terrible disappointment for him.

My dear Christian, so much has happened since last I wrote and none of it good, but why burden you with my endless troubles? I have a bed and a roof over my head and three meals a day, so I should not complain. God will look after us.

I pray daily that He will show me the way out of this noisy, filthy, disease-ridden city full of scoundrels and liars and thieves—a city of men who want to get rich any way they can as soon as possible—a city on a great river which they have filled with poisons and excrement so that no fish can be taken from it. There are lakes nearby, but on Sunday I am too tired to walk so far, and when I *have* gone I found them crowded with ignorant people who spend a fortune on a pole and then stand and beat the water with it! They fling the line to and fro until it is tangled around their necks and meanwhile they curse and drink whiskey and drop garbage on the ground and talk disgusting talk. This is no place for a decent man. I am saving my money toward the day when I can go north, where they say the lakes are pure and bountiful and uninhabited. When I reach there, I will write again.

Muus saved $165 in four months by refraining from all entertainment, and the following September he rode the train north to St. Cloud, where he continued on foot, looking for a good lake where Norwegian was spoken. He walked through a pouring rain, carrying his rucksack under his thin coat, singing hymns to give himself strength, and felt weak when he reached the settlement of New Munich two days later, and collapsed on the street, feverish and out of his mind, and was treated there for consumption by a Mrs. Hoppe who decided the poor man was dying and put him on a wagon for Lake Wobegon, where, at least, he could expire among his countrymen. The wagoneer, approaching the town, saw no life in his passenger, lying under the canvas, and dumped him in a ditch, knowing what a lot of trouble a person has when he drives into town with a dead man, and there Muus awoke a few hours later. His fever was gone, and the sun shone down on him. He heard water lapping. He crawled out of the ditch and saw he was thirty feet from the shore of a fine lake.

Out on the water, a man sat motionless on a log raft, holding one end of a line. Muus felt as weak as a baby and his throat was parched, so he was surprised at the strength of his voice as it hollered out of him: "How are they biting?"

"Pretty good," the man yelled back.

"Is there room for two?"

"Are you a fisherman?"

"Yes."

"Then there is room." And he poled the raft to shore, helped the formerly dying man onto the raft, and the two of them spent several hours pulling a good string of sunfish and crappies out of the still water among the weeds and water lilies. The man was Magnus Oleson, and he and Muus did not exchange three words all afternoon. In fact, it wasn't until dark that Magnus got around to asking if Muus was ill, and by that time, he was not.

He was the first Norwegian bachelor farmer in Lake Wobegon. He farmed three acres north of the lake, only enough to keep him stocked with beans and tobacco, and his real occupation was fishing, which he did every day except Sundays. Every fish he caught, he smoked in a stone smokehouse as big as the shack he lived in, which was beside the smokehouse. People wondered about him, of course. He didn't join the Norske Folke society or the Lutheran church, though he attended church faithfully, taking his place in the "doubters' pew" at the rear, and he never spoke up when the emigrants gathered for the weekly reading of their mutual copy of the Minneapolis *Tidende* and, strangest of all, he got no mail. He was not known at the post office. He was barely known at all.

He was generous with his smoked fish, though, and always carried a few in his shirt for distribution, and to those who got some, he was not so strange. They figured that a man who could make the finest smoked fish they ever tasted was entitled to some leeway in his private life. The minister got a fish every Sunday, and the Norske Folke got a big bundle for Christmas, and any Norwegian who took sick found a large smoked fish at the front door the next day, placed on the lintel to keep it away from cats and dogs. The fish was good for any kind of intestinal problem and was credited with having saved the lives of several who were wasting away until the sweet smell made them strong enough to sit up and eat it, including Anna Torgerson, fading fast from dysentery, who recovered and married him, July 6, 1873, after which he fished only every other day.

Magnus and Katherine had three daughters before she died giving birth in 1871, so the Norwegian Bible was passed to the eldest girl, Hildur, and then to her daughter. Hildur married Oskar Tollefson after his first wife died, and they had seven children, including Amelia (b. 1885) who married Peter Ingqvist, begetting nine, including Esther (b. 1906), who married Gustaf Bunsen, by whom she had four children, including Clarence (b. 1925), who now has the Bible, his sister Eva having given it to him as a wedding present when he and Arlene were married, after Eva learned she could not have children. After fathering the Katherine Oleson branch, Magnus married again in 1872, had three more children by Mari Tollerud, a hired girl at the Watsons' who dumped dishwater on him when he first proposed, and, after her death fourteen years later of consumption, married a third time, Ada Tommerdahl, the widow of a minister who drowned, with four sons, with whom he lived until his death in 1911 at the age of seventy-five, the patriarch of a great house of descendants, now mostly scattered and gone off to places almost as strange as America was to him. A fine portrait of the old man taken when he was sixty-eight and strong as a horse, his white beard like a buttress and his eyes still clear and sharp despite this print having been photographed from a photograph of a photograph—this portrait hangs in a vast white living room in La Jolla, in a mobile home outside of Abilene, in a stone house in the province of Michoacan, Mexico, in a dreadful driftwood frame above a purple plush couch in a Chicago condo, and God only knows where else aside from Lake Wobegon, of course, where you see it almost everywhere you look. Anyone who looks hard at him gets a good hard look back telling you to buck up, be strong, believe in God, and be about your business.

By 1904, when the picture was taken by his grandson John Tollefson, who had a studio in the Central Building, Magnus Oleson had seen more history than a person could put in a book, not that he was a man to think about writing one. His letters home to Norway began to peter out when the Tollefson party rode into town and ceased abruptly when Katherine

Shroeder arrived: just *stopped*. He had written them because he was lonely and had no one to talk to, and the day she came, the literary chapter of his life snapped shut and he began another that we can only guess at. We know that in 1871, while still in mourning for his first wife, he set a record for planting corn, using the old hand planter and covering the seeds with his foot: sixteen acres in one day—it's in *The New Albion Sun* (formerly the *Star*). We know that in 1876 he sold 257 bushels of wheat at $1.75 and eight years later the price was down to 35¢. A bushel made about forty pounds of flour, and at less than a penny a pound, he felt somebody was cheating him so he took up potato farming and kept a small dairy herd; the 1883 class consisted of Lily, Jenny, Bessie, Molly, Daisy, Helen, and Flora. His horses were named Norma and Fanny, two gray mares that cost him $400, and their children were Gypsy and Blaze whom his children rode to high school in town the first year there was one, 1885. He served on the school board for ten years and donated firewood. In 1894 he donated $10 to the Women's Suffrage & Temperance Union (W.S.T.U.), of which his daughter Anna was a founder, and the following year donated a pig toward the purchase of an organ ($259 from Brunelle & Sons, Chicago) for the Norwegian Lutheran Church, of which his grandson John Olaf Quist was choirmaster. He liked music. He enjoyed having his feet tickled. He was a heavy reader. He subscribed to four newspapers, one English (the St. Paul paper through which he had found his wife, not the *Sun*, which was too Republican for his taste) and three Norwegian, the *Posten*, the *Budstikken* (later the *Tidende*), and *Nordisk Folkebladet*, in which he faithfully followed the funny strip "*Ole og Tina*" which popularized the words "*Uffda!*" and "*Ishda!*" His contempt for bankers was exceeded only by his disgust for lawyers. "Honesty in a lawyer," he said, "is like a hen's hind legs." He kept all his teeth except two, which were extracted for 50¢ apiece by a man named Ronning who practiced dentistry with a pair of pliers. During the farm depression of the 1890s, he sold his two hundred sixty acres to Elmer Tollerud, the husband of his granddaughter Viola, and moved to a house in town. He never visited Minneapolis, never rode in an automobile, but in 1906 at the annual county fair put on by the Agriculture Society, of which he was a charter member, he rode solo in a hydrogen balloon to the end of its tether, about three hundred feet, and looked down at the crowd, many of them related to him, and at a town he had observed for more than fifty years, and stayed aloft for his full five minutes. When he died, he was buried next to Katherine after a service that, according to his wishes, included a good sermon in Norwegian and the singing of "*Hvor Finner vel Hjertet sin Saligste Ro?*" ("Where Does the Heart Find Its Most Blessed Peace?").

"No innocent man buys a gun and no happy man writes his memoirs," said Raymond Duff Payne, and yet there's so much we'd love to know about the early years of our town which is buried in silence. A few dim recollections from ancient relatives who were asked for information only after they got feeble, by an earnest grandchild, about matters that no longer much interested them. The letters are for the most part lost; they were all mailed. The photographs are for the most part formal. No picture exists of a Saturday night dance, for example, of the thousands put on in houses before the Alhambra Ballroom (& Roller Skating Rink) was built in 1887, and yet it was (along with church) one of the bedrocks of Norwegian life.

The first Social Circle was formed in 1871 by Oskar, six families who took turns hosting the weekly dance when they all could "turn loose" after a week of digging. People walked miles to a dance, even in the winter. It began at seven P.M. and went for four hours, with a big lunch and coffee served after, but often they went until four in the morning. Little houses *packed* with people, the furniture piled, hauled upstairs or out in the yard. Some played whist, but everyone danced. Oskar and brother Paul played violins and their mother the piano (if there was a piano, otherwise Mr. Jaeger played his harmonica). Paul was so good, his father let him off the hard work so his hands wouldn't get stiff. They sat on top of the piano, the house was so crowded. Little boys dashed in and plunked some bad notes and ran away. They played *polskas* and schottisches, *springleiks, masurkas,* and of course the *vals.* To a woman who had risen at five A.M. for six days in a row to make a fire, haul water, feed poultry, milk, pump water for the livestock, and *then* do laundry and cook and clean house and perhaps also help out in the field, the Saturday dance was a bright spot that she worked toward.

"We worked hard but we had fun then," old Mrs. Berge murmured to a grandson whose name she couldn't remember. She couldn't even remember the work so well. "Anything that needed doing, we did it ourselves." She did however remember the dances. She came from Norway to work for Carl Ingqvist and family for $3 a week, seven days a week with Saturday night and Sunday morning off. "They were good to me." They took her to the Circle. Sixty years later she remembered the dancers and the music clearly. "The room was full of people laughing, hopping up and down."

———————

In 1878, something about a hill made August Krebsbach think of Bavaria, the contours and the two spruce in the dusk, and he said, "Halt!" and climbed down off the wagon and tasted the dirt. It was April, his children were tired of riding, and his wife, Clara, was pregnant. The register of deeds shows 180 acres purchased April 18 for $2700, $2000 secured by the New Albion National Bank, and the elevator records show that in his first season he tried potatoes, the next year corn. In 1880, there was a misunderstanding over credit, and Mr. Peabody at the elevator "initiated proceedings" that sent the sheriff and county clerk to roust the Krebsbachs out of bed at gunpoint and seize two beds and an oak dresser. Shots were fired, a brindle cow was killed, and the family was threatened with prison, all of which appears in the records simply as a credit of $21.

From this shameful incident began the Krebsbachs' enmity toward town, which lasted long after the sheriff shot himself and Mr. Peabody departed with several thousand dollars that didn't belong to him. August paid off the bank, then never set foot in New Albion or Lake Wobegon again. The names of August and Clara vanished from the church roll, their three boys and two girls left school, their trade went to the merchants of St. Hubert. Only the tax assessor noted their existence. Even the fire that burned their house to the ground went unnoticed in the newspaper. That is thought to have happened in 1891, in January. How the family survived, nobody knew. Perhaps they lived with their animals until spring, or else they may have moved temporarily to St. Hubert. St. Hubert dried up and blew away fifty years ago, so there is no record there, and whatever the Krebsbachs' neighbors knew about them, they didn't consider it worth telling their children, and the story is gone. August and Clara may be buried in the St. Hubert cemetery, a sad story itself. The promoter who sold the lots also sold gravestones of an inferior grade of granite, which disintegrated. The ruins were picked up and put in one big pile which you can see today next to County 49, across the road from some old stone foundations.

The boy who got the farm was Manfred, Fred to the few who knew him, who married a St. Hubert girl and led an unexceptional life except for his great isolation, although after she died in childbirth, he was known to visit town on occasion and even hoist a beer at Barney's, howbeit in silence. Old-timers remember him as "the red-faced man" who never spoke other than what was necessary to buy things. One day, Rev. Olaf Hauge drove out to Krebsbachs' and spent an evening, and they became Lutherans, he and his sister, Mrs. Winkler, whose husband had run off, and her two boys. Whatever this taught Fred about forgiveness and regeneration did not change his habit of silence—for one thing, he was a German Lutheran and the church was Norwegian and worshiped in Norwegian until 1934, when a monthly English service was added; and for another, the former county clerk was a deacon. Fred endured baptism and never entered church again until he was carried in for his funeral (1929). He did send the boys, though, and with Leon and Roman, the grudge finally ended. They never discussed it with anyone else, it ended without comment after forty-nine years when Fred died.

Roman was the older, a heavy man; he lived in a pair of blue bib-overalls that he stretched fore and aft, belly and shanks, a very admirable figure of a man, with hands big as legs of lamb, a ruddy face, a distinguished band of white across his forehead where the hat left off, and a white dome above the fringe of curly brown hair. He was an admirable horseman in his day, then an admirable mechanic; he was admired for sheer strength, having once lifted a steer and put it on a wagon; he was admired for never being at a loss for words and never wasting any either. He even spat tobacco admirably—pooching his cheeks and putting the thin brown line exactly where he wanted it, not a big blow, just a real nice spit, very graceful and discreet.

Most of all, he was a good worker, *steady* (one of the finest words one man could say about another); he didn't slack off; he was good for twelve, fifteen hours of work a day. He was generous in trading work with his neighbors, he didn't keep a count of it, and when he worked for them, it was the same as working for himself. They called him, he came, and he carried his end and some of theirs. Clarence Bunsen said that Roman Winkler could not be convicted of horse theft anywhere in Mist County if they found the horses in his bedroom.

He had to be a good worker, the farm being poor as it was, though you couldn't tell it from looking at that clean white house, the red barn and the row of outbuildings (granary, pig barn, chicken coop, tractor shed, and tool shed) which was as trim and well-kept as an Army post though he got no help from his brother Leon.

Neither brother ever married, so far as we knew (though Leon spent a few years in the Philippines with the Navy and hinted at other arrangements there). For almost all of Leon's life, they lived under the same roof.

Leon, the younger, was slight of build, had thin wrists and delicate fingers and went around in jeans, a blue sweater, and a stocking cap. He had a faraway look in his eye so that, talking to him, eventually you'd look over your shoulder to see what he saw back there, and he had the ability to look at work for days at a time. Some days he stayed in bed until afternoon. Bed, after all, was where he found himself when he woke up, he felt fine there, and he could think of no reason to get out, because his bookcase was by the bed, and books were all he needed. He could crawl into a book and pull the covers over him and stay until it got dark, and then go back to sleep. He bought books at auctions, he bought them C.O.D., and every week he came to town with Roman and hauled a bagful out of the library.

Being Roman's brother, he was not talked about, only a little, and that mostly pretty tolerant, even when he went off on one of his bright ideas, which didn't last more than a day or two. Once he decided to put on *Coriolanus* and talked four people into coming to a rehearsal, which he forgot to attend. Another time he started to build an ocean-going yacht in the barn, then loaded potatoes in the hull. The boat broke up and Roman used the lumber to make a ramp to load hogs on the truck.

Drink wasn't his problem, inspiration was. Once he sat all night under Hazel Bunsen's bedroom window, presumably thinking about her, which frightened Hazel, who was young and practical, but he got over her sometime around breakfast and walked home.

When they were younger, the brothers had some fierce arguments about work and responsibility, but as they got old, they were able to say it all in a few words. "Oh, *Leon*." "Ah, Roman,"

Roman farmed, kept house, cooked, did laundry, did everything but make Leon's bed in the morning, though Leon said in his own defense that sometimes he was on the verge of doing chores only to find that Roman had already. He also said that Roman tried to make more of the farm than it was, which was true. Whatever God intended that land to be, it certainly wasn't a showplace for seed corn or the home of purebred Poland hogs. Roman worked, Leon said, as if he could by sheer effort pull the corn up out of the ground and make it grow. Leon said that he worked, too. On a book, though he wasn't ready to show it to anyone, which would distill the wisdom of the ages into a single volume. This book, when finished, would change people's minds about him, but he was in no hurry to finish it, knowing that work that lasts comes slow.

Then one day Leon announced he was leaving home, at the age of sixty-two. Roman had dreams at night in which he rounded up pigs who were loose in the corn, and they kept Leon awake. So he went over the hill and made him a sod house in the meadow. Dug down six feet and put up walls of turf blocks and laid old lumber across the top and laid on a sod roof, and he moved in with his books and bed and a woodstove. "My brother who lives in the dirt," Roman said, but he was lonely without him and came down in the evening with Leon's hot supper in a pie tin.

Leon didn't lack for visitors the last few years. He planted flowers on the roof, which bloomed beautifully in the summer and also in the winter, germinated by the heat of the stove. People drove out to see it, a patch of bright colors in the snow, and dropped in to see him. He climbed out of bed, marked his place in the book, snipped off some roots from his ceiling, and boiled up tea. He died in a bed full of books, with an encyclopedia on his chest, open to a page of pictures of flowers. Roman pulled the covers over his face, hauled out the woodstove, hitched the team to the two main timbers, clucked twice, and buried Leon under a ton of dirt. After a couple of years, rains had leveled the mound, and Roman, who was forgetful in his old age, plowed the meadow and planted corn. In that one patch, he got the corn he always wanted, seven and eight feet high, like a squadron of soldiers. "*Ja*, that's the best I ever had," he said. "I just wish that my brother Leon could be here to see it."

———————

Jonson Ingqvist drove a black Buick touring car with leather upholstery though his home was only two blocks from the bank, and he kept a lake home on Sunfish Bay a quarter-mile from home, and he was said to own fourteen suits, all of them blue. In 1908, he went to Minneapolis for the big Hallingdal picnic, having promised his mother he'd look up her old friends and tell them she was sick and hadn't long but knew she would see them in Heaven. He wore a white linen suit, a white shirt, a straw hat, and a gold stickpin, and on his hip he carried a silver flask of brandy. He knew he would need it, spending a day with his countrymen. He walked from his hotel to the Milwaukee Depot and when he boarded the train to Minnehaha Park, his heart sank, it was as if he had lost everything he had worked for and been thrown back into a former life. The car was packed, so was the next one, with families carrying boxes and baskets that smelled of fried pork and meatballs. The people smelled of lye soap. They were as excited as if it were a train to Niagara Falls and all jabbering in a language he only knew how to be polite in. The park was less than five miles away, but Jonson wished the train had a first-class car where he could sit and talk to men in English.

The picnickers rushed off the train at Minnehaha station and made a beeline for the pavilion to claim a good table. He strolled across the bridge over the creek and had a look at the Falls and hiked along the creek to the Mississippi and back, and by then, the speeches had begun, the worst part of the ordeal. One gasbag after another climbed up on the platform, struck a pose, and launched into a hymn to Norwegian virtue that would have made angels blush, but, judging from the applause, was received by the crowd as no more than their due—grocers, millhands, streetcar conductors, journeymen carpenters, all turned their faces towards the sun of Norwegianness, even the ones in back who couldn't hear a single word of it—and after an hour, Jonson walked away and into the bushes and drew out the flask. "She will see you in heaven," he mumbled.

About six years ago, Lake Wobegon High decided to cut out commencement speeches by the valedictorian, salutatorian, and class orator because they all sounded the same. That was the year Charlene Holm made valedictorian. Her family marched to school, and the manure hit the ventilator. They wanted her in plain view with a gold tassel and words coming out of her mouth. As it turned out, Charlene's speech was on "Service to Others" and was based on Christ's words to the rich young man: "Give all that you have to the poor and follow me." The Holms thought it was the greatest speech ever given in English. Her dad didn't hear a word of it, he was taking 8mm color movies. But you can forgive the Holms their pride, if you remember back to 1926.

In 1926, Norwegian royalty visited Lake Wobegon, arranged by Jonson Ingqvist, who was a big contributor to the Republican party and knew the governor well enough so the governor had once been to his home for coffee one afternoon and a hundred children stood out on the front lawn to watch him drink it. So when Jonson heard that King Haakon VII would be visiting Minnesota, he put in his bid with the governor and got the King, for almost two hours, 2:30 to 3:45 P.M., on May 14, 1926. The town learned about it in early April, and people got down to serious yard work.

The Germans pooh-poohed the visit at first. They pointed out that King Haakon VII wasn't even Norwegian, he was a Danish prince whom the Norwegian parliament had imported when Norway split off from Sweden in 1905. And this was America, where every person is as good as another. But when the good Norwegians of Lake Wobegon thought of the King coming to visit, they got so excited they had to sit down.

In Norway, their ancestors had been dirt poor and never saw royalty, let alone hung around with them, so the King's visit was a sign that they had made good in America. At the same time, they had been so busy making good, they had begun to forget old Norway. So the King's visit was like the past coming to greet them, as if their grandfather rose from the dead and came to shake their hand and say, "You done good. I'm proud."

They set to work making themselves worthy. They polished up their Norwegian. They bought new clothes. They painted. They fixed up. In 1926, most farmers came to town in wagons, so they cleaned up Main Street and said, "No more horses there until after the visit." They created a Norwegian children's choir where none had been before, and drilled those children in six Norwegian songs. (The children, now almost seventy, still remember the words.) And each of them imagined the long black car pulling up at their house, and the tall man walking up to their door to "wisit," and the bows and the curtsies, and he sits down at their table and has his krummkake and coffee and he says, "*Smake saa god. Vaer saa god. Du er saa snille. Mange takk. Mange mange takk.*" ("It tastes so good. Very good. You are so kind. Many thanks.")

Then came the bad news. Mr. Ingqvist decided that since the visit would be so short and the King's schedule was busy, the sensible thing would be to let him lie down and rest. Why show him things he'd seen a thousand times before? Why sing him songs he knew already? No, the King deserved true hospitality. He'd come to town, sit a moment with the Ingqvists, and then he could go upstairs and have a nap. No choir, no crowds. Quiet. The King should have quiet.

To Mr. Ingqvist this was a simple, sensible, humane, decision, and he'd invited the King, so there was no more to be said.

Then Mrs. Ingqvist decided they would invite some of her family, the Tollefsons, and then the Berges got in and the Olesons, and soon there were twelve people who would have coffee with the King and then sit quietly downstairs while he rested. The Rognes family, Paul and Florence, was devastated, and never forgave the insult. Paul never did business with Mr. Ingqvist again, which wasn't easy since he owned the bank. Florence was Mrs. Ingqvist's cousin, they were best friends as girls, and they didn't speak after that. It was soon after that Mrs. Rognes began her career, domineering the Ladies' Circle at church. Mrs. Holm, mother of Charlene, is Florence's daughter.

It didn't change matters much when, the day before the visit, the King got sick in Minneapolis and couldn't come. He'd been in America one week and had attended six *lutefisk* dinners and was resting in his suite at the Nicollet Hotel. It was only three years after President Warren G. Harding had died from eating something on a tour, and the governor was horrified at the thought of the King expiring in Minnesota of an excess of hospitality, so he was put on toast and tea, and a Norwegian count named Carl was sent in his place. Then Mr. Ingqvist changed his mind. Count Carl wouldn't be tired, so they could go ahead and have a big do.

Count Carl was a big bear of a man with heavy black eyebrows and a rumbling voice, and was a good eater. They gave him a dinner at the Sons of Knute lodge and he ate everything put before him. Then the children's choir sang their six songs, and with the first note of music, Count Carl's head fell to his chest and he slept the sleep of the innocent. He snored through the presentation and awoke with the applause and jumped up and took a bow. He spoke for five minutes in Norwegian, got in his car, and left. If he noticed how nice the yards looked, he didn't mention it to anybody.

This changed nothing. People were humiliated by the original insult. This hurt has diminished gradually as the people who weren't invited have died. Now almost all of them are dead.

Last year, a little act of forgiveness took place at Lake Wobegon Lutheran, in the basement, in the furnace room. Luther Rognes, Florence's oldest son, came up from the Cities for the dedication of the new gas furnace that he donated. He decided to name it for his parents, so he and Pastor David Ingqvist, the great-nephew of Jonson Ingqvist, held a small ceremony. They drilled four holes above the little window that looks in at the pilot light and attached a simple brass plate: The Paul and Florence Rognes Memorial Furnace. Luther had a bottle of brandy. He poured a little in two Dixie cups and smashed the rest against the furnace. "Well," said Pastor Ingqvist, "I think you christened it. Tell me this," he said, "do you want an announcement in the church bulletin?"

"I don't know. What would people think?"

"I suppose they would think it was funny. Naming a furnace after your parents. Not many people would do it, I suppose. Why *did* you?"

Luther thought. "My parents were the proudest people I've ever known. My mother wouldn't let even relatives in the house except on Sunday when it was clean. My father drove forty miles to deposit his money because he didn't get invited to meet the King of Norway in 1926. If they could choose a memorial for themselves, I'm sure they'd prefer a carillon, but I always thought—if pride were kindling, our family could heat the church for twenty years. So—"

"Well," David says, "if I dedicated the gas tank to the memory of my great-uncle, we'd have us a complete set. Here's to you, Luther. Good health." And they drank a toast and smashed the Dixie cups underfoot and turned out the light and went to lunch. The brass plate to the memory of Paul and Florence above the window; inside, the little flame flickering. It was a good furnace all last winter, they didn't have a single problem with it: it ran real quiet and when they turned up the thermostat early Sunday morning, she went from fifty to seventy in about an hour flat.

SUMUS QUOD SUMUS

Why isn't my town on the map? — Well, back before
cartographers had the benefit of an aerial view, when
teams of surveyors tramped from one town to the
next, mistakes were made. Sometimes those towns
were farther apart than they should have been. Many
maps were drawn by French explorers in the bows of
canoes bucking heavy rapids, including Sieur Marine
de St. Croix, who was dizzy and nauseated when he
penciled in the river that bears his name. He was
miles off in some places, but since the river formed
the Minnesota-Wisconsin border, revision was politi-
cally impossible and the mistakes were inked in,

though it left thousands of people sitting high and dry on the other side.

A worse mistake was made by the Coleman Survey of 1866, which omitted fifty square miles of central Minnesota (including Lake Wobegon), an error that lives on in the F.A.A's Coleman Course Correction, a sudden lurch felt by airline passengers as they descend into Minnesota air space on flights from New York or Boston.

Why the state jobbed out the survey to drunks is a puzzle. The Coleman outfit, headed by Lieutenant Michael Coleman, had been attached to Grant's army, which they misdirected time and again so that Grant's flanks kept running head-on into Lee's rear until Union officers learned to make "right face" a 120-degree turn. Governor Marshall, however, regarded the 1866 survey as preliminary—"It will provide us a good general idea of the State, a foundation upon which we can build in the future," he said—though of course it turned out to be the final word.

The map was drawn by four teams of surveyors under the direction of Finian Coleman, Michael having left for the Nebraska gold rush, who placed them at the four corners of the state and aimed them inward. The southwest and northwest contingents moved fast over level ground, while the eastern teams got bogged down in the woods, so that, when they met a little west of Lake Wobegon, the four quadrants didn't fit within the boundaries legislated by Congress in 1851. Nevertheless, Finian mailed them to St. Paul, leaving the legislature to wrestle with the discrepancy.

The legislature simply reproportioned the state by eliminating the overlap in the middle, the little quadrangle that is Mist County. "The soil of that region is unsuited to agriculture, and we doubt that its absence would be much noticed," Speaker of the House Randolph remarked.

In 1933, a legislative interim commission proposed that the state recover the lost county by collapsing the square mileage of several large lakes. The area could be removed from the centers of the lakes, elongating them slightly so as not to lose valuable shoreline. Opposition was spearheaded by the Bureau of Fisheries, which pointed out the walleye breeding grounds to be lost; and the State Map Amendment was attached as a rider to a bill requiring the instruction of evolution in all secondary schools and was defeated by voice vote.

Proponents of map change, of "accurates" as they were called, were chastised by their opponents, the so-called "moderates," who denied the existence of Mist County on the one hand—"Where is it?" a moderate cried one day on the Senate floor in St. Paul. "Can you show me one scintilla of evidence that it exists?"—and, on the other hand, denounced the county as a threat to property owners everywhere. "If this county is allowed to rear its head, then no boundary is sacred, no deed is certain," the moderates said. "We might as well reopen negotiations with the Indians."

Wobegonians took the defeat of inclusion with

their usual calm. "We felt that we were a part of Minnesota by virtue of the fact that when we drove more than a few miles in any direction, we were in Minnesota," Hjalmar Ingqvist says. "It didn't matter what anyone said."

In 1980, Governor Al Quie became the first governor to set foot in Mist County, slipping quietly away from his duties to attend a ceremony dedicating a plaque attached to the Statue of the Unknown Norwegian. "We don't know where he is. He was here, then he disappeared," his aides told reporters, all the time the Governor was enjoying a hearty meatball lunch in the company of fellow Lutherans. In his brief remarks, he saluted Lake Wobegon for its patience in anonymity. "Seldom has a town made such a sacrifice in remaining unrecognized so long," he said, though other speakers were quick to assure him that it had been no sacrifice, really, but a true pleasure.

"Here in 1867 the first Norwegian settlers knelt to thank God for bringing them to this place," the plaque read, "and though noting immediately the rockiness of the soil, remained, sowing seeds of Christian love."

What's special about this town, it's pretty much like a lot of towns, isn't it? There is a perfectly good answer to that question, it only takes a moment to think of it.

For one thing, the Statue of the Unknown Norwegian. If other towns have one, we don't know about it. Sculpted by a man named O'Connell or O'Connor in 1896, the granite youth stands in a small plot at a jog in the road where a surveyor knocked off for lunch years ago and looks down Main Street to the lake. A proud figure, his back is erect, his feet are on the ground on account of no money remained for a pedestal, and his eyes—well, his eyes are a matter of question. Probably the artist meant him to exude confidence in the New World, but his eyes are set a little deep so that dark shadows appear in the late afternoon and by sunset he looks worried. His confident smile turns into a forced grin. In the morning, he is stepping forward, his right hand extended in greeting, but as the day wears on, he hesitates, and finally he appears to be about to turn back. The right hand seems to say, Wait here. I think I forgot something.

Nevertheless, he is a landmark and an asset, so it was a shame when the tornado of 1947 did damage to him. That tornado skipped in from the northeast; it blew away one house except for a dresser mirror that wasn't so much as cracked—amazing; it's in the historical society now, and people still bring their relatives to look at it. It also picked up a brand-new Chevy pickup and set it down a quarter-mile away. *On a road. In the right-hand lane.* In town, it took the roof off the Lutheran church, where nobody was, and missed the Bijou, which was packed for *Shame*, starring Cliff DeCarlo. And it blew a stalk of quackgrass about six inches into the Unknown Norwegian, in an unusual place, a place where you wouldn't expect to find grass in a person, a part of the body where you've been told to insert nothing bigger than your finger in a washcloth.

Bud, our municipal employer, pulled it out, of course, but the root was imbedded in the granite, so it keeps growing out. Bud has considered using a pre-emergent herbicide on him but is afraid it will leave a stain on the side of his head, so when he mows, simply reaches up to the Unknown's right ear and snips off the blade with his fingernails. It's not so noticeable, really; you have to look for it to see it.

The plaque that would've been on the pedestal the town couldn't afford was bolted to a brick and set in the ground until Bud dug it out because it was dinging up his mower blade. Now in the historical society museum in the basement of the town hall, it sits next to the Lake Wobegon runestone, which proves that Viking explorers were here in 1381. Unearthed by a Professor Oftedahl or Ostenwald around 1921 alongside County Road 2, where the professor, motoring from Chicago to Seattle, had stopped to bury garbage, the small black stone is covered with Viking runic characters which read (translated by him): "8 of [us] stopped & stayed awhile to visit & have [coffee] & a short nap. Sorry [you] weren't here. Well, that's about [it] for now."

Every Columbus Day, the runestone is carried up to the school and put on a card-table in the lunch-room for the children to see, so they can know their true heritage. It saddens Norwegians that America still honours this Italian, who arrived in the New World and by accident, who wasn't even interested in New Worlds but only in spices. Out on a spin in search of curry powder and hot peppers—a man on a voyage to the grocery—he stumbled on the land of heroic Vikings and proceeded to get the credit for it. And then to name it *America* after Amerigo Vespucci, an Italian who never saw the New World but only sat in Italy and drew incredibly inaccurate maps of it. By rights, it should be called Erica, after Eric the Red, who did the work five hundred years earlier. The United States of Erica. Erica the Beautiful. The Erican League.

Not many children come to see the runestone where it spends the rest of the year. The museum is a locked door in the town hall, down the hall and to the left by the washroom. Viola Tordahl the clerk has the key and isn't happy to be bothered for it. "I don't know why I ever agreed to do it. You know, they don't pay me a red cent for this," she says as she digs around in a junk drawer for it.

The museum is in the basement. The light switch is halfway down the steps, to your left. The steps are concrete, narrow and steep. It's going to be very interesting, you think, to look at these many objects from olden days, and then when you put your hand on the switch, you feel something crawl on it. Not a fly. You brush the spider off, and then you smell the must from below, like bilgewater, and hear a slight movement as if a man sitting quietly in the dark for several hours had just risen slowly and the chair scraped a quarter-inch. He sighs a faint sigh, licks his upper lip, and shifts the axe from his left to his right hand so he can scratch his nose. He is left-handed, evidently. No need to find out any more about him. You turn off the light and shut the door.

What's so special about this town is not the food, though Ralph's Pretty Good Grocery has got in a case of fresh cod. Frozen, but it's fresher than what's been in his freezer for months. In the grocery business, you have to throw out stuff sometimes, but Ralph is Norwegian and it goes against his principles. People bend down and peer into the meat case. "Give me a pork loin," they say. "One of those in the back, one of the pink ones." "These in front are better," he says. "They're more aged. You get better flavor." But they want a pink one, so Ralph takes out a pink one, bites his tongue. This is the problem with being in retail; you can't say what you think.

More and more people are sneaking off to the Higgledy-Piggledy in St. Cloud, where you find two acres of food, a meat counter a block long with huge walloping roasts and steaks big enough to choke a cow, and exotic fish lying on crushed ice. Once Ralph went to his brother Benny's for dinner and Martha put baked swordfish on the table. Ralph's face burned. His own sister-in-law! "It's delicious," said Mrs. Ralph. "Yeah," Ralph said, "if it wasn't for the mercury poisoning, I'd take swordfish every day of the week." Cod, he pointed out, is farther down in the food chain, and doesn't collect the mercury that the big fish do. Forks paused in midair. He would have gone on to describe the effects of mercury on the body, how it lodges in the brain, wiping the slate clean until you wind up in bed attached to tubes and can't remember your own Zip Code, but his wife contacted him on his ankle. Later, she said, "You had no business saying that."

"I'll have no business, period," he said, "if people don't wake up."

"Well, it's a free country, and she has a perfect right to go shop where she wants to."

"Sure she does, and she can go live there, too."

When the Thanatopsis Club hit its centennial in 1982 and Mrs. Hallberg wrote to the White House and asked for an essay from the President on small-town life, she got one, two paragraphs that extolled Lake Wobegon as a model of free enterprise and individualism, which was displayed in the library under glass, although the truth is that Lake Wobegon survives to the extent that it does on a form of voluntary socialism with elements of Deism, fatalism, and nepotism. Free enterprise runs on self-interest.* This is socialism, and it runs on loyalty. You need a toaster, you buy it at Co-op Hardware even though you can get a deluxe model with all the toaster attachments for less money at K-Mart in St. Cloud. You buy it at Co-op because you know Otto. Glasses you will find at Clifford's which also sells shoes and ties and some gloves. (It is trying to be the department store it used to be when it was The Mercantile, which it is still called by most people because the old sign is so clear

---

*The smoke machine at the Sidetrack Tap, if you whack it about two inches below the Camels, will pay off a couple packs for free, and some enterprising patrons find it in their interest to use this knowledge. Past a certain age, you're not supposed to do this sort of thing anymore. You're supposed to grow up. Unfortunately, that is just the age when many people start to smoke.

on the brick facade, clearer than the "Clifford's" in the window.) Though you might rather shop for glasses in a strange place where they'll encourage your vanity, though Clifford's selection of frames is clearly based on Scripture ("Take no thought for what you shall wear. . . .") and you might put a hideous piece of junk on your face and Clifford would say, "I think you'll like those" as if you're a person who looks like you don't care what you look like— nevertheless you should think twice before you get the Calvin Klein glasses from Vanity Vision in the St. Cloud Mall. Calvin Klein isn't going to come with the Rescue Squad and he isn't going to teach your children about redemption by grace. You couldn't find Calvin Klein to save your life.

If people were to live by comparison shopping, the town would go bust. It cannot compete with other places item by item. Nothing in town is quite as good as it appears to be somewhere else. If you live there, you have to take it as a whole. That's loyalty.

This is why Judy Ingqvist does not sing "Holy City" on Sunday morning, although everyone says she sounds great on "Holy City"—it's not her wish to sound great, though she is the leading soprano; it's her wish that all the sopranos sound at least okay. So she sings quietly. One Sunday when the Ingqvists went to the Black Hills on vacation, a young, white-knuckled seminarian filled in; he gave a forty-five minute sermon and had a lot of sermon left over when finally three deacons cleared their throats simultaneously. They sounded like German shepherds barking, and their barks meant that the congregation now knew that he was bright and he had nothing more to prove to them. The young man looked on the sermon as free enterprise.* You work like hell on it and come up a winner. He wanted to give it all the best that was in him, of which he had more than he needed. He was opening a Higgledy-Piggledy of theology, and the barks were meant to remind him where he was: in Lake Wobegon, where smart doesn't count for so much. A minister has to be able to read a clock. At noon, it's time to go home and turn up the pot roast and get the peas out of the freezer. Everybody gets their pot roast at Ralph's. It's not the tenderest meat in the Ninth Federal Reserve District, but after you bake it for four hours until it falls apart in shreds, what's the difference?

So what's special about this town is not smarts either. It counted zero when you worked for Bud on the road crew, as I did one summer. He said, "Don't get smart with me," and he meant it. One week I was wrestling with great ideas in dimly lit college classrooms, the next I was home shoveling gravel in

---

*He is no longer in the ministry. He is vice-president for sales at Devotional Systems, Inc., maker of quadraphonic sanctuary speakers for higher fidelity sermons, home devotional programs on floppy disks, and individual biofeedback systems in the pews. Two wires with electrodes hang from each hymnal rack, which the faithful press to their temples as they pray, attempting to bring the needle on the biometer into the reverence zone. For some reason, prayer doesn't accomplish that so well as, say, thinking about food, but DSI is working on it and thinks this may be a breakthrough in the worship of the future.

the sun, just another worker. I'd studied the workers in humanities class, spent a whole week on the labor movement as it related to ideals of American individualism, and I thought it was pretty funny to sing "Solidarity Forever" while patching potholes, but he didn't, he told me to quit smarting off. Work was serious business, and everybody was supposed to do it—*hard* work, unless of course you thought you were too good for it, in which case to hell with you. Bud's wife kept telling him to retire, he said, but he wasn't going to; all the geezers he'd known who decided to take it easy were flat on their backs a few months later with all their friends commenting on how natural they looked. Bud believed that when you feel bad, you get out of bed and put your boots on. "A little hard work never killed anybody," he told us, I suppose, about fifteen thousand times. Lean on your shovel for one second to straighten your back, and there was Bud to remind you. It would have been satisfying to choke him on the spot. We had the tar right there, just throw the old coot in and cook him and use him for fill. But he was so strong he might have taken the whole bunch of us. Once he said to me, "Here, take the other end of this." It was the hoist for the backhoe. I lifted my end, and right then I went from a 34- to a 36-inch sleeve. I thought my back was going to break. "Heavy?" he said. *Nooo.* "Want to set her down?" *Nooo. That's okay.* "Well, better set her down, cause this is where she goes." *Okay.* All my bones had been reset, making me a slightly curved person. "Next time try lifting with your legs," he said.

People who visit Lake Wobegon come to see some-body, otherwise they missed the turn on the highway and are lost. *Ausländers*, the Germans call them. They don't come for Toast 'n Jelly Days, or the Ger-mans' quadrennial Gesuffa Days, or Krazy Daze, or the Feast Day of St. Francis, or the three-day Mist County Fair with its exciting Death Leap from the top of the grandstand to the arms of the haystack for only ten cents. What's special about here isn't special enough to draw a major crowd, though Flag Day— you could drive a long way on June 14 to find another like it.

Flag Day, as we know it, was the idea of Herman Hochstetter, Rollie's dad, who ran the dry goods store and ran Armistice Day, the Fourth of July, and Flag Day. For the Fourth, he organized a double-loop parade around the block which allowed people to take turns marching and watching. On Armistice Day, everyone stepped outside at 11 A.M. and stood in silence for two minutes as Our Lady's bell tolled eleven times.

Flag Day was his favorite. For a modest price, he would install a bracket on your house to hold a pole to hang your flag on, or he would drill a hole in the sidewalk in front of your store with his drill gun powered by a .22 shell. *Bam!* And in went the flag. On patriotic days, flags flew all over; there were flags on the tall poles, flags on the short, flags in the brack-ets on the pillars and the porches, and if you were flagless you could expect to hear from Herman. His hairy arm around your shoulder, his poochlike face close to yours, he would say how proud he was that so many people were proud of their country, leaving you to see the obvious, that you were a gap in the ranks.

In June 1944, the day after D-Day, a salesman from Fisher Hat called on Herman and offered a good deal on red and blue baseball caps. "Do you have white also?" Herman asked. The salesman thought that white caps could be had for the same wonderful price. Herman ordered two hundred red, two hundred white, and one hundred blue. By the end of the year, he still had four hundred and eighty-six caps. The inspiration of the Living Flag was born from that overstock.

On June 14, 1945, a month after V-E Day, a good crowd assembled in front of the Central Building in response to Herman's ad in the paper:

> Honor "AMERICA" June 14 AT 4
> P.M. Be proud of "Our Land &
> People". Be part of the "LIVING
> FLAG". Don't let it be said that Lake
> Wobegon was "Too Busy". Be on
> time. 4 P.M. "Sharp".

His wife Louise handed out the caps, and Herman stood on a stepladder and told people where to stand. He lined up the reds and whites into stripes, then got the blues into their square. Mr. Hanson climbed up on the roof of the Central Building and took a photograph, they sang the national anthem, and then the Living Flag dispersed. The photograph appeared in the paper the next week. Herman kept the caps.

In the flush of victory, people were happy to do

as told and stand in place, but in 1946 and 1947, dissension cropped up in the ranks: people complained about the heat and about Herman—what gave *him* the idea he could order *them* around? "People! Please! I need your attention! You blue people, keep your hats on! Please! Stripe No. 4, you're sagging! You reds, you're up here! We got too many white people, we need more red ones! Let's do this without talking, people! I can't get you straight if you keep moving around! Some of you are not paying attention! Everybody shut up! Please!"

One cause of resentment was the fact that none of them got to see the Flag they were in; the picture in the paper was black and white. Only Herman and Mr. Hanson got to see the real Flag, and some boys too short to be needed down below. People wanted a chance to go up to the roof and witness the spectacle for themselves.

"How can you go up there if you're supposed to be down here?" Herman said. "You go up there to look, you got nothing to look at. Isn't it enough to know that you're doing your part?"

On Flag Day, 1949, just as Herman said, "That's it! Hold it now!" one of the reds made, a break for it—dashed up four flights of stairs to the roof and leaned over and had a long look. Even with the hole he left behind, it was a magnificent sight. The Living Flag filled the street below. A perfect Flag! The reds so brilliant! He couldn't take his eyes off it. "Get down here! We need a picture!" Herman yelled up to him. "How does it look?" People yelled up to him. "Unbelievable! I can't describe it!" he said.

So then everyone had to have a look. "No!" Herman said, but they took a vote and it was unanimous. One by one, members of the Living Flag went up to the roof and admired it. It *was* marvellous! It brought tears to the eyes, it made one reflect on this great country and on Lake Wobegon's place in it. One wanted to stand up there all afternoon and just drink it in. So, as the first hour passed, and only forty of the five hundred had been to the top, the others got more and more restless. "Hurry up! Quit dawdling! *You've* seen it! Get down here and give someone else a chance!" Herman sent people up in groups of four, and then ten, but after two hours, the Living Flag became the Sitting Flag and then began to erode, as the members who had had a look thought about heading home to supper, which infuriated the ones who hadn't. "Ten more minutes!" Herman cried, but ten minutes became twenty and thirty, and people snuck off and the Flag that remained for the last viewer was a Flag shot through by canon fire.

In 1950, the Sons of Knute took over Flag Day. Herman gave them the boxes of caps. Since then, the Knutes have achieved several good Flags, though most years the attendance was poor. You need at least four hundred to make a good one. Some years the Knutes made a "no-look" rule, other years they held a lottery. One year they experimented with a large mirror held by two men over the edge of the roof, but when people leaned back and looked up, the Flag disappeared, of course.

PROTESTANT

Our family was dirt poor, which I figured out as a child from the fact we had such a bad vacuum. When you vacuumed the living room, it would groan and stop and you had to sit and wait for it to groan and start up, the vacuum like mad before it quit again, but it didn't have good suction either. You had to stuff the hairballs into it. I also knew it because Donald Hoglund told me. He asked me how much my dad earned, and I said a thousand dollars, the most money I could imagine, and he shrieked, "You're poor! You're poor!" So we were. And, in a town where everyone was either Lutheran or

Catholic, we were neither one. We were Sanctified Brethren, a sect so tiny that nobody but us and God knew about it, so when kids asked what I was, I just said Protestant. It was too much to explain, like having six toes. You would rather keep your shoes on.

Grandpa Cotten was once tempted toward Lutheranism by a preacher who gave a rousing sermon on grace that Grandpa heard as a young man while taking Aunt Esther's dog home who had chased a Model T across town. He sat down on the church steps and listened to the voice boom out the open windows until he made up his mind to go in and unite with the truth, but he took one look from the vestibule and left. "He was dressed up like the pope of Rome," said Grandpa, "and the altar and the paintings and the gold candlesticks—my gosh, it was just a big show. And he was reading the whole darn thing off a page, like an actor."

Jesus said, "Where two or three are gathered together in my name, there am I in the midst of them," and the Brethren believed that was enough. We met in Uncle Al's and Aunt Flo's bare living room with plain folding chairs arranged facing in toward the middle. No clergyman in a black smock. No organ or piano, for that would make one person too prominent. No upholstery, it would lead to complacency. No picture of Jesus, He was in our hearts. The faithful sat down at the appointed hour and waited for the Spirit to move one of them to speak or to pray or to give out a hymn from our Little Flock hymnal. No musical notation, for music must come from the heart and not off a page. We sang the texts to a tune that fit the meter, of the many tunes we all knew. The idea of reading a prayer was sacrilege to us—"if a man can't remember what he wants to say to God, let him sit down and think a little harder," Grandpa said.

"There's the Lord's Prayer," said Aunt Esther meekly. We were sitting on the porch after Sunday dinner. Esther and Harvey were visiting from Minneapolis and had attended Lake Wobegon Lutheran, she having turned Lutheran when she married him, a subject that was never brought up in our family.

"You call that prayer? Sitting and reciting like a bunch of schoolchildren?"

Harvey cleared his throat and turned to me with a weak smile. "Speaking of school, how are you doing?" he asked.

There was a lovely silence in the Brethren assembled on Sunday morning as we waited for the Spirit. Either the Spirit was moving someone to speak who was taking his sweet time or else the Spirit was playing a wonderful joke on us and letting us sit, or perhaps silence was the point of it. We sat listening to rain on the roof, distant traffic, a radio playing from across the street, kids whizzing by on bikes, dogs barking, as we waited for the Spirit to inspire us. It was like sitting on the porch with your family, when nobody feels that they have to make talk. So quiet in church. Minutes drifted by in silence that was sweet to us. The old Regulator clock ticked, the rain stopped and the room changed light as the sun broke through—shafts of brilliant sun through the windows and motes of dust falling through it—the smell of clean clothes and floor wax and wine and the fresh bread of Aunt Flo which was Christ's body given for us. Jesus in our midst, who loved us. So peaceful, and we loved each other too. I thought perhaps the Spirit was leading me to say that, but I was just a boy, and children were supposed to keep still. And my affections were not pure. They were tainted with a sneaking admiration of Catholics—Catholic Christmas, Easter, the Living Rosary, and the Blessing of the Animals, all magnificent. Everything we did was plain, but they were regal and gorgeous—especially the Feast Day of St. Francis, which they did right out in the open, a feast for the eyes. Cows, horses, some pigs, right on the church lawn. The turmoil, animals bellowing and barking and clucking and cats scheming how to escape and suddenly leaping out of the girl's arms who was holding on tight, the cat dashing through the crowd, dogs straining at the leash, and the ocarina band of third-graders playing Catholic dirges, and the great calm of the sisters, and the flags, and the Knights of Columbus decked out in their handsome black suits—I stared at it until my eyes almost fell out, and then I wished it would go on much longer.

"Christians," my uncle Al used to say, "do not go in for show," referring to the Catholics. We were sanctified by the blood of the Lord, therefore we were saints, like St. Francis, but we didn't go in for feasts or ceremonies, involving animals or not. We went in for sitting, all nineteen of us, in Uncle Al's and Aunt Flo's living room on Sunday morning and having a plain meeting and singing hymns in our poor thin voices while not far away the Catholics were whooping it up. I wasn't allowed inside Our Lady, of course, but if the Blessing of the Animals on the Feast Day of St. Francis was any indication, Lord, I didn't know but what they had elephants in there and acrobats. I sat in our little group and envied them for the splendor and gorgeousness, as we tried to sing without even a harmonica to give us the pitch. Hymns, Uncle Al said, didn't have to be sung perfect, because God looks on the heart, and if you are In The Spirit, then all praise is good.

The Brethren, also known as the Saints Gathered in the Name of Christ Jesus, who met in the living room were all related to each other and raised in the Faith from infancy except Brother Mel who was rescued from a life of drunkenness, saved as a brand from the burning, a drowning sailor, a sheep on the hillside, whose immense red nose testified to his previous condition. I envied his amazing story of how he came to be with us. Born to godly parents, Mel left home at fifteen and joined the Navy. He sailed to distant lands in a submarine and had exciting experiences while traveling the downward path, which led him finally to the Union Gospel Mission in Minneapolis where he heard God's voice "as clear as my voice speaking to you." He was twenty-six, he slept under bridges and in abandoned buildings, he drank two quarts of white muscatel every day, and then God told him that he must be born again, and so he was, and became the new Mel, except for his nose.

Except for his nose, Mel Burgess looked like any

forty-year-old Brethren man: sober, preferring dark suits, soft-spoken, tending toward girth. His nose was what made you look twice: battered, swollen, very red with tiny purplish lines, it looked ancient and very dead on his otherwise fairly handsome face, the souvenir of what he had been saved from, the "Before" of his "Before . . . and After" advertisement for being born again.

For me, there was nothing before. I was born among the born-again. This living room so hushed, the Brethren in their customary places on folding chairs (the comfortable ones were put away on Sunday morning) around the end-table draped with a white cloth and the glass of wine and loaf of bread (unsliced) was as familiar to me as my mother and father, the founders of my life. I had always been here.

Our family sat in one row against the picture window. Al and Florence and their three, Janet and Paul and Johnny, sat opposite us, I saw the sky and the maple tree reflected in my uncle's glasses. To our left, Great-Aunt Mary sat next to Aunt Becky and Uncle Louie, and to our right were Grandma and Grandpa and Aunt Faith, and behind them was Mel, sitting on the piano bench. His wife, Rita, was a Lutheran. She only came occasionally and when she did, she stood out like a brass band. She used lipstick and had plucked eyebrows and wore bright hats. Brethren women showed only a faint smudge of powder on their cheeks and their hats were small and either black or navy blue. Once Rita spoke up in the meeting—Al had stood up to read from the Lord's

Word, and she said, "Pardon me, which chapter did you say?"—and we all shuddered as if she had dropped a plate on the floor: *women did not speak in meeting*. Another time, Sunday morning, she made as if to partake of the bread as it was passed, and Grandpa snatched it away from her. It had to be explained to Rita later that she could not join in the Lord's Supper with us because she was not in fellowship.

We were "exclusive" Brethren, a branch that believed in keeping itself pure of false doctrine by avoiding association with the impure. Some Brethren assemblies, mostly in larger cities, were not so strict and broke bread with strangers—we referred to them as "the so-called Open Brethren," the "so-called" implying the shakiness of their position—whereas we made sure that any who fellowshiped with us were straight on all the details of the Faith, as set forth by the first Brethren who left the Anglican Church in 1865 to worship on the basis of correct principles. In the same year, they posed for a photograph: twenty-one bearded gentlemen in black frock coats, twelve sitting on a stone wall, nine standing behind, gazing solemnly into a sunny day in Plymouth, England, united in their opposition to the pomp and corruption of the Christian aristocracy.

Unfortunately, once free of the worldly Anglicans, these firebrands were not content to worship in peace but turned their guns on each other. Scholarly to the core and perfect literalists every one, they set to arguing over points that, to any outsider, would have seemed very minor indeed but which to them were crucial to the Faith, including the question: if Believer *A* is associated with Believer *B* who has somehow associated himself with *C* who holds a False Doctrine, must *D* break off association with *A*, even though *A* does not hold the Doctrine, to avoid the taint?

The correct answer is: Yes. Some Brethren, however, felt that *D* should only speak with *A* and urge him to break off with *B*. The Brethren who felt otherwise promptly broke off with them. This was the Bedford Question, one of several controversies that, inside of two years, split the Brethren into three branches.

Once having tasted the pleasure of being Correct and defending True Doctrine, they kept right on and broke up at every opportunity, until, by the time I came along, there were dozens of tiny Brethren groups, none of which were speaking to any of the others.

Our Lake Wobegon bunch was part of a Sanctified Brethren branch known as the Cox Brethren, which was one of a number of "exclusive" Brethren branches—that is to *non*-Coxians, we were known as "Cox Brethren"; to ourselves, we were simply *The* Brethren, the last remnant of the true Church. Our name came from Brother Cox in South Dakota who was kicked out of the Johnson Brethren in 1932—for preaching the truth! So naturally my Grandpa and most of our family went with Mr. Cox and formed the new fellowship.

The split with the Johnsons was triggered by Mr. Johnson's belief that what was abominable to God in the Old Testament must be abominable still, which he put forward at the Grace & Truth Bible Conference in Rapid City in 1932. Mr. Cox stood up and walked out, followed by others. The abomination doctrine not only went against the New Covenant of Grace principle, it opened up rich new areas of controversy in the vast annals of Jewish law. Should Brethren then refrain from pork, meat that God had labeled "Unclean"? Were we to be thrown into the maze of commandments laid out in Leviticus and Deuteronomy, where we are told to smite our enemies with the sword and stone to death rebellious children?

Mr. Johnson's sermon was against women's slacks, and he had quoted Deuteronomy 22.5, "The woman shall not wear that which pertaineth unto a man, neither shall a man put on a woman's garment: for all that do so are abomination unto the Lord thy God," but Mr. Cox, though he was hardy pro-slacks, felt Mr. Johnson failed to emphasize grace as having superseded the law, and when Mr. Johnson said, "An abomination to God under the law is still an abomination to God under grace," Mr. Cox smelled the burning rubber of Error and stood up and marched. He and the other walkouts proceeded to a grove of trees and prayed for Mr. Johnson's soul, and Mr. Johnson and those seated inside did the same for them. The split was never repaired, though as a result of being thought in favor of slacks, the Cox Brethren became death on the subject. My mother never wore slacks, though she did dress my sister in winter leggings, which troubled Grandpa. "It's not the leggings so much as what they represent and what they could lead to," he told her. He thought that baby boys should not wear sleepers unless they were the kind with snaps up the legs. Mother pointed out that the infant Jesus was wrapped in swaddling clothes. "That doesn't mean he wore a dress," Grandpa said. "They probably wrapped his legs separately."*

Intense scholarship was the heart of the problem. We had no ordained clergy, believing in the priesthood of all believers, and all were exhorted to devote themselves to Bible study. Some did, Brother Louie and Brother Mel in particular. In Wednesday-night

---

*Brethren history is confusing, even to those of us who heard a lot on the subject at a young age—the Dennis Brethren, for example: I have no idea whether they left us or we left them. Ditto the Reformed Sanctified, and the Bird Brethren, though I think that Sabbath observance was involved in our (i.e., the *Beale* Brethren, what we were called before 1932 when we Coxes left the Johnson wing) dispute with the Birds, who tended to be lax about such things as listening to the radio on Sunday and who went in for hot baths to an extent the Beales considered sensual. The Beale, or Cold Water, Brethren felt that the body was a shell or a husk that the spirit rode around in and that it needed to be kept in line with cold baths. But by the time I came along, we listened to the radio on Sunday and ran the bath hot, and yet we never went back and patched things up with the Birds. Patching up was not a Brethren talent. As my Grandpa once said of the Johnson Brethren, "Anytime they want to come to us and admit their mistake, we're perfectly happy to sit and listen to them and then come to a decision about accepting them back."

Bible reading, they carried the ball, and some nights you could see that the Coxes of Lake Wobegon might soon divide into the Louies and Mels.

One summer night, they set to over the issue of speaking in tongues, Louie arguing that this manifestation of the Spirit was to be sought earnestly, Mel holding that it was a miraculous gift given to the early church but not given by God today. I forget the Scripture verses each of them brought forward to defend his position, but I remember the pale faces, the throat-clearing, the anguished looks, as those two voices went back and forth, straining at the bit, giving no ground—the poisoned courtesy ("I think my brother is overlooking Paul's very *clear* message to the Corinthians . . . ," "Perhaps my brother needs to take a closer look, a *prayerful* look, at this verse in Hebrews . . .") as the sun went down, neighbor children were called indoors, the neighbors turned out their lights, eleven o'clock came—they wouldn't stop!

"Perhaps," Grandpa offered, "it would be meet for us to pray for the Spirit to lead us," hoping to adjourn, but both Louie and Mel felt that the Spirit *had* led, that the Spirit had written the truth in big black letters—if only some people could see it.

The thought of Uncle Louie speaking in tongues was fascinating to me. Uncle Louie worked at the bank, he spoke to me mostly about thrift and hard work. What tongue would he speak? Spanish? French? Or would it sound like gibberish? Louie said that speaking in tongues was the true sign, that those who believed *heard* and to those who didn't it was only gabble—what if he stood up and said, "Feemalator, jasperator, hoo ha ha, Wamalamagam-anama, zis boom bah!" and everyone else said "Amen! That's right, brother! Praise God!" and *I was the only one who said, "Huh?"*

Bible reading finally ended when Flo went up to bed. We heard her crying in the bathroom. Al went up to comfort her. Grandpa took Louie aside in the kitchen. Mel went straight home. We all felt shaky.

It was soon after the tongues controversy that the Lake Wobegon Brethren folded their tent and merged into another Cox Assembly in St. Cloud, thirty-two miles away. Twenty-eight Brethren worshiped there, in a large bare rented room on the second floor of the bus depot. We had often gone there for special meetings, revivals, and now we made the long drive every Sunday and every Wednesday night. Grandpa fought for this. "It is right for brethren to join together," he said. Louie agreed. Mel didn't. He felt God had put us in Lake Wobegon to be a witness. But finally he gave in. "Think of the children," Grandpa said. One fear of Grandpa's was that we children would grow up and marry outside the Faith if only because we knew nobody in the Faith except for relatives. Faced with the lonely alternative, we'd marry a Lutheran, and then, dazzled by the splendid music and vestments and stained glass, we'd forsake the truth for that carnival down the street. Grandpa knew us pretty well. He could see us perk up on Sunday morning when the Lutheran organ pealed out at ten-thirty. The contrast between the church of

Aunt Flo's living room and the power and glory of Lutheranism was not lost on him. Among other Brethren boys and girls, nature would take its course, and in due time, we'd find someone and make a Brethren family. Grandpa was looking to the future.

The shift to St. Cloud changed things, all right, and not all for the better.

My mother hated the move from the start. She had no Scripture to quote, only a feeling that we had taken a step away from the family, from ourselves. We had walked to Flo's house, we had sat in Sunday school class in her kitchen and celebrated the Lord's death in the living room. The bread we broke was bread Flo baked, and she also made the wine, in a pickle crock in the basement. Flo's two cats, Ralph and Pumpkin, walked in and out of the service, and along toward the end, having confessed our unworthiness and accepted our redemption by Christ, the smell of Flo's pot roast, baking at low heat, arose to greet us. Before it was Flo's and Al's, the house had been Grandpa's and Grandma's— Mother had known this room since she was tiny, and though she bowed to Grandpa's wishes, she felt in her heart that she was leaving home. Sunday in St. Cloud meant a long drive, and Mother was a nervous rider who saw death at every turn. She arrived at the St. Cloud assembly in a frazzled state. The second-floor room was huge and bare and held no associations for her. The long silences were often broken by the roar of bus engines and rumble of bus announcements downstairs. Waiting for the Spirit to guide us to a hymn, a prayer, a passage from Scripture, we heard, "*Now boarding at Gate One . . . Greyhound Bus service to Waite Park . . . St. Joseph . . . Collegeville . . . Avon . . . Albany . . . Freeport . . . Melrose . . . and Sauk Center. All aboard, please!*"

Whenever a special Bible study meeting was scheduled for Sunday afternoon at three, we couldn't drive home after morning meeting, have dinner, and get back to St. Cloud in time, so one Sunday our family traipsed over to a restaurant that a friend of Dad's had recommended, Phil's House of Good Food. The waitress pushed two tables together and we sat down and studied the menus. My mother blanched at the prices. A chicken dinner went for $2.50, the roast beef for $2.75. "It's a nice place," Dad said, multiplying the five of us times $2.50. "I'm not so hungry, I guess," he said, "maybe I'll just have soup." We weren't restaurantgoers—"Why pay good money for food you could make better at home?' was Mother's philosophy—so we weren't at all sure about restaurant custom: could, for example, a person who had been seated in a restaurant simply get up and walk out? Would it be proper? Would it be *legal*?

The waitress came and stood by Dad. "Can I get you something from the bar?" she said. Dad blushed deep red. The question seemed to imply that he looked like a drinker. "No," he whispered, as if she had offered to take off her clothes and dance on the table. Then another waitress brought a tray of glasses to a table of four couples next to us. "Martini," she said, setting the drinks down, "whiskey sour, whiskey sour, Manhattan, whiskey sour, gin and tonic, martini, whiskey sour."

"Ma'am? Something from the bar?" Mother looked at her in disbelief.

Suddenly the room changed for us. Our waitress looked hardened, rough, cheap—across the room, a woman laughed obscenely, "Haw, haw, haw"—the man with her lit a cigarette and blew a cloud of smoke—a swear word drifted out from the kitchen like a whiff of urine—even the soft lighting seemed suggestive, diabolical. To be seen in such a place on the Lord's Day—*what had we done?*

My mother rose from her chair. 'We can't stay. I'm sorry," Dad told the waitress. We all got up and put on our coats. Everyone in the restaurant had a good long look at us. A bald little man in a filthy white shirt emerged from the kitchen, wiping his hands. "Folks? Something wrong?" he said. "We're in the wrong place," Mother told him. Mother always told the truth, or something close to it.

"This is *humiliating*," I said out on the sidewalk. "I feel like a *leper* or something. Why do we always have to make such a big production out of everything? Why can't we be like regular people?"

She put her hand on my shoulder. "Be not conformed to this world," she said. I knew the rest by heart: ". . . but be ye transformed by the renewing of your mind, that ye may prove what is that good and acceptable and perfect will of God."

"Where we gonna eat?" Phyllis asked. "We'll find someplace reasonable," said Mother, and we walked six blocks across the river and found a lunch counter and ate sloppy joes (called Maid-Rites) for fifteen cents apiece. They did not agree with us, and we were aware of them all afternoon through prayer meeting and Young People's.

——————

The Cox Brethren of St. Cloud held to the same doctrines as we did but they were not so exclusive, more trusting of the world—for example, several families owned television sets. They kept them in their living rooms, out in the open, and on Sunday, after meeting and before dinner, the dad might say, "Well, I wonder what's on," knowing perfectly well what was on, and turn it on—a Green Bay Packers game—and watch it. On Sunday.

I ate a few Sunday dinners at their houses, and the first time I saw a television set in a Brethren house, I was dumbfounded. None of the Wobegonian Brethren had one; we were told that watching television was the same as going to the movies—*no*, in other words. I wondered why the St. Cloud people were unaware of the danger. You start getting entangled in the things of the world, and one thing leads to another. First it's television, then it's worldly books, and the next thing you know, God's people are sitting around drinking whiskey sours in dim smoky bars with waitresses in skimpy black outfits and their bosoms displayed like grapefruit.*

———————————————————————

*Clarence Bunsen: "Most Brethren I knew were death on card-playing, beer-drinking, and frowned on hand-holding, and of course they wouldn't go near a dance. They thought it brought out carnal desires. Well, maybe theirs lay closer to the surface, I don't know. Some were not only opposed

That was not my view but my parents'. "Beer is the drunkard's kindergarten," said Dad. Small things led to bigger ones. One road leads up, the other down. A man cannot serve two masters. Dancing was out, even the Virginia reel: it led to carnal desires. Card-playing was out, which led to gambling, though we did have Rook and Flinch—why those and not pinochle? "Because. They're different." No novels, which tended to glamorize iniquity. "How do you know if you don't read them?" I asked, but they *knew*. "You only have to touch a stove once to know it's hot," Mother said. (Which novel had she read? She wasn't saying.) Rock 'n' roll, jazz, swing, dance music, nightclub singing: all worldly. "How about Beethoven?" I asked, having heard something of his in school. "That depends," she said. "Was he a Christian?" I wasn't sure. I doubted he was.

On the long Sunday-night drive home, leaning forward from the back seat, I pressed them on inconsistencies like a little prosecutor: if dancing leads to carnal desire, how about holding hands? Is it wrong

---

to dancing but also felt that marching in formation was wrong, so we called them the Left-Footed Brethren. Some others were more liberal, Mr. Bell for example, he thought cards were okay so long as you didn't play with a full deck. The Bijou used to show good movies but the Brethren and some Lutherans ganged up on Art and made him stop, so now you have to drive to St. Cloud if you want to see unmarried people together in one room with the door closed. It's a shame. I think if the church put in half the time on covetousness that it does on lust, this would be a better world for all of us."

to put your arm around a girl? People gamble on football: is football wrong? Can you say "darn"? What if your teacher told you to read a novel? Or a short story? What if you were hitch-hiking in a blizzard and were picked up by a guy who was listening to rock 'n' roll on the radio, should you get out of the car even though you would freeze to death? "I guess the smart thing would be to dress warmly in the first place," offered Dad. "And wait until a Ford comes along." All Brethren drove Fords.

In Lake Wobegon, car ownership is a matter of faith. Lutherans drive Fords, bought from Bunsen Motors, the Lutheran car dealer, and Catholics drive Chevies from Main Garage, owned by the Kruegers, except for Hjalmar Ingqvist, who has a Lincoln. Years ago, John Tollerud was tempted by Chevyship until (then) Pastor Tommerdahl took John aside after church and told him it was his (Pastor Tommerdahl's) responsibility to point out that Fords get better gas mileage and have a better trade-in value. And he knew for a fact that the Kruegers spent a share of the Chevy profits to purchase Asian babies and make them Catholics. So John got a new Ford Falcon. It turned out to be a dud. The transmission went out after ten thousand miles and the car tended to pull to the left. In a town where car ownership is by faith, however, a person doesn't complain about these things, and John figured there must be a good reason for his car trouble, which perhaps he would understand more fully someday.

The Brethren, being Protestant, also drove Fords,

of course, but we distinguished ourselves from Lutherans by carrying small steel Scripture plates bolted to the top of our license plates. The verses were written in tiny glass beads so they showed up well at night. We ordered these from the Grace & Truth Scripture Depot in Erie, Pennsylvania, and the favorites were "The wages of sin is death. Rom.6:23" and "I am the way, the truth and the life. Jn.10:6." The verse from John was made of white beads, the Romans of lurid red, and if your car came up behind a Brethren car on the road at night, that rear verse jumped right out at you. It certainly jumped out at me the night I drove Karen Mueller back from Avon, where we had had two whiskey sours apiece on her fake ID. I was going seventy on the old post road when we flew over a hill and there was a pair of taillights and what looked like a red stripe between them. I hit the brakes, we skidded at an angle so that for one split second, looking out the side window, I saw "The wages of sin is death" like a flashbulb exploding in my face, and then we were halfway in the ditch. I hit the gas, and we passed Brother Louie on the low side, and I got Karen home before eleven, and nobody was the wiser except me. "You're a wonderful driver. You saved our lives," Karen said, but I knew the truth. Drinking whiskey sours with a Catholic girl and thinking lustful thoughts, I had earned death three times over, and God was reminding me of this at the same time as He took the wheel for those few seconds, probably because He had a purpose for Brother Louie's life.

Perhaps God had a purpose for mine, too, but He

must have wondered why I showed so little curiosity about what it might be. My own purpose was escape, first in my dad's car (a Ford Fairlane station wagon) and then in the car he gave me (a 1956 Tudor sedan). Both of these cars had verses bolted to the plates, so I carried pliers with me and pulled over just outside town and removed the evidence of our faith and put it in the trunk. Then I raced off and did what I could to debauch myself, and, on the way back, sometimes reeling from the effects of a couple of Grain Belts and half a pack of Pall Malls, I bolted the verses back on.

The Grace & Truth catalog offered many items with Scripture emblazoned on them, including birthday cards ("Ye must be born again"), a Gospel mailbox with handsome nameplate and "My Word shall not pass away. Matt.24:35" painted on the lid, a telephone-book cover ("Let no corrupt communication pass out of your mouth, but that which is good to the use of edifying. Eph.4:29"), a doormat ("Now ye are no more strangers and foreigners, but fellow-citizens with the saints, and of the household of God. Eph.2:19"), a wastebasket ("Touch not the unclean thing. 2Cor.6:17"), and even an umbrella ("Giving thanks always for all things. Eph.5:20"). There were paper napkins and placemats in the Bible Families, Familiar Parables, Our Lord's Miracles, and Bible Prophecies series—once, my friend Lance came to supper and found Armageddon and the Seven-Headed Beast under his plate. Grace & Truth even offered matchbooks. If a smoker asked for a light, you could give him the book ("Your body is the temple of the Holy Ghost, therefore glorify God in your body, which is God's").

Testimony was the aim of this merchandise. The Grace & Truth people believed that unregenerate man has hardened his heart against God and that the Spirit works to exercise and open the heart but that these openings of grace may be very brief, perhaps only a few seconds, during which the wicked may repent—especially if God's Word is before them. Thus, the need to place Scripture in plain view. A fellow motorist's heart might be opened on the road; our license-plate verse would be right there at the right moment to show the way.

I felt that so much Scripture floating around might tend to harden some hearts, that Scripture should be treated with reverence and not pasted to any flat surface you could find—at least, that was what I said when Brethren asked why I didn't carry a "The Peace of God Passeth All Understanding" bookbag to school. In fact, I was afraid I would be laughed off the face of the earth.

My dad's car sported a compass on the dashboard, with "I am the Way" inscribed in luminescent letters across its face, clearly visible in the dark to a girl who might be sitting beside me. "Why do you have that?" she might say. "It's not mine, it's my dad's," I'd say. "I don't know why, I guess he likes it there." I wanted her and me to be friends and our conversation to head in the direction of personal feelings. The Importance of Being Free and Sharing Love, and not toward the thorny subject of obedience, which tended to put a damper on things. The compass wasn't easily removed; you'd have to get behind the instrument panel to remove the nuts. I thought of covering it with masking tape, but that might only draw attention to it. So I hung my cap on it.

Brother Louie wasn't so timid. His car (a Fairlane four-door) was a rolling display of Scripture truth, equipped not only with verses on the license plates but also across the dashboard, both sunvisors, the back of the front seat, all four armrests, the rubber floormats, the ashtray and glove compartment, and just in case you weren't paying attention, he had painted a verse across the bottom of the passenger side of the windshield—"The earth is full of the goodness of the Lord"—for your edification as you gazed at the scenery. Brother Louie kept a plastic bucket by his left leg, where he kept Gospel tracts, rolled up and wrapped in bright cellophane, which he tossed out at mailboxes as he drove along. The cellophane was to protect the Word from rain and also to attract the eye. And finally, one year, he found a company in Indiana that advertised custom-made musical horns. Louie's horn played the first eight notes of the Doxology. It sounded like a trumpet. He blew it at pedestrians, oncoming traffic, while passing, and sometimes just for his own pleasure. On occasion, vexed by a fellow driver, he gave in to wrath and leaned on the horn, only to hear "Praise God from Whom all blessings flow". It calmed him down right away. The horn cost Louie more than a hundred dollars, and when he traded in the Fairlane on a Galaxie, he took the horn along.

Brother Louie was assistant cashier at the First

Ingqvist State Bank, which entitled him to a cubicle, three feet of oak paneling topped with two feet of frosted glass. He sat in there and received loan applicants, the small-time ones, and also some depositors. Many older people who remembered their elders' memories of the failure of the New Albion Bank in the Panic of 1873 did not quite trust a bank per se and were uneasy about shoving their money under the grill to Mary Dahl, who was nineteen years old and chewed gum. They wanted Louie to accept it personally.

It was touching to see Mrs. Fjelde and Mrs. Ruud and Mrs. Diener, old farm ladies in farm-lady dresses and their best black hats with the veils, their cotton stockings and old cloth coats, shuffling into Louie's cubicle. Sitting by his desk, enjoying the little ritual conversation. "Good morning. You certainly look well." "Thank you, Louie. Actually, my back has been bothering me." "I'm sorry to hear that." "Oh, it's nothing. I'll feel better when it warms up." Some weather talk. "How's Lena doing? and Harold? What do you hear from Elsie?" Louie knew everybody by name. Some news, and then the grand moment: reaching in her purse for the coin purse, emptying the egg money out on the desk. A few crumpled ones, a lot of quarters and dimes. Louie, impressed: "Well, look at that! Doing pretty well, I'd say." The careful count of the treasure. Filling out the deposit slip. The customer inquiring about Louie's wife, Gladys, and his four daughters. Some customers could make a fifteen-minute transaction out of less than five bucks. At the end, Louie stood up and held out his hand. "Thanks," he said. "Appreciate your coming in." And out they went.

Brother Louie, a heavy-set young man with a full head of black hair and elegant mustache who had a weakness for two-toned summer shoes and red bow ties, grew old and fat and bald at the bank, where he stayed assistant cashier for thirty years until he retired in 1961, after forty-five years of employment there. It never occurred to me until he retired that once Louie had wanted to make something of himself in the banking business.

In the flush of pride that accompanied retirement — his picture appeared on the front page of the *Herald Star* along with an extensive article, "Town Lauds Louie For Years of Service," and a photo of a Certificate of Distinguished Citizenship that Hjalmar, using his considerable influence, had wangled for Louie from Governor Elmer L. Andersen himself, signed by him *and* by Minnesota's Secretary of State Joseph L. Donovan, and presented to Louie at a banquet at the sons of Knute temple, attended by everyone, even Fr. Emil — Louie went so far as to show me his scrapbook and talk about his salad days, which was utterly unlike him: on Louie's Grace & Truth shaving mirror was, "Not me, but Christ in me, be magnified," and he lived by that precept. I never knew a man who tried so hard to avoid the personal pronoun.

In the scrapbook, along with photos of his parents (who glared at the photographer as if this moment was a terrible insult, even though they had paid for it) and of him and Gladys in the front seat of a Buick roadster (his only non-Ford car) and souvenirs of a honeymoon in the Black Hills, was a certificate from the St. Paul College of Commerce proclaiming in fancy script bedecked with patriotic bunting that Louie had successfully completed a course in finance and banking and earned the degree of Associate of Commerce. It was dated 1931.

He earned the degree studying at night, and when it came in the mail, he said, "I told Gladys we were moving to the Cities. It was our chance."

"We packed everything we owned in the back of the Buick and took off a week later. Sandy and Marylee stayed with their grandma. They cried to see us go, they thought Minneapolis was on the other side of the world, where there were missionaries. We had a flat this side of St. Cloud and another near Anoka and then one in Osseo. Gladys thought I could've checked those tires before we left, which I had, but I was too mad to talk about it, so we hauled in around midnight at the Cran Hotel on Hennepin Avenue, which looked to have reasonable rates in the tourist guide, and got a room. The lobby was dirty, and there were old men sitting around the lobby in their undershirts, and the desk clerk was rude. He said, 'Whaddaya want?' Gladys wouldn't let me pick up the change. She said, 'You don't know where that money has been.' The room was small and it smelled of disinfectant. I opened the closet and almost fell to my death—no floor, it was a shaft of some sort, it went down to the basement; I dropped my shirt in it. We got undressed for bed, and now we were wide awake. Gladys said, 'Someone died in here, that's why the Pine-Sol. I'm not about to get into a death-bed.' She said she would prefer to sleep on a park bench. So we got dressed and snuck down the back-stairs to avoid notice. We drove to the Hotel Nicollet. It was a swank place with walnut paneling and potted palms and a carpet like walking in mud. Well, we must've looked like orphans in the storm because the clerk asked if we had reservations and then he got snooty with us, he said, 'Ordinarily we're full weeks in advance. You really should have written on ahead a long time ago. But you're lucky, I do have a room for $15.' Gladys thought it was the weekly rate. She said, 'No, we're only staying the one night.' But I knew. I looked him straight in the eye and I said, 'You wouldn't happen to have something better, would you?' I didn't want him to think we were green. No, he said, so I said we'd take it and I peeled off a twenty, my only one. Gladys was in shock, and so was I. We got to the room which was like a royal suite, and we couldn't sleep for thinking about all that money. Fifteen dollars! Gladys said, 'What made you say that?' Well, it was pride talking, worldly pride. I was so ashamed. I thought of the girls, the things I could've done for them with that money. I sat up all night thinking. I decided that if Minneapolis had that effect on me, that I'd rather spend what I didn't have than admit to not having it, then I'd better go back where I belonged, and the next day we did. And then I told a lie: I said I'd looked for a job and didn't find one good enough. It took me a long time to get Minneapolis off my conscience."

The Brethren did not hold with ambition of

worldly success, and their hopes for their children were modest ones: to earn an honest living, take pleasure in the Lord, and suffer trouble cheerfully. College was not necessary, nor was a well-paying job. Mr. Milburn of the St. Cloud Brethren earned a good dollar as a wholesale hardware salesman for Benson Brothers, but salesmanship forced a man to put his faith on the shelf—if a client cursed and told dirty jokes, he'd have to bite his tongue. Farming was the most godly livelihood, and show business was the least. When Bernie Carlson ("Mister Midwest"), host of the popular "Happy Day" and "Farm Hour" shows, got fired for a drunken remark to the Sweetheart of Song, it was noted as "what happens to people who get too big," the logical consequence of success. Bernie was "big" in nobody's eyes but ours. WFPT in Freeport was a Quonset hut in a cornfield by the tower. Nevertheless, he drove a white Olds and was on the radio, so he was pointed out to me as a sign of "what happens." I was ten and I liked to read from the newspaper into a cardboard tube, cupping a hand behind my ear to hear if I had Bernie's deep bass tones.

On Memorial Day, two great bands of marchers assemble in the morning, the Catholics at Our Lady and everyone else at the Lutheran church, and the Catholics are definitely the flashier outfit. Twelve Knights of Columbus led by Florian Krebsbach will lead them in their smart black suits and satiny capes with silver sabers at their sides and gorgeous white plumes on their black tricorn hats, followed by Father Emil in gold-embroidered surplice, and the five Sisters leading the classes from Our Lady School, including the flutaphone band in red capes, tooting "Immaculate Mother." We pass Our Lady on the way to the Lutheran church, and the Catholics are a wonder to behold. Florian, a mechanic by trade, now gives off the aura of an Admiral of the Fleet; gold and silver medals adorn his chest as he stands with the other Knights, smoking a last Lucky, and gives a nod to us poor Protestants slouching by. The Catholic boys' drum and bugle corps wears purple sashes with white fringe, the boys' honor guard carries a dozen flags including six American (five large, one immense), the Order of St. Benedict, the Marian Society, the St. Joseph's Circle and the long green banner of the Little Sisters of St. Margaret, *and* six white carbines for the rifle salute. They could add two senators and an elephant and it wouldn't be any more magnificent than it is.

The municipal Lutheran procession is nothing but a bugler, two flags, the Sons of Knute, and a big crowd. "Christians don't go in for show," my father says, explaining the difference. We aren't Lutheran, but there are only two parades to choose from; if we Brethren put on our own, it would look like a few people going out to lunch. "Christ commanded us to be humble," he adds. Well, I guess we've got that commandment in our hip pockets. We're humble to the point of being ridiculous. We look like POWs.

We march first, and the Catholics march after us.

We walk up the hill to the cemetery behind Gary and LeRoy in the cruiser, the bubble light flashing, and the poor old Knutes wobble along and everyone else bring up the rear, and as we turn the corner onto Taft, we hear the clatter of drums and a burst of flutaphone toots and Florian hupping the Knights, and I turn to see the Catholics swing out onto Taft and head for our rear. Our numbers are approximately equal, but if they attacked, they would roust us in a minute. I've read *Foxx's Book of Martyrs*, and it's hard to forget: scenes of faithful Huguenot believers praying quietly and praising God and forgiving the hordes of Catholics who pile kindling at their feet. If the Knights were to tie me to a telephone pole and pile dry brush around me and call on me to renounce my faith while a Catholic Boy Scout prepares his flints, what would I do then? I guess I'd renounce, all right. Kiss a statue, hold a crucifix, do what they said. I could always cross my fingers at the time and prevent a real conversion. God would know I didn't mean it.

Our Prairie Home Cemetery is divided into Catholic and Us; they have their gate and we have ours, and a low iron fence with spikes separates the two. After service, while our elders stroll among the stones, we boys practice jumping the fence. Little kids stand by and watch this, lost in admiration. You make your first jump when you're nine or ten and the fence comes up to your thighs, an awesome feat because if you missed, of course, you'd fall on the spikes and be impaled and die there. Nobody could save you. You'd flop around like a fish on a hook and be buried immediately. When you clear the fence, then you have to jump right back over or else. "You can't come here," David Krueger told me. He was Catholic. He had a heinie and a fat face and was "after" me at school. He got me. "This is holy. Get the hell out." I broke away from him and vaulted back to our side. Then he jumped over and we chased him back. Then we stood and exchanged views.

"Catholics stink."

"You stink so bad you think everybody does. You stink so bad, you make flowers stink."

"The Pope is dumb, he can't even speak English."

"You're so dumb you're going to hell and you don't even know it."

"Am not."

"Am too."

That was afterward. First, our crowd gathered in silence on the slope above the obelisk erected in 1889 by the Grand Army of the Republic in grateful memory of those brave men who laid down their lives for their country and conducted a formal service out of which, had they been watching, those brave men surely would have gotten a big kick. The ladies' sextet, decked out in white dresses, gathered to one side of the obelisk along with (then) Mayor Hjalmar Ingqvist and Pastor Tommerdahl, and the school-children's committee to the other, under the eye of Miss Lewis. For once, we needed no shushing; the presence of death hung heavy in the sweet summer air, as the killdeers called their name and the meadowlarks warbled and other relatives eased themselves down on the fresh grass, and the somber reality of the committee's task weighed on us.

All eight of us, chosen on the basis of good behavior, had memorized three pieces—the Gettysburg Address, "In Flanders Fields," and the Twenty-third Psalm—but we did not know which child would be called on to recite until the moment for that piece arrived and Miss Lewis put her hand on the victim's shoulder. It was an agonizing wait: your mind raced through the lines—

> In Flanders fields, the poppies blow
> Between the crosses, row on row—

That was easy, but then what? Something about larks singing, which was stuck to "Four score and seven years ago" and "He maketh me to lie down,"—and when you tried to pull out the line about the larks, your hot little mind coughed up a wad of odds and ends, a whole bird's next of lines ("Pepsi-Cola hits the spot, twelve full ounces, that's a lot"), and you tried to catch Miss Lewis's eye with a silent message: *I can't do it*. She looked straight ahead.

The Sons of Knute honor guard stood at the gate smoking and fiddling with their rifles, waiting for the crowd to shut up, then they marched double-file up the drive, all eight of them. On the gravel, their shoes ground out a sort of beat for a few steps and then the curve and the incline threw them off stride and they hauled up to the obelisk shuffling, almost dancing, trying to get back in step, until the Grand Oya yelled *Halt*. They turned to face us, and the sight of them did nothing for our confidence. They looked exhausted by the march. They wore the remnants of old Army clothes, whatever still fit them, and they made me think I'd rather die young in battle than grow up to be a Knute. All in all, they were not the men you'd pick to fire rifles around a crowd.

Pastor Tommerdahl took two steps forward, bowed his head, and prayed. It was a long one, taking in a good deal of American history, and gave me time to worry about the Gettysburg Address, the first hurdle of the program. The awful moment arrived. Karen was tapped for the Address, stepped forward, and said it perfectly. The ladies' sextet then offered "Abide With Me." They got to use a hymnal, one more unfair advantage of being older. I pulled for them to hit a clinker, I wished they'd hit one so bad that people would laugh out loud, and then they did—Mrs. Tollefson screeched like an old screen door—and I stifled a sudden laugh and it came out as a fart. Miss Lewis poked me, and I stepped forward, thinking it was time for "Flanders Fields," and had to be yanked back.

John Potvin was tapped for the poem, my classmate who we called "Wiener." He stepped forward, got the first two lines out, stopped, and swayed in the breeze. "That mark our place," Miss Lewis hissed between her teeth. He said that "And in the sky!" she hissed. He said that, and she gave him the line about larks, but his mind was shot and then he ducked and turned around and I saw the dark spot on the front of his pants. Leonard Tollefson finished the poem and had to be prompted, too. This made all of us except Karen feel sick to our stomachs. Normally, the

Twenty-third Psalm was a cinch, but it had now escaped me and I knew it had escaped the others—I could smell the sweat and hear lips moving. "The Lord is my Shepherd." That was all of it I had, that and the valley of death.

Pastor Tommerdahl again, with a few remarks. He spoke about the gallant men of the First Minnesota who held their position at Gettysburg against the rebel onslaught, our own men falling and dying in the tall grass that July afternoon and their comrades coming forward to repel the Confederate charge with bayonets, wrestling with the enemy in hand-to-hand combat—as his raspy voice went on and on, I let my mind drift away to my grandfather, born in 1860, three years before Gettysburg, in New Brunswick, his father's family having gone there from England about the time of the American Revolution. His mother's fled there about the same time from America. Her ancestors were loyal subjects of the King, who lived in Connecticut and Massachusetts and lost everything in the war except the clothes on their backs. School had taught us to regard the Loyalists as turncoats, like the Confederates, who fought on the side of Error, but I imagined them as farmers like my uncles, who had gone along minding their own business until one day someone like Miss Lewis had butted in and told them to shape up or else, and they refused.

The disobedience of my ancestors was a wonderful thought; I imagined myself back there with them. Taking up a rifle and fighting against America! Shooting at George Washington, the Father of Our country! Shooting the white wig right off his head! A terrible wicked idea, it made me shiver to think it but I kept right on thinking. Standing in the row of condemned children, heads hanging, awaiting our humiliation—suddenly gunfire from the line of trees! Miss Lewis clutches her bosom and falls to the gravel, and enemy troops swarm up the hill—but they aren't enemies! They're my relatives! They hoist me up to their shoulders. "You're safe now," they say.

And then it happened. I felt her bony finger on my shoulder. I took two steps forward. Faces grinned at me from the crowd. My brother smirked. The Knuters smiled, their rifles in hand. I looked down at the dirt and let fly with the psalm, my heart pounding in my ears, and when I got to "I will dwell in the house of the Lord forever," I expected to fall down dead. I stepped back, watching the spot in the dirt where I would fall. Miss Lewis then led the crowd in "America," a confident first verse followed by a second and third that were inaudible except for the sextet who had hymnals, and after a moment of silence, I heard the Oya holler, the slap of hands on rifle butts, the clinks of the bolts, and then the guns went off with a mighty blast so close that we felt the heat and the ladies' sextet scattered in shrieks, and we heard the shots rip through leaves.

Some ripped through the leaves of the oak tree where Harold Olson sat on a lower branch with his bugle, waiting to sound Taps, picked for this honor on the basis of ability and citizenship. He jumped ten feet and ran down the hill and stopped and tried to play Taps from there, but after being shot at, his concentration was gone—it didn't sound like Taps, it sounded like someone had picked up a bugle and was trying it out. He fooled with Taps for a while and quit. The Oya yelled, "Company dismissed!" Little boys dove in to grab the brass shell casings. My Aunt Flo put her arms around me. She said that the Twenty-third Psalm was the best part of the whole program and she was so proud of me she could hardly stand it. We walked around the cemetery, looking up our dead relatives.

For the coronation of Queen Elizabeth II in 1953, Miss Lewis brought a radio to school and we listened to it at our desks. The horse troops clopped by and battalions of drums, then a band of bagpipes, which we had never heard before, and so she drew a picture on the blackboard. We recognized it instantly as a penis and scrotum, and so did she when she heard the buzz and stepped back for a look, so she made the bag rounder and made the pipe stand up, which fascinated us even more, and finally she erased it and turned and said, her face glowing, "Small minds think small thoughts." Soon another bagpipe band marched by, and Jim whispered to me, "They're playing their pants." That made stuff come out my nose. "Leave the room right now," she said. I went out in the hall and sat on the top stair and looked down the stairwell. Three flights to the basement. Above the stairs, a round window divided into four panes by a wooden cross, its crossbars flared out in the molded frame. The stairwell looked like the front of a church—Westminster Abbey, maybe, although through the window I could see roofs of stores on Main Street and the lake. That, I imagined, was the Atlantic Ocean.

Elizabeth II ascended the stairs slowly, in time to faraway music. She wore a gold crown encrusted with diamonds, a long white dress, a mink coat, golden slippers, and carried a jeweled scepter under her arm like a twirler's baton. Behind her came ladies and a footman holding a radio on a cushion and an archbishop praying, and when she reached the landing below me, she looked up and gave me a dazzling smile. She climbed the stairs until she stood before me, I not daring to look up, staring at my black Keds. She said, "You of all my subjects have been truly faithful and good, and so I hereby do make you my knight forever and ever, and grant you your heart's desire." And she touched the top of my head with the scepter and was gone.

Processions often occurred to me when I was alone, or I walked in one if I happened to be walking at the time, to school or home from school or to the lake. Crowds clapped silently from the ditches, and great men looked down from reviewing stands on the housetops. Honor guards snapped to attention, *Hup-thunk-bam!* "Sir—" the captain said. "At ease, Captain," said I. The band played "Minnesota, Hail To Thee." I walked with a slight limp from my war wounds, carrying a softball bat—"You're wounded, sir. Let me—" "I'm all right, Captain. Others have suffered far worse than I." "Yes, sir." My voice echoed in the vast stadium amid the silent throng: "I am-m-m-m deeply-ly-ly-ly hon-on-on-on-ored," and indeed I was deeply and continually honored wherever I went, whenever I was alone.

Life in a small town offered so little real ceremony. Every morning we Boy Scouts raised Old Glory in front of school, a satisfying moment, the triangle unfolded, the eyelets clipped to the lanyard, salutes all around, and up she went, snapping in the wind, but so short—why not a prayer, a speech, a few maneuvers, some rifle shots? We of the school safety patrol got to wear Sam Browne belts and carry red "Stop" flags on poles; at my post on the corner of Main and McKinley, I made little kids stand and wait until something big like a truck came along so I could stop it and march them across, but only little kids would wait; the bigger ones just laughed and ran across the street.

I was eleven. A bad age for a boy so starved for ceremony, because as I got good at it, other kids were losing interest. My older sister and her friends had gone in for weddings in the woods, dress-up affairs, and I'd be usher one day and ringbearer another, then once got promoted to minister, stood on a stump, held a candle, and said "Dearly beloved" and read from Corinthians, and was *good*, but then they got interested in bike-riding with boys, which didn't include me.

Little kids weren't much fun because I had to tell them everything to do, which is all right if you're playing Army but not if you are King Vincent I of Altrusia ascending the throne in a royal-blue chenille robe—then the Altrusians are supposed to pay homage and lay precious gifts at your feet and make good bows and go down on bended knee and back away from the throne bowing, and it ruins the occasion if King Vincent has to tell them *how* to pay homage, they are supposed to just do it. I was extremely good at these events and couldn't see why other kids weren't. You'd go along in the ceremony— this time it's Crazy Horse and the Sioux Chieftains in a council of war, asking the Great Spirit to bless them as they go after the cowboys—and everyone is doing a fairly good job of talking Indian and tossing the sacred dirt to the four winds and passing the war pipe, then one kid says, "Let's do something else. Let's go swimming," and it ruins it. Or one of them turns and shoots you. "What are you *doing*? You can't shoot people here!" I yelled. "You're dead," he said. Two of the Tollefsons and Karen Skoglund and I played office on the Skoglunds' back porch; they had two desks, two telephones, and good paper from Skoglund's dimestore, receipts and bills and carbons, but they scribbled any old thing and expected you to believe it, then didn't bother to add up the numbers right. Karen was president, of course, which was fine, but when she got tired of office work and went in to watch television, she told us we had to stay. "You've got to get out those shipments," she said. I quit.

When I was twelve, the summer of 1954, Jim and his brother Sheldon and I had Senate hearings for a week in their basement where they had a Ping-Pong table. It was Jim's idea—he had seen this on television and knew how it went—but I was a better Senator McCarthy than him, so he became a detec-

tive who helped the committee and Sheldon, of
course, was a Communist. He was good at it—we
had him dead to rights, piles of proof that he spied
and gave secrets to the Russians, most of the proof
in writing! and he sat there across the table with a
gooseneck lamp aimed at him and lied his head off.
Then he was Senator McCarthy and I was a Communist, a General John LaClaire who committed
treason from the very heart of the Pentagon, a desperate criminal and atheist who sneered at the Committee and then one day during hard questioning about
his chummy correspondence with Stalin—the Committee had birthday cards in its possession—he
leaped up and pulled a .45 automatic and was shot
down dead by Senator McCarthy and sprawled
across the table, his soul gone to hell. That day, the
Committee adjourned, its job done, and we spent
part of August as detectives on the trail of three classmates whom we suspected of smoking cigarettes in
the woods. We found a few butts near the old fort on
Adams Hill and kept up surveillance for a day or two,
then laid a trap. We left fresh cigarettes on a tree
stump, cigarettes we had put cat hairs into, and
observed our suspects for signs of nausea. We caught
one, Paul, and made him confess. It was a good
summer.

Funerals, however, were my favorite. Funerals
expressed my deepest feelings at the time; grief, of
course, and the sadness of life, but also bravery and
great dignity—funerals were dignified because we
had a real corpse—our black spaniel, Cappy, and a
series of cats, and a parakeet named Pete. Other

people held funerals for paper dolls such as Hedy Lamarr, but we thought that was childish. We had the real goods.

Our funerals were based on the funeral of Aunt May, who died an old, old lady, of cancer, and whose funeral was the first our parents let us attend. I was seven. My mother didn't think I should go because it might be "too much" for me, and the words "too much" rang out in my ear: *too much?* I had had far too little, I thought that too much would be just about enough. She and Dad discussed it quietly on the front porch one Sunday afternoon while I wiped dishes. I liked to walk around while I wiped and, taking a pass by the open door, heard my name spoken in Dad's low voice and stopped and knelt by the window. He was saying I had reached the age of accountability and the funeral might turn my mind toward eternal things. "Well," she said, "I don't know," and I knew I was going to get to go.

My mind had been on eternal things for a while, at least on death, the door to eternity. I knew that dead people were buried in boxes in the ground, and I often wondered what they did there, in the dark with no food, no radio, no books. Grownups did have, I knew, an ability to sit still for a long time, but death seemed like quite a feat even for them, even knowing that the Lord would come and get them and they would fly up to heaven.

Aunt May lay in Lundberg's Funeral Home, which was also the Lundberg's home. They lived on the second floor and in back. Mary Ellen Lundberg was eleven and was in my sister's class. She and her sister

Protestant

Leila sang at funerals, including Aunt May's, their blond hair in curls and their white dresses ironed and black shoes shined, "Asleep in Jesus, blessed sleep" and "Called From Above." Mary Ellen said that dead bodies are cold and hard, the blood is all drained out of them, and sometimes they sit up in the coffin. But Aunt May didn't look like she was going anywhere. My dad held me up to look at her. "It's like being asleep," he whispered, but to me she looked no more asleep than a piece of lumber. She looked dead as a doornail.

We sat in back of the long room filled with black folding chairs, so still you could hear the old ladies fanning themselves. Dry coughs and solemn whispers, and faint odor of flowers and mothballs. Men in their blue Sunday suits. They walked softly, hardly letting their feet touch the floor. When Mr. Lundberg shut the lid on Aunt May, he did it as if she was made of spun glass and might shatter. Mrs. Lundberg played the organ softly, pumping the pedals, the bellows wheezing, and then Mary Ellen and Leila (Leila who punched me in the stomach once) sang in tiny voices, "Abide with me, fast falls the eventide." And Uncle Al got up to read about the corruptible putting on incorruption in a voice I never heard before, not like his voice at all but thin, like the voice of a ghost.

I imagined my own self dead and lying in a coffin, this solemn crowd gathered here in honor of me, and me a little ghost sitting by my big dad, enjoying the elaborate delicacy and gentleness of my funeral. Standing outside waiting to ride up to the cemetery and then at the cemetery and later at Flo's house,

189

people who never said boo to me before did now and put a hand on my head, petted me like a cat. May's brother Roy, an old man who once yelled at me for coming in his yard to get a baseball, put his old hand on my head as he talked to Dad, and scratched my hair and kneaded my neck muscles. "You got a good boy here," he said. Ordinarily, men like Roy weren't sweet like that, but sweetness was all over that funeral, even Leila was sweet. She said, "You should come and play in our yard sometime, we got a swing," evidently thinking I was all broken up over Aunt May, but I wasn't, I was enjoying every minute of it.

Our funerals did not quite achieve the Aunt May standard, hard as we tried. For one thing, Mother made us do it right away when the dead body was found, no time to plan things properly, we had to get busy and dig a hole. For another, our funerals attracted a few who laughed out loud during the service, and when we told them to beat it, they said, "It's just a dumb old cat!" We could've killed them. Especially the Krebsbachs, who sang off-key on purpose and when we put the box in the hole, they sang under their breaths, "The worms crawl in, the worms crawl out, the worms play pinochle on your snout." But we did our best.

Our cat Pinky was hit by a car. My sister found him in the road by the ballpark. She ran home, crying her head off, and she and I went to get him with the coaster wagon. She didn't want to look. I put the white doily from the dining room table over him (knowing I'd *get it* later, but it was right that Pinky should have a nice piece of cloth) and lifted him into the wagon, and we went home and I got a shoebox and started digging by the lilacs and she went around to invite the guests. We got five *Little Flock* hymnals out of the piano bench and picked out two songs. We set up folding chairs by the grave. The funeral was at three o'clock. Then the sad task of laying Pinky in the shoebox—and then he didn't fit because his legs were stiff, so we got a hatbox and dug a bigger hole. We put him in the shade, the doily wrapped around his little orange body except for his face. Donna Bunsen arrived and Janet and Judy Peterson and Jim and Marlys Mueller and Margaret Nute. They said they were sorry and shook our hands and then we got started.

"Let us sing Number 203," I said. We sang "Abide with me" and I stood up and read about the corruptible in a voice like Uncle Al's. We sang "Away in a tent where the gypsy boy lay, dying alone at the close of the day," and then I couldn't think of how to pray, so we had a silent prayer. I closed my eyes and thought about our cat, how I had fed him that morning not knowing it was his last breakfast, how glad I was that I had stolen half a can of tuna for him (though I was sure to *get it* for that, too), and how I would never see him again ever. I thought of him in heaven, chasing birds, where it is always warm and sunny and there are no cars. I thought about us children: would one of us eat breakfast one morning and then go out and be hit by a car? Yes, I was sure it would happen, and right then my tears started flowing in earnest. Marlys put an arm around me. And then a crab apple flew in and bounced a few feet from Pinky.

It was Casper Krebsbach, firing from the side of the garage, crouched behind the garbage can. "Casper, you creep!" my sister yelled. Marlys said, "Don't pay any attention to him. That's what he wants. Ignore him." But it was hard to ignore hard green crab apples lobbing in, and finally my sister made a dash for him. She caught him by the shirt and swung him around and threw him down and pounded him twice, *hard*, on his back, before he got away. Then we stood around the hole, put the cover over Pinky, set the box in the hole, and knelt, gently pushing handfuls of dirt over him. We patted the dirt into a mound and laid a half-slab of sidewalk on it, and wrote, in orange crayon, "P I N K Y our cat 1950 A.D. We love you. R.I.P." and went in and had macaroons and grape nectar on the porch. We sat in a circle and conversed as people do after funerals. "How is your mother?" I asked Marlys. "She is very fine, thank you," she said. "Is your family planning a vacation this summer?" "Yes, we plan to visit the Black Hills in August, Lord willing." "Lord willing" was a phrase learned in church, denoting the uncertainty of the future. It seemed appropriate after burying a cat.

SUMMER

In winter, we sit in the house
Around a blazing fire.
In summer, we sit on the porch
Like birds on a telephone wire.

Society of summer evenings in Lake Wobegon was formal and genteel. We didn't bolt our food and jump up from the table but waited for the slowest eater, me, who hated all vegetables except pickles, and cleared the table, and two of us did dishes, a race between washer and wiper. By then, it was six o'clock. Children of age could go out bike-riding, the younger ones played in the yard. Mother and Dad worked in the yard, except Wednesday, which was prayer meeting, and then sat on the porch, and one by one we joined them.

The porch is about thirty feet long, almost the width of the house, and six feet, eight inches wide. The porch is enclosed with ten-foot-tall screens and we sit in old brown wicker chairs, rocker, couch, except me. I lie on the floor, feet to the house, and measure myself against that wonderful height. A six-eight person can pretty much write his own ticket.

"They say we're supposed to get some rain," Ralph said, stopping by our porch,* "but then they've been

---

*Porch society is described by Gaylord Gibbon in his *Etiquette Along the Mississippi* (p. 28), a book not found in our house but it applied to us anyway:

The backyard is for privacy. Only people walking in the alley will bother you, and they're the sort who would anyway. The porch is sociable, but certain rules apply:

- Even if you're screened from public view, it's polite to call out hello to passers-by you know. It's up to them to stop or not. It's up to you to invite them in or not. The porch is a room of your house, not part of the yard. Only peddlers or certain ministers would barge right in.
- If you say, "Why don't you come up and sit for a bit?," it is customary for them to decline politely. If the invite was legit, it should then be repeated.
- *An invite to the porch is not an invite to the house.* Its terms are limited to a brief visit on the porch, no refreshments necessarily provided unless the occupants have such at hand.
- When the host stands up and stretches or says,

saying that for a week." The grass is brown, and you can taste dust in your mouth. A cloud of dust boils up behind Mel's car when he comes with the mail, and then he doesn't stop at the mailbox. Not even a shopper today or the phone bill (*Who called Minneapolis last month? Three dollars! What do you think this is, the Ritz Hotel?*). Not even a free pamphlet from Congressman Zwickey's office, something from the U.S.D.A. about keeping cool.

The dog days of August, they're called, but you get them in July, too, days when dogs camp under the porch where the dirt is cool and damp or lie panting in the shade, big grins on their faces. Good old Buster. Phyllis and I trimmed him one afternoon and kept trimming until we got him trimmed all even, he was clipped down to the stubble. A dog heinie. He seemed grateful. We ran the hose on him and he lay in the sun and got a dog tan.

Nobody in this family lies in the sun. You work in the sun, you lie in the shade. We don't have air-

---

"Well—," the visitor should need no further signal that the visit has ended. Only an oaf would remain longer. If the host says, "You don't have to run, do you?," this is not a question but a pleasantry.

Humankind knows no finer amenity than the screened porch. It is the temple of family life, and the sacred preserve of the luxurious custom known as "visiting." Compare it to the barbarity of the "business lunch," the hideous conversational burden of the cocktail party, and the prison that is the formal dinner, the porch visit shines with civility.

conditioning, of course. "If you'd work up a little sweat out there, the shade ought to feel good enough for you," is Dad's thinking. Air-conditioning is for the weak and indolent. This isn't the Ritz, you know. Be thankful for a little breeze.

It was luxuries like A/C that brought down the Roman Empire. With A/C, their windows were shut, they couldn't hear the barbarians coming. *Decadence*: we're on the verge of it, one wrong move and *k-shoom!* the fat man sits on your teeter-totter. You get A/C and the next day Mom leaves the house in a skin-tight dress, holding a cigarette and a glass of gin, walking an ocelot on a leash.*

---

*A/C, dishwashers, automatic transmissions, frozen dinners, and liberal theologians.

Some people move away, they get A/C first thing and crank it up to Cold. They drape themselves over it. Then they find a church where God is the gentle mist rising from the meadow and the smile on a child's face. They don't want to get sweaty anymore if they can help it. Some people dive right into decadence and make up for lost time, such as Wendell Tollerud who became a big noise in life insurance, has two cars (automatic with A/C), a one-acre ranch house (A/C, all the conveniences), membership in the Presbyterian church, and bought a lake home to get away in, which, he found to his horror, had no indoor plumbing. It was in virgin wilderness up north where septic tanks are forbidden. He paid the price of the cabin for a stainless-steel Swedish catalytic toilet (indoor) that converts shit to a fine white ash like powdered sugar. Wendell had had eighteen years of outdoor biffies and they held no further attraction. He wanted one you could sit in and not be reminded of all the people who've been there before you.

What about the Ingqvists, they have air-conditioning.

We're not the Ingqvists.

What about Fr. Emil?

He has hay fever.

Father's hay fever was so bad last summer, he could hardly breathe. His face was puffy, he went around with a hanky in his hand. He went to the North Shore for some relief in August, but one week, alone with all that scenery was all he could bear. So he's got an immense NorthernAire in his bedroom window and he lives up there.

It was when Mrs. Hoglund got one that people talked. There was nothing wrong with her, so who did she think she was? She said she got it for Janice who broke out in heat rash, but Janice only visited for a week or two and always in June. "Well, it was probably a mistake," Mrs. Hoglund said, "but as long as I have it, I might as well get the use of it." So we'd sit on our porch on an August evening, quietly perspiring, and hearing her machine humming next door. If only there were a way to connect air-conditioning to health or education. An article in the *Digest*: "Air-Conditioning: Man's New Weapon Against Malaria." COMFORTABLE CHILDREN SCORE HIGH IN SCHOOL, STUDIES SHOW—KEEPING COOL ALSO CUTS CASES OF POLIO, SAYS DR. But school is out, and Mother thinks air-conditioning causes colds. When I remark on the heat, she simply says, "Make the best of it. Life is what you make it." Her answer to any complaint without specific symptoms. "Life is what you make it."

I feel that the saying "Life is what you make it" points directly *toward* air-conditioning. Mrs. Hoglund is making the best of it, obviously. She is sitting and enjoying a fine program on television (which we don't have either) and is cool as a cucumber.

"We could try having an air conditioner and see if we like it, and if we don't, we can send it back."

I sit, all hot and bothered, suffering, and mention this. Mother says, "Go outside. Do something. Take your mind off it." But outside is not the answer. I want to be inside with cold air blowing at me. I've *been* outside in the garden working. The rule around here is that you finish your work first before you take off and play, which means that I waste the cool of the morning slaving over vegetables I don't like, and when I'm finally free to take off, it's too hot to do much. I get my golf club, a mashie niblick, out of the garage and play an imaginary game I invented, called Championship Golf: wherever I hit the ball, wherever it stops, that's where the hole is. I'm the champion, but it's boring to be so good, and it's hot. I sit under a tree with two other kids, talking about what we would do if we had a million dollars. I would buy a large cool house with a swimming pool and hire some servants. Bringing me glasses of cold nectar is what they would do, and cranking up the air conditioner.

Despite the heat and no rain, gardens come on like gangbusters, faster than we can haul in the stuff and give it away. Ralph sells no produce in July and August, not an ounce. Cans of Libby's tomatoes gather dust on his shelves. Tomatoes are free for the asking, sacks of tomatoes are thrust on you after church.

Nothing has changed in the garden since then.

Slaving in her half-acre spread, August 1984, Mrs. Luger doesn't recall the garden fever that hit her and the Mister last winter* when months of cold weather set them off on a seed binge, and they careened through the catalog like submarine sailors on shore leave, grabbing everything in sight.

By May 1, twenty little tomato plants in sawed-off milk cartons had taken over the kitchen dinette. Two large boxes from Gurney's cooled their heels on the chairs. Mr. Peterson and his Allis-Chalmers plowed the half-acre on his plowing route through town, and Mr. Luger worked it with a rake, busting up the big clods, making a flat brown table. May Day dawned warm and sunny, and the two veterans nodded at each other over morning coffee. It was V-Day.

By July, Mr. and Mrs. started to feel they'd set something in motion back there that was getting out of hand, and now, late July and August, the glacier is moving in on them for good. The pressure cooker has been running full blast for days, Ralph is out of Kerr lids, but vegetables fill up the fridge, the kitchen counter—quarts of tomatoes have been canned, still

---

*When Bertha Ingqvist, David's mother, said one April, "I don't believe I'll put in a garden this year," they knew she didn't have long. When you no longer care about fresh tomatoes and sweet corn, then death is near, and so she died the first week of June and now she is enriching the soil up there on the hill.

more tomatoes move in. The Mister reaches for the razor in the morning, he picks up a cucumber. Pick up the paper, underneath it are three zucchini. They crawled in under there to get some shade, catch a few Zs, maybe read the comics. Pumpkins are moving in to live with them. At night they check the bed for kohlrabi. Turn out the lights, they hear rustling noises downstairs: a gang of cauliflower trying the back door. Go to sleep, dream about watermelon vines reaching out and wrapping their spiny little fingers around your neck, the Big Berthas, the forty-pounders. Those cantelope they planted, the Dauntless Dukes: why plant twelve hills? Why not two?

"I like to have extra just in case and also it's nice to have some to give away," says Mrs. Luger, her hair melted to her head from an afternoon of canning. *But everyone else has some to give away.*

Back in April, she'd have killed for a tomato. Not the imported store tomatoes that were strip-mined in Texas, but fresh garden tomatoes that taste like tomatoes. That's how my mother felt, too, back then in my youth, so in May she set out thirty or forty tomato plants to satisfy our tomato lust and now, going into August, fresh tomatoes are no more rare or wonderful than rocks, each of us has eaten a bushel of them and there are plenty left where those came from.

One night, she and I snuck over to the Tollefsons' after their lights went out and left a half-bushel of tomatoes on their back step.

On this morning in August when I am thirteen, it's hot by ten o'clock. I poked along over the Post

Toasties as long as I could, then my mother sent me out to pick tomatoes. Rudy and Phyllis were already out there. I picked one and threw it at a crab apple tree. It made a good *splat*. The tree was full of little crab apples we'd have to deal with eventually, and a few of them fell. My brother and sister stood up and looked: what did you *do?* we're gonna tell.

I picked the biggest tomato I saw and took out a few more crab apples. Then I threw a tomato at my brother. He whipped one back at me. We ducked down by the vines, heaving tomatoes at each other. My sister, who was a good person, said, "You're going to get it." She bent over and kept on picking.

What a target! She was seventeen, a girl with big hips, and bending over, she looked like the side of a barn.

I picked up a tomato so big it sat on the ground. It looked like it had sat there for a week. The underside was brown. Small white worms lived in it. It was very juicy. I had to handle it carefully to keep from spilling it on myself. I stood up and took aim, and went into the wind-up, when my mother at the kitchen window called my name in a sharp voice. I had to decide quickly. I decided.

A rotten Big Boy hitting the target is a memorable sound. Like a fat man doing a bellyflop, and followed by a whoop and a yell from the tomatoe. She came after me faster than I knew she could run, and I took off for the house, but she grabbed my shirt and was about to brain me when Mother yelled "Phyllis!" and my sister, who was a good person, obeyed and let go and burst into tears. I guess she knew that the pleasure of obedience is pretty thin compared to the pleasure of hearing a rotten tomato hit someone in the rear end.*

---

*One slow week years later, the *Herald-Star* carried a photo of the Lugers looking at their garden under the headline GARDENS DOING WELL, RESIDENTS SAY — SWEET CORN, TOMATOES, ON TARGET, ACCORDING TO REPORTS. I thought my targeted tomato would have made a great photo, and also the cheeseburger I bought at the Chatterbox when I was four with a dollar I stole off the kitchen counter. My father arrived just as Dorothy put the beautiful cheeseburger in front of me; he said, "You come with me," and I said, "I'll be there in a minute." He dragged me away without a bite. No burger since has looked so good to me. I still miss it. Wake up nights hungry and see it.

In *Gene Autry and the Mystery of Big Mesa*, a gang of desperados rode into town when Gene was away, and one named Big Pete rode his horse into Mrs. Adams's Dry Goods Store, grabbed one end of a bolt of calico and rode away with it up the street, trailing a long flag of bright blue cloth that got longer and longer. A bad man, and yet I couldn't get that picture out of my head, and though I knew it was wrong to tie all those sheets together the day after washday and run out the front door and tow them around the house, whooping at my horse Bob, forty feet of white sheets is quite a sight. Throwing the tomato was a great moment. It was a fabulous cheeseburger.

"Don't you know it's wrong to steal?" he said. Of course, I knew. In the Bible, people who innovated tended to get smote, and that at a time when God smote hard: when He smited you stayed smitten, smiting was no slap on the wrist. Mrs. Tollerud illustrated this in Sunday School with a flannelgraph: a cloth-covered board on which she

"Look at what he did!" she said, but Mother just said that that was enough of *that* and to get back to work. That was fine with me. Later Phyllis caught me coming out of the bathroom and pinched me. In my baby picture, still displayed on the piano, she held me on her lap and looked down at me with pure devotion. I couldn't help telling her how much her attitude had changed. I told her not to be so unhappy. "Life is what you make it," I said. "You should get out and enjoy yourself more." As I said it, I jumped back in the bathroom and locked the door. She pounded on it, then pretended to go downstairs, but I could tell fake footsteps and I stayed put. "I can hear you breathing," I said. I stayed put for all of one *Reader's Digest* and part of another. A door slammed downstairs. My mother called my name. I yelled for help. She came upstairs. "She's hiding. She's after me," I said. "Don't be silly," Mother said, "there's nobody here but me."

———

placed cloth figures and moved them around. The liberals got kicked out of Paradise, they got flooded upon, and Pharaoh, though decent in some ways, when he didn't obey God, God made a mess of Egypt, dumping locusts, frogs, blood, lice, hail, and flies on them and then turning day to night. She took down the figure of Pharaoh the ruler and put up the figure of Pharaoh with his hands over his face. It made us think twice about striking out in new directions. But knowing right from wrong is the easy part. Knowing is not the problem.

The all-time biggest tomato ever raised in town was Irene Bunsen's in 1978, the year the Whippets beat Albany when Wayne Tommerdahl whacked the ole tomato into the eighth row of soybeans with the bases loaded in the ninth. One day in early July, Irene saw that her tomato had championship potential, which in a town full of fierce competitors who've seen some biggies was a tomato to get excited about, particularly for Irene, who was known for her black thumb because she had bad luck with marigolds. Everyone else's would come up like a drill team and Irene's got sick and drooped, and some women made cutting remarks such as, "Gee, you're the first person I ever knew who had trouble with marigolds. Mine grow like weeds."

The contender tomato was situated high on the plant, which she had staked up, so she was worried it might lose its grip. She pounded in two more stakes and made a little hammock out of mosquito netting for the tomato to lie in. It weighed close to twenty ounces. Her sister Arlene grew a two-pounder once, but Clarence ate it before the jury arrived, so it didn't count. The record was twenty-four.

Irene nursed it up to twenty-two. She was so proud of it, you'd've thought she made it in her basement. You'd've thought she invented tomatoes. She tore the other tomatoes off the plant on the theory they were taking nourishment away from the champ. She rigged a hanky to protect it from sunburn and one night she woke up in a storm and ran out to make sure it wouldn't blow down. Clint woke up when she left and looked out the window. He saw her in the flashes of lightning, kneeling by the tomato plant, holding onto the stakes.

As it closed in on the record, she checked it twice a day for bugs and whatnot, and it was during a routine check that she bumped the hammock. The champ took a dive, hit the deck, and split wide open. Irene ran in the house and called her sister who ran right over. Irene was bawling so hard she couldn't see, so Arlene went out and scooped up the remains and went to work. She stuffed its insides back in, patched it with masking tape, and took a basting syringe and replenished its bodily liquids. She put it in a plastic bag, and they took it in to Ralph for the weigh-in.

"It looks like it blew up," he said.

Arlene said, "Well, that's between you and me. It had a little accident, but it's still a tomato. Weigh it."

Twenty-five ounces. If you added three for all it went through, it'd be twenty-eight, but twenty-five was good enough for the record.

The next year, there were no remarks about Irene and her fatal effect on plants. Nobody looked at her yard and said, "Look at that. Her marigolds don't even bloom." Irene didn't plant marigolds. She put in tulip bulbs, bought from a nursery in North Dakota, a special breed that can take any punishment and stay on their feet, a cross between the Hardy Mojave and the famous Yukon Yellow, the tulip of the tundra. Her tomatoes didn't do so well the next year, but as Clint said, once you've produced the all-time champion, you have nothing more to prove. You're No. 1. You can sit back and let the others try to beat your mark.

Buster's hair grew back. My sister forgot about the tomato. She went with Wally Pilcher for a few months, they drove around in his Ford, she gave him a wallet-sized photo of herself looking up in a dreamy way, it rode around on Wally's big butt. I didn't like him because he had one long eyebrow and he called me Sport. I put a potato in his tailpipe. One day mother got a block of ice and turned the electric fan on it and we sat in the cool breeze, drinking iced tea, like royalty.

"It's so hot I can hardly get my breath," she said.

"I don't think it's healthy to get so hot," I said. "I'll bet we could find a used air conditioner in St. Cloud. You see ads in the paper all the time."

"You stopped breathing once when you were five weeks old. Did I ever tell you that?"

No, she certainly hadn't.

"I was about to take a bath and then I thought I'd better check the crib, so I went in and you weren't moving at all. I thought you were dead. I snatched you up and tore out of the house to the Jensens and pounded on the door, and right then you let out a cry. Anyway, we took you to the doctor.

"What did the doctor say?"

"He wasn't sure. He didn't think it was a seizure. I guess it was just one of those things that happens sometimes." Then she got up to make a salad for supper.

That's how Mother told stories. Never enough detail, and she always left you hanging at the end. If she had gone ahead and run the bath water, I'd be dead right now. And it was "just one of those things that happens sometimes"? I felt a little weak myself. I had about gotten over the fear that I'd stop breathing during the night, all those years I used to remind myself to breathe, and now this. So it *wasn't* dumb to think that your breath could stop at any time. It could happen right now, sitting on a white kitchen chair in a cool breeze and drinking iced tea. Fall over dead on the linoleum. Thirteen years old, dead.

Three years before, the Heglunds brought their boy home from the doctor with six months to live. He and I had been friends once, then he threw a rock at me and we drifted apart, and soon after he came down sick with the flu. Or so they thought until the doctor had a look and heard a ratchety sound in his heart. There was nothing to be done about it. They put his bed against the upstairs window so he could look out, and one day our class got out of school to go stand in the street and wave at him. It was August but the Heglunds got him a Christmas tree, and all his relatives sent presents, including a movie projector. One day he got a letter from the governor, which his sister brought to school: we all got to hold it. Nobody talked about him, it was too sad, and gradually we forgot about him. When he came back to school in December, nobody made a fuss over him. His death had pretty well worn out our interest in him, and we had nothing left for his resurrection. Mrs. Heglund told my mother that she got sick of him lying in bed, which was a mess, and one day she hauled him out and sent him to school, and the exposure to cold air improved him, and soon he was running around and being his usual dumb self.

Exposure to heat was killing me; August 12, 101°: why? Dallas, 98°. Miami, 96°. You don't have to be Einstein to see the unfairness of it. What happened to the forces of nature that socked us with −30° six months ago, were they on vacation? By rights, we should be cool and comfortable, being so far north, but instead we woke up and at eight o'clock the last of the cool was burning off, the State Farm thermometer out the window over the sink was slowly percolating to the top. Sitting eating soggy Cheerios on the morning of a hot one, a day that promised nothing but a lawn to mow and then a blank afternoon reading back issues of the *Geographic*, I knew that summer was an experiment that didn't work. It looked good in May as things warmed up and Miss Lewis's classroom turned rank and sour, and for a few weeks of June a person could fill his time with projects, but by August summer was dragging on the ground and only a good thunderstorm could bring it to life. Standing in the dormer window as black and purple clouds boiled up in the west, I pretended I was the captain of the house, sailing straight into it, and when the lightning came closer, blazing bolts ripped the sky and the bomb went off at the same instant and Mother yelled at everyone to go to the basement, I stayed on deck and secretly wished for a tornado.

Father Emil's vacation is in August; his fifteenth annual bus tour of Civil War battlefields, he is now the senior member of his bus. They added Nashville this year, otherwise it was the same. "You keep discovering new things every year, though," he says, and he finds to his surprise he is becoming more sympathetic to the Confederacy, partly the work of sweet-talking waitresses who say, "Hah, yew doin'? C'd ah git yew s'm pah? Mo' cawfee, honey?" The tour spent a night in a town east of Knoxville, and he walked to a tavern across the highway from a revival tent and sat in the dark, where a man told him a long story about a man who kept three wives for twenty years and none of them knew about the others. The man in the dark was a son of the second wife. He said, "Daddy was too much for one woman. I guess he was the best-loved man who ever was. We just all wrapped ourselves around him. When he finally got sick, he just went off and shot hisself. He didn't do it at home, though, I'll say that for him. He didn't want to make his family have to clean up after him." When Father left, it was two hours later, and across the highway they were singing at the tops of their voices about the love of Jesus. The South was wrong, but nothing is simple. Lee coming home to commit treason for friends he didn't agree with: was that right? Maybe, Father thought when he was on vacation. He walked from monument to monument, green pasture once heaped with the dead; he wondered about his own troops: would they march so far on pitiful rations, with no decent shoes? His fellow passengers complained about heat, air-conditioning, too much salt on the chicken, poor TV reception in motels. Riding down from the Blue Ridge to Chancellorsville, where the hapless Hooker was whipped by an army half its size under Lee, where Stonewall Jackson was mortally wounded, and on to Fredericksburg, scene of Burnside's humiliation—history and tragic blunders and terrible slaughter on every hand wherever you looked—a woman in the seat in front of him said, "I tried to watch *Donahue* this morning, it was like it was coming from the moon." A force of thirty-six tourists but he doubted they had the wherewithal to hold up a gas station.

With Father's return imminent, the parish bade farewell to his sub, Father Frank. The Kruegers threw a cocktail party for him in their backyard where they have a concrete patio and a glass-top table with umbrella (green-striped) attached. The guest list was small; not many Catholics in town are comfortable around a priest in a sportshirt and yellow shorts, drinking gin and saying, "*Damn*, this is good, Jack. *Dry*. Mmmmm. What did you do? Just *think* about vermouth, for Christ's sake?" For his farewell homily, Father Frank developed the Twenty-third Psalm into a golf course where He maketh the ball to lie in the fairway and leadeth it around the water hazards. Yea. Though we walk through the rough, we will fear no bogey, for He prepareth the green before us in the presence of sand traps, and our putt runneth over to the cup and dwells there. Father Frank is on the back nine of life these days and thinks it's the best part of the course. He looks good. Close-cropped gray hair, good tan, and—well, should you say this about a priest? Should you even think it?—good legs. Hell, yes! he'd say, just because I'm a priest doesn't mean you can't look! He hugs women and gives them a good smack on the lips.

In 1975, Jack Krueger worked all spring and

summer to start a Country Club in town. A loan guarantee under the Rural Recreation Development Program got the ball rolling, and Jack took an option on forty acres of Old Man Tollerud's pasture and woodlot. No investors stepped forward for weeks; people wanted to know who else had signed up—they didn't want to be the first; the membership fee was $1,000. Maybe it'd sell better if they knew what they were buying, thought Jack, so he paced off two hundred yards on the pasture, put a can in a hole, mowed the grass short and Roto-tilled three sand traps. He invited prospects to try their hand. Mr. Tollerud, however, refused to remove the Holstein hazards, and when the first foursome approached the tee, cows moved in for a closer look. Clint Bunsen's ball hit one amidships, and she turned her head and gave him a look as if she'd heard someone curse. They played the hole and then came back and played it again. Clarence Bunsen told Jack, "I can't imagine doing this all afternoon." But, as he told Clint later, it was the principle of the thing. A golf club would be the first organization that it cost a pile of money to join. Sons of Knute you get in for $10 initiation and eating a raw egg and memorizing a few lines of Norwegian. Church you join when you're born, for nothing. "If I had a thousand dollars and I wanted people to know I had it, I wouldn't have to join a club, I could walk around town with the money on a forked stick," Clarence said. "I could wave it right in people's faces." Because he wouldn't join, Clint didn't, and when Clint didn't, people thought it might be fishy, and by August, the Holsteins had trampled the first hole. You couldn't tell it had ever been.

"Nothing ever changes in this town," said Jack. "It's hard to get people interested. You set off the fire alarm and they just get up and go to lunch."

The fire siren goes off at noon and six every day but Saturday (noon only) and Sunday (*Be still and know that I am God*). That is how we tell time, that and the progress of the sun across our sky. Some people wear a watch—on the one hand. On the other they don't look at it very often.

As children we got so we could tell time by the sun pretty well, and would know by the light in the room when we opened our eyes that it was seven o'clock and time to get up for school, and later that it was almost ten and then almost noon and almost three o'clock and time to be dismissed. School ran strictly by clocks, the old Regulators that Mr. Hamburger was always fiddling with, adding and subtracting paper clips on the pendulum to achieve perfect time, but we were sensitive to light, knowing how little was available to us as winter came on, and always knew what time it was—as anyone will who leads a regular life in a familiar place. My poor great-grandpa, when his house burned down* when grandma left the bread baking in the summer kitchen oven to go visit the Berges and they built the new one facing west

---

*In his desk, they say, was thousands in gold dust brought back from Colorado, the family fortune—all lost in the

instead of south: they say he was confused the rest of his life and never got straightened out even when he set up his bed in the parlor (which faced north as his former bedroom had): he lived in a twilight world for some time and then moved in his mind to the house he'd grown up in, and in the end didn't know one day from another until the day he died. "Yeah, though I walk through the valley of the shadow of death, I will fear no evil," but there's more than one kind of shadow, and when a man loses track, it can kill him. Not even the siren could have saved my great-grandpa. He died of misdirection.

The siren isn't set off by a clock but by Bud Mueller who takes a nap in the fire truck and sets his alarm clock for noon if the nap starts early. He gets up, pulls the siren lanyard, and goes back to snooze for another half hour. His breathing sounds like the cardboard flap you pin to the back wheel of your bike to make a motorcycle. At six, he sounds the siren on his way home to supper and usually is a few minutes fast.

At noon, as the siren dies slowly at the end of its long scream, almost everyone in town puts down one thing and picks up another. Fr. Emil picks up his

---

blaze, thus changing our history these past hundred years. All of us think of it often. The new house became a chicken coop later, and I wonder if the gold didn't sit in the dirt and generations of chickens crawl under the boards and eat it. In that case, the golden yolks of our boiled eggs were truly golden and so are we now. I loved eggs. I may be worth hundreds of dollars.

breviary and prays for the poor people. "My God, rich people have the time to praise You if they want to, but the poor people are so busy, accept their work as praise because, my God, they don't have time for everything." A lot of poor people knock off work right then and have them some dinner, such as the Commercial Hot Beef Sandwich at the Chatterbox: two slices white bread, two big dollops mashed potato, three chunks pot roast, and dark gravy poured over everything—you also get string beans and a slab of pie—$1.75. The Chatterbox gets as loud as the school lunchroom at noon with all the good eaters piling in, and sometimes the siren sets off an alarm in Dorothy. She straightens up, standing over the gravy pot with a ladle in her hand, and looks like she could brain somebody with it. She is a big lady and with that hairnet on, her head looks like a helmet. The big booths in back are full of hefty guys jammed in tight—they roll Horse with dice out of leather cups and turn and holler at guys lumbering in the front door, so there is dice clatter and loud volleys of talk across the room and the crash of plates— she looks like she could clear the room in about eleven seconds flat. "You know, I think I'd sell this place for about half of what anyone in his right mind would want to pay for it," she says to nobody in particular. It's packed today because it rained so hard last night nobody could get into the fields this morning and a lot of them wound up in town. Big butts of pear-shaped gents in coveralls lined up on the stools like the 1938 Chicago Bears as seen by Bronko Nagurski. Platters of the Commercial on the counter

("Twenty-six years I stood back here and watch them eat—if I got some hogs and a trough, I'd feel right at home": Dorothy) and big forkloads of chow hover above the gorge, meanwhile Al who hasn't yet got his dinner hunkers at the end and clears the phlegm from his head with one expert snort. It's a deep liquidy snort of a sort that Flora would never allow at home, but here at the Box he cuts loose as if it were no more than a little cough, a mere *ahem*, and then he eases up one cheek and releases a whistle of a fart. Bob next to him is offended. "Take a dump while you're at it," he says. "Gotta eat first," says Al.

Carl Lundberg eats alone, a hot beef sandwich plus a BLT plus apple pie. He's feeling sour and a good lunch might cheer him up. None of the Lundbergs slept well last night. The heat makes them nervous and jumpy, even in their sleep. Lundbergs always were restless in bed, except Betty, but then she was an Olson before she married Carl. She's the type who lies on her back, folds her hands, and wakes up eight hours later without a wrinkle, even in bed with Carl who swims in his sleep. He treads water in heavy seas, yelling to search planes overhead. So do Carl, Jr., Benny, Wilbur, and Donny, who sleep upstairs in the Lundbergs' little house, four big boys in bunkbeds. In daytime, they're placid enough, all big-boned, phlegmatic ("Those Lundbergs," my grandma said, "they can sit with the best of them"), but at night they toss and turn and holler out and sometimes go for walks.

Something about hot sticky weather brings the Lundbergs out at night. When Gary and LeRoy make the midnight round in the cruiser, they're never surprised to see a Lundberg lumbering down the street. Once Donny sleepwalked all the way to the ballpark and crouched behind the plate, calling for the fast one. They've climbed fences in their sleep, gotten into gardens, tramped on tomatoes, knocked over beanpoles. Wilbur woke up in a tree once. And in a town where nobody locks the doors or knows where the keys are, some people have been awakened by a Lundberg on the premises, coming up the stairs in his shorts.

Even restless and afoot, they're sound sleepers. You have to shake a Lundberg and yell at him, and then when he wakes up, he's never in a good mood. He's apt to shake you back and yell, "What are you doing t'me? Getcha hands offa me!"

One hot night, four Lundbergs took a hike, aroused by thunder and lightning, aroused but not awakened. Their neighbor Mrs. Thorvaldson, widow of Senator K.'s brother Harry, called the constables. Carl, Jr., had pitched into her marigolds and the other three were moving around on her lawn. "They're having dreams, and I don't want to be part of it," she said.

Gary and LeRoy hauled Carl, Jr., out of the flowers and herded the others to their own yard and, rather than wake them, tied clothesline to their ankles and tethered them to a tree. Of course, when Carl walked to the end of his rope, he fell like a load of bricks. He awoke then, mad about the rope, the light in his face—"This isn't right," he said, as LeRoy untied him. "You got no *right* tying up people in their sleep. We were *asleep*. You woke us up. *You* can't do that."

LeRoy said he was sorry. "Sorry!" Carl said. "Sorry isn't good enough." Next day, he had forgotten the whole thing. When Dorothy asked him how he was, he said, "I didn't sleep too well last night. Somebody put sticks in my bed. I got scratches all up and down my legs. I don't know. Sometimes I wonder."

In the booth across from Carl, Harold and Marlys Diener sit on one side, wedged in by Willard Diener, and across from them are Rollie Hochstetter and brother Walter. "If Harold don't treat you right, you give me a call," Willard says to Marlys with a friendly leer. *You big dummy*, she thinks. She is crushed between them and can hardly handle her fork and finish her lemon meringue pie. She just mentioned to Harold that she wants to go to St. Cloud and see a movie, she doesn't care which one, they haven't been to a movie for months without the kids along. They are slowly getting over a big argument of months before, March in fact. He got so mad he threw the Bible out the bedroom window right through the glass. She was showing him the verse where it says, Husbands love your wives, or words to that effect. He grabbed it and threw it. The argument started out to be about breakfast: he was going to make French toast and didn't put oil in the frying pan, and she said, "Don't you know how to do this?" and he said, "It's not my job." He talked about wives being obedient to husbands, so she wanted to show him the other side. He threw it out the window. It was *cold* out, so he had to spend an hour cleaning shards of glass out of the window and cutting a new pane and installing it, which didn't improve his disposition, and that night after supper he said, "If you'd spend a little less time at your mother's gabbing and a little more around here, this place'd be something a person could call *home*."

"Sometimes I think Mother's *is* my home," she replied.

"Well, anytime you decide, you just let me know."

"Well, maybe I'm in the process of deciding."

They had gone to the bedroom so the children wouldn't hear. They were in there for fifteen or twenty minutes, then Dawn came in. "Daddy, Todd broke the biffy," she said.

The little boy had dropped his Brussels sprouts in the toilet and covered them up with a couple of pounds of toilet paper, and then flushed, and flushed again, flooding the bathroom floor. Harold got a clothes hanger and fished the glop out of the bowl, and Marlys mopped. He said, "This always happens. If you'd just pay attention to the kids once in a while, maybe they'd learn something about discipline."

"I can't do everything myself!" she said. She slammed the door shut and yelled some more things at him—she forgot what she said, but something connected, something she had been saving up for a long time, and when he heard it, he said, "That's it. I don't have to take this anymore."

He marched straight to the front door and threw it open. A blast of cold air hit him. She was right behind him, saying, "Go head! Walk out! Leave us! I don't care!" Behind her, peeking around her, were the kids. They never heard this sort of talk, they weren't allowed to go to movies that featured this sort of dialogue—only to family movies.

Harold turned and marched past them to the bedroom. He felt ridiculous. He had been about to utter his exit line, "You don't need to tell *me* you don't care, I *know* you don't care," when he remembered it was March and he was barefooted. He was going to say the line and slam the door. Instead, he had to go back for socks. He yanked clothes out of the drawer and threw them on the floor, looking for his long wool socks, meanwhile he kept repeating himself:

"I've had it. A man can only take so much."

"There's a limit to how much a man can take."

"I've come to the end of my rope."

"A man can take just so much and no more."

The children drifted away. Marlys went to make coffee. The moment was lost for him. He wandered into the kitchen to ask if she had seen his wool socks, and she said no, would he like a cup of coffee? He said okay. "To go?" she whispered. He didn't hear her. After a while, he said, "Sometimes I don't know what keeps us together."

"If it wasn't for winter, I think I'd be a divorced woman," she told her mother the next day. Her mother said, "You keep your house so cold. You oughta turn up the heat so you can wear your good nightie."

That wasn't the problem.

Crushed between Harold and Willard, their elbows in her side, Willard breathing on her, she felt like *that* was something she deserved a little vacation from. Even the night he came so close to leaving, Harold had *that* on his mind about ten minutes later. She went to bed with her back turned to him and wouldn't roll over, but the bed had a trough down the middle (from *that*), and when she was half asleep and her grip on the mattress loosened, she fell into the trough and there he was, waiting.

"What movie you going to see?" Willard said. "Maybe I'll come and keep you company."

"Anything that doesn't have naked people in it," Harold said. "Marlys sees naked people and it makes her sick."

"Depends on the person," she said. Willard thought that was the funniest thing he ever heard in his life.

Fr. Emil comes in for lunch. Harold: "Shhhh. Father hear us talk, we'll be here till Tuesday." With Father is Father Willetz, visiting from St. Cloud, a priest who wears a turtleneck. Father stands by the coatrack, pretending to read the auction notices and ballroom posters. Actually he is scouting the room for the right place to sit, a strategic problem for a priest who simply wants to eat lunch and not necessarily be asked what he thinks about those Benedictines who got hold of St. Mary's in Finseth. St. Mary's was a gorgeous church until the Benedictines came through and told people they ought to clean out the statuary and the high altar, which the people did, and do you know what they used for an altar? A *lunch* table! from the cafeteria! Set right out on the floor where everybody could see it—why? Why tear the church apart so you can see the priest say Mass?

Fr. Emil has been asked about St. Mary's often enough, by sitting near the wrong people who feel obliged to make conversation on holy things. He says a prayer, asking God to grant him a secular lunch. He reads the wall—

Bill Larson and his Stearns County Cavaliers are playing the St. Anna Coliseum. Johnny (Mr. Sway). Swendson (formerly of "Let's Get Together!" on WCCO) coming in August. A thank-you note from the Bloodmobile.* A wedding dance at the Avon Ballroom on July 22nd for Mary Paterek and Virgil Loucks (imagine, a youth named Virgil, he must be the youngest Virgil in Minnesota, maybe the last of the Virgil line). An auction of household goods July 14 (and some farm machinery and misc.) at the Albert Diener farm, lunch on the grounds, three o'clock sharp. Albert is seventy-two. He never thought this would happen to him, his legs getting weak.

---

*The Red Cross gave Ralph a pin for giving the most blood during the drive that ended Memorial Day. The pin arrived from Minneapolis the first of August, and Ralph and Margaret Krebsbach went to the *Herald-Star* for the presentation, where Harold has the Speed-Graphic mounted for portraiture—most official presentations take place there, in front of Harold's display of fine printing: NO TRESPASSING, HUNTERS WILL BE PROSECUTED, KEEP OUT, BEWARE OF DOG, PRIVATE. Margaret accidentally stuck Ralph when she pinned it to his shirt, and he didn't bleed a drop. "It was only a scratch," he said, but he didn't feel well at all.

"Father?" says Father Willetz.

"Sorry." There's an empty booth across the floor from the jukebox. Father Emil knows that with him sitting there, nobody will play music.

For three weeks of agony last February, Dorothy was gone on vacation to Tucson, and her cousin Flo from Burnsville, who is too nervous to run around at noon with a dozen orders in her head, filled in. "I don't know how you do it," she told Dorothy, and she was right, she didn't. Flo has her own way, a daily menu like a hot-lunch program—you plunk down your $2.50 and get Luau Pork Chops with pineapple and marshmallow dainties and cherry-cola Jell-O salad, or, if it's Tuesday, Tuna Mandalay with Broccoli Hollywood, End of the Trail Bean Salad, and Yum Yum Bars or Ting-A-Lings (your choice). Liver casserole au gratin appeared once, and Chicken Surprise and potato-chip cookies. Flo herself did not eat lunch, or drink coffee. Her coffee had an oil slick on top.

Good old Norwegian cooking: you don't read much about that, or about good old Norwegian hospitality. At Art's Bait & Night O'Rest Motel, guests find the cabins are small, the chairs are hard, and the floors are studded with exposed nails. For decoration, an exciting wildlife picture, and for relaxation, you get two cast-iron lawn chairs with a scallop shell that makes a twenty-four-hour impression on your back, even through a shirt. In Cabin One is a hand-lettered sign tacked to the wall beside the door. "Close the damn Door," it says. In Cabin Two, you will read, "Don't clean Fish on the Picnic tables. How many Times do I have to Repeat myself? Use the table by the Botehouse. That's What it's there for. Anyone caught Cleaning Fish on Picnic Tables gets thrown out bag + baggage. This means You. For Pete Sake, use your goddamn Head." Underneath that gruff exterior is a man who means every word he says. Every summer you will see at least one car high-tailing it out of Art's with a red-faced man at the wheel and the back seat full of scared children. The man is livid. If Bambi walked out of the woods, he might not swerve to miss her. At the end of Art's long dirt road, he turns east on the gravel, skidding half sideways, the back wheels spinning, stones flying like they were shot from guns, and he stomps it and hits eighty on the quarter-mile straightaway to Hansens', hits the brake, and takes that long deceptive turn around Sunfish Bay sliding up into the left lane, his wife saying, "Stop. Stop right here and let us all out." What has burned his bacon is the utter shame of it. The humiliation. He caught the sunnies about a hundred yards off the dock, one, two, three, four, big ones, and rowed back to show them off. He was so excited, he cleaned them right away for breakfast, on the picnic table, intending to wash it off afterward. Then a skinny, sawed-off sonuvabitch with a face like a bloodhound's came up from behind, grabbed the knife away from him, and said, "Get the hell out of here. You got five minutes and then I get the shot-gun." He waved the knife at him. The man was ber-serk, one of those psycho-rural types you see in movies, unshaven, drooling brown spit, who take in city-folk for the night so they can murder them in their beds. A vacation is ruined. He had to run around the cabin throwing stuff into suitcases, hustling sleepy kids into the car, grabbing up wet swimsuits and towels, while his wife said, "Can't you just talk to him?" and the maniac stood outside the door saying, "If you can't read a simple goddam sign and follow one simple goddam instruction, then you can just get your fat butt the hell out of here." Right in front of the children. And he wouldn't give back the knife. Careening along the dirt road, the dad's gorge begins to rise for good, and down the straightaway, he completely rethinks his position on gun control. The speedway turns are to compensate for his not decking the man on the spot and cutting his scrawny throat. Oscar Hansen has seen a lot of cars almost spin out on the long turn and come up through his barbed wire. He's thought about putting up a sign:

CALM DOWN.
HE'S LIKE THAT TO EVERYBODY.

Other residents come to mind as people who if you were showing a friend from college around town and you saw them you would grab his arm and make a hard U-turn, such as Mr. Berge, not because he might be drunk but because whether drunk or sober he might blow his nose with his index finger the old farmer way. Farmers still do this in the field, though most of them know that town is a different situation, but not Mr. Berge and his friends, the Norwegian bachelor farmers. Their only concession to town is a slight duck of the head for modesty's sake. To them, the one-hand blow is in the same league with spitting, which they also do, and scratching in the private regions. They never learned the trick of reaching down deep in your pocket and feeling around for a dime until you solve the problem. When ill at ease, such as when meeting your friend, they are apt to do all three in quick succession, spit, blow, and scratch—*p-thoo, snarf, ahhhhh*—no more self-conscious than a dog.

"It's better to apologize than to ask permission," says Clarence, arguing for greater boldness in life. The bachelor farmers, however, do neither. On a warm day, six of them may roost on the plank bench in front of Ralph's, in peaceful defiance of Lutheranism, chewing, sipping, snarfling, and p-thooing, until he chases them away to the Sidetrack Tap (they're bad advertising for a grocery store, the heftiness of them seems to recommend a light diet) and then they may not go. Mr. Munch may just spit on the sidewalk, study it, and say, "I don't see no sign says No Sitting." "You get up, I'll paint one for you," says Ralph. They may wait a good long time before they go.

"Tellwiddem," says Mr. Fjerde.

"Tellwid *all*uvem," says Mr. Munch.

The Norwegian bachelor's password. *Tellwitcha.*

We are all crazy in their eyes. All the trouble we go to for nothing: *ridiculous.* Louie emerging from his job at the bank, white shirt and blue bow tie, shiny brown shoes, delicately stepping across the street for lunch: *dumb bastard.* Byron Tollefson bending over grass, pulling the odd stuff out: *stoopid.* Your college chum, gesturing at the cornices of brick facades and saying, "Marvelous!": *talks like a goddam woman.*

In time, you learn not to die of shame, as you did at sixteen and eighteen and twenty-one, when you meet one while in the company of a fine friend—you learn to let the friend figure things out for himself, you don't yank him into Skoglund's to look at postcards until the coast is clear. Which is odd, considering that it's true, as Clarence once said: in their hearts, the bachelor farmers are all sixteen years old. Painfully shy, perpetually disgruntled, elderly teenagers leaning against a wall, watching the parade through the eyes of the last honest men in America: *ridiculous.* Clarence mentioned this when I was eighteen and complaining about my father's lawn compulsions—grass is *meant* to get long, it's part of nature, nature *is* growth. "You should talk to the Norwegian bachelors, you have a lot in common," he said. I said to myself: *ridiculous.*

———

It's noon of a July day, not a cloud in sight, and a long stone's throw from the Box, a long beanpole of a kid with hair the color of wet straw stands in the front door of the big green house and holds a cup of coffee. In his pajamas, still, at noon. The Tollefson house, the green one with two cast-iron deer peacefully grazing in front of the dark screened porch, a rusted Monkey Wards swing set in back. The Tollefson boy who has been up until two in the morning for weeks reading books, still basking in the glow of graduation and getting the sons of Knute Shining Star Award (a $200 scholarship). His mother, Frances, is still basking, too, and that's why, when she comes up behind him, she touches him lightly on the shoulder and says gently, "Still in your pajamas, Johnny?"

He flinches as if she were a snake. He sighs. "The answer to your question, Mother, is yes. These are my pajamas and I'm in them."

"Would you like a little lunch?"

"No, I'm not hungry."

"I could fix you breakfast."

"I just said I'm not hungry."

"What's wrong?"

"Nothing is wrong."

"Are you sure?"

He sighs. He's cornered with her there behind him. He walks over to the brown cane chair by the porch swing and slouches down in it. It's hard to get comfortable if you're tall, you have to ease down until you balance on a particular vertebra a few notches above the coccyx. He finds the bone he wants, puts his feet up on the swing, sets his sad blue eyes on the Krebsbach house across the street, and wishes she would leave him alone. Why is it the people who follow you around asking what's wrong are the ones who wouldn't know if you told them?

What's wrong is this—and it isn't this exactly, this is only one thing of many—it's his mother's plan that at two o'clock they pick up his grandma and Aunt Mary and his uncle Senator K. Thorvaldson, and the whole motley bunch drive to St. Cloud to see him register at St. Cloud State College for fall quarter.

"It's only registration! It's like getting a driver's license! It takes ten minutes! What's the big deal?" he said to her three days ago when she announced this idea.

"I thought you'd be pleased. They're so proud of you. They want to be there."

How do you tell your mother that there's something funny about your old relatives? They talk funny, and they look funny. It's less noticeable in Lake Wobegon, but put them in a big city like St. Cloud and *everybody sees it*, like they have signs around their necks that say "Hick." People in St. Cloud have some shine to them and look comfortable in their clothes as they stroll along St. Germaine, going about their business affairs, and if you asked one of them for directions to a good restaurant, they'd tell you that, but his old relatives dress up like scarecrows, Uncle Senator wears baggy black pants and an old white shirt buttoned up to the neck and no tie and hightop kangaroo shoes, and if you asked him for directions he'd give you the story of his life.

For three days they've gone around and around.

"Why don't you and *them* go register? You don't need me."

"Oh, Johnny, it's such a little thing."

"If it's so little, how come they have to go?"

"I can't tell them they can't come now, they'd be so hurt."

"Well, you should've thought of that when you invited them."

His dad said, "If we're not good enough to be seen

228

with you in public, then maybe it's time you started packing."

"I don't see what that has to do with the fact that I am perfectly capable of going to St. Cloud without taking my whole family along."

"There's a lot you don't see and I doubt if you ever will."

"I don't know what that's supposed to mean."

Why couldn't his family be more like the Flambeaus? Emile and Eileen Flambeau in the Flambeau Family mystery series he has read every one of which twice. Emile is a Nobel laureate microbiologist whose travels around the world in search of elusive viruses seem to put him time after time in the vicinity of violent crimes committed by rings of dope smugglers, whom Emile brings to justice with the use of superior intelligence, his own and that of his wife, the former screen star, and his teenage son, Tony Flambeau. The Flambeaus live in a spacious apartment at the Sherry-Netherland Hotel overlooking Central Park in Manhattan, where they relax and have fun after their strenuous adventures, and what impresses him is the way Emile and Eileen treat Tony as a mature person and also the way the Flambeaus do what they *feel* like doing—*when* they feel like doing it, not like in Lake Wobegon. There is no noon siren in Manhattan when everyone has to sit down immediately and eat a hot beef sandwich, no six o'clock siren when you dig into a tuna casserole made with cream of mushroom soup. The Flambeaus keep irregular hours. Once they went to Chinatown at three in the morning for shark fin soup, and another time they went for a long walk together down Fifth Avenue and dropped in at Xenon and danced and went to a movie and wound up sailing out through the Verrazano Strait in the *Ginny B.* as the sun rose over the Atlantic. It's the little things that impress him about the Flambeaus, such as Tony's sixteenth birthday, when Eileen said, "Tony, Emile and I would love it if you'd join us for a glass of wine on the balcony," and Tony said, "Thanks, Eileen. Should I open the Pouilly-Fuissé?" To call your parents by their first names, to sit around drinking fine wine with them—this never happens in Lake Wobegon!

No point in thinking about Flambeaus now. He's squashed in the front seat between his mother and Grandma, who reeks of face powder and lilac water. Aunt Mary and Senator K. are spread out in back. The windows are rolled up tight because Grandma can't stand drafts. She leans forward, her jaw set, gripping the shiny black purse as if someone would snatch it from her, the thick specs magnifying her eyes so she looks like a lizard. A lizard with a mustache. Aunt Mary is Grandma's younger sister who never married, and it's not hard to see why men looked at her and thought they could make it through life without her by their side. Aunt Mary talks the way other people chew gum. His dad can stand her for about five minutes, then he goes out and starts up the lawn mower. Wraps the cord around her neck and gives it a yank. In the car, she narrates the trip. Up ahead is a house moving down the road on a flatbed truck—"Look. A house on the road! Ain't that something. Look at those sheep. Boy, there are lots of them, aren't there. Boy, that's a big building. Sure is warm today, isn't it."

Aunt Mary reads billboards out loud. Petters' Furs & Fabrics, All You Need To Sew, See Us About Winter Coat Storage. O'Connell's Midnight Club, Cocktails and Dancing, Appearing Nightly The Duke Bryan Combo. Don't Drive So Fast Among the Pines, Aunt Mary Likes to Read Our Signs—Burma-Shave.

And Uncle Senator K. Thorvaldson—who else has a great-uncle named Senator? How do you explain to people that he was named that because his mother liked the sound of it? If he was normal, it might be okay, but he's even battier than the others. At least Aunt Mary talks about what's there but Uncle Senator drifts in and out of the present; anything in the world can remind him of anything else going back to boyhood where in fact he hangs out most of the time, so the sights of the modern world are pretty amazing to him, such as motor vehicles ("We useta go to St. Cloud, it took us all day and Mama packed us a dinner and we slept at the Uelands'. Can you believe that, Johnny? Now look at us") or ballpoint pens ("Did you ever see how these work, Johnny? Boy, the guy what thought it up sure was a smart one, don't you think"), or even good weather surprises him. Aunt Mary reads signs into your left ear and Uncle Senator leans forward and yammers into your right. "Oh Johnny, you'll remember this day as long as you live. What a day! Look at the sky! Oh, God is good, isn't he. Ah, it's a good day."

Now, as they come down Division Street and turn onto the campus of St. Cloud State College, he slouches deeper into the front seat, ducks his head, puts his hand up to his face. He wants to become somebody at this school. He wants to write for the literary magazine *Cumulus*, but what if when he brings in his poems and stories, the editor looks up and says, "Oh yeah, I remember you—you were driving around in a beat-up car with a bunch of funny-looking people"?

And people *are* staring at them. Groups of girls turn and look, and a couple of guys with tennis racquets, distinguished underclassmen carrying briefcases, everyone turns and takes a gander at the yokels—of course! "Ma!" he cries. "Ma! You're going the wrong way! This is a one-way street!"

"Oh, for goodness' sake. This is so confusing. I'm doing the best I can."

A car honks. Another car honks. A garbage truck swerves and lets out a long blast.

"Pull in the parking lot!" he hisses. "Turn! Here! *Turn!*"

Aunt Mary and Senator don't notice this, they're too busy noticing the size of buildings, but Grandma takes his hand in hers—she is trembling. God knows why. She thinks something terrible is just about to happen, God knows what. The idea of one-way traffic is as foreign to Grandma as outer space. For all she knows, the car is about to blow up in flames. She pulls out a hanky and wipes her eyes. This unnerves his mother, who is already shaken.

"Mother," she says, "don't you start in or I'm going to go right to pieces!"

Grandma weeps. They sit in the car in the middle

232

of an empty parking lot. His mother is weeping. Senator says, "Where do we go, Johnny? Where is your school building? Boy, I never seen the likes—it looks like a hundred schools!" Aunt Mary thinks she will stay in the car, she can see everything just fine from here.

"Excuse me, please," he says, and his mother climbs out, and he climbs out and turns to her. "You almost killed us," he says. "Why don't you stay in the car, I'll be back in fifteen minutes, and then I'll drive us home."

"I'm sorry," she says. He turns and walks away, fast. She says something else to him but he doesn't stop. He walks across the lawn and around the front of Meister Hall and as soon as he's out of sight, he sits down on the steps, pulls a cigarette out of his pocket—one he has saved for this very moment— and lights it expertly, cupping his hand, and exhales. Looking across the street, he imagines that he is Tony Flambeau. Emile and Eileen sent him out on the plane—"You don't need us along, we'd only get in your way," Eileen said, even though he begged them both to come, knowing how much fun it would be. What great parents! Actually, they're his best friends. But she was right: it is time for him to strike out on his own. Here at St. Cloud he will have the freedom to develop more as an individual. Which is exactly what they want for him. How lucky to have such wonderful parents! He will miss Manhattan, but he'll soon make new friends here, and of course they'll all know about the famous Flambeaus and ask him about his adventures, but he'll be able to tell the phonies from the true friends, and his true friends he'll invite to New York for Christmas break—Eileen is great about welcoming Tony's pals to their spacious apartment. Feeling terribly lucky, Tony Flambeau snuffs out the smoke, and ambles toward the registration office, his hands stuck in his pockets, a guy without a care in the world, a guy who shows every sign of becoming a very big success.

Byron Tollefson didn't accompany them to St. Cloud because he was busy at the Co-op Elevator, trying to iron out a misunderstanding with a man in Minneapolis who felt that the elevator, owed $1564 for sunflower seeds. Byron knew the seeds had never arrived, but the voice on the phone had an invoice in front of him and couldn't be made to understand that a piece of paper is one thing, a shipment of seeds is another.

To Byron, the boys in Minneapolis were a lot like his son: didn't know anything, thought they knew everything, talked in that smart voice and so damn persistent until you lost patience and wanted to smack them.

Byron valued patience. Nothing worthwhile comes easy. Life is full if disappointments. You learn this growing up on a farm. Forty acres of corn burns up in July or is flooded out or beaten to a pulp by hail. You learn to look at it and say, "Well—" And after you've looked at disaster, disappointment falls into place in the natural order of things. The lack of a car to drive to a dance, the lack of a good shirt to go in, the lack of time to go at all—these aren't disasters, not like to his son.

The world had changed. Father Emil spoke about this to the Commercial Club a few weeks before. Byron was Lutheran, but he gave Father Emil a lot of credit. Father Emil had spoken the week before Father's Day and said that agonistic liberals had cut fatherhood off at the knees. These liberals aimed to destroy authority and stability, and so had undermined the Father. Look at television, Father had said—Dad is shown as a dummy who stumbles around and breaks things and gets into trouble, usually to be rescued by a small child or a pet. Children watch hours of this junk every week. Their fathers allow them to watch it because fathers want to be pals, not meanies. But children can find other children to be pals. Children need fathers to be fathers.

Father Emil thought that fatherhood could be restored, but Byron thought maybe things had gone too far. Guys who hung around the elevator often talked about their boys and things the boys did that they the fathers would *never* have dared to do. Guy Peterson the other day had mentioned his boy, Guy, Jr. The boy had refused to do chores. Said he didn't feel like it. "You sick?" Guy asked him. No, the boy said, he felt depressed. Guy was baffled by that. He didn't know what depression had to do with the fact there were forty Holsteins that had to be milked and the stalls cleaned and their feed put down. He didn't see how depression entered into the picture at all. "If I had ever said that to my dad, he woulda walloped me one upside the head, given me something to be depressed about." That was in the old days when it was different.

My dad was of the old regime. He dispensed discipline, some Bible instruction, and a good example of industry and manly conduct, but he didn't hang out with us. Once he made a boomerang from a scrap of plywood, cut it on the jigsaw, shaped it on the belt sander, gave it two coats of lacquer and presented it to me for my birthday, but he no more would've taken me out and showed me how to throw it than he would've climbed up in our treehouse and read comics. He drew the line at fatherhood.

I took the boomerang myself to Tollerud's cornfield and after thirty, forty throws like throwing an ordinary stick, got off a good one, sidearm, the gift skimming six feet above the ground for a couple hundred feet, then rising and rising and circling back and making an incredible perfect descent to my throwing hand. Incredible. I felt I had performed a miracle so impossible as to make me immortal, and, of course, I never threw the boomerang again. You only need to be immortal once.

He wasn't there to see it. That night while he washed up for supper, he asked if the boomerang worked, and I said yes. "Good," he said.

I wanted to tell him how perfectly it flew, what an amazing little piece of wood he had made, but my dad did not deal in compliments or engage in small talk with children. This sounds harsh, and yet the memory of that perfect flight is a finer memory, I think, for it being mine alone, without him leaning over me in the cornfield, placing my little fingers on the wood, demonstrating, crowding me out of the picture.

Grownups were so immense, slow moving, carrying great burdens; they sank into chairs with a great sigh and remained there for long periods as we fetched a newspaper, got ice cream for them, rubbed their necks. "Rub my neck, wouldja," one would say and so we did as the poor thing groaned. They had so many aches and pains, we never expected them to play with us. Aunt Flo did, sometimes, take her ups and give the ball a whack, but she only visited the game, she didn't stay in it.

They kept to the porch in the summer when they weren't working, sunk into porch chairs. Their dogs barked. Their eyes burned. They had dust in their mouths, we got them Kool-Aid. "I don't know when I've felt so exhausted before," they said day after day, always beating their old record. Their weariness was honorable, even awesome. They had done everything they could do for us. We could ask no more.

So: to tiptoe out on the porch on Sunday afternoon and find three old guys in suits, my uncles, giggling over a good one they had pulled twenty years before. *Giggling*.

Our porch featured heavy wicker chairs you could hide behind and listen. "Oh, no! Oh, no, don't remind me!" Uncle Art bending over, having a coughing fit, spilling coffee on his good brown suit. Men who in dealing with me were paragons of prudence and thrift and maturity and knew the value of a dollar and giving an hour's work for an hour's pay and meeting your responsibilities, actually *giggling* as they remembered "the look on his face" when he saw his T-Model Ford on top of the chicken coop, or when he bit into his sandwich, or when he opened the door and found the pig in the bedroom.

Grow up, my sister said after she took a bite of Grape-Nuts that she had shaken salt on, knowing I had put sugar in the shaker, but actually I had switched it back so it really was salt in the shaker. *Grow up*.

My uncles were old, in their forties, but when one of them remembered it—that deal they pulled on him and then lay in the weeds, waiting for him to walk into it—they all remembered it as if it were happening right then. "Here he comes." "Shhhhhh." "What if he doesn't—" "Don't worry. He will." And he did. *Wham!* The pail fell! Cowflop all over! He slipped and sat down in it!

Tipping the privy with their cousin Phil inside. He had arrived from Minneapolis in a linen suit and had a bad case of the trots. He was visiting the privy every fifteen minutes. The fourth visit, he was just getting comfortable when his world overturned. The privy fell forward, landing door-down. Phil thought it was the result of something he had done, so he didn't yell. They heard him say, "Oh, dear. Oh, dear," as he picked himself up, and saw his guilt-stricken face peering out one of the seats.

Hanging bells on the bedsprings on Art and Millie's wedding night. Art had an idea they were going to, but in his great passion he forgot and jumped in bed like Christmas morning. Then he tried not to move too much, but it still tinkled, and finally he had to climb out of the rack and unfasten them, all sixty-seven. The wire was wound tight, the boys had spent all morning on the project.

Days of fear and trembling until it blew over. And then years of reminiscence.

In fact, wrassling that hog up the stairs, they already were thinking what a wonderful story it would be—boy, they're not going to believe this one. Boy, we're going to be talking about this one for a long time to come.

Got the pig up on the bed. Fed him corn until he quieted down. He went to sleep. They tiptoed downstairs. They waited.

Taking the ladder away when Mr. Tollerud was up on the barn roof.

The toads at the revival meeting.

The dead cat in the stovepipe.

The pie-eating contest at the county fair, 1941, between Harald Ingqvist and Florian Krebsbach, each of whom had been given a good pep talk by the boys, promised $10 if he won and told that Lena Tommerdahl would go skinny-dipping with him afterward. Hard to believe they fell for this, but Harald and Florian hated each other, so they approached the pie table in a frenzy. They ate so fast, they didn't notice how greasy the apple filling was, which the boys had pumped full of mineral oil, until it was much too late. The boys cheered them on, screaming at them to *go-go-GO*, and Harald and Florian ate slower and slower, gobs of filling on their faces, until they stopped and looked around, stupefied by pie, and tried to stagger to the trees, but truth struck them before they got there. "They blew up," said Uncle Tommy. "It even came out their noses."

And now they are whispering about something else, and one by one they sneak outside. "Where are you going?" I ask. "We have to go look at Al's garage floor," says Tommy. "We poured the concrete yesterday, and I think we might've poured it upside down."

"Can I come?"

"No, we'll be back soon as we check that concrete."

When I came along, the age of privy-tipping had passed, the age of car explosives was almost over. Carl Krebsbach wore it out when he sent away for $20 worth of car bombs. They worked just fine; he hooked one up to the ignition, the victim turned the key, *BANG!* he jumped, hit the ceiling, leaped out, ran around, ha ha ha. The trouble was, you get an awful lot of car bombs for $20, and Carl used up the joke before he used up the supply. The age of gunpowder dragged on and on until everyone was sick of it.

The flame flickered briefly on the Fourth of July. Major arms shipments came in from the Dakotas in May and June, fireworks being illegal in Minnesota; ammo was stored up, heavy artillery and bombs and rockets were moved to the front, and on the eve of the Fourth, light skirmishes broke out between the town constables, Gary and LeRoy, and the insurgent forces, who competed to see how close to the old Chevy cruiser they could set off the charges. After dark, the law cruised down the alley at about four knots, its long white beam sweeping the backyards, Gary and LeRoy peering out the open windows—*did they see us?* Yes! Run! *No wait.* Now, good old Larry, the one who can play Taps with his armpit, darts into the alley and fires a colossal rocket that arcs gracefully over the cruiser, where it explodes a few feet in front of the hood ornament with a shower of purple sparks and a blast that rattles garage doors, and the Chevy's taillights burn bright red as Gary hits the brakes and throws it in reverse, burning rubber, and you and four boys run like rabbits through Mrs. Mueller's yard—*Unnnhhhhhh!* What happened? *I ran into the birdbath.* Come on, get up! *No, you guys go on, I'll just lie here and die.*

"I saw you!" the law yells. "I know who you are!" It yelled that at us for years, meanwhile more and more trash barrels got bent out of shape from cherry bombs dropped in them to see the cloud of ash come up and hear that big boom. Watching the Volunteer Fire Department set off the official fireworks was not the same, even when the Roman candles exploded horizontally into the old people's section and the lame leaped out of their lawn chairs and ran.

One August evening, we sat on the porch, too hot to read, waiting for the sun to go down, when Senator K. Thorvaldson came by and said he had a present for us. It was in the paper bag. Three rockets, about two feet long.

My sister wanted to fire one and save the others for later, which was ridiculous. My brother and I just laughed at her. We stuck the rockets in a row on the lawn and fired them one-two-three. The fuses hissed, the rockets whooshed straight up and whammed, and dropped tiny wooden soldiers on paper parachutes. When the last soldier fell to earth, she said, "See? Now that's it. If you'd've saved some we'd still have two left over."

I could see her point. I said, "I wish we could have fireworks every night."

"If you had them every night, you'd get tired of them," Dad said. "It's just like anything else."

I said I didn't think I could ever get tired of fireworks. I thought we ought to keep a big supply of them and shoot off some every night, about ten or fifteen.

"Well, we can't and that's all there is to it."

I knew he'd say that. I could've said it for him, I knew how he talked. I could've done the whole conversation and saved him the breath. "Please? No. Absolutely not. Oh, Dad. No—I said no, I meant no. But—. That's enough—no means No."

He cut our hair on the porch, my brother and I taking turns on the high chair. The gentle *snip-snip-snip* of the scissors made me think he was in a good mood, and so I'd save up a good idea like fireworks or a vacation trip to the nation's capital, a little home-improvement idea such as TV or air-conditioning, for when he worked on my head. He was good at barbering and proud of his work and when he had almost finished and was doing the last little snips, not even cutting hair, just clicking the scissors near the head and admiring the job and in a sense admiring *me*, I would say in a careful voice (having sat still for fifteen minutes, phrasing this in my mind), "I was reading a book about Washington, D.C. A guide-book. You know, you really learn a lot of history by seeing it. They say it's something everybody should do, go to Washington." Or, "I counted up the money I've saved and it's almost enough for an accordion. I figured out that, with what I have, I could buy one now and pay you back for the rest by Christmas."

But I knew the answer, because the principle was clear. It's good to wait, nothing should come easy, you'll appreciate it more if you work for it. *You'll appreciate it the most if you never get it*, I thought.

That wasn't how the Flambeaus lived in The Flambeau Family Series: scarcity wasn't the guiding light in their lives. Emile and Eileen and son Tony, when they were in the Congo in *The Case of The Strange Safari* and the Land Rover went over a cliff and the native guide M'Bulu ran jabbering into the under-brush when he saw the skull on the rock and the three Flambeaus were sleeping on the dirt and eating nuts and berries, they did this because they had to, not out of some misguided notion it was good for their character, and you knew that when they solved the case and went home to Manhattan, they'd have themselves a night on the town and drop fifty or sixty bucks without blinking. You never read about Tony asking Emile for, say, an accordion or some rockets, and Emile saying, No, you get that, you'll enjoy it for five minutes and then get tired of it. Tony was treated like an adult, and he got to live life to the full. He wasn't always being told to wait. The Flambeaus' life was fraught with peril, Count Dumont was sworn to vengeance after they drove him from his Caribbean island stronghold, and when you live under a sword like that, you don't cut corners. Our life was fraught with peril, too—accidents could happen anytime, the house burn, a car go out of control, lightning strike, and next thing, your parents would be weeping over your small, still form, feeling terrible for having denied you so much pleasure—well, why wait until it's too late?

If doing without makes you appreciate things more, I guessed that the people of Lake Wobegon should be the happiest people in the world. No purple mountain majesty there and no alabaster city, just waves of grain and the Co-op Elevator.

I liked what Pastor Tommerdahl said at Mrs. Lundberg's funeral. He spoke on the text "So teach us to number our days that we may apply our hearts unto wisdom," and to him, it meant that we should live each day as if it were our last. Mrs. Lundberg was the Asparagus Lady. She had a half-acre of it, my favorite vegetable, so delicious and it needed no planting, no weeding: it just jumped out of the ground by the thousands. Asparagus was the only extravagant thing about Mrs. Lundberg; otherwise she was like us.

If you lived today as if it were your last, you'd buy up a box of rockets and fire them all off, wouldn't you?

———————

Muriel Krebsbach, daughter of Hazel and Fred, got rheumatic fever when she was nine and lay in bed a year and when she came back to school, she was excused from recess and spent the time reading books. She was skinny and mopey and had black stringy hair.

Fred ran away in 1953, while going to St. Cloud to buy a cold chisel. Muriel was twelve. Even before Fred absconded, Hazel considered Muriel no better than an invalid, and after he left, Hazel really cracked down. Muriel was sent to bed at the slightest symptom and warned against overexerting herself, and soon she didn't need to be told. Any sudden moves, her mother was right there to give her a look. Anyone asked her how she was feeling, her mother was there to answer for her: "Not too good, thank you. She's been kind of puny and listless."

One summer afternoon when she was seventeen, she was taking a nap, her second or third, and dreamed that a pig in a white straw hat came out of the woods and said, "Play me a tune and I'll dance for you." So she played a tune and the pig danced. Not well, but all right.

When she woke up, she went in the kitchen to take her pills, and Hazel said, "Cut up some tomatoes, but be careful with the knife." The first tomato Muriel sliced had a hollow center in the shape of a heart. She thought about it and decided it was a sign, and what it meant was: open your heart.

Muriel liked to look for signs and omens. She liked to sit on the porch and think, The next man I see is the man I will marry, though the next man always turned out to be nobody special—Mr. Berge returning a shovel, Elmer coming to haul away the trash; or she would close her eyes and open the Bible and put her finger on the page, and whatever verse she touched, that would be God's special message to her, even though it might be "And Jared lived an hundred sixty and two years and he begat Enoch."

The morning after the dream, however, she put her finger on the Bible and read, "And ye shall wash your clothes on the seventh day, and ye shall be clean, and afterward, ye shall come into the camp," which struck Muriel as a message you must act on immediately or else you will never get another clue in this world.

Washing her clothes was no simple matter with Hazel there. Hazel knew whenever Muriel drew a deep breath. But when her mother turned to see to the bacon, Muriel spilled cranberry juice on herself and headed for the basement. Hazel came after her. "Let me do that," she said, but God had told Muriel to wash her clothes, and so she did, and took a bath and got dressed and snuck out of the house and headed for the camp.

The only camp she knew was the clearing in the woods that we boys called "the camp," where we played Indians. We weren't there, we were too old for that, and the littler kids had another camp. Our camp was up on the hill behind school, a good steep climb, and when she got to the top, her heart was pounding so hard she sat down on a stump to rest, but she was excited. She wasn't supposed to be there, and if someone saw her and asked, "What are you doing, Muriel?" she'd have to tell a lie, and she didn't lie well, so they'd know she was lying and they'd take her home and tell her mother.

It was thrilling to think about. She decided that if someone came along and asked what she was doing, she'd say, "I'm waiting for my destiny," and if they didn't like it, they could lump it.

She listened to the wind in the trees, listening for a voice in the wind. She looked at clouds, thinking she might see a face, a picture, some sign. She thought, the next man who walks into the woods is the man I will marry. She wished she had brought her Bible.

It was a blazing hot day, even in the shade. She lay down on the grass by our campfire pit. She kept looking up, looking around: something was just about to happen that would open up her dry life and make it bloom like a tiger lily. A miracle, a vision, it was trembling on the verge like a drop on the faucet.

Our Lady of Perpetual Responsibility was going to walk out of the sumac and tell her a story, give her a message, as Our Lady had done with the children at Fatima. The Pope would send a bishop to ask for the message, but Muriel would say, No, Our Lady told me to keep it secret until 1980. The good people would build a shrine here, and Muriel would tell them to write on it, "Ye shall wash your clothes on the seventh day, and ye shall be clean." In Lake Wobegon, women always wash on Monday, the second day, and Saturday would be a big change for them, but they would do it, and then something else would happen. A poor beggar would arrive on Saturday morning and ask her to wash his clothes. (Was this the significance of the pig?) *Ish*, his clothes stink like a cesspool, but she washes them anyway, using extra Oxydol, and they come out gleaming white, like in commercials, and when he puts on his clothes, he becomes a prince and he gives them a million dollars. And this would be the message from Our Lady: be nice. A simple message, one everyone has heard before, and maybe she *wouldn't* save it until 1980, maybe she would take that message straight to the people right away: "Be nice. Be nice to each other. Be nice to me," and people would see it and obey. Boys who teased her by singing "Muriel, Muriel, looks like a body at a burial" would say they were sorry. She'd have a million dollars. She'd send half to the Pope and keep the rest to build a nice shrine and maybe a house up here, and she would come out on the balcony and bless the pilgrims: "Be nice, Remember to be nice."

They would have a yard like the Hagendorfs', with a stone grotto and waterfall, colored lights, iron deer, and wind chimes. Perhaps the waterfall would have healing powers, and crippled children would be dipped in it and stand up and walk. Instead of being cooped up, they would get better right away.

All of this seemed to her *just about to happen* all afternoon as the faceless clouds floated by and she prayed for God to make it happen, *something*, it didn't have to be great, just any little thing He could give her, and finally she settled for a shaft of sunlight that broke momentarily through a hole in one cloud—not a tremendous shaft as in pictures of angels descending to earth, but a shaft nonetheless, which seemed to indicate Hope. When you look for your destiny, she thought, you see everything more clearly, even if the destiny doesn't exactly come. When the sun broke through the cloud, she felt exalted. She could almost hear an organ playing, like the organ on "Friendly Valley," where June was in such a pickle now that Walt had gone to Chicago without marrying her, and yet the organ seemed to say that good things will happen if you're only patient.

Muriel went home and got her bawling-out from Hazel and, as Hazel remarked, "I say it and it goes right off you like water off a duck"—it was true, it didn't make her feel bad at all.

When Fred did not return from his trip for the chisel, Hazel looked around to see if he had left her a note explaining that he'd be gone overnight. She had said good-bye to him when he went out the door and he hadn't mentioned a long trip then, but he was taciturn and full of secrets. His taste for Ever Clear pure grain alcohol was a secret to her for years, as were the mail-order books he kept in his workbench. One day she went to look for a C-clamp and saw a grimy picture of a bosomy dame in black net stockings and harness like a telephone lineman's. She learned about the Ever Clear one morning when the toaster burst into flames and she grabbed his cup and threw the coffee on the fire. The coffee exploded. Then she had an idea why he always poured his own and what was in the bottle marked DON'T THROW OUT under the sink.

On his workbench she found a note he had written

to himself the morning he left, a list of jobs to do around the house. It began:

> (1) Replace back steps.
> (2) Take squash out of basement & build new shelfs.
> (3) New tailboard for truck.
> (4) Shower head.

And it continued on to:

> (31) Tear out tile around tub & retile. (1st fix pipe)
> (32) New water heater?
> (33) New siding on garage wall. Maybe NE side too.
> (34) Check roof.

Evidently he had decided to sit down and get his life in order, and then when he looked at what needed to be done, he panicked and ran. Thirty-four items on the list, and he was thirty-four years old. When she noticed that, she knew that it was more than coincidence. It was a sign that he had reached his limit as Fred and would never come back. He had left his wallet behind, too. Evidently, he was going to be somebody else for a while.

SCHOOL

School started the day after Labor Day, Tuesday, the Tuesday when my grandfather went, and in 1918 my father, and in 1948 me. It was the same day, in the same brick schoolhouse, the former New Albion Academy, now named Nelson School. The same misty painting of George Washington looked down on us all from above the blackboard, next to his closest friend, Abraham Lincoln. Lincoln was kind and patient and we looked to him for sympathy. Washington looked as if he had a headache. His mouth was set in a prim, pained expression of disapproval. Maybe people made fun of him for his long, frizzy hair, which resembled our teacher's, Mrs. Meiers', and that had soured his disposition. She said he had bad teeth—a good lesson for us to remember: to brush after every meal, up and down, thirty times. The great men held the room in their gaze, even the back corner by the windows. I bent over my desk, trying to make fat vowels sit on the line like fruit, the tails of consonants hang below, and colored the maps of English and French empires, and memorized arithmetic tables and state capitals and major exports of many lands, and when I was stumped, looked up to see George Washington's sour look and Lincoln's of pity and friendship, an old married couple on the wall. School, their old home, smelled of powerful floor wax and disinfectant, the smell of patriotism.

Mine was a vintage desk with iron scrollwork on the sides, an empty inkwell on top, a shelf below, lumps of petrified gum on the underside of it and some ancient inscriptions, one from '94 ("Lew P.") that made me think how old I'd be in '94 (fifty-two) and wonder who would have my place. I thought of leaving that child a message. A slip of paper stuck in a crack: "Hello. September 9, 1952. I'm in the 5th grade. It's sunny today. We had wieners for lunch and we played pom-pom-pullaway at recess. We are studying England. I hope you are well and enjoy school. If you find this, let me know. I'm 52 years old."

But Bill the janitor would find it and throw it away, so I only scratched my name and the date next to Sylvester Krueger's ('31), a distinguished person whose name also appeared on a brass plaque by the library, "In Memoriam. Greater love hath no man than that he lay down his life for his friends."

It was an honor to have Sylvester's desk, a boy who probably sat and whiled away the hours with similar thoughts about Washington and Lincoln, cars, peckers, foreign lands, lunch. School was eternity, a quiet pool of imagination where we sat together and dreamed, interrupted by teaching, and thought of the boy Lindbergh (from Little Falls, a little east of us), the boy Lincoln, Wilbur and Orville, Lou Gehrig, all heroes, and most of all, I imagined Sylvester who left the room and died in France where his body was buried. Strange to think of him there, French guys mowing the grass over him and speaking French; easy to think of him here, working fractions under George Washington's gaze.

His mother came to school one day. Maybe it was Arbor Day, I remember we planted a tree in the memory of those who died for freedom, and I wasn't one of the children chosen to shovel the dirt in. Bill the janitor dug the hole, and the filling honors went to the six children who were tops in school citizenship, which didn't include me. They were lunchroom and hall monitors, flag-raisers, school patrol, and I was a skinny kid with wire-rim glasses who had to do what they said. Mrs. Krueger was a plump lady in a blue dress who put on her specs to read a few remarks off a card. I studied her carefully on account of my special relationship with her son, Sylvester. She was nervous. She licked her lips and read fast. It was hot. Some kids were fooling around and had to be shushed. "I know Sylvester would be very proud of you and glad that you remember him," she said. The little sliver of tree was so frail; it didn't last the spring. Bill had dug the hole in left field and the tree got stomped in a kittenball game at the All-School Picnic. Mrs. Krueger looked like a person who was lost. Mrs. Meiers walked her to the corner, where she would take McKinley Street home. I tagged along behind, studying. Mrs. Krueger seemed to have very sore feet. At the corner, she thanked Mrs. Meiers for the very nice ceremony. She said, "A person never forgets it when they lose a son, you know. To me, it's like it was yesterday."*

The same day we planted the tree, our all-school picture was taken by a man with a sliver of a mustache who crouched behind his tripod and put a cloth

---

*Once a bat got loose in Mrs. Krueger's house and swooped from room to room and scared her silly. She lay on the floor, then crawled to the phone and called Gary and LeRoy to come and kill it, meanwhile her big cat Paul, named for her late husband, sat on the highboy studying the bat's flight and in one well-timed leap knocked it to the floor where Gary and LeRoy found it. They offered to look around the house for more bats. They took their time about it, never having seen her house before. Upstairs, although she lived alone, they found five single beds each neatly made and the covers turned down, and the kitchen table was set for two. The radio was on, playing one Glenn Miller tune after another. Out in the squad car, they searched the radio for Glenn Miller and couldn't find any. LeRoy went back in, thinking he might have left his glove or something, and her radio was still playing Glenn Miller. "Tuxedo Junction."

over his head. Jim told me we could be in the picture twice—at both ends of the group—by running around back while he shot it, but I left the right end too soon and got to the left end too late, and so appeared as two slight blurs. I looked at the print and thought of Sylvester and me.

School gave us marks every nine weeks, three marks for each subject: work, effort, and conduct. Effort was the important one, according to my mother, because that mark showed if you had gumption and stick-to-itiveness, and effort was my poorest showing. I was high in conduct except when dared to do wrong by other boys, and then I was glad to show what I could do. Pee on the school during recess? You don't think I would? Open the library door, yell "Boogers!" and run? Well, I showed them. I was not the one who put a big gob on the classroom doorknob during lunch though, the one that Darla Ingqvist discovered by putting her hand on it. Of all the people you'd want to see touch a giant gob, Darla was No. 1. She yanked her hand back just as Brian said, "Snot on you!" but she already knew. She couldn't wipe it off on her dress because she wore such nice dresses so she burst into tears and tore off to the girls' lavatory. Mrs. Meiers blamed me because I laughed. Brian, who did it, said, "That was a mean thing to do, shame on you" and I sat down on the hall floor and laughed myself silly. It was so *right* for Darla to be the one who got a gob in her hand. She was a jumpy, chatty little girl who liked to bring money to school and show it to everyone. Once a five-dollar bill—we never had a five-dollar bill, so all the kids crowded around to see it. That was what she wanted. She made us stand in line. It was dumb. All those dumb girls took turns holding it and saying what they would do if they had one, and then Darla said she had $400 in her savings account. "Liar, liar, pants on fire," Brian said, but we all knew she probably did have $400. Later Brian said, "I wish I had her five dollars and she had a feather in her butt, and we'd both be tickled," which made me feel a little better, but putting the gob on the knob, knowing that Darla was monitor and had the privilege of opening the door, *that* was a stroke of genius. I almost didn't mind Mrs. Meiers making me sit in the cloakroom for an hour. I put white paste on slips of paper and put them in the pockets of Darla's coat, hoping she'd think it was more of the same.

It was Booger Day. When Mrs. Meiers turned her back to write her loopy letters on the board, John Potvin whispered, "Bunny boogers. Turkey tits. Panda poop," to Paul who was unprepared for it and laughed out loud. Mrs. Meiers snatched him out of his seat and made him stand in front, facing the class, a terrible humiliation. Everyone except Darla felt embarrassment for poor Paul; only Darla looked at him and gloated; so when Paul pretended to pull a long one out of his nose, only Darla laughed, and then she stood up in front and he sat down. Nobody looked at her, because she was crying.

On the way home, we sang with special enthusiasm,

School

On top of old Smoky, two thousand feet tall,
I shot my old teacher with a big booger ball.
I shot her with glory, I shot her with pride.
How could I miss her? She's thirty feet wide.

I liked Mrs. Meiers a lot, though. She was a plump
lady with bags of fat on her arms that danced when
she wrote on the board: we named them Hoppy and
Bob. That gave her a good mark for friendliness in
my book, whereas Miss Conway of fourth grade
struck me as suspiciously thin. What was her problem? Nerves, I suppose. She bit her lips and squinted
and snaked her skinny hand into her dress to shore
up a strap, and she was easily startled by loud noises.
Two or three times a day, Paul or Jim or Lance would
let go with a book, dropping it flat for maximum
whack, and yell, "Sorry, Miss Conway!" as the poor
woman jerked like a fish on the line. It could be done
by slamming a door or dropping the window, too, or
even scraping a chair, and once a loud slam made *her*
drop a stack of books, which gave us a double jerk. It
worked better if we were very quiet before the noise.
Often, the class would be so quiet, our little heads
bent over our work, that she would look up and
congratulate us on our excellent behavior, and when
she looked back down at her book, *wham!* and she
did the best jerk we had ever seen. There were five
classes of spasms: The Jerk, The Jump, The High
Jump, The Pants Jump, and The Loopdeloop, and we
knew when she was prime for a big one. It was after
we had put her through a hard morning workout,
including several good jumps, and a noisy lunch

period, and she had lectured us in her thin weepy voice, then we knew she was all wound up for the Loopdeloop. All it required was an extra effort: *throwing* a dictionary flat at the floor or dropping the globe, which sounded like a car crash.

We thought about possibly driving Miss Conway to a nervous breakdown, an event we were curious about because our mothers spoke of it often. "You're driving me to a nervous breakdown!" they'd yell, but then, to prevent one, they'd grab us and shake us silly. Miss Conway seemed a better candidate. We speculated about what a breakdown might include— some good jumps for sure, maybe a couple hundred, and talking gibberish with spit running down her chin.

Miss Conway's nervous breakdown was prevented by Mrs. Meiers, who got wind of it from one of the girls—Darla, I think. Mrs. Meiers sat us boys down after lunch period and said that if she heard any more loud noises from Room 4, she would keep us after school for a half hour. "Why not the girls?" Lance asked. "Because I know that you boys can accept responsibility," Mrs Meiers said. And that was the end of the jumps, except for one accidental jump when a leg gave way under the table that held Mr. Bugs the rabbit in his big cage. Miss Conway screamed and left the room, Mrs. Meiers stalked in, and we boys sat in Room 3 from 3:00 to 3:45 with our hands folded on our desks, and remembered that last Loopdeloop, how satisfying it was, and also how sad it was, being the last. Miss Conway had made some great jumps.

School

1. Can you name other American Presidents whose pictures make you feel uneasy?
2. If you wrote a message to the child who will have your desk in thirty years, what would you write?
3. Do you think the author should have worked harder in school?

Yes, I should have, and also in Scouts. Einar Tingvold, our Scoutmaster, quit Scouting the year after I joined and I knew it was frustration with me that drove him out.

Three decades later, I keep running into my failure in Scouting. I cannot identify trees, flowers, fish, or animal tracks. I know only four knots: the square, the half-hitch, the one I tie my shoelaces with, and the bowline hitch, which is useful if you're in a pit and rescuers throw down a line, which has never happened to me.

Every Tuesday night in the basement of the Lutheran church (the Catholics had their own troop, run by Florian Krebsbach, that met at Our Lady), Einar tried to coach us in semaphore signals, animal tracks, knots, and the Code of the Trail. He was a skinny old guy with a white crewcut and black horn-rimmed glasses; his Adam's apple bobbed like a cork as he sat on a bench murmuring woods lore to the

259

good Scouts who sat cross-legged around him, taking it all in. I was curious about the Adam's apple.

What does it look like? Like a piece of apple, some kid said; the chunk of apple that Adam ate and got original sin. I doubted that God would put a piece of apple in our throats, but the sight of Einar's, rattling and jumping around as he talked, made me think that, apple or not, it was definitely loose in there. A person could choke on it. Einar's even slipped to the side, did somersaults, came almost up into his mouth when he swallowed.

Einar also had ropy spit, a fact I discovered when he got angry at us for flipping cards into a hat when we should have been practicing our semaphore signals. "You guys don't care, do you! You really think you can sit on your duffs and let other guys do the work! Well, I don't need you here! You can go sit someplace else as far as I'm concerned." Some secret ingredient of his saliva made it stick to his teeth and tongue as his mouth moved, producing ropes of spit in there, long liquid stalagmites that made different formations for each word. It was very interesting. I tried to do it in front of a mirror and couldn't, not even with a mouthful of spit.

Why did we need to know semaphore code? Einar said it was handy for sending messages in the outdoors at a distance of up to a half-mile. "Imagine you're camping on a hill and another troop is on another hill a half-mile away. Suddenly you need medical help. You flash a mirror at the other camp to get their attention. They train their binoculars on your camp, and meanwhile you take two shirts and tie them to sticks. Now you're ready to send a message, using semaphore code. This is why we need to learn this. Imagine if someone were sending you an urgent message and you couldn't read it. Help could be delayed for hours. Someone might die as a result."

Einar's answer only raised a lot of questions in my mind (1) What hills? You'd need to have pretty high hills to be able to see a fellow Scout waving his flags a half-mile away, even with binoculars. We don't have hills like that around here. Usually, we camp in a ravine, down near the creek so we don't have to haul the water so far. Flags in a ravine aren't going to do anyone any good. (2) What binoculars? None of us Scouts had a pair. Einar had one, but what good would that do if he was with us, the troop that needed urgent medical help? All he could do with his binoculars then would be to see that the other troop couldn't see us. (3) What other troop? No other Scout troop camped around where we camped out in Tolleruds' pasture (with its one extremely *low* hill). The only people to see our semaphore signals would be the Tolleruds, and probably they'd think it was just some kid waving a couple of shirts. (4) If we needed urgent help, why not get in Einar's car and drive to the doctor's? Einar always had his car when we went camping. That's how we got there. Why stand around waving at a nonexistent troop on a hill that wasn't high enough and probably misspelling words in the process ("UNGENT/SEND HEAP/I'M BADLY CURT") when we could hop into Einar's Studebaker?

I raised some of these doubts with Einar one night

during semaphore practice. We were paired up and told to send messages back and forth, and when Einar found out that Donald Scheid and I were only pretending to wig-wag and were really whispering the messages, he grabbed me by the shoulder, shook me, and told me it was time I started getting serious about Scouting. I told him that I *was* serious but that I didn't think semaphore signaling was a useful skill. I mentioned the fact that he always took his car on camping trips.

Whenever Einar got extremely mad, he turned on his heel and walked away. Something seemed to snap shut inside him, he couldn't talk to you. His back stiffened, his face flushed, his fists clenched, and he had to go straight outdoors and calm down or otherwise he would kill you. (Once on a camping trip, when we put a juicy booger on the tab of the zipper on his tent, and then when we stayed awake until two A.M. giggling about it, Einar suddenly jumped up and walked away. He took our breakfast with him, three dozen eggs that he threw one by one at a clump of birch trees.)

When I pointed out that his car would be more useful in the event of a medical emergency than semaphore signals, he walked away from Boy Scouting for about fifteen minutes. When he returned, Donald was telling Speedy Gonzalez jokes. They were the first Speedy Gonzalez jokes we had ever heard, and we were flopping around on the floor, sobbing and grabbing our pants to keep from peeing in them.

Einar stood and watched us. It took us a while to come to attention. We'd get almost to attention and then the thought of Speedy would make one boy break down and that got the rest of us going. Einar stood the whole time and didn't move a muscle, just stared us down. When the snickering had mostly died out, he made a speech that we had heard once before, after the tent zipper. He said he had gone into Scouting because he wanted to help boys grow up into fine young men, and most boys had done exactly that. They had become the sort of fine young men who defended their country in Germany and the Pacific and in Korea. Those boys knew how to have fun but also when to be serious. We were not like them. We were, in fact, the sorriest excuse for Scouts he ever saw in all his years. We were the laziest and most disobedient and *worthless* Scouts—in fact, he wouldn't even call us Scouts—the most worthless *children* he'd ever seen. Ever! We did not deserve any of this—the great tradition of Scouting, the sacred outdoor lore learned from the Indian and passed down by generations, the honor of the scout uniform—we did not deserve this because we had dishonored that uniform as surely as if we had thrown it in the dirt and spit on it! He had never known boys like us before. He didn't know what to do with us. He knew that, under the laws of Scouting, he ought to kick us out right away—take away our neckerchiefs and khaki shirts, our clasps, our badges— ought to cancel the camping trips, and if our parents asked why, well, he would tell them. That's what he ought to do. But he thought that every boy deserved a second chance. We had been given many second chances. This was going to be our last second chance.

There would be no more after this one. If we continued to dishonor the uniform, then it would be all over for us: "And you—" he said, his gaze sweeping the room, "*you* will become the first boys in the history of this town to have your badges stripped from you."

———

Twelve P.M.: as the last moan of the noon siren fades away, twenty-seven boys are led from the church basement and marched under close guard to Main Street where, in front of the Central Building, the town of Lake Wobegon stands in ranks, facing, on three sides, a patch of asphalt where the boys, disheveled, their eyes downcast, their faces crimson with shame, are ordered to form a row. Under the blazing sun, the crowd listens as Scoutmaster Einar Tingvold reads the Bill of Dishonor, all thirty items. A bugler plays Retreat. In the silence that follows, the crowd can hear clearly every rip as the Scoutmaster tears insignia from each Scout in turn—troop number, merit badges, insignia of rank—and places the bits of cloth on a small bonfire. At a shouted command (" 'Bout face!"), the crowd turns its back to the miscreants, then disperses quietly into the bright afternoon, as the boys, tears streaming down their dirty faces, stand and watch the flames devour the last little scraps of their Scouting careers. They will carry this mark for the rest of their lives. Doors will slam in their faces, old friends will turn away, even loved ones will whisper behind their backs: "He dishonored the uniform. He did not deserve to be a Scout."

I heard quite a few snuffles around me when Einar talked about stripping our badges. I did not snuffle myself because I had nothing he could strip. Two years a Scout and I hadn't even made Tenderfoot. Second Class seemed very far away and First Class or Eagle only a dream. I joined Scouts because it was fun to hang around with my friends and go on camping trips: not for the Scout part but for the stuff we thought up including stuff that made Einar mad. What he was talking about, the dishonor and all, made no sense to me. What honor?

Listening to Einar was one time I felt superior to grownups, hearing them thunder and yell and knowing they had no power over me. Dave Ingqvist was shattered by the thought of being stripped; he had a shirtful of badges, he stood out from the crowd like Audie Murphy in a battalion of postal clerks, he was a Scout's Scout. He was State President of Scouts for Christ, and the same year he went to Boy's State and was elected governor of Minnesota, which didn't surprise me. I was only surprised to find out he was Governor-for-a-Day. I thought he was elected for good. He was brave, reverent, and clean, though perhaps lacking in the trustworthiness department. *I* didn't trust him, anyway, not after he told Einar about the tent zipper.

Now he is Pastor Ingqvist, a good man, and I've forgiven him, though not entirely. He was the only boy who had the complete uniform—Scout pants, shoes, cap, belt, even Scout shorts for summer wear—the rest of us only had shirts and neckerchiefs. I thought he should give his uniform to the poor, me, and let me have his Schwinn too.

Mrs. Meiers had a Reading Club on the bulletin board, a sheet of brown wrapping paper with a border of book jackets, our names written in her plump firm hand and after each name a gold star for each book read, but she has given it up because some names have so many stars. Her good readers are voracious and read their weight in books every week, while the slow readers lag behind. Daryl Tollerud has read two books, Mary Mueller has read sixty-seven, and her stars are jammed in tight behind her name. In the encyclopedia, I'm up to Customs of Many Lands and she is up to Volcanoes. She is the queen of Reading Club and she knows it. Girls want to sit next to her at lunch. Donna Bunsen is second with forty-six. Her close friends believe that Mary writes her book reports from book jackets. *Look at this: "Little House on the Prairie* is a book about the Ingalls family living in South Dakota . . ." *She didn't read that book, the big cheater.* Marilyn Peterson put a slip of paper in a book in Mary's desk. It said, "You big cheater," she put it in at the end of the book. Mary didn't say anything about it. "See?" Marilyn said. "She didn't read that book."

It took me a long time to learn to read. I was wrong about so many words. *Cat, can't. Tough, through, thought. Shinola.* It was like reading a cloud of mosquitoes. Donna in the seat behind whispered right answers to me, and I learned to be a good guesser, but I didn't read well until Mrs. Meiers took me in hand.

One winter day she took me aside after recess and said she'd like me to stay after school and read to her. "You have such a nice voice," she said, "and I don't get to hear you read in school as much as I'd like."

No one had told me before that I had a nice voice. She told me many times over the next few months what a *wonderful* voice I had, as I sat in a chair by her desk reading to her as she marked worksheets. "The little duck was so happy. He ran to the barn and shouted, 'Come! Look! The ice is gone from the pond!' Finally it was spring."

"Oh, you read that so well. Read it again," she said. When Bill the janitor came in to mop, she said, "Listen to this. Doesn't this boy have a good voice?" he sat down and I read to them both. "The little duck climbed to the top of the big rock and looked down at the clear blue water. 'Now I am going to fly,' he said to himself. He waggled his wings and counted to three. 'One, two, three.' And he jumped and—" I read in my clear blue voice. "I think you're right," Bill said. "I think he has a very good voice. I wouldn't mind sitting here all day and listening to him."

One word I liked was *popular*. It sounded good, it felt good to say, it made lights come on in my mouth. I drew a rebus: a bottle of Nu-Grape + U + a Lazy Ike. *Pop-u-lure*. It didn't occur in our reading book, where little children did the right thing although their friends scoffed at them and where despised animals wandered alone and redeemed themselves through pure goodness and eventually triumphed to become

Top Dog, The Duck of Ducks, The Grand Turtlissimo, The Greatest Pig of Them All, which, though thrilling, didn't appeal to me so much as plain *popular*. "The popular boy came out the door and everybody smiled and laughed. They were so glad to see him. They all crowded around him to see what he wanted to do."

Morning and afternoon, school recessed and we took to the playground; everyone burst out the door except me. Mrs. Meiers said, "Don't run! Walk!" I always walked. I was in no hurry, I knew what was out there. The girls played in front. Little girls played tag and stoop-ball, hopscotch, skipped rope; big girls sat under the pine tree and whispered. Some girls went to the swings. Boys went out back and played baseball, except for some odd boys who lay around in the shade and fooled with jackknives and talked dirty. I could go in the shade or stand by the backstop and wait to be chosen. Daryl and David always chose up sides and always chose the same people first, the popular ones. "Let somebody else be captain!" Jim said once. "How come you always get to choose?" They just smiled. They were captains, that was all there was to it. After the popular ones got picked, we stood in a bunch looking down at the dirt, waiting to see if our rating had changed. They took their sweet time choosing us, we had plenty of time to study our shoes. Mine were Keds, black, though white ones were more popular. Mother said black wouldn't show dirt. She didn't know how the wrong shoes could mark a person and raise questions in other people's minds. "Why do you wear black tennis shoes?" Daryl asked me once. He had me there. I didn't know. I guessed I was just that sort of person, whether I wanted to be or not. Maybe not showing dirt was not the real reason, the real reason was something else too terrible to know, which she would tell me someday. "I have something to tell you, son." She would say it. "No! No!" "Yes, I'm afraid it's true." "So that's why—" "Yes. I'm sorry I couldn't tell you before. I thought I should wait." "But can't I—" "No, I'm afraid not. We just have to make the best of it."

Nine boys to a side, four already chosen, ten positions left, and the captains look us over. They chose the popular ones fast ("Brian!" "Bill!" "Duke!" "John!" "Bob!" "Paul!" "Jim!" "Lance!"), and now the choice is hard because we're all so much the same: *not so hot*—and then they are down to their last grudging choices, a slow kid for catcher and someone to stick out in right field where nobody hits it, except maybe two guys, and when they come to bat the captain sends the poor right-fielder to left, a long ignominious walk. They chose the last ones two at a time. "You and you," because it makes no difference, and the remaining kids, the scrubs, the excess, they deal for as handicaps ("If I take him, then you gotta take *him*"). Sometimes I go as high as sixth, usually lower. Just once I'd like Daryl to pick me first. "Him! I want him! The skinny kid with the glasses and the black shoes! You! Come on!" But I've never been chosen with any enthusiasm.

I think that if Wally ("Old Hard Hands") Bunsen

were here, things would be different for me; he and I would be close friends. He was a true champion, a man among men, known for his kindness as well as athletic prowess. He saved a boy from drowning once, and another time he brought a crippled kid to the ball game to see him hit a double off Carl Hubbell. That was in the season he spent with the Chicago Cubs.

Born, Lake Wobegon, August 1, 1910. Died, Lake Wobegon, June 11, 1936. I know those dates by heart. The year 1933 he was with the Cubs, and batted .348 from April to July, and then came home. He died while batting for Lake Wobegon Volunteers (who later became the Whippets), vs. Albany, bottom of the seventh inning, with men on first and third (later known as "The Dead Man's Spread"). He batted left, threw right, was 6'2" and weighed 181 pounds. His golden hair was parted down the middle, and he wore a gold ring on his right hand. The little finger of his right hand was cut off in a corn picker, 1931. The little white house next door to Dieners' was his house; he slept on the back porch, even in winter, and his dog's name was Buddy. His parents' names were Clara and Oscar. He was smart as a whip and if he hadn't played ball he would have been an inventor. He made a gasoline-powered sled, an automatic apple-corer, and an electric water fountain for his mom's rock garden.

Two pictures of him hang in the Sidetrack Tap: one in his Cubs uniform, his bat cocked, and the other with Jack Dempsey, who is kissing him on the cheek, a great tribute when you think about it. What sort of man would the Heavyweight Champion of the World kiss? A man's man, of course. I wasn't allowed in the Sidetrack as a boy, but I went in—just to have a look at the pictures, and they were permanently imprinted in my mind, and from his wonderful grin I began to imagine him as a personal friend.

Wally Krebsbach: "He had wings on his feet and a whip for an arm. He ran, he threw, he came to bat, and it was all play to him. He just laughed out there, it was so natural to him. A beautiful ball-player. God gave him the talent and he had no trouble with it. The outfield was his home and any ball hit near him just naturally belonged in his hand. He came to bat and had no trouble in his mind, he was meant to hit."

His trouble with the Cubs lay in his glove. Growing up in Lake Wobegon, being poor, he learned to play without one, and by the time he could afford to have it, he was such an excellent bare-handed fielder he didn't bother with a glove. Thus the nickname "Old Hard Hands." His palms were like leather. In 1931, a Cubs scout went to look at a prospect in Duluth, and the hotel clerk said, "Dobbins? Hell, you ought to see a guy in this little town near St. Cloud, he could put Dobbins in his back pocket." So the scout came to town, in his gabardine suit with a bottle of rye in his valise and took one look at Wally shag flies and waved $500 in his face as if he was trying to wake him up. "One thing, kid, you gotta get a glove," he said. Wally was about to leave for spring training the next January, but his father got sick, so he stayed until he recovered, which wasn't until May, and the year after that he went to Florida and put on the uniform.

"Dear Folks," he wrote. "Arrived this morning and went straight to the park for practice. The grass is brown and the ground is hard as cement, but guess it will do. Tried on so many gloves and none felt just right so just picked the smallest one and hoped for the best. Ran for an hour and felt better, then lunch. Food here is all fried. Felt queasy after, but swung the bat okay and then came back to the hotel, which is small but clean. The others went to a movie. Miss you all."

He begged the Cubs to let him play barehand, but they said it was against the rules. "You will get accustomed to it," they said. He was so good in every department, they figured it would be easy for him to learn this one little thing. A man who stood at the plate so relaxed and easy, then cocked his lip, lifted his left foot, and the next you saw was him trotting slowly towards first—a man who if he did have to leg it cruised on the basepaths so deceptively fast, the centerfielder trotted in and picked up Wally's single and went to lob it to the cut-off man and saw Wally ambling into second—a man whose eye in the field was so keen, he was momentarily distracted by a pigeon gliding into the grandstand or a shooting star—a man who people would have paid just to watch him throw a ball home, so hard it hummed, so true the catcher never moved his feet—surely, a man so talented could learn to wear a glove on his left hand and catch with it.

"He could've but his heart wasn't in it," says Wally

Krebsbach. "It didn't feel right to him. It threw him off balance. It took the fun out of the game. He actually got headaches from it. And then he dropped a couple, and that made him ashamed and then he came home. They offered him more money but he just laughed. It wasn't worth it to him."

"If they'd let him play the way he wanted to, barehanded, he would've been the greatest they ever saw, but they wouldn't, so he came home."

"He wasn't the same. He looked forty. His hands shook. Then he had a run of bad luck. His dad passed away. That was hard on him. And then his girl told him she didn't love him anymore—that took all the spirit out of him. Nobody could cheer him up after that. He told me—he said, 'Buddy, she says to me, she says, "My daddy says you're nothing but a ballplayer and you'll never hold down a regular job, but that doesn't matter to me. I could love you anyway." She says, "It's your hands being so hard. I just can't get used to it." Can you believe that, Buddy?' he says. He couldn't believe it. He said, 'A man is *supposed* to have hard hands, ain't he? Who has soft hands? Nobody but fruitcakes and bank clerks.' He was broken up over her for weeks."

"And then he got the idea from the way people talked that he'd been a failure, that if he was any good he'd be in Chicago. And that just killed him. He knew it wasn't true, it was that they thought it that killed him. He knew how good he was, he didn't have to prove it by going someplace else. A man is just *good*, he can be good anywhere. This was his own family who looked down on him, though, so it tore him apart. Clarence's dad, that's Wally's brother, he gave him a hard time about quitting the team and embarrassing the family, as if he had any right to talk about it. Well, Wally didn't have a job, he was living off what he'd earned from the Cubs, and he was lying around in that sleeping porch, thinking too much, just living from Sunday to Sunday for the Volunteers games. One Saturday night he comes down here and asks for a drink. My old man was bartending, he says no. So Wally left. Where he found it I don't know but he found enough to last him all night because when he came to the game next day he was suited up and that was about all. He looked like death on toast."

"He never should have played. Dutch and me, we argued with Henneman to send him home, but there was naturally a big crowd to see him play so play he did. I never saw a man sweat so much. his eyes bugged out. He flopped on the bench and almost passed out. Then he dropped one in the top of the seventh. It wasn't important, we were up by six runs, there were two outs, we said, 'Shake it off,' but it bothered him so that when he came up to bat, he was set to kill one. And instead it killed him."

"It was the bottom of the seventh, Roy on first and me on third, no outs, a count of two-and-two, and he stepped out of the box and looked down toward me, but he wasn't looking *at* me because his eyes wouldn't focus. He was clearing his throat and I thought he was choking so I called time and ran in, but he wasn't choking, he was crying. He says, 'I'm no good.' I said, 'You're the best. You're the best there ever was.' And then I went back to the bag."

Wally stops. He can't finish the story. He shuts his eyes and tears squeeze out from his eyelids and fall down his poor old face. Up and down the bar, old guys look away and touch their eyes. The alarm clock ticks by the cash register, and you can hear the electric clock hum in the Cold Spring beer sign. The big fan above the door hums. Everything else stops at the Sidetrack when he comes to that point in the story everybody has heard him tell so often.

The rest is: Wally Bunsen swung at the next pitch, an inside fast ball across the letters, and fouled it off into his own head and fell across the home plate and died. They said he never knew what hit him. Some of his family said that was what comforted them in this terrible tragedy, that he hadn't had to suffer, but of course he had suffered a great deal more than they knew.

When I thought of him, I imagined him as my best friend and him and me taking off to go fishing together. I even practised what we would say. He'd say, "Nothing beats fishing." And I'd say, "*You're* not just talking."

In August, Coach Magendanz gets in his Chevy wagon and drives around recruiting Leonards for football season. The late Leonard Halvorson, for whom the high school teams are named, recruited in September with an emotional speech to the student body about school pride and about rival schools who at the moment were planning our disgrace, but Coach likes to go one-on-one and establish a personal rapport with his prospects. "You coming out for football?" he says to a big boy he's found mowing hay in a ditch. The boy is not sure. "You queer?" Coach asks. "If you are, I don't want you." The boy thinks he may after all. Coach has fifteen or twenty certains on his list and needs to round up as many undecideds. He looks for size, speed being rare among Norwegians and Germans, and for malleability or what he calls *attitude*. In football, it's kill or be killed, and he needs some killers. "There is an animal in you and I intend to bring it out," he tells the team the first day of practice. The new boys glance at each other—it isn't what they learned in Luther League. He picks out two big boys to stand up and face each other. "Okay, Stuart," he says, "rip his shirt off." Stuart advances. "You going to let him rip your shirt off, Stupid?" Coach yells. Stupid isn't. They go at it in the hot sun, fooling around at first but then the animal in them comes out. They grunt and pant, rolling in the dirt, getting wristholds, leg holds, ripping each other's shirts off, until Coach calls them off. "That's football," he says. "Any pansies in the bunch can get up and leave right now."

Some of us who are more sophisticated drift by the practice field on our bikes. It isn't Goodhue Field but Sandburr Field at the county fairgrounds; Goodhue is grassy and Coach likes to start on dirt. Forty boys do pushups in unison, then stand up for the burpies. We wave to them, on our way to go swimming. He looks at us and we don't hear what he says to them; he says, "I gueth they can't take their eyeth off you guyth." We hear about it later, and far from being sophisticated, we are filled with terror. All those afternoons we went skinny-dipping, the curiosity about what each other looked like—is something terrible going on? Are we that way? Perhaps we are, otherwise why are we so uncertain about girls? We don't talk about this. But each of us knows that he is not quite right. Once, at the river, Jim made his pecker talk, moving its tiny lips as he said, "Hi, my name's Pete. I live in my pants." Now it doesn't seem funny at all. *If it's not wrong, why were we worried somebody would come along and see?*

My Uncle Earl centered the line of the great Leonards team of 1932 that beat Minneapolis Roosevelt in the days when football was football, before shoulder pads or hot showers. A Saturday afternoon in November in Memorial Stadium at the University, the teams fought to an o—o tie as the sun set. Uncle Earl's shirt hung in shreds, one eyes was swollen shut, his left hand was broken from being stepped on, and blood ran down his legs into his shoes that squished when he walked. But the huge crowd wouldn't go home without somebody winning, so the game went on in the dusk. The Leonards had only fifteen on the squad, and some were hurt worse than him, so he stayed in. The two lines crouched and heaved forward, and the weary Leonards fell back, until the ball was on their two-yard-line, first and goal for the Teddies. The referee had a flashlight. He shone the light on the ball as the teams lined up. The crowd roared, all rooting for Roosevelt. Then the light failed, and Uncle Earl, crouched ahead of the ball, hollered "Hup!" and grabbed it. The lines crashed together. Leonards yelled "Fumble! Fumble!" A

Leonard fell and the Teddies tore his uniform off trying to get the ball. But Uncle Earl had it under his arm, and he had walked toward the sideline with it and was strolling up the field. He walked ninety-eight yards for the winning touchdown and when they got the flashlight fixed, there he was under the goalposts. He played against me and my cousins when we were little. He picked up the ball and walked the length of the yard with six of us hanging on him.

When I was fourteen, he came up to bat one hot July afternoon in the Father-Son softball game and looked at me playing third base and pointed his bat at me. I crouched; my mouth was dry and my heart pounded. He waited for a low pitch and drove it straight down the baseline—a blazing swing, a white blur, a burst of chalk dust—I dove to my right just as the ball nicked a pebble—it bounced up and struck me in the throat, stopping my breath, and caromed straight up in the air about fifteen or sixty-five feet. Blinded by tears, I hit the ground face first, getting a mouthful of gravel, but recovered in time to catch the ball and, kneeling, got off a sharp throw in the vicinity of first which caught him by a stride. I was unable to speak for twenty minutes. That play was some proof that I was all right. Everyone saw it and said it was great; even guys who didn't like me had to say that, because it was.

FALL

A hard frost hits in September, sometimes as early as Labor Day, and kills the tomatoes that we, being frugal, protected with straw and paper tents, which we, being sick of tomatoes, left some holes in. The milkweed pods turn brown and we crack them open to let the little seeds float out across the garden on their wings of silvery hair. The milk of the milkweed is said to be poisonous. Toward the end of September, the field corn is ready to be picked, about the same time as the sun (represented by an orange in Miss Lewis's hand) is directly over the equator of the pea, thus making day and night of equal length, the northern hemisphere of the pea (us) tilting away from the orange and toward the darkness. The orange is smaller than the one Senator K. Thorvaldson gives me for Christmas, the glorious Florida orange. "Here, Chonny," he says, "you put this in your stocking." He has forgotten my name—he gives oranges to so many kids—but he likes me and wants me to be on a first-name basis. On a cold December morning, the orange gives off the sweet essence of Florida, a spectacular smell, almost as good as Vick's Vaporub. But Christmas is a long way off, beyond the planets of Halloween, Armistice Day, and Thanksgiving.

One Saturday in October, Mayor Clint Bunsen puts up his storm windows, and the next Saturday everyone does, including Byron Tollefson and his boy Johnny, home from college, who asks, "Why do we have to do it today just because everyone else is?" He also wonders why they don't get aluminium combinations with the storm enclosed that you just slide up or down instead of taking down screens and lugging these ancient storms up from the cellar and washing them and hoisting them up: it about breaks your back, and the second-story ones you got to hump up a ladder which won't reach unless it's at an 89° angle so you climb straight up the cliff bucking a hundred pounds of glass and if a gust catches it or the legs slip or if you take a deep breath or lean back one degree or if you have a serious thought in the back of your mind, you're a goner.

Byron has the radio on to the Gophers, who are getting pounded by Ohio State in heavy static, so it's hard to follow exactly, it's a sort of general overall disaster. Sounds like a short-wave transmission from the Russian front, but they're in Columbus, and the long, long wave of crowd noise means another Buckeye TD, which makes it 51–7. "Our Gophers are definitely being outplayed today," the announcer remarks. It has put Byron in a tough mood. "Don't tell me about it. Just *do* it," he says and he points up to the front bedroom window, number fourteen (XIV scratched in the sill and in the side of the storm), and braces his foot on the bottom rung. Byron can't lift the big ones on account of his back, which he sprung the day they moved into this house, carrying the refrigerator; and he doesn't climb because his sinuses are affected by heights.

It was chilly the next night, and the night after that. Father Emil's hay fever began to subside to two hankies per day. There had been no mention of the Feast Day of St. Francis in the bulletin, so Sister Arvonne asked him straight out if he wasn't going to have the blessing of the animals. "Oh, I don't know," he said. "It's so hard on the grass. They tear up the sod and then it freezes and you got hoofprints in the spring."

"If it's your allergies you're thinking about, we could get Father Todd," she said.

"Oh, it's not the allergy, it's the commotion. You know —" and he paused profoundly — "we have to think twice about providing ammunition to the unbeliever. What troubles me about the blessing of the animals is the circus aspect. People see this, they think, Well, there go the Catholics. I think, Sister, we could bless animals without having them on the premises, same as the criminals or the lepers—you wouldn't ship in a bunch of lepers so we could pray over them, would you?" Meanwhile, he thought: Father *Todd?* Bring in Father *Todd?* The T-shirt priest? The last time he got talked into Father Todd was for an Easter sunrise vigil for Catholic youth, which the man presided over in a *T-shirt*. With a picture of Our Lord on water skis that said "He's Up!" What would the man do on St. Francis's Feast Day? Probably wear antlers and talk about Our Brother the Buffalo.*

"Well," she said, "I know people who have their heart set on it, so if we're going to disappoint them, let's not do it at the last minute. And what's wrong with a show? Entertainment *began* in the Church, after all. People need it."

A reference, perhaps, to Father's part in the town council debate on installing a community TV antenna on the water tower. He was going to stay away, and then he heard that Principle was melting among the Protestants so he felt obliged to carry the ball. Long

---

Father Emil: "He went to St. Clement's and appeared to be okay but then he went to Minneapolis and fell in with a liberal crowd and got assigned to Holy Childhood in Golden Valley where they call God *Mother* and play guitars and he preaches about nutrition and stuff. I'm not sure but I *believe* that's the parish where some people got up a petition demanding that Father Todd do his share of baby-sitting so now he puts in two Sundays a year in the crib room. I believe that he is a chaplain at the Excelsior Amusement Park, too."

ago, he used to ask his parishioners to sign a pledge to turn their TVs to the wall at 5 P.M. Friday and leave them turned until Sunday after Mass, but it didn't work out. People turned their TVs toward the wall at such an angle that the picture was received by a mirror and transmitted back to them. More houses every year put up ugly thirty-foot antennas to pull in St. Cloud. So he went and gave a speech against television. Television dulls the moral senses, breaks up the family, distracts people from religious obligations, and tempts children with all manner of junk. Pastor Ingqvist then gave the case for educational programs and went out of his way to mention the Pope's visit to New York, the extensive TV coverage, the value of watching this, etc. Father Emil said that if you want to know what the Holy Father said, you could find it in *The Catholic Bulletin;* if you just want to see him climb in and out of limousines, then watch TV. Clint Bunsen said he doubted they could afford it anyway with Bud needing a new hydraulic lift for the snowplow. Bob Peterson said if the snow plowing went like last year, people would be spending lots of time indoors and needing entertainment. Bud challenged him to name one day when the streets weren't clear by noon. Bob said there were so many it was hard to pick one. Clint called for order. Then Harvey spoke about the danger of electrocution. Since time immemorial, boys have climbed the water tower. It's dangerous, it's wrong, but sooner or later a boy must do it, and with a TV antenna, there is always the danger of electricity getting loose. The water tower sweats, so all you'd need would be a few volts, and boys would fall like flies. "Then we'll be *on* television," he said. "They'll all come with their cameras to take pictures of the service in the gymnasium and those little white coffins all in a row." The vote was four opposed, one abstention.

Saturday. Opening day of duck hunting. At three A.M. a basement light shines in the squat brick lodge of the Sons of Knute where Elmer is brewing three giant pots of coffee, a special Knutes blend, double-strength with two raw eggs per pot, guaranteed to open a dead man's eyes. Other necessities have been hauled the day before to the Pete Peterson Memorial Blind—two fourteen-foot fiberglass duck decoys, a duckboat to retrieve the kill, carpet strips for the blind—and Edgar is bringing the brandy. Elmer had a good golden retriever once, named Duke, but he got too fond of coffee laced with brandy; two years ago he plunged in and paddled out for a dead duck and chewed it up and couldn't be trusted again. The giant decoys were borrowed by Pete Peterson (1910–1978) from his friend Walt who built them for the 1972 Minneapolis Duck Show and who didn't need them back. Walt's theory was that ducks fly too high to see life-sized decoys, that giant decoys would appear life-sized from cruising altitude (though making the lake seem dramatically smaller by comparison) and thus would exert greater draw. Each decoy can hold two hunters, but unfortunately, the immense superstructure makes the vessels unseaworthy, and they leak slightly, due to the holes in the bottom for the uprights, and the hunters within—one of whom puts his head and shoulders in the duck's head (which the other rotates with a hand-crank) and fires through the nostrils on the bill, an awkward shot at best, made more so by the tendency of the decoy to tip when a large man, excited by quacking aloft, jumps to his feet and pokes his shotgun out and begins to blast—tend to get wet and discouraged. A third decoy, the U.S.S. *Pete*, sank with Gus aboard in the fall of 1974. Gus heard incoming mallards and jumped to his hunting station, the *Pete* rolled to starboard, and Gus, trying to right it, stuck his big foot through the fiberglass shell and she descended into the drink tail first and he had to blow the head off to get out.

The Memorial Blind, named for the unlucky man whose lakeshore property it was dug into, is a trench with a bench where eight can sit camouflaged by haybales and wait for their prey. But the thought of eight Knutes firing guns from that small space is too much even for them, so four marksmen occupy the blind, two serve as ballast in the decoys, and the others, eight or ten, remain in the weeds behind the lines, ready to provide supporting fire. Opening Day morning is chilly and often rainy, and they need the brandy to keep warm, and more coffee to keep sober, and brandy in *that* coffee to keep calm and also because the coffee tastes better if it's well-laced, so by sunrise a Knute is in a fraternal mood, full of loyalty to his pals of the mystic order of the hunt and to departed friends now manning the pearly blinds in the duck shoot in the sky, such as Pete Peterson.

Poor Pete. Cancer got him. He always knew it would and in his last years kept a desperate watch for it—the Seven Danger Signs was taped to his bathroom mirror—but without much hope: every day revealed a possible sign, something unusual, a little change of weight, a thickening, a *slight* lump, *some* soreness, a redness of the stool, a sore that was slow to heal (older guys heal slower)—then, that fateful Friday, he felt a definite lump of the back of his head and was dizzy and found blood on his toothbrush. Lois was off to clean the church and he panicked—jumped in the car in his pants and T-shirt—it was Dr. DeHaven's day off and besides, Dr. DeHaven didn't believe his cancer theory—so he headed for St. Cloud to a new doctor, and only a panicky man would have passed the semi the way they said he did, on a long right-hand curve going up the hill toward Avon, and there he suddenly met his end and found his peace in the grille of a gravel truck.

"It was his time," said Elmer at the time, reflecting the general Knute philosophy of death as a lottery, and yet they miss him so much every year, the Duck Hunter's Duck Hunter. A man who lived for the hunt, lived by the lake about a beer can's throw from the blind, and took his gun to bed with him in season, the bedroom window being a four-foot single-pane spring-action sash-loaded window that dropped into its housing when he yanked the rope tied to the bedpost, permitting a good shot from a mattress position. His last fall, he bagged two from bed with one shell in a heavy drizzle an hour before dawn, barely awake, his head still on the pillow—that's how good a shot he was. Lois jumped three feet straight up, she yelled, "What in the name of creation!" and hit the floor and was at the door in one jump. "Mergansers," he said.

Action is slow in the blind. Seven A.M. and only clouds have flown over and birds too small to shoot, nonmeaty birds like sparrows and those white-breasted ones, and the hunters are thinking of former days. "It was better hunting before you had jet planes," says Mr. Nordberg. "Something·about the sound, it's hell on ducks. It ruins their instincts, you know, so they don't fly bunched up to much in formation, you get more loners than you used to."

"Well, that's the trend everywhere you look now," says Elmer, and indeed this seems true, of man as well as duck. Everyone out for himself, no loyalty, no interest in others, just grab whatever you can get. It's sad to think about the way things have gone downhill. "I'm glad I don't have much longer," says Mr. Nordberg. "I'm glad I lived when I did. I'd hate to be young and have that to look forward to." Tears come to his eyes as he says it. "There were no times like the old times." This reminds Elmer of Pete. He stands up stiffly and proposes a toast to their old friend. Mr. Berge is asleep and Swanny doesn't feel so good. He has been sitting on a hemorrhoid the size of a Concord grape, no position gives him relief, and all the anesthetic he has put away has not helped either. Elmer and Mr. Nordberg haul in the decoys and Bob and Cully climb out. Ivar and Phil, Johnny, Gus, and

Sig and Bernie come up from the rear. Edgar pulls the last bottle out of the Porta-Bar chest. "To Pete," he says. "God love him." They pass the bottle around. It truly does seem like the end. Of these grizzled old comrades in their big jackets and brown ponchos, gray-haired veterans of so many hunts, good pals and true, the finest men by God that you could ever hope to meet—who knows which ones will never see another October? They all are well into heart-attack country now, where life's road gets steep and a man is easily winded. Women go on and on but men drop like flies around this age. "To all of the brothers who have gone before, God love them," says Elmer.

"Ike. George. Val—" Mr. Berge stops. The roll of the dead is too long, and he's afraid he will forget one. The bottle goes around again, a shorter trip as they are standing closer, shoulder to shoulder. Edgar says they should buy a Last Man bottle and bury it in the blind for the survivor to come out and have a toot on in their memory. "It wouldn't last long, somebody'd sneak out and finish her up," says Cully looking at Mr. Berge who is insulted. "This is no time for that kind of talk. My God. You can't be decent then keep your mouth shut for Chrissake."

Elmer feels so tired he'd like to curl up in the car and sleep all day. "You'll outlive us all," says Edgar to Mr. Berge, trying to cheer him up. "The hell I will. Cully will and he can buy his own bottle. I ain't paying for it."

Cully goes off to take a leak. Swanny has to go home and get in a sitz bath. He came in Edgar's car so Edgar has to go too and Bernie. Sig and Ivar think

288

they'll be going. "Why? What's the rush?" says Elmer. Well, they just think they may as well. "*Why? What's the problem? Afraid the wife's gonna chew your ass?*"

Well, no, Sig says, it's just that he came out to hunt, not to stand around and get soused—"*Soused! Soused?* You got your nerve to stand there and say that! I dare you to say it again! Look at me and say it! Look at me! You're saying I'm drunk then have the decency to look me in the eye!" Johnny steps in between Sig and Elmer. "I'm going," says Phil. "I never saw the likes of you guys. What would Pete think? he'd be ashamed." Phil leaves and Sig decides to go with, and Johnny. Cully comes back and goes with them. That leaves Elmer and Gus. They sit down in the blind. "What are you thinking?" asks Gus. "Let's hang it up." "You know," says Elmer, "I don't think nothing is ever going to be what it was ever again. We've about seen the last of it. I'm getting too damn old."

———————

Uncle Virgil Bunsen, a former Knute, died during hunting season so the Knutes honor guard was in good form for the graveside salute, and attendance was good what with hunting being poor. His death caught almost everyone by surprise, though: they hadn't known he was alive. He moved to Nevada in 1925 and didn't keep in touch, so not many people at his funeral knew him well enough to feel as bad as they knew they ought to. They went to be sociable.

The few who wept did it out of custom and because they didn't want to pass up the opportunity.

Clarence had got the news on Monday from his cousin Denise, Virgil's daughter, who asked Clarence to handle the arrangements because she couldn't be there. "I think Dad would've wanted to be buried up there; he hated Nevada. Anyway, Burt and I have to go to Hawaii for two weeks. It's something we've been planning for a long time and, anyway, I want to remember Dad the way he was. I can't see what good it would do me to be there, I don't know anybody and funerals depress me. I think we have to look ahead. Not look back. You know.'

Who was Burt? Her husband, Clarence guessed, but which one? The last he heard she was married to a Ray. And where was Aunt Ginny? "Oh, she died about six years ago," Denise said. "I thought Dad wrote to you."

The upshot was that he had to get up at six A.M. and go to the Minneapolis-St. Paul airport, find a certain freight terminal, sign a receipt for Uncle Virgil, and talk a young man in a suit into letting him put the box in the panel truck instead of hiring a hearse. The man told him that he was only an assistant manager and didn't make the rules. He said, "Would you want people hauling you in an old truck after you pass on?" Clarence said, "It depends who the people are." Back home, he dropped off the box at Lundberg's Funeral Home and went to persuade Pastor Ingqvist to give Uncle Virgil the benefit of the doubt and provide a Christian burial, then he called

Elmer about the honor guard, and about four o'clock he headed up to the cemetery with Bud to help dig.

"It looks like rain for tomorrow," Bud said. "That's why I didn't want to wait. You ever dig a grave in the rain? It feels like you're digging your own." Clarence worked the pick and Bud shoveled. The two little Diener boys rode up on their bikes and sat down to watch. The men took turns in the hole. The plot was between Clarence's Uncle Frank, the oldest boy who never married, and an Alphonse Herberger whom he had never heard of: 1881–1924. It was going to be a tight fit, they could see as they got down to four feet, and Bud said he hoped Virgil was the sort who got along. Clarence was sweating. He shuddered each time he raised the pick and bought it down. Pieces of what looked to be Frank's coffin kept turning up beneath his feet and he was afraid of bringing up a bone. The boys were hoping for just that. They peered down when Clarence climbed out. "What do dead people look like when they've been buried a long time?" one asked.

Bud leaned on his shovel and sucked his teeth and looked at them thoughtfully. "Weeel, we don't ordinarily dig them up to find out," he said, "but ever so often now and then we have to, like with the boy — what was his name now? The one who died of diphtheria? You remember, Clarence. Oh, well. Anyway, he was about your age. A wonderful boy. He had a brown collie dog used to follow him like a shadow and the two of them liked to swim together and they'd go fishing and in the winter they slid down the hill, you never saw a boy and a dog so close as those two were. Well, the boy got sick, and he just got worse and worse. He was too weak to walk but they hitched that dog up to a wagon and he pulled the boy around town every day until one day he was too sick even for that and one week later he was dead."

"Well, of course, his parents were heartbroken and his brothers and sisters. They sat around crying their eyes out for two days, looking at that poor child lying in the coffin, but the collie dog took it even harder. He wouldn't eat a bite, he didn't sleep, he just sat by the coffin and cried, the way dogs do, moaning, and when the boy was buried, the dog lay on his grave and wouldn't leave, so they left him here."

"Well, sir, it was two days after the burial, the dog came tearing down the hill like he was crazy, barking and yipping and wouldn't quit. They tied him up but he kept on until finally the father said, 'I believe he wants us to follow him,' and sure enough. They untied him and he took off for the cementry and stood on the boy's grave and howled, and when the people got up there, the dog began to dig in the dirt. The father said, 'He's trying to tell us something,' so they got shovels and dug as fast as they could, and got down to the little coffin and lifted it out and opened it up."

"Well, sir, what they saw inside, it just tore their hearts out, it was so horrible. People took one look, and turned away, sick. The boy's eyes were wide open and his face looked like he was screaming. His face was all bloody and so was his hands. He had clawed the cloth off the lid and scratched the wood and had torn off his clothes and scratched his face to ribbons. You see, they had buried him alive."

The Diener boys did not move a muscle as Bud told them this: they looked as if he had clubbed them over the head. Clarence got back in the hole to pick some more.

"His father was never the same after that. He completely lost his mind. He became like a little child. Every day he sat in the yard and just hummed and talked to hisself and the dog sat there with him. It was the saddest thing you ever saw. And now the boy and his father and his dog are all dead, buried up there around back of the maple tree. I can show you their grave if you want to see it."

The boys whispered, No, they didn't want to. They picked up their bikes and coasted off down the hill. They coasted very slowly. Bud laughed. "Well," he said, "you ask a question, you get an answer." He studied the hole. "Don't be afraid to dig down around Frank," he said. "It's only dust, you know."

Clarence's one clear memory of Virgil was from a family trip out West, when Clarence was nine or ten. He remembered eating hamburgers in buns (his family always had them on bread) and leaving the cafe and his father put him up on his lap and let him drive the car. His mother said, "Clinton, he's only nine!" Or ten. In Nevada, they stopped at Virgil's house, a little white house, and Virgil came out to see them. They stood around, and he didn't invite them in. Aunt Ginny wasn't feeling well. They all went for a walk. It was hot and the air smelled of gasoline. They walked along some railroad tracks and past a water tank, and next thing, Virgil was forty, fifty feet out in front of them. Walking like he forgot they were there. That night, they stayed in tourist cabins. "Uncle Virgil doesn't have room for all of us," his mother explained. His father snorted. He said, "Virgil never did have room." Years later, from his father, Clarence heard a passing reference to bad blood between Virgil and Clarence's grandfather, which had to do with cattle and led to Virgil moving away and which apparently never got patched up.

Clarence put himself out for the funeral, as several people remarked to him afterward: "This was real good of you, Clarence. You did the right thing." He made four big sprays of evergreen and dug up enough about Uncle Virgil to make a decent obituary and when Pastor Ingqvist said he couldn't stay for the graveside service, Clarence handled that himself. He read the Twenty-third Psalm, and then, even though it gave him a bad case of the shakes, he faced them, all sixteen of them, and said, "Uncle Virgil left here when I was pretty little and I only saw him once after that, so I don't have much to say about him. I do know that it was because of an argument that he left. I wish I knew more. I'm glad to have him back and I hope that he is finally at rest. I hope that all of us will take a lesson from it, to settle our arguments as quick as we can. I say this especially to the younger ones. Life is short. The Bible says, don't let the sun go down upon your wrath. Settle these things. It isn't true that time heals all wounds, sometimes they get worse if you don't do something about them. I didn't mean to talk this much, but I know I've done things to make people mad and I ask you to forgive me for them and I forgive you for anything you ever did to me." He stopped, not certain how he should end it. Finally, he just reached for the ropes. They lowered Virgil into his grave and shoveled in the dirt and made a nice mound over him. They shook hands and got in their cars and went home to supper.

Eloise was a little put out with Bud afterward. "I don't see why Clarence had to help with the grave," she said. "That's your job, after all."

"I didn't make him. But I'll tell you this, they don't pay me enough to get away with treating me like a servant."

She said, "But servants always get paid less."

He said, "Well, there's the problem, isn't it?"

Clarence sat in his green easy chair and Arlene fixed him a cup of Sanka. She kissed him on the top of his head. "You did good, honey," she said.

"I went down there early so I could have a look at him," he said. "The coffin was sealed shut and I had to get a clawhammer to pry it open. It was stuffed with those green pads, like house-movers use. I pulled those out and there he was, you know, I didn't recognize him at all. It was like I'd never seen him before in my life. A complete stranger. All I had to show it was my uncle was a piece of paper with his name on it. Like an invoice. You know, my dad never wrote to him, never talked about him. Something about cattle—he and Grandpa thought Virgil cheated them, and that was the end of him. Stopping to see him in Nevada, that was Mother's idea, and I remember her trying to be friendly and Dad and Virgil not saying more than two words to each other. When my cousin called, she offered me $500 to take care of the funeral. My God. She was surprised I wouldn't take it. She said it'd cost her twice that to hire a funeral director. Good Lord."

———

"So I slow down and roll down my window and I says, 'Do you need a ride?' and he says, 'No, I'm running.' Well, I could see that. That's why I offered. So then I go on to Ralph's and head home and there he is again—running back the way he come. I know they do this but I can't see it: why would you run so hard to get to where you were in the first place?"

"Beer an' a bump. And don't give me that Jim Beam. Last time I drank it, I got so damn sick I was afraid I'd die. And then I was afraid I wouldn't."

"Wayne, you're so dumb, you *deserve* to be a Democrat."

"Look at yourself, Oscar. You're drunk, you're personally repulsive, and you believe in Reagan. What's left for you, Oscar? Next thing you'll be living in your car, eating bugs off the grille."

"I don't have to take that from you, you—"

"You! Wayne! Out!"

"How come me? I didn't start it! Throw *him* out!"

"He hasn't finished his beer."

"Wally, these nuts are *rotten*. Lookit this!"

"So get some other ones."

"You eat a whole bag of nuts and you don't know they're rotten?"

"Lookit this! Jeez!"

"I read an article in the Minneapolis paper about rotten nuts. It affects your sex life. That's the truth."

"There's a chestnut tree out there and he's getting them chestnuts and I know it and he knows it too. Damn Norskie's so damn stubborn: I followed him out there one day last fall and he drives around all damn afternoon rather than have me find out where the damn thing is. Cheap sonofabitch. I don't know how some people can go to church on Sunday!"

"I tell you, the price is so ridiculous—next year I'm putting in forty acres of zinnias. I'm sick of looking at corn. Long as I'm gonna go broke anyway, may as well have fun doing it. Put in zinnias and sit out there in a lawn chair and read the paper."

"Wally! this *beer's* flat, dammit. What you trying to do to me? I work all day and the old lady chews me out for coming down here and now you're trying to keep me sober?"

A good night at the Sidetrack Tap: Mr. Berge has borrowed ten bucks from Senator K. and won two more at pinochle, and now he is up and dancing to Rusty Hintges's old song: "I can't wait to drive you home, Just call me Mr. Smith. Tonight it's time for love, And baby, you're the one I'm with." Rusty grew up near here and Mr. Berge once gave him bus fare to Nashville and years later got a box of 45s from him in payment, including this one, but it's not the memory of old Rusty that warms his heart, it's the fact that ten minutes ago two young women walked in and sat by him at the bar. Not so beautiful by day, perhaps, but in dim light they look like movie stars. Mr. Berge, who doesn't draw much attention from women including his wife, is thrilled to pieces. One is Roxanne and the other is Suzie. They're from St. Cloud. Just driving through. He insists on buying them beers, which guarantee him five minutes, and he starts out with a couple of Ole and Lena jokes, which they like okay, so he tells them a dirtier one, about Ole and Lena's wedding night. He gives them cigarettes. He offers to give them a ride home. "We got a car," says Suzie. "Well, I could give the other one a ride home then," he says. "You don't live together do you?" Actually, they do. "Well, maybe you could give me a ride, then," he says. Their attention is wandering. He offers to dance with one of them, but they don't want to dance. "I dance pretty good," he says, and gets up and dances.

In his own mind, having had a few, he dances *real* good, but Merle laughs at him. "Hey, Berge, how's your wife and my kids?" The girls think this is pretty funny. He hitches up his pants and sits down. Merle has moved in at the other end, next to Suzie. "This is Merle," Mr. Berge announces, "Merle is my best buddy, ain't that right?" Merle snorts. "These ladies are from St. Cloud, now ain't that a deal, Merle? We don't get all that many of you up here. God, you're so pretty. Anybody tell you that before? You remind me of the Soderberg Sisters. Ever hear of them? God, they were pretty. Talented? Jeez, they had it all. *Ja,* they went right from here to the National Barn Dance. Did you know that? Huh?"

The girls had never heard of the National Barn

Dance so they don't know what a great compliment it is to be compared to the Soderberg Sisters. "I used to know 'em both quite well," Mr. Berge plunges on, feeling his way. "I used to take 'em around to dances when I was a bartender at the Moonlite Bay supper club." Moonlite Bay burned to the ground in 1954, but for Mr. Berge, it still is the ultimate in swank. Memories of the dance floor with spring suspension, Eddie Flores and His Saxophone Troubadors onstage behind little band desks, and forty booths with table-cloths and candles in glass bowls that reflected the mirror on the back bar. O fabulous Moonlite Bay . . . but Merle leans forward and laughs at him. "You never bartended at Moonlite Bay!" he says. "I was in there a hundred times and I never saw your ass in there."

"I never saw *your* ass in there! And I bartended there for three years! I was there when Tommy bart-ended! Jerry Heinrich! Mike Gutknecht! Ask any-body!"

"You're such a big liar," says Merle, "you gotta get your neighbor to call your dog!" The girls think this is funny. Merle says to Suzie, "Where'd you find him? Out in the ditch?"

Mr. Berge plays it cool, he doesn't want to scare them. He tries to stare Merle down. "What you so quiet about?" asks Merle.

"I figure if you know so much, maybe I'll learn something from you. Tell me some more, Merle. What else are you an expert in?"

This works pretty good. Roxanne pats his hand and tells him not to get upset. She says to have fun.

He tries to hold her hand but she needs it to light another cigarette.

"Who gives a shit if you bartended at the Moonlite Bay or not?" says Merle. "I know I don't. Do you?" he asks the girls.

Roxanne turns to Mr. Berge. "Was that near here?" she says. He tells her a little about the Moonlite Bay. The tables, the candles, the long bar, the band—"It was the most gorgeous place you ever seen," he says, but then he thinks that maybe, being from St. Cloud, she's seen a lot of clubs like that, so he mentions that John Dillinger once hung out there. A good story. It works! She says, "I saw a movie about Dillinger with Warren Oates, I think."

(Who's Warren Oates? Is he her boyfriend?) Mr. Berge goes with Dillinger. "*Ja*," he says, keeping an eye on Merle who is trying to distract Suzie, "Dillinger and his gang come up from Chicago for a rest. They figured nobody up here knew him. But we knew. Ha! We spotted him the minute he walked in."

"I was pretty young at the time. Just a kid." He mentions this so Dillinger won't date him.

"He was a decent guy. He bought a beer and left a dollar tip. One of the other bartenders was going to call the sheriff but I says to him, I says, 'Hey, he didn't do anything to you. Leave him be.' That's my philosophy. Nobody gives me trouble, I don't give them trouble. I remember he sat at this table facing the door and he unbuttoned his jacket and I seen he had a bulge in his pants."

Merle thinks that's the funniest thing he ever heard

in his life. He repeats it three times. He laughs his head off; he pounds on the bar.

"I meant his gun, dammit!"

Roxanne pats his hand again and tells him not to get angry. 'Let's just have fun," she says. This time he holds her hand. She says he's sweet. He leans forward and kisses her on the cheek. She laughs and says his whiskers tickle. He kisses her again. She turns and says to Suzie, "Well? What do you say?"

His heart is pounding, he is so much in love. His hands tremble. He excuses himself to go to the bathroom. There, he takes a leak and then, seeing his poor old self in the mirror, he washes his hands and his face. He spits out his tobacco and rinses his mouth. He doesn't have a comb on him, but he wets down his hair and does the best he can with his hands. When he comes out, they're gone.

He runs outside. A car's taillights are way down Main Street, they flare up as it brakes and turns onto the country road. He looks that way a long time, thinking they might turn around and come back.

Inside, Merle takes one look at him and says, "What happened to you? You fall in?"

"Where did they go?"

"Back to St. Cloud. They had to get to work in the morning."

"Oh? Where do they work?" If he knew that, he could give them a call.

"I didn't ask." Merle pays up with Wally, and while he's waiting for change, Mr. Berge wants to ask him more about the girls, like what kind of car was it? Did he get their last names? Where in St. Cloud do they live? What *type* of work do they do? But of course Merle wouldn't tell him even if he did know which he probably doesn't, and why give Merle one more laugh tonight. —Time to go home and see the Mrs.—But first, a whiskey for the road.

Tasting the whiskey, he feels as bad as he's felt all day. They were so beautiful. Why wouldn't they dance? All he wanted was to have some fun. Couldn't he have fun too?

But then as he thinks about it, he starts to feel better. If they came in once, they'll come in again. Maybe tomorrow, maybe next week, but sometime. When they do, he'll be watching for them. He's going to wear a clean shirt tomorrow and get his hair cut. He's going to bring a gift he can give them if they come back. Too bad it's September and the roses are dead. But tomorrow afternoon, he'll cut two African violets from Mrs. Berge's plant and come down to the Sidetrack early.

A big storm blew in on Wednesday, the day before Thanksgiving, that nobody saw coming, not even Bud who knows weather like my father knows the Great Northern and calls the storms as they roll in from the coast. This one caught Bud leaning toward autumn.

Freezing rain fell in the morning, turning to heavy snow, and by suppertime we had thirteen inches on the ground and more coming, falling sideways in front of a stiff west wind, and you couldn't see the house across the street. Wally closed the Sidetrack at five o'clock. It's illegal to sell alcohol in town when you can't see across the street; and when Clarence closed up Bunsen Motors across the street and turned off the blue Ford Motor sign, Wally couldn't see anything over there, so he called it a day even though Mr. Berge had Mr. Lundberg on the run at cribbage and was closing in for the kill and was furious, of course. He yanked his overcoat off the hook and jammed his arms into it and glared out the window at the snow, waiting for a good sharp remark to come to mind. "Well," he says, "I think I'll go home."

Clarence walked five blocks home which he had been doing for a few weeks since he read an article about the heart, which his daughter Barbara Ann sent him along with a picture of a bicycle clipped from the Sears catalog. She and her husband were due for Thanksgiving dinner, and from the looks of things, they wouldn't make it. *Nuts!* Clarence liked it when she lectured him about his health, which she did now with every visit—"Daddy," she said in that sweet tone that led right into the legumes. Legumes, garlic, hard breathing, whole grain cereals, and no cigars and no red meat, plus whatever she had read about recently, maybe the benefits of eating raw cotton or the dangers of chewing on lead pencils. He argued with her only to stimulate further class discussion. "Your grandfather lived to be eighty-four and he lived on cigar butts, fried chicken skin, and as much Rock 'n Rye whiskey as he could sneak downstairs for without arousing Grandma's suspicions. He kept the bottle in the cellar in his tool chest. The last three years, after he went blind, it was pretty hard for him

to explain why he needed hammer and nails."
Daddy.

He had been looking forward to her Thanksgiving health homily (maybe a tip on eating raw yams or some new data on cranberry sauce and how the pancreas feels about it). She made him feel like a well-loved man. That she would think a small-town Ford dealer could become Mahatma Gandhi. To most people, Clarence was Clarence, always would be. When he thought of her great faith that he might switch to grass and berries and grow young and run marathons, her fond hope of his longevity, he was moved to tears. As he was by her improbable gifts: walking shorts, *kim chee*, Walt Whitman's *Leaves of Grass*. As he was by Arlene's choice of lilac wallpaper for their bedroom: amazing woman. His daughter Donna sent him Whitman's Chocolate Cherries and thought lilac was ridiculous.

Over his old brown overcoat, like a shawl, Clarence wore a red wool serape that had hung in his office closet since he wore it to work in a blizzard the March before. It was a gift from Don Eduardo, Eddie Bunsen, his cousin, a postal supervisor at the Minneapolis post office until he retired to a village in the mountains of Michoacan. Clarence sent him a Christmas card every year. *Feliz Navidad*. Don Eduardo and Donna Marie live in a two-room hut overgrown with flowering manzanita, the Airstream they took to Mexico now serving as a chicken coop. He sent Clarence pictures of beautiful brown people, fabulous landscapes that breathed flowers and rain, and the red serape—when Clarence wore it, he felt like he was back in the Thespian Club as the *generale* in "A Message for Garcia." He thought of those brown faces with high cheekbones and grave handsome expressions, people at rest before the camera, with nothing to fear at all. That was their handsomeness—courage. Calm courage. Not having to impress anybody. Peace.

Beating his way home, the serape to cover his face, he could smell the animal whose hair this was and his own stale cigar breath. He thought, I got to quit smoking, I'm losing my sense of smell, usually I only smell myself. The snow smelled clean, but like a hospital. For the third or fourth time that day, he thought, *I am dying*.

The thought came to him, struggling home; *you don't have to be very smart to be an adult. Most people are working on half-throttle.* Take this storm, for example. Depressing to see autumn snap shut—what a fine November, then suddenly the fuse blows and she's all over, no warning. But to see Wally in the front door saying, "I just wonder if the kids are going to make it up from the Cities tonight"—no, not if they have a brain in their head, they're not going to try to make it anywhere. A foot of snow with a good wind behind it can make you a person in a news story if you're not careful. Couldn't he see? This was a blizzard.

And the phone lines to the Cities were busy all evening. He tried twice and Elizabeth at the exchange said, "I got you on the list, Clarence. I'll ring you. You're still tenth."

"What's taking them so long?"

"Oh, you know."

People at this end were calling people at that end, and the other end didn't know any more than they did—he tried a third time, and there was Art Diener on the party line with his son-in-law in St. Paul, saying, "How does it look down there?" "Looks pretty bad." "So what do you think?" "Hard to say." "I guess we'll have to wait and see." "I think that's all we can do." "Well, let us know." "Okay." It's in critical situations such as this that the telephone is supposed to be such an advance in communications, but what's there to say? "What's it doing down there?" "Snowing." "Yeah, same here."

"You'd think these people weren't *from* here!" Clarence said to Arlene. "You'd think they never *saw* winter before!"*

Hjalmar and Virginia Ingqvist's oldest, Mrs. Keith (Christine) St. Clair, called them from Los Angeles at noon (ten A.M., P.S.T.) to say, "I can't believe it! I'm so excited! We'll be there in just a few hours! I can't wait! No, there's nothing wrong. Why? No, I just called to say hi. Good-bye," and then she and her orthodontist husband and the three children flew to

---

*"Short memory makes everything more entertaining, even weather. Four definite seasons every year, four big surprises. People talk about weather most of the time, usually like children. 'Smell that! It's spring!' Then, 'Jeez, it's a hot one.' Then, 'Looka those leaves, wouldja.' Each change wipes the slate clean, so when it snows, they look out the window and say, 'Well, heaven's sake. Look at that, willya.' People are easily amused here." (*Up from Minnesota*, Whyte; Spartan, 1964.)

Minnesota in three hours. Amazing. You leave California, have two glasses of champagne and eat lunch, and the next thing you know you're back in the old North Star State. Except they weren't. They were in Sioux Falls, S.D. Traffic at Minneapolis-St. Paul was backed up with only one runway open. A few hours later, they were still in Sioux Falls, on their sixth cup of vending-machine coffee apiece, and the children were sick of Space Invaders and were draped on their parents and aiming sharp kicks at each other. A few hours after that, they were in Minnesota (though, from the look of the airline terminal, it could've been anywhere in America), and a few hours after *that* they left the airport on a bus heading for downtown Minneapolis. An hour later, they were almost downtown. Up in the air it was the twentieth century but in the blizzard on the ground it was the Middle Ages. Peasants trudged along the road, their heads down, or struggled to free their oxcarts from the mire, lacking only oxen to do it. Their sheer bulk in the heavy clothing made the people look like beasts. A bearded man got on the bus. He was immense. His feet were like clubfeet in two moon boots, and his giant leather paws hung at his side. In the dimness, his fur cap appeared to be his own matted hair, on a head shaped like a gorilla's. His breath and spit were frozen on his hair face. He smelled of wet fur. Christine turned away. He looked as if he had emerged from a cave where he had spent the Ages since Bronze eating half-cooked mastodon and grunting to his women. Christine was cold. She wore a thin London Fog raincoat over her pink shirt and blue jeans. Her feet were wet, in brown loafers. "Put your arm around me," she told Keith. He grunted and put his arm around her. "If I had known it was going to be like this—" she said.

In 1887, her great-grandfather Sveeggen, a boy of twelve, was lost in a blizzard between the barn and the house where he'd gone to do chores. His family had gone to town; he was the oldest of six children. He looked out the barn door into the wind and was sure he saw a ghostly mass of house and black roof ahead so he plunged out into the blizzard and was blinded by white light and everything disappeared, house and barn behind him—he counted twenty, thirty, forty, fifty steps, trying to walk straight into the wind, then turned left, took thirty steps. Then right. And turned back, and knew he was lost and would die—and then the house caught fire. He saw the dull orange glow and walked toward it and stood by the back steps as flames shot out the roof and it all collapsed—he was cold on one side, burning hot on the other—and got his bearings straight and ran into the blizzard and ran smack into the side of the barn, where he spent the night, lying next to the cow, Tina, holding his broken nose. It was the great experience of his life, which he never forgot. "*Hvor er Gud Fader mild, vi alle var fordervet i synd.*" ("How kind is God the Father, we were all lost in sin.") Having lost his life, he entered the new one with a sweet disposition. He planted trees, raised cattle, married, and had seven children, and seldom spoke a harsh word. His nose was never set. He pitched ten tons of hay the day he was married; in their wedding picture,

308

he sits, smiling, his eyes bright beside his ruined beak, a man who took a hard wallop and now everything is easy for him.

To Dede, washing pots and pans in the back of the Chatterbox, the snow came as quite a thrill. It has been so long since she had seen snow, she had almost forgotten about it. Tiny white crystalline flakes falling through the air, billions of them, which when you take some in your hand and study them, no two are the same. You can't study them long because they melt in your hand, but no two are the same, that's what they say. But who said this? Who would do a study of billions of snowflakes to prove no repetition? She scraped at the crusted noodles on the bottom of the big aluminum bake pan and looked out the little window fogged with grease at the faint white yard. One more year that Merle wouldn't get that '52 Chevy pickup running. Too late now. It would be a deadster through April when he'd talk about it again. When the Chevy was newer, they went to movies in it at the Cloud-Nine drive-in near St. Cloud and necked in a half-hearted way. Merle didn't seem to understand that a man is supposed to lead the way, not sit there and wait for lightning to strike. A man should be passionate, make mistakes if he has to, get out of line. She could keep him in line but he never got out. He parked the pickup behind the Cafe when they were still going together. It needed a new carburetor, which somehow he never got around to. "That's a good old truck, she's got a lot of miles left in her," he had been saying for six years now. Meanwhile, he married a skinny girl with bad skin from Bowlus, whose name Dede couldn't remember, and had two kids. Dede guessed that What's-her-name didn't cook, judging by how often they ate out, about four times a week, and the kids ate like pigs and ran around with snot running down their faces. No two people are exactly alike, was what her mother said, but Merle and his family seemed common as dirt to her. They lived in a trailer by his dad's chickenhouse, surrounded by trash and filth. It took a good snowfall to make that place look decent.

Bud was the only customer. He had been out with the plow, but there wasn't much he could do. The state plows weren't out yet, he said. So he sat and drank coffee. "She's going to be a hard winter," he said to Dorothy. "You can tell by watching the squirrels. The way they walk around hunched over. They know. They're thinking about it."

"You say that every year. I'd like to know what an easy winter is. I don't believe I've been in one."

"Well, your winter of '35 was a mild winter. Or was it '38? One of the two. School never closed and I don't believe we got more than forty inches of snow."

Forty inches is above my bosom, Dede thought.

"It was nothing like '51 or '65. Whew! sixty-five."

Dorothy swabbed the deck and tried to recall 1965.

"Remember the water main froze?" Bud laughed at this grim memory; he had to put his coffee down. He wiped his eyes. The main froze solid, cutting off water to the north side of town. It was Saturday evening. People who were taking baths didn't notice it but the showers started running boiling hot, and people had to jump out. He wished he'd been there to see it. Soap all over them. Yelling. Thinking someone had flushed a toilet. People take water for granted. It comes out of a tap like some God-given right. Some of them had to get dressed, covered with dry soap, and drive to their mother's on the south side to rinse off. That was the night they appreciated old Bud for once. It was thirty-five below, he had to jump-start the backhoe. He knew right where the trouble was, it was exactly where he had told them for years it would be if they didn't spend the money to re-lay the line, and that's where she was all right. It took him three hours to uncover the pipe, the ground was so hard. Men standing around the hole with flashlights, utterly useless. The sort of help who watch you do it and then when the pipe appears, they all yell, "I think you got it, Bud!" Thirty feet of pipe he uncovered and laid hot coals on, and then it was two in the morning and hardly a soul around. Gone to bed so they could get up for church. Oh yeah. Go to church. Real good. But they hadn't called Father Emil or Pastor Ingqvist when the water went out, now did they? No sir. Church is a comfort, all right, but your water and your sewer, those are necessities. And roads. People can skip church, but they do not skip water or sewer. When it really comes down to it, it comes down to plumbing. And plowing in the winter. But you got a bunch of windbags on the town council who don't know pipe from a hole in the ground, want to spend money on a library but think water and sewer is some sort of natural fact, like a river, what can you do? This museum of antiques they call a system, you just do what you can and hope for the best. And you hope that when the thing falls apart the members of the town council are sitting on their toilets reading books from the library. Man in the can reading *Giants in the Earth*. Goes to flush, no water. Goes and gets water, pours it in, but the pipe is clogged, and his mess runs out all over the floor. Right then is when he finds out something. Then he wakes up finally.

The council's annual debate on snowplowing and the use of street salt came in October. Item 3, Line 2, Additional Expenditures; Salt: $287.38. The War of the Roses. Ladies of the Garden Club were present as were some gentlemen who own ancient cars, to cry out against salting the streets to melt the ice. Salt eats car bodies, it kills grass and flowers. Salt the street, then it snows again, Bud plows, and the blade throws the salt on your lawn, and your roses gasp and shudder in their deep sleep and give up the ghost. Ladies speak against the salt holocaust, and then Florian stands up and says a few words about his '66 Chevy. Forty-two thousand miles on her—he has two doormats glued to his garage floor where, when the car is parked, they're in place to wipe your feet on before you climb in—she's like new all over, not a spot of rust. Salt will destroy this car as surely as if you took a hammer to it. Ella Anderson speaks up for the tulips. Then Mrs. Langen in behalf of the cemetery, where the dead rest in their pleasant garden, attended by lovely plants which speak to us of the promise of resurrection and eternal life. Salt will turn the cemetery into a dump. When this happens, she thinks she will move elsewhere. There is no need for salt, it is simply a lazy man's scheme for getting out of snowplowing—and all eyes turn to Bud, the czar of salt, and once again Line 2 is defeated on a voice vote.

This year, Bud didn't go. Eloise wouldn't let him. His blood pressure has been up, and the doctor took him off salt last spring, and she was afraid the annual salt talk would make blood come out his eyeballs. Bud has said his piece on salt many times and it's like talking to a stone wall. Plowing cannot remove ice. Sand can't do the job alone. You need salt. Otherwise, you come to January and old people are trapped at home as surely as if you nailed the doors shut, sidewalks are deadly, streets are sheer suicide, and he (Bud) just hopes that when someone goes sailing off an icy road into a tree, that it is someone from the Garden Club and that, in the last moment before her body is hurled through the broken windshield like meat into a grinder, she thinks about the importance of road maintenance.

Mayor Clint Bunsen sat through an hour of argument, trying to keep it from veering off into greener pastures. "I'm opposed to salt, too," said old Mr. Diener, "but I don't think it's the greatest danger we face here—which is (and I think everyone knows it): what is going on now in our schools. The other day—" and Clint no sooner put out that fire when Mrs. Langen got going on the need for a War Memorial. She knew for a fact that the Army was *giving* away old artillery pieces for use as monuments, and why the council couldn't get one, she had no idea—Salt was too mundane for these philosophers, they wanted to get at the big issues. "Excuse me," he kept saying, 'but the motion on the floor right now is to spend money on salt."

He thought about the legislature in St. Paul. People have told him he should run. Senators sit in big armchairs at mahogany desks and bat around millions of dollars. The councilmen sit on folding chairs behind a folding table and listen to endless discussion of $287.38. Mr. Diener suggests that the salt money could be donated for cancer research instead; this terrible disease rages through the land, killing young and old alike including some dear friends of his whom he recalls with tears in his eyes, and though $287.38 may not seem like much, he quotes a poem ("For want of a nail, the shoe was lost") to show that little things may be crucial.

They voted 4–1 against salt, Clint being the one in favour. Councilman Diener, nephew of Mr. Diener, moved that in the interest of avoiding bitterness and rancor they make the vote unanimous. They voted 3–1 for unanimity, Councilman Bauser abstaining.*

---

*A memorable council meeting was that of 5/16/62 to discuss a motion to hold a special election to vote on a bond issue to repair sidewalks and install new streetlights. It was the late Leo Mueller who suggested that with a little more inner light ("Thy Word is a lamp unto my feet"), fewer people would need assistance walking home. He hinted

In Minneapolis, a fleet of orange snow plows and salt trucks moved out of the city truckyard at three A.M. Thanksgiving morning. The snow had stopped and the wind let up. State plows were out on the high-

---

that it was Lutherans who were walking into trees. It was the late Mr. Osterberg who said, "Men love darkness rather than light because their deeds are evil. John 3:19," and "Let the lower lights be burning, cast a gleam across the wave," and, in defense of sidewalk repair, "Prepare ye the way of the Lord, make his path straight." "Wide is the gate and broad is the way that leadeth to destruction," said Leo's friend, Mr. Luger, pointing out that our earthly pathway is not meant to be easy. Hjalmar Ingqvist, then the mayor, asked the speakers to please limit themselves to pertinent argument and be brief, and they all turned on him. Louie reminded him of Christ's admonition in the Sermon on the Mount, "When they bring you unto magistrates and powers, take ye no thought how or what thing ye shall answer, or what ye shall say. For the Holy Ghost shall teach you in the same hour what ye ought to say." What seemed "pertinent" to Hjalmar was not necessarily pertinent to the Holy Ghost who was leading them, and should one be brief where truth was at stake? The discussion began to range widely in the field of personal morals. At ten o'clock, Hjalmar banged his gavel, said he was tired, and moved for adjournment, but all he got was an uproar. How could he think of sleep at a time like this? Now was the time for wakefulness. People cited the watchman who slept, the sleeping apostles, the parable of the wheat and the tares, until Hjalmar said, "I'm going home to bed. Turn out the lights before you leave." He didn't run for reelection. "Politics brings you into contact with all the people you'd give anything to avoid," he said. "I'm staying home."

ways, a string of flashing blue lights moved along I-94 north from downtown along the river. The city crews started downtown, clearing the streets and salting them and loading snow into dump trucks. When Christine stirred at seven, Sixth Street was black and dry in front of the Dyckman Hotel, through she didn't know it. On the bedside table was a card advertising the Thanksgiving buffet at the Dyckman's Chateau de Paris restaurant. A happy family sat at a gleaming table admiring the huge turkey as a friendly waiter hovered overhead. The tablecloth was snowy white, no spills. The children were handsome and beautifully dressed. Candles glowed. All you could eat for $12.95. Wine from the Chateau cellar. Flaming desserts. Arturo and His Boulevard Violins. Keith and the children were asleep. Christine eased out of bed and into the bathroom and ran a hot bath. A telephone hung on the wall. She called home. "It doesn't look like we'll make it," she said. "It looks like we'll be up on Friday."

She called Chip in St. Paul and Corinne in Edina, and they both said, Fine, dinner at the hotel sounded good. Meet at ten for brunch, take a walk, go to a movie, eat dinner at five.

That was the plan until the others drove downtown and noticed that the streets were in pretty good shape. They had gone to bed hearing dire warnings on WCCO—"no travel advised"—and woke up to hear. "No unneccessary travel advised," but now WCCO, the Good Neighbor to the Great Northwest, was sounding less dogmatic about it, and Charlie Johnson was taking calls on "Party Line" from listeners who advanced their own views of weather conditions, more liberal than the official line. "How does it look out there?" he asked. "Not so bad, Charlie. Pretty good. Wind's died down, and the plow went by an hour ago." He pointed out that the weather bureau still advised no unnecessary travel. "Well, she looks pretty good here," they said. "I think we're going to go."

The Ingqvist children met in the hotel lobby at ten. and decided they would feel bad spending Thanksgiving there with the roads looking good. Corinne said, "The folks listen to 'CCO. They'd never say so but they'd feel terrible if they knew that we could've come and just didn't. You know Mom. She's crazy about holidays. I'll bet she's got the turkey in the oven already and she's already got her pies out of the freezer."

"Think we should call?" Keith asked.

"Naw," said Chip. "Let's surprise them."

As it turned out, Virginia did have her pies out of the freezer, but they were Swanson's frozen chicken pot pies. At one o'clock, she was sliding them into a 450-degree oven when Hjalmar yelled, "Guess what?"

She had no idea. Something on television?

"They're here."

"Who? Is this a joke?" Then she heard them coming through the door. It was them all right. The grandchildren tore in, and there were coats to be taken off and boots, and hugs and kisses all around, and in all the pandemonium, it took the children awhile to notice that something was different. The house smelled different. It didn't smell like Thanksgiving; it smelled like room freshener.

Christine went back to the kitchen to help her mother make coffee. She said, "Were you thinking we wouldn't make it?" Her mother ran water in the teakettle and got the coffee down from the cupboard. "You know," she said, "there's a recipe for macaroni and cheese I've always been meaning to try. It's the one where you boil up about three pounds of macaroni, and then you grate cheese on it. It only takes about five minutes."

Barbara Ann Bunsen and her husband Bill pulled into the Bunsen driveway about one-thirty. "We made love," she explained to her mother. "Otherwise we would've been here earlier."

"Well, it certainly is good for your complexion," said her mother.

Bill had a new mustache that did not quite fill his upper lip. He held a casserole of refried beans that smelled of garlic. He took his time wiping his feet, not sure where he should go from the doormat ("Welcome")—to the kitchen?—An easy chair? Stand and talk for a while, then sit down? "Come on in, make yourself at home," said Clarence. "*Duane!*"

Arlene snapped on the oven light where the bird sat, dark and golden in its pan, glittering, and snapped it off.

"That," she said, "is my twenty-eighth Thanksgiving turkey."

"It's perfect."

"It's a turkey anyway. I kind of lost interest after the tenth."

"I like your glasses."

"Thank you."

They looked at each other. Barbara Ann wore blue jeans and an embroidered blue shirt. She was letting her dark brown hair grow long again. Arlene's had dramatic grey streaks and she didn't know what to do with it, or with her new glasses, only two weeks old: she took them off. Clear plastic frames, the only pair on the rack that didn't look ludicrous on her, meanwhile Clifford handed her one after another, each worse than the others. "These are quite attractive," he said. "These are real popular this year." Cat's-eyes with rhinestones, goggles, granny specs. *Why be picky at your age?* he seemed to be saying.

"Hi, Mama."

They hugged each other.

"I love you," they said. "I love *you*."

"So," said Clarence, sinking into the couch. Bill had sat in Clarence's chair. "How's that chair? Comfortable for you? What you been doing with yourself?" Then he remembered: drinks. Of course. "A drink!" he said. "You care for a drink?"

"Sure. What do you have?"

Clarence wasn't sure. Some bottles down the basement in an old library bookcase. Did it matter? "How about brandy?" he said. He thought he could make up one of those. "Fine."

Bill crossed his legs and tried to look comfortable. It was one-thirty. Four, five hours to go. Duane stuck his head in and saw him. "Oh, hi," he said and disappeared.

At the in-laws', Bill felt as if he had walked into the wrong class, medieval history instead of civics which he had studied for, and everyone but him knew the right answers. Names, dates, stories of which they only used the punch line ("I didn't know that was your horse!" "*Svensk*"), obscure references. If his wife had been offered a brandy, she'd say, "Just up to the first bird," referring to a childhood tumbler with four painted chickens down the side. *The whole town is like this*, he thought. *A cult*.

Duane didn't understand why he couldn't invite a friend of *his* to Thanksgiving, someone *he* could talk to. The answer was, "Because they have their own families."

"They see their families all the time. Maybe they'd like to get away once in a while."

"Some other time."

"But—"

"No."

Everything in the kitchen was the same except the mixer was moved to the counter by the stove. Barbara Ann found, to her not very great surprise, that she knew it by heart; she got the colander out and rinsed strawberries; the meat platter was on top of the fridge, the gravy boat down behind the cereal, the sieve was nesting in the mixing bowls. She got out the big bowl, moved the mixer back to its old home by the toaster, and was about to mash the potatoes when, on an impulse, she opened the small cupboard high over the sink. There was the little china Pilgrims, their log cabin, two pine trees, and one surviving Indian who looked like Uncle Stan. The smoke was broken off the cabin chimney where she had dropped it while setting the table eighteen years ago. Four people at that dinner were now dead: Grandpa B., Ryman and Monie, Aunt Faith. Grandpa sat on the couch and took her for a ride on a horse on his knee: "*Up* the hill—clop, clop, clop—and *down* the hill—clip-clop, clip-clop, clip-clop—and across the pasture, jiggety-jiggety-jig." When she broke off the smoke, the Pilgrims had no fire, they sat around eating sandwiches and devilled eggs. Her father's table grace was unchanged in her lifetime; it was: "Dear Heavenly Father, bless this food to our bodies and watch over all Thy children as we gather once again to give thanks for Thy love and Thy many gifts. Amen." Still, she thought she would try to steer him away from bacon and toward yogurt.

WINTER

When I was fifteen, a girl I wrote three poems for invited me to Christmas Eve so her parents could see that I wasn't as bad as many people said, and after a big meatball supper and a long thoughtful period between her dad and me as she and her mom cleared the dishes when he asked me what I intended to do with myself, we went to the ten o'clock candlelight service at Lake Wobegon Lutheran. My mind wasn't on Christmas. I was thinking about her. She had never seen the poems because they were too personal, so she didn't know how much I loved her.

The lights went out, and the children's choir began

its slow march up the aisle, holding candles and singing *"Hjemmet paa Prairien"* ("Home on the Prairie")—"To our home on the prairie, sweet Jesus has come. Born in a stable, he blesses his own. Though humble our houses and fortunes may be, I love my dear Savior who smiles on me"—and in the dark, the thin sweet voices and illuminated faces passing by, people began to weep. The song, the smell of pine boughs, the darkness, released the tears they evidently had held back for a very long time. Her mother wept, her father who had given me stony looks for hours bent down and put his face in his hands, her lovely self drew out a hanky and held it to her eyes, and I too tried to cry—I wanted to cry right along with her and maybe slip my arms around her shoulders—and I couldn't. I took out my handkerchief, thinking it would get me started, and blew my nose, but there was nothing there.

I only cried later, after I walked her home. We stood on her steps, she opened the door, I leaned toward her for one kiss, and she turned and said, "I hate to say this but you are one of the coldest people I ever met." I cried at home, in bed, in the dark. Turned my face to the wall and felt hot tears trickle down my face. Then woke up and it was Christmas morning.

Now an older guy, I've gotten more moist and when the decorations go up over Main Street from Ralph's north to the mercantile, I walk down alone to look at them, they are so beautiful—even old guys stand in wonder and are transported back to childhood, though of course these are the same decorations as when we were kids so it doesn't take much imagination. The six-foot plywood star with one hundred Christmas bulbs, twenty on each point, was built by Mr. Scheffelmacher's shop class in 1956; I flunked the quiz on electricity and didn't get to work on it. I sanded the edges a little, though I had flunked wood too. Later, I flunked the ballpeen hammer and was kicked out of shop and into speech class—Mr. Scheffelmacher said, "All you do is talk, talk, talk, so you might as well learn how." I begged him to let me stay in shop, which was getting into sheet metal and about to make flour scoops, but he said, "You couldn't even pass wood. You couldn't even make a decent birdhouse!" and he was right. My birdhouse leaked, and the birds were so mad about it, when I tried to caulk the roof, they attacked me, Mr. and Mrs. Bluebird. So I dragged myself into speech and had to make up the work I had missed: five speeches in one week: humorous, persuasive, extemporaneous, impromptu, and reflective, and suddenly, talking, which had been easy for me at the shop bench, became impossible. I dragged my feet to the front of the room, afraid my loafers would flap (they had been my brother's), and stood there, a ridiculous person six-feet-three and a hundred fifty pounds, trying to keep my jaw slack as I had practiced in a mirror to make up for a small chin, and mumbled and got hot across the eyes and had to say, "Anyway, as I started to say . . ." which Miss Perkovich marked you down for three points for because "Anyway" showed disorganization, so I failed speech, too, but speech was the end of the line—if you couldn't speak, where could you go? To reading? I sat in speech and drew stick men hanging on the gallows, listening to Chip Ingqvist's reflective, entitled "A Christmas Memory," which was about his dear old aunt whom he visited every Christmas, bringing sugar cookies, and was so good he did it twice in class and again for school assembly two weeks after Christmas and then in the district speech tournament, the regional, and the state, and finished first runner-up in the reflective division, and yet it always sounded so sincere as if he had just thought of it—for example, when he said, "And oh! the light in her eyes was worth far more to me than anything money could buy," a tear came to his voice, his eyes lit up like vacuum tubes and his right hand made a nice clutching gesture over his heart on his terrific brown V-neck sweater, which I mention because I felt that good clothes gave him self-confidence, just as the clothing ads said and that I might be sincere like him if instead of an annual Christmas sweater I got a regular supply. Anyway, Christmas decorations sure bring back a lot of memories for me.

Depending on your angle, the stars seem to lead the traveler toward the Sidetrack Tap, where the old guys sit and lose some memory capacity with a glass of peppermint schnapps, which Wally knows how to keep adding to so they can tell the old lady they only had one. After one of those continuous drinks, they try not to look at the bubble lights on the little aluminum tree on the back bar. Bud is there, who gets a twinge in his thighs around Christmas, remembering the year the ladder went out from under him as he was hanging decorations, and he slid down the telephone pole, which was somewhat smoother after he slid down than before. In addition to the large star, you see smaller ones that look like starfish, and stubby candles, and three wise men who in their wonder and adoration appear a little stupid, all made by shop classes on a jigsaw, and angels that, if you look at them a certain way, look like clouds. The manger stands in front of Our Lady church, the figures (imported from Chicago) so lifelike, it gives you the chills to see them outdoors—it's so cold, they should take their flight to Egypt! The municipal Christmas tree stands in front of the Statue of the Unknown Norwegian who seems to be reaching out to straighten it. It leans slightly toward the south, away from the wind.

One bitter cold night, a certain person stepped out of the Sidetrack Tap and crossed the street under the clear starry sky toward the gay lights of the municipal tree and noticed that he needed to take a leak. It was three blocks to home, and the cold had suddenly shrunk his bladder, so he danced over toward the Unknown and picked out a spot in the snow in the dark behind the tree where nobody would see him.

It was an enormous relief at first, of course, like coming up for air after a long submersion, but it also made him leery to be so exposed right out on Main Street. So many dark windows where someone could be watching, and what if a car came along? They'd know what was up. Him, profaning a monument to the Norwegian people. "I should stop—right now!" he thought. His capacity, though: it was amazing!

Like a horse. Gallons, already, and it didn't feel like he could put the cork back in. Then he saw the headlights. Only for a moment, then the car turned the other way, but in that moment he hopped six feet to one side and stood in shock until the taillights disappeared, and only then did he hear the hiss of liquid on the hot bulb and look and see what he was doing. He was peeing on the tree! Pissing on Christmas! Then the bulb burst. Pop!

'Oh God, what a pig I am!" he thought. He expected the big spruce to fall on him and crush him. Pinned under the tree, found the next morning, frozen to death with his thing in his hand. The shame to his family. The degradation of it. Finally he was done (*you pig!*). There was a stain in the snow as big as a bathtub, and another one where he had stood before. He dumped handfuls of clean snow on them, but it turned yellow. Then he walked home, got a snow shovel, came back, and carried his mess, shovel by shovel, across the street to the side of the Sidetrack Tap, and brought back shovels of clean snow to fill in. He smoothed it over and went home to bed.

It was not such a happy holiday for him for the recollection of what he had done (*pig*), which if any of his children had done it he would have given them holy hell. He bought them wonderful presents that year and a gold watch for his wife, and burned when they said what a great guy he was, and it wasn't until January after the tree came down that he started to feel like he could drop in at the Sidetrack Tap and relax with a couple of beers.

We get a little snow, then a few inches, then another inch or two, and sometimes we get a ton. The official snow gauge is a Sherwin-Williams paint can stuck to the table behind the town garage, with the famous Sherwin-Williams globe and red paint spilling over the Arctic icecap. When snow is up to the top of the world, then there is a ton of snow. Bud doesn't keep track of the amount beyond that point because once there is that much snow, more doesn't matter a lot. After the ton falls, we build a sled run on Adams Hill, behind the school, with high snow embankments on the turns to keep our sleds on the track at the thrilling high speeds we reach once the track is sprayed with water and freezes. Everyone goes at least once, even Muriel. Up at the Pee Tree, you flop on your belly on the sled and push off, down an almost straight drop of twenty feet and *fast* into a right-hand turn, then hard left, then you see the tree. It is in the middle of the track and will bash your brains out unless you do something. Before you can, you're in the third turn, centrifugal force having carried you safely around the tree, and then you come to the jump where some cookies are lost, and the long swooping curve under the swings, and you coast to a stop. You stand up and look down and see that you've almost worn the toes of your boots. You had the brakes on and you didn't notice.

At the swimming beach, the volunteer firemen have flooded the ice to make a glass sheet and hung colored lights in a V from the warming house to the pole on the diving dock. The warming house is open, the ancient former chickenhouse towed across the ice in 1937 from Jensens'; when he gave up poultry after some exploded from a rich diet that made their eggs too big. When Bud fires up the cast-iron Providence wood stove, a faint recollection of chickens emanates from the floor. The stove stands in the middle, the floor chopped up around it where decades of skaters stepped up and down to get feeling back in their feet, and the benches run around the walls, which are inscribed with old thoughts of romance, some of them shocking to a child: news that Mother or Dad, instead of getting down to business and having you, was skylarking around, planting big wet smackers (XXXXX) on a stranger who if he or she had hooked up with her or him you would not be yourself but some other kid. This dismal prospect from the past makes a child stop and think, but then—what can you do?—you lace up and teeter down the plywood ramp and take your first glide of the season. It's a clear night, the sky is full of stars and the brilliant V points you out toward the dark, the very place your parents went, eventually, holding hands, arms crossed, skating to the Latin rhythms of Cully Culbertson and His Happy Wurlitzer from the *Rexall Fun Time* album played through a mighty Zenith console put out on the ice, where some of the oldsters still cut a nice figure. Clarence and Arlene Bunsen, for two: to see him on the street, you'd know he has a sore back, but on the ice, some of his old form returns and when they take a turn around the rink in tandem, you might see why she was attracted to him, the old smoothie. Once two people have mastered skating the samba together, it isn't that much harder to just get married, says Clarence. She has bought a new pair of glasses, bifocals, that, when she looks at him, bring his ankles into sharp focus, slightly magnified.

In some homes, decorations don't appear until Christmas Eve afternoon, except for the Advent wreath on the supper table, its candles lit every night during supper. Catholics believe in abstaining before a feast—it sharpens the appetite—so Father Emil gives up his 9 P.M. finger of brandy for weeks so that his Christmas Eve brandy will taste more wonderful, even when Clarence brought him a bottle of Napoleon brandy far more wonderful than the Dominican DeLuxe Father buys for himself. "None for me," he said. "Oh, come on," Clarence said, 'you only live once." Clarence is Lutheran but he sometimes drops in at the rectory for a second opinion. It is Father's opinion, however, that a person does not only live once, so he put the Napoleon on his bookshelf behind *War and Peace* where he would remember it. Even on Christmas Eve, one finger is the correct portion, by him, and it's a miserable mistake to think that two would be twice as good, and three even better, or putting both hands around the bottle and climbing into it. That's no Christmas. The true Christmas bathes every little thing in light and makes one cookie a token, one candle, one simple pageant more wonderful than anything seen on stage or screen.

The Kruegers ask him over to watch the Perry Como Christmas special out of respect for their tremendous contributions over the years, he goes, and sits in glum silence watching tanned, relaxed people sing "O Little Town of Bethlehem" on a small-town street like none he's ever seen. A man appears on the screen to talk about Triumph television sets as the perfect Christmas gift, as behind him a viewing couple turn and beam at each other as if TV had saved their marriage. The Kruegers enjoy martinis, a vicious drink that makes them sad and exhausted, and the Mister gets up during commercials to adjust the picture, making it more lurid—greenish faces like corpses of the drowned, then orange, the victims of fire—and then the Krueger boy says, "Oh, *Dad*," and fixes it to normal, but even that looks lurid, like a cheap postcard. They sit, enraptured by it, but what dull rapture: not fifteen words spoken between them in the whole hour until, in the middle of "Chestnuts," the phone rings—it's Milly's sister in Dallas—and though it's only a commercial, Milly doesn't take her eyes off the screen, doesn't make a complete sentence, just says "uh-huh" and "oh" and "all right, I guess" as if the lady demonstrating the dish soap is her sister and her sister is the telephone salesman. A dismal scene compared to church, people leaning forward to catch the words coming from their children's mouths, their own flesh and blood, once babes in arms, now speaking the Gospel. What would the Kruegers do if during Perry's solo the doorbell rang and they heard children singing a carol on the porch?—would they curse them?

The German club from high school goes caroling, most of them Catholic kids but it's Luther they sing: *Vom Himmel hoch da komm ich her, Ich bring euch gute neue mar*. Luther League goes out, Catholic youth, Lutheran choir, Miss Falconer's high school choir, the Thanatopsians troop around and warble in their courageous ruined voices, Spanish Club, G.A.A., 4-H, even Boy Scouts sidle up to a few doors and whisper a carol or two. *O Christmas tree, O Christmas tree/How brightly shine thy candles*. The Scouts carry candles, which drip onto their jackets. Jimmy Buehler, Second Class, whose mother confiscated his phonograph because AC/DC's song "Highway to Hell" made her nervous, is their best singer; his sweet tenor leads the others. *And from each bough, a tiny light/Adds to the splendor of the sight*.

The carols that Miss Falconer's choir sings along Elm Street are a relief from the *Hodie* they practiced so hard for the Christmas assembly. Day after day, they sat and looked at the floor, which reeked of disinfectant, and breathed quietly through their mouths as she stood over them still as a statue, and said, "Well, maybe we should cancel the whole concert. I'm not getting one bit of cooperation from you." She sighs at the shame of it and folds her arms. In a school this small, you don't get to specialize: one day Coach Magendanz is trying to bring out the animal in you, and then you are Ernest in *The Importance of Being*, and then you are defending the negative in the question of capital punishment, and the next day you're attempting sixteenth-century polyphony. "Tenors, open your mouth, you can't sing with your mouths shut. Basses, read the notes. They're right in front of you."

So great is the town's demand for Christmas music,

some of them are going straight from this practice to Mrs. Hoglund's at the Lutheran church or to Our Lady choir practice and a different *Hodie* under Sister Edicta, a rehearsal in parkas in the cold choir loft, Father Emil having blanched at the latest fuel bill and turned the thermostat down to fifty-five. A cold Advent for Catholics, thanks to Emile Bebeau, the itinerant architect who designed this pile in 1878, no doubt intending the soaring vaulted ceiling to draw the hearts of the faithful upward; it also draws heat upward, and the parish is in hock to a Lutheran fuel-oil supplier. Father is dreaming of a letter from Publishers' Sweepstakes: "Dear Mr. Emil: It's our great pleasure to inform you—" or an emergency check from Bishop Kluecker, though Our Lady is not a diocesan parish but a mission of the Benedictines and Father reports to an abbot in Pennsylvania who observes the rule of silence, at least in financial matters.

The Son of Knute don't carol in person, God having given them voices less suitable for carols than for wallies and elmers, but they do sponsor a choir of fourth-graders who learn two Norwegian carols well enough to sing them in dim light and make the rounds in the snow after supper, alternating carols house to house. One is usually enough to make any Knute wipe his eyes and blow his nose—*Jeg er så glad hver julekveld, Da synger vi hans pris; Da åpner han for alle små, Sitt søte paradis.* ("I am so glad on Christmas Eve, His praises then I sing; He opens then for every child The palace of the King")—and two might finish him off for good. Even Hjalmar, who sat like a fencepost through little Tommy's rare blood disease on "The Parkers" while Virginia put her head down and bawled, even Hjalmar hears *Jeg er så glad hver julekveld;* his pale eyes glisten, and he turns away, hearing his mother's voice and smelling her *julekake,* the Christmas pudding, Mother sitting in a chair and working on her *broderi,* a pillowcase with two *engler* hovering over the *krybbe* where Jesus lies, the bright *stjerne* in the sky. "*Glade Jul!*" the fourth-graders cry, and back come Hjalmar's own boyhood chums in fragrant memory to greet him. "Hjally! Hjally!" they call, standing in the frame of bright windowlight on the brilliant snow of 1934.

Custom dictates that carolers be asked in and offered a cookie, a piece of cake, something to nibble, and so must every person who comes to your door, otherwise the spirit of Christmas will leave your house, and even if you be rich as Midas, your holiday will be sad and mean. That is half of the custom; the other half is that you must yourself go visiting. Everyone must get at least one unexpected visitor, otherwise they'll have no chance to invite one in and Christmas will be poorer for them. So, even if when they open the door, their thin smile tells you that you have arrived at the height of an argument, and even if, as you sit and visit, sulfurous looks are exchanged and innuendos drop like size—12 shoes, you are still performing a service, allowing them to try to be pleasant, even if they don't do it well.

Baking begins in earnest weeks ahead. Waves of cookies, enough to feed an army, enough to render an army defenseless, including powerful rumballs and fruitcakes soaked with spirits (if the alcohol burns off in the baking, as they say, then why does Arlene hide them from her mother?). And tubs of *lutefisk* appear at Ralph's meat counter, the dried cod soaked in lye solution for weeks to make a pale gelatinous substance beloved by all Norwegians, who nonetheless eat it only once a year. The soaking is done in a shed behind the store, and Ralph has a separate set of *lutefisk* clothes he keeps in the trunk of his Ford Galaxie. No dogs chase his car, and if he forgets to change his *lutefisk* socks, his wife barks at him. Ralph feels that the dish is a great delicacy and he doesn't find *lutefisk* jokes funny. "Don't knock it if you haven't tried it," he says. Nevertheless, he doesn't offer it to carolers who come by his house because he knows it could kill them. You have to be ready for *lutefisk*.

Father Emil doesn't knock *lutefisk*; he thinks it may be the Lutherans' penance, a form of self-denial. His homily the Sunday before: we believe that we really don't know what's best for us, so we give up some things we like in the faith that something better might come, a good we were not aware of, a part of ourselves we didn't know was there. We really don't know ourselves, our own life is hidden from us. God knows us. We obey His teaching, even though painful, entrusting our life to Him who knows best.

The faithful squirm when he says it. What comes next? they wonder. No Christmas this year? Just soup and crackers? Catholic children see Lutheran children eating candy that the nuns tell them they should give up until Christmas and think, "Ha! Easy for nuns to talk about giving up things. That's what nuns do for a living. But I'm twelve—things are just starting to go right for me!"

Lutherans also get a sermon about sacrifice, which the late Pastor Tommerdahl did so well every year, entitling it "The True Meaning of Christmas," and if you went to church with visions of sugarplums dancing in your head, he stopped the music. Santa Claus was not prominent in his theology. He had a gift of making you feel you'd better go home and give all the presents to the poor and spend Christmas with a bowl of soup, and not too many noodles in it either. He preached the straight gospel, and as he said, the gospel is meant to comfort the afflicted and afflict the comfortable. He certainly afflicted the Lutherans.

I only heard his sermon one year, and I liked it, being afflicted by Christmas, knowing how much I was about to receive and how little I had to give. I was ten, my assets came to eight bucks, I had twelve people on my list and had already spent three dollars on one of them: my father, who would receive a Swank toiletries kit with Swank shaving lotion, Swank deodorant, Swank cologne, Swank bath soap on a rope, and Swank hair tonic, an inspired gift. I walked into Detwiler's Drugstore and there it was, the exotic Swank aroma that would complete his life and bring out the Charles Boyer in him, so I said, "Wrap it up," and was happy to be bringing romance into his life until the cash register rang and I realized I had five bucks left and eleven people to go, which came to forty-five cents apiece. Even back then forty-five cents was small change.

I imagined a man walking up and giving me fifty dollars. He was fat and old and had a kind face. "Here," he said, and made me promise I wouldn't tell anyone. I promised. He gave me two crisp new twenty-five-dollar bills, a rarity in themselves and probably worth thousands. A Brink's truck raced through town, hit a bump, and a bag fell out at my feet. I called the Brink's office, and they said, "Nope. No money missing here. Guess it's your lucky day, son." Crystal Sugar called and said that the "Name the Lake Home" contest winner was me, and would I like the lake home (named Mallowmarsh) or the cash equivalent, fifteen grand?

But there's nothing like a sermon against materialism to make a person feel better about having less. God watches over us and loves us no less for knowing what we can't afford. I took the five dollars and bought small bottles of Swank lotion for the others, which smelled as wonderful as his. If you splashed a few drops on your face, you left a trail through the house, and when you came to a room, they knew you were coming. It announced you, like Milton Cross announced the opera.

Dad was so moved by his gift, he put it away for safekeeping, and thanks to careful rationing over the years, still has most of his Swank left.

Father Emil still has the bottle of Napoleon brandy.

I still have wax drippings on the front of my blue peacoat.

The *Herald-Star* still prints the photo of Main Street at night, snowy, the decorations lit, and underneath, the caption "O little town of Wobegon, how still we see thee lie"—the same photo I saw in the paper when I was a boy. That's Carl's old Chevy in front of Skoglund's, the one he traded in on the Chevy before the Chevy he's got now. He's sorry he traded it in because the new one is nothing but heartache. The one in the photo ran like a dream.

The Christmas pageant at Our Lady has changed a little since Sister Arvonne took the helm. Under Sister Brunnhilde, it was as formal as a waltz, but it had a flaw in that the speaking parts were awarded to the quietest, best-behaved children, while the rambunctious were assigned to stand in silent adoration, which often meant that the speakers of glad tidings were stricken with terror and had to be hissed at from the wings while a heavenly multitude stood by and smirked and poked each other.

Sister Arvonne is a reverent woman, like Sister Brunnhilde, but is much smaller and light on her feet, so her reverence takes other forms than kneeling, such as reform, for example. It was Arvonne who took the pruning shears and whacked the convent lilacs into shape; over-grown bushes that had been sloughing off for years she cut back and the next spring they got down to the business of blooming. So did she when the new edict came down on nun dress. She put her wimple on the bust of Newman and developed a taste for pants suits. Some old *Catholische* thought it was the end of the world, but looking at her, they could see it wasn't. She zipped around like it was eight o'clock in the morning. Around the same time, the new liturgy was greeted with a long low moan from the faithful and even from the unfaithful—Arvonne's sister Rosalie who had not uttered a Pater Noster since the early days of the Eisenhower administration nevertheless mourned the Latin mass as if it were her dear departed mother—but Arvonne didn't pause for a moment. "English," she told Rosalie, "is an excellent language. Look at Shakespeare. Look at Milton—hell, if a Congregationalist could write like that, think what you could do if you actually knew something."

Sister Brunnhilde had directed the pageant forever, and, massive woman that she was, seemed permanently in place, like a living pulpit, but Sister Arvonne bided her time, listened to Sister complain about how unappreciated and unacknowledged this annual burden was, sympathized with her, drew her out, and when she had drawn Sister so far out that she couldn't go back, Sister Arvonne sweetly sliced off the limb and took over.

She set out to cut down on smirking by creating more speaking roles. She brought in Zacharias and Elizabeth and tried to write some lines for Joseph:

No room?? But my wife is great with child!
Here, Mary. You lie down and I'll get the
    swaddling clothes.
Should we put the baby in the manger?
Is it a boy or a girl?

The last one appealed to her in a way, but all of them struck her as *forced* somehow and she gave up on him. She had never been clear about Joseph. The shepherds, too, were a problem. They had only one line, and as she well knew from her own acting experience, one line is harder than a hundred. You practice "Let us go to Bethlehem and see this thing which is come to pass, which the Lord has made known unto us" a hundred times, and yet there's no telling what will come out when it's your turn to shine. Intense rehearsal of one line may drive it deeper into the brain, to where you can't remember it that night and can't forget it for the rest of your life. She gave the shepherds a good speech from the Book of Isaiah.

"They'll never remember it," said Sister Brunnhilde who came to rehearsal one day to help out. "It's too complicated. They're all mumbling. Nobody will hear a word they're saying."

"It'll be beautiful. Besides, everybody knows the story anyway," said Sister Arvonne, and she was right of course.

A cloud of incense drifted down the center aisle behind Zacharias as he marched forward, praising God, his short arms upraised, swinging the censer like a bell, and the cloud enveloped him where he knelt at the steps to the altar, when the angel Gabriel jumped out and shouted, "Fear not!" Gabriel, exceedingly well dressed, announced that Z. would have a son, named John, who would be great in the sight of the Lord. "I am an old man!" cried Zacharias. And Gabriel struck him dumb, for his unbelief. His wife, Elizabeth, also old, helped him away, and you could tell that she believed they'd have a baby, she was counting the days. When the Blessed Virgin came in to grind corn, you could see that she was very shy, and you hoped the angel would speak softly. He waited in the shadows, adjusting his magnificent wings, grooming himself, and then walked up behind her. "Hail Mary, full of grace, the Lord is with thee. Blessed are thou among women." She fell down. He told her, "And behold thou shalt conceive in thy womb, and bring forth a son, and shalt call his name Jesus." He told her about Elizabeth, which seemed to make her feel better. She said, still lying on the floor, "Behold the handmaid of the Lord; let it be according to thy word."

Elizabeth helped her up, and they hugged each other. Mary said the Magnificat. John was born and Zacharias recovered his tongue and gave a speech about the tender mercy of God who had visited his people, to give light to them who sit in darkness in the shadow of death, to guide our feet into the way of peace. And then the lights went out for a spooky minute or two, during which you knew something had gone wrong and everything was about to come to a big crashing halt, but the lights came on and there was the manger and Mary and Joseph. Shepherds were lounging a little way away, where the angel made his third appearance, illumined by powerful beams, and cried, "Fear not!" and they all fell down. A heavenly choir joined him in song. Wise men appeared, coming up the aisle, uncertain whether they were doing the right thing. "Where is he that is born King of the Jews? For we have seen his star in the east and are come to worship him." They met the gang of shepherds going west and all went in together and knelt down at the manger. Gifts were given, prayers said, and some of the shepherds remembered most of the long prophetic passage from Isaiah. "Behold the Lamb of God who taketh away the sins of the world," one said.

And then silence. The children huddled together on their knees, heads bowed, such a peaceful sight and yet you wondered if it was the end or what came next—nobody moved, Mary and Joseph knelt like statues, nobody said a word. They remained in perfect adoration until the organ began to play and then, remembering that it was time to go, they got up and left, and the pageant was over.*

———————

The tree enters a few days before Christmas, a fresh one bought from Mr. Fjerde or Mr. Munch, two

———————

L. W. Lutheran once bought (by mistake) twenty copies of (rehearsed for almost a week) a Christmas pageant entitled "The New Christmas," in which, on page four, they found:

> And the spirit of truth came upon them, and it gave them a great brightness, and naturally they were worried. And the spirit of truth said, "Don't worry. I've come with good news that should make you really happy, for there is born today a child who shall be a symbol of new beginnings and possibilities. And suddenly there was the spirit of truth a multitude of truths, praising goodness and saying, "It's wonderful! Peace on earth and real understanding among people."

The purchase price was nonrefundable.

adjoining bachelor farmers who share a small forest of evergreens where you can cut one for yourself. Mr. Fjerde is a silent man, and when you bang on his door, your tree in hand, he won't even tell you the price; he waits to hear your offer and then nods or looks studious until you come up a dollar. But Mr. Munch will talk your ear off, and to hear him tell it, he never meant to raise Christmas trees, they simply snuck into his property one day, and if he ever has the time he'll clean them out with a backhoe.

"They grow like goddam weeds, you know," he says, "and they eat the hell out of your soil—that's good soil there, a guy oughta be doing something with it, it's a shame to let it go like I have. Goddam, I think next spring I maybe oughta get in there with some herbicide, get them cleaned out. Or I could burn them. *Ja*, I think maybe I'll burn them."

Mother can't bear to hear swearing, so she sits in the car with the windows rolled up and choir singing on the radio. "You stay here," she tells me, but I go with Dad up to Mr. Munch's back door for the thrill of it. Bachelor farmers disobey almost every rule my parents ever laid down; the yard is full of junk under the snow, including a broken-down sofa, a washing machine, an old icebox leaning against a tree with its doors hanging open and more junk inside it. A hill of old tin cans sits about a can's throw from the back door. Mr. Munch is unshaven, a cloud of white hair on his head; his clothes are dirty, brown juice runs down his chin, his breath smells of liquor. "He's not fit to live with decent people," Mother told me when I asked why he lived alone. And yet he seems to have gotten away with it; he is as old as my grandpa. God hasn't struck him with lightning, the way you might think.

He ducks into his little house to get two dollars' change from his cigar box, and I see that he does not clean his room either. Old breakfast scraps on the plate on the table—what a luxury to get up and walk away from a meal! He carefully counts out the two dollars into Dad's hand, and says, "You be careful with that tree now. Those things are like explosives, you know. I sold these people a tree, I think it was last year, and two days later they was all dead. It blew up one night and burned them all so you couldn't tell one from the other. I tell you I wouldn't have one if you paid me. Even fresh—they can go off like a bomb, you know. *Boom!* Just like that."

"Merry Christmas," Dad said.

"God help you," said Mr. Munch.

News of incendiary Christmas trees was no news to Mother. She knew all about fire hazards. Oily rags never spent a night in our house. A paintbrush in a can of thinner was allowed half an hour to get clean, and then the thinner went down the drain with fifty gallons of water behind it. Extension cords that looked frayed or suspicious were bound up in Scotch cellophane tape. A jar of flour sat on the counter by the stove, ready in case of fire; once, the gas flame under the spaghetti sauce flared up and Mother went for her flour, but we ate the sauce anyway—"It's only flour," she said, "same as in the noodles"—though it stuck to the roofs of our mouths like Elmer's glue.

344

Any unusual sound from the furnace, a wheeze or sigh, and she could see (1) fuel oil leaking on the floor and making an immense dark pool creeping closer and closer to the pilot, or (2) carbon monoxide drifting up the ducts and flowing invisibly into our lives. Our fireplace was used only under supervision, and even after she had doused the coals with water, she often couldn't sleep and tiptoed down and laid on another quart or two.

As a result, I grew up with a passion for fire and sometimes lit a few farmer matches in my room for the sheer pleasure of it, and one year, two days before Christmas, when the Mortensons' house burned down (they didn't *know* that the tree caused it, but it could've) when I was staying at Uncle Frank's farm, I felt terrible for having missed it. I also felt bad for wanting to have seen it, because they lost everything in the fire including all their presents, an awful tragedy, but nonetheless one I was sorry to miss.

Dad's fear was that Christmas would throw him into the poorhouse. Mother felt that each of us should get one big present every year in addition to the socks, Rook game, paddleball set, model, ocarina, shirt, miscellaneous gifts: one *big* one, like a printing press or a trike or Lincoln logs. Dad thought the ocarina should be enough for anybody. He for one had never been given a toy as a child but *made* his own toys, as everyone did then, out of blocks of wood and string and whatnot, and was content with them, so the thought that a boy *needed* a large tin garage with gas pumps out front and crank-operated elevator to take

345

the cars up to the parking deck was ridiculous to him and showed lack of imagination. "I don't want to know," he said when Mother walked in with a shopping bag full, but then he had a look, and one look made him miserable. "Twelve dollars? *Twelve dollars?*" He believed that spending was a tendency that easily got out of hand, that only his regular disapproval kept Mother from buying out the store. It all began with Roosevelt who plunged the country into debt and now thrift was out the window and it was "Live for today and forget about tomorrow' with people spending money they didn't have for junk they could do without and Christmas was a symptom of it. He went into the Mercantile to buy a pair of work socks and saw a German music box that made him wonder what the world was coming to. Eight dollars for a piece of junk that played "Silent Night," which was maybe worth seventy-five cents, but there was Florian Krebsbach buying the thing who owed money to a list of people as long as your arm. That was Christmas for you.

The twin perils of the poorhouse and the exploding tree made for a vivid Christmas. Where the poorhouse was, I didn't know, but I imagined it as a gray stone house with cold dank walls where people were sent as punishment for having too much fun. People who spent twelve dollars here and twelve dollars there, thinking there was more where that came from, suddenly had to face facts and go to the house and stay in it and be poor. I might go with Dad or I might be farmed out to relatives, if the relatives wanted me, which probably they wouldn't, so I'd live in a little cell at the poorhouse and think about all the times I had begged for Dad to buy me things. I would eat rutabagas and raw potatoes and have no toys at all, like Little Benny in *The Mysterious Gentleman; or, The Christmas Gruel; A True story of an Orphan in the East London Slums*, except that Little Benny was patient and never complained or asked anything for himself and was adopted by a kind benefactor and brought into a life of fabulous wealth and luxury in a Belgravia mansion, whereas I, a demanding and rebellious and ungrateful child, was heading in the opposite direction, toward the dim filthy room and the miserable pile of rags for a bed and the racking coughs of our poor parents, dying of consumption from hard labor to earn money to buy the junk I demanded.

On the other hand, the danger of Christmas-tree fire some night killing us all in our beds seemed to point toward a live-for-today philosophy, not that we necessarily should go whole-hog and buy everything in the Monkey Ward catalog, but certainly we could run up a *few* bills, knowing that any morning could find us lying in smoldering ruins, our blackened little bodies like burnt bacon that firemen would remove in small plastic bags. Simple justice demands that a person who dies suddenly, tragically, at a tender age, should have had some fun immediately prior to the catastrophe. If your mother yells at you and you go off on your bike feeling miserable and are crushed by a dump truck—that would be a much worse tragedy than if it had been your birthday and you had gotten nice presents, including the bike, and were killed in a good mood.

Then one Christmas I opened a long red package and found a chemistry set, exactly what I wanted, and sat and stared at it, afraid to look inside. For Mother to buy me one, given her feelings, was more than adventurous, it was sheer recklessness on her part, like a gift of Pall Malls and a bottle of whiskey. The year before, I tried to aim her toward the Wards deluxe woodburning kit, pointing out that I could earn money by making handsome Scripture plaques, but she said it was too dangerous. "You'll burn down the house with it," she said. So, a year later, to get a chemistry set, complete with Bunsen burner, fuel, a little jar marked "Sulphur," and who knew what else, I didn't dare show how happy I was. "Thank you," I said, humbly, and put it aside and tried to look interested in what other people were getting, afraid that if I got too excited about chemistry, she'd want to have a closer look at it.

After a little elaborate politeness, thanking her for the nice socks and wonderful underwear, admiring my sister's dollhouse, I slipped away to the basement and set up my laboratory on a card table next to the laundry tubs. The instruction book told how to make soap and other useful things I didn't need, and omitted things I was interested in, such as gunpowder and aphrodisiacs, so I was on my own. I poured some liquid into a peanut butter jar and dumped some white powder in it—it bubbled. I poured a little bit on the table as an experiment and it hissed and ate a hole in the leather, which made me think, if it had spilled on me it would have eaten my hands off down to the wrists. Would it eat the jar? Would it eat the drain pipe? Had the makers of Junior Scientist included chemicals so deadly they might destroy a house? Upstairs, everybody was enjoying Parcheesi, unaware of the danger. I got out a tube of thin metal strips that I thought must be solder, and lit a match to melt some onto a plastic cowboy to give him a coat of armor, but instead the strip burst into fierce white flame as bright as the sun—I dropped it on the floor and stomped it to bits. My cowboy's face was gone, his head a blackened blob drooped down on his chest—what I would look like if I kept fooling around. I packed away the chemistry set and stuck it on the shelf behind the pickled beets. Eight dollars wasted. My poor father. Little Benny sold matches on the streets of London in bitter weather to buy medicine for his sick father, but I was a boy who played with fire and came close to killing everybody. Poor me, too. My big present was a big joke. What was Mother thinking of?

I went upstairs and moped around in the doorway so they could see me, but they were too busy having a good time. I went up to my room to mope around up there, maybe someone would come and find me and ask what was wrong, but time passed and nobody did. Mother called up the stairs to ask if I was hungry, but when I yelled that I wasn't she didn't come to find out why. I went to the stairs to yell down that maybe I'd just go to bed, and as I was about to yell, I looked in the door to my sister's room and saw the dollhouse.

It was a two-story white house, two bedrooms upstairs, living room, dining room, and kitchen. I had helped her carry it to her bedroom and set it on the floor by her bed and arrange the furniture, and now the Peabodys were about to enjoy their Christmas dinner. Upstairs, their plastic beds were permanently made; downstairs, a perpetual fire glowed in the fireplace, their two tabby cats curled up on the floor.

Minutes later, the big olive-drab B–17 revved up its engines and roared off the flight deck and down the dark hallway. The poor helpless family, Phoebe and Pete Peabody and little Petey and Eloise, sat in their elegant dining room, their movable arms placed politely on the table, their smiling little faces turned toward the turkey, as the hum of the deadly aircraft came closer and closer. Their great protector was miles away, engrossed in Parcheesi. They sat in pathetic dignity as the craft circled overhead and finally came in on its bombing run, dropping tons of deadly Lincoln logs. Pete was the last to die, sitting at the head of the table, a true hero, and then it was all over and Christmas lay in ruins with clouds of smoke rising from it, and the bomber returned to the carrier, its crew jabbering and laughing in Japanese. But little Petey wasn't dead! He rose painfully from under a pile of furniture and limped out of the house. He was badly injured and would have to spend some time in a hospital until his burns healed, but somehow he would get over his frightful loss and grow up and be a normal, happy person.

After Christmas, time drifted awhile; beyond Christmas there was nothing to look forward to. The tree got dry and was finally hauled out half-naked of needles and I set it on fire. New Year's Day was an imitation, Christmas without gifts, and New Year's Eve passed without much notice, Mother and I trying for three years to stay awake by playing Parcheesi until one year we made it over the top to midnight. On the radio at eleven, Ben Grauer came on from Times Square to narrate the amazing descending ball of light that marked the New York New Year, and Guy Lombardo and his Royal Canadians played from the Waldorf, which was exciting to imagine—the elegant Ben in a tuxedo standing on the rooftop watching the meteor fall, the handsome Guy and his band in their scarlet tunics like Sergeant Preston's, playing saxophones on horseback, their faithful huskies lying nearby—but it would have been more exciting to watch it on television, which we didn't have. At midnight our time, nothing happened. Mother and I hoisted a glass of grape Kool-Aid. I said, "Here's mud in your eye," and tossed it back, screwed up my face, and said, "Ha!" "Where'd you get that?" she said. On television, of course. She reminded me that watching television was as bad as going to the movies. The next morning she went next door to the Holmbergs' to borrow sugar and visited awhile and watched some of the Tournament of Roses.

Christmas, years later. I got five dollars from Grandma, a big raise from the one dollar she gave to little kids, and bought a bottle of Jade East cologne with it, the kind Chip Ingqvist used, the name of which I found out by making fun of him for smelling like rotten fruit. "It's Jade East," he said, smiling his superior Ingqvist smile. "It's what they wear at the U." With a splash of it on my neck and wearing the new Christmas sweater, I headed for the skating rink after supper, feeling like I was cut out for romance. I was sixteen. Six feet, three inches tall, and I walked with a peculiar springing stride, like a pogo stick, which sometimes I looked behind me and saw a little kid imitating. The Jade East was supposed to take care of that, and also I tried to saunter.

The town was buried in three feet of snow. Downtown was dark except for the Sidetrack where a red sign flashed "BEE . . . BEE . . . BEE" inside the strips of orange and green neon around the front window. The lamp over the door made a cone of light, as if the step were a stage and Mr. Berge might emerge, sway back and forth, and say, "O what a noble mind is here o'erthrown!", but only Ronnie came out. He pulled his collar up and his stocking cap down and headed the other way. It was so cold, he got small as he walked, contracting his middle, like a turtle pulling himself in.

So still on a cold night. I could hear his boots crunch in the snow, could hear a car not quite starting a long way away, and then the door slamming when the guy got out and him hitting the hood with his fist. The volume of the world was turned up so the air molecules hummed a deep bass note. If the fire siren went off it would knock a person into the middle of next week. The moon rose over the frozen lake; the light seemed to come out of the snow. Buried in three feet of light. And colors jumped out, hundreds of lovely shades of shadows, browns and grays and blacks. If a woman with bright red lipstick appeared, a person would fall over backward.

On this cold night, the skating rink was a carnival. The music I could hear when I left my house, and now I saw the long V of colored lights hung out across the rink from the warming house. Its windows blazed white. Pairs of skaters flowed counterclockwise in a great loop to "The Blue Skirt Waltz," and little kids buzzed around the big slow wheel as it turned. I looked for the girl I loved, who I had met the night before.

She was older, eighteen or nineteen, and had worn bright lipstick and sat down beside me in the warming house and slowly unlaced her leather boots and took them off and then her socks. My face turned red. In the Age of Imagination, before the Age of Full Disclosure, the removal of any article of clothing was inspirational. She was a cousin of the Ingqvists, up from Minneapolis for Christmas break, and had a way about her that set her apart. Her hair, for example, was jet-black and cut short as a man's. She wore a short skirt and tights, but unlike other girls whose tights were lumpy from long johns, hers were tight. She leaned against me and said, "Got a cigarette?" No girl asked me that before, because I didn't smoke, but for her sake, I said, "Yeah," thinking I *might* have one—it certainly was worth a look, and who would say no at a time like that?—then said,

"Oh, I just remembered. I forgot mine at home." She said, "Oh, well. I think I got two in my purse." She offered one to me. I didn't smoke, but then I was young, I'd been held back, it was time to get started on these things, so I said, "Thanks." She gave me the book of matches. As I lit one and held it toward her mouth, she held my hand to steady it, and although I knew that you didn't make babies this way, two hands together holding a match, I thought it must be similar. We took deep drags and blew out big clouds of smoke, then she leaned back and inhaled again, and I leaned forward and put my head between my knees. Not sick exactly, I was simply appreciating it more than most people do. I was sixteen, I experienced everything deeply.

This night she was there again, sitting on the bench against the wall, with my friend Jim who was not smoking but who was inhaling her smoke as deeply as he could. "Dorene's from Minneapolis," he told me. I ignored him. "I got to show you something," I told her. "Whenever you're done here.'

As we walked up the hill toward Main Street, I wasn't so sure what I could show her in Lake Wobegon that would be interesting, so I made up a story about a woman named Lydia Farrell who had lived here in love with the memory of a boy who had drowned. I picked out Florian Krebsbach's house as the home where Lydia spent fifty years in solitude, cherishing the few brief moments she spent with young Eddie before his boat overturned in a sudden storm. The moral was that we must seize our few bright moments and live deeply. It surprised me, how easily I did this and kept her interested. We walked up to the Ingqvists, both enjoying Lydia's sweet sad life, and then she asked me if I skied. I said, "Sure." I never had, but how would I know I couldn't unless I tried? So the next afternoon, I was squeezed next to her in the back seat of the Ingqvists' Lincoln, Chip driving, eight of us in the car, going goodness knows where.

Unbelievable to me, being in the same car with Ingqvists and that whole Ingqvist crowd, sharp dressers in those Norwegian ski sweaters you couldn't find in town and who never had asked me before so much as to come in their house. But Dorene, who was even finer than they, had seen something in me. She was from Minneapolis but had spotted some personal quality of mine that other people had never seen, and I was determined not to let her down. I imagined her turning to me with a smoky Minneapolis look and saying, "Kiss me," and so had practiced kissing, using my thumb and forefinger as practice lips. I had also gone to the library and skimmed through a book about skiing. I felt prepared to do either one.

A long drive during which they all talked about college and how much harder it was than high school. "You have to study six or seven hours a day," Chip said. I said I didn't think it was so hard. They laughed: 'What do you know?" I said I'd read a lot of college books. "Like *what?*" A lot of different things, I said. Dorene held my hand. She said, "It isn't hard for everybody. Some people have a harder time in high school, then they do real good in college."

I was grateful for that, but by the time we got to where we were going, I was much less confident about everything. It was dark. A plywood Swiss chalet sat between two spruce at the end of the parking lot, and beyond it strings of lights ascended a hill much steeper than what seemed possible in Minnesota. (Maybe we were in Wisconsin.) They got their skis off the car carrier. I was going to say, "That's all right, you go ahead, I feel like I'm coming down with something. I'll just wait in the building. I'll be okay. You go ahead"—and then she put a pair of skis and ski poles in my hands and said, Let's go, so I went.

I put on the skis, which she refastened so they wouldn't fall off, and showed me where to stand, next to her, holding hands, and the big wheel groaned in the wheel house and the bench came up behind and scooped us up and we rose into the dark. "I can't ski," I said; she said, "I know." We kissed. We slid off at the top and I staggered after her to the edge of the precipice where Chip Ingqvist stood, adjusting his binding. He grinned at me and flung himself off. She told me to relax, stay loose, bend my knees, and if I lost my balance to just sit down—and she jumped over the edge and I did too, and followed her down in a series of short rides. Skiing, sitting down, skiing. I lost momentum in the sittings so at the bottom where other skiers flashed across the flats to the chalet and plowed to a stop, I had to walk. She was gone when I got there. I sat in the chalet for an hour with some people from Minneapolis who hoped they could make it to Colorado in February, then she appeared, limping. She twisted her ankle while getting off the lift and had made the long trip down in pain. I examined it as if ankles were my specialty, a top ankle man called in from Minneapolis. "Can you walk on it?" I asked. She said, "I don't want to sit in here with all these people feeling sorry for me," so we went to the car, her arm around my neck, mine around her waist. We sat in the car for awhile. After awhile, I said, "I never did this before," but she seemed to be aware of that.

January. It was cold—got down to thirty-some below a couple nights, according to old guys who get up to pee—so that when Lyle turned the key in the ignition, his blue Impala gave a low moan, like Roland Park in *Blood on the Saddle* when he saved Don Decatur's life by jumping between him and the outlaw ambush at the Little Crazy River and lay in the tumbleweeds and Don said, "Take it easy. Don't try to talk. You're going to be all right," but you knew Roland was a goner when he let out that moan. Then he sagged in Don's arms and went limp. So there was no getting around it: the car was dead.

She was a good car. Lyle bought her in 1978, six years old but in terrific shape thanks to Virginia Ingqvist's fear of driving after she totaled a previous Chevy, even Lyle's brother-in-law Carl Krebsbach, a shrewd man about cars, agreed that Lyle got a heck of a good deal. Lyle just didn't have the knack of starting her up on cold mornings. His tendency was to get angry and flood the carburetor. Of course he had jumper cables, like everybody else, but that required a live car to start his deadster, most likely

Carl's next door, and Lyle cringed at the thought of asking. Carl's Chevy pickup roared to life every morning; Lyle heard it as he shaved, and sometimes he nicked himself. It made a sound like "nonagenarian-rn-rn-rn." Carl gunned it a few times—in a boastful way, Lyle thought, like a lion roaring after intercourse. And then Carl would come over, let himself into the kitchen, pour a cup of coffee, and offer to start Lyle's. Or he said, "Where's your keys?" and just went out and did it. "Don't bother, I don't need the car today," Lyle said, "I feel like walking," but Carl believed a car should be started in cold weather whether you drove it or not.

Sometimes Carl poked his head in the garage as Lyle stood at the side of his dead pal. Carl opened the hood and fiddled with the carburetor, and said, "Here, let me try it," and the car picked up its head and started. Maddening. An impossible problem, you're resigned to it, and then a cheerful guy reaches over casually with one hand and solves it. Lyle is the science teacher at the high school, he can explain cold, but he can't accept it, having grown up in Torrance, California. He's lived in Minnesota since 1971, a transplant that didn't take. Even now, when December rolls around and the first blizzard rolls in from Montana as regular as the North Coast Limited, he looks out the window and wonders, "What's going on here? What's the matter?" And when it's thirty below, he feels that something is definitely wrong. Then cool Carl shows up in his immense parka and insulated rubber boots and a big grin on his face and says, "It's a cold one. Boy, I think we mighta set a record."

Carl has the golden touch. Once Carl caught a walleye off Art's Point that raced toward the boat and leaped almost into Carl's arms. Landed in the boat, and later when Carl cleaned him he found an Indian-head penny, a high school ring (class of 1954, which was Carl's class), and a piece of tinfoil off a bottle of pink champagne *that Carl himself had drunk*. Late one night in 1955, trying to get over the girl he had given his ring to who had told him to get lost. She took the ring off her necklace and threw it in the lake. "There. Go get it," she said. Carl was heartbroken. He returned to the spot with his champagne, got drunk, couldn't remember what he had done with the foil. Now he knew. Both had come back to him by way of a tremendous fish as a sign that his life would be happy. He kept the ring and the penny and threw the foil back in the lake, for more good luck. "I've got the ring right here if you want to see it," he told Lyle. It fit him perfectly. Lyle was amazed. "And the fish?" he asked. "In the freezer," Carl said. He looked straight at Lyle: "Now that's what I call fishing."

Once a deer walked up behind Carl as he stood in the woods the first Saturday of deer-hunting season, waiting for a deer. ("You know that road about a hundred yards beyond Winkler's? Little dirt road heads west off the gravel? Well, you go beyond that and to your right you'll see a road goes east, just a couple ruts in the weeds. You follow that into the woods and it comes to a foundation where this guy is supposed to have lived with a Chippewa woman who was a faith healer. She could talk it right out of people, TB, cancer, heal broken bones, anything, but he was jealous and he killed her and he set fire to the house and burned himself up. You can't miss the foundation, there's an old rusted-out woodstove sitting in the middle of it—you go beyond that and there's a path goes between two chestnut trees and up the hill. You can see the water tower from the hill. You head in the opposite direction and you come down into a ravine. It's an old creek bed. That's where I was.") He was waiting for his deer when he felt a cold nose touch his hand. He did the standing broad jump, bounced off a birch tree, turned around and saw the deer. A doe, a big one. His first thought was that she had escaped from the Pet-the-Tame-Deer Park on Highway 10, and his second was that his three cousins from Minneapolis were near by who he left because he was nervous being around them the way they carried their rifles. Eugene had a way of gesturing with his that gave Carl the willies: "I'll go this way and you head up *there*" and jabbed the thing and the muzzle was looking straight at Carl's gut. Carl knocked it away and grabbed Eugene's jacket and called him an idiot. Eugene's brothers, Dave and Nick, thought Carl was being harsh. Carl walked away from them. Now he thought he didn't want to be near anything that moved, with the cousins around God knows where, and especially not a deer. He walked away, she followed. He turned and clapped, but evidently she'd been trained to come when someone clapped. He ran a little ways down the ravine and up the bank to the edge of a meadow, she had no trouble keeping up. He lay down in the tall grass, hoping she'd get bored and go away, but she stood and looked down at him with her big brown eyes. *Git! Go on! Shoo! Haw!* He was afraid she'd step on him and break his arm. That'd be a good one: "How'd you break your arm, Carl?" "Deer stepped on it." "Oh, where were you?" "In the woods, deer hunting." The deer nuzzled his pockets. He gave her half of a Salted Nut Roll. He said, "Look, it's not supposed to be this way." He felt like he was in a Walt Disney cartoon. She stood over him, drooling Nut Roll, her front legs straddling his leg, looking down at him. ("Her face was as close as yours is to mine, and I've seen deer before but not like this one, her eyes looked almost human. And then I knew what I had to do. I didn't want to but I had to. So I got up and did it before I changed my mind.")

"You didn't," Lyle said.

"Of course I did. She didn't have anything going for her, nothing. No fear. She wouldn't run. She was just as trapped as if she was hitched to a tree. If she walked up to my cousins, they'd shoot her of course but they'd hit her in the rear end, and *then* she'd run, and she'd crawl off in the bushes and die for the rest of the day. I shot her in the back of the head and she dropped like a stone, she didn't even twitch. I cleaned her and carried her to the truck. I gave her to the Dieners. I couldn't see eating her myself. And I never went hunting with those jerks again."

This seemed brutal to Lyle, but also possibly heroic. The sureness of it. *He knew what he had to do and he got up and did it before he changed his mind.* But also brutal. He asked Carl how it felt, what were his feelings at the time. Carl said, "I don't know what you mean."

Lyle asked his sister-in-law Margaret one day if she was ever worried that Carl might go over the edge. Lyle had read about guys who suddenly went crazy with a shotgun, which he didn't mention to her, not wanting to alarm her, but he thought Carl was possibly the type.

She said, "He went over the edge when he met me."

One fine day in 1957 they went to see *Dracula* at the Alhambra, which she had seen before, and right when the French doors were open in the young woman's boudoir, the curtains blowing in, the mist rolling up from the moors, the bat flew in, and suddenly Dracula was bending over the bed—right then she leaned over and kissed Carl on the neck.

She had thought of Carl as a calm fellow until then. In fact, it was one of her few remaining doubts about him as a husband, that he might be too calm. Other faults she had improved. He smoked so much at first he smelled like burnt toast, and his hair oil was 10W-30, and she changed all that and also helped him learn to eat food and converse at the same time, quite a trick for a boy from a big family whose only sound at dinner was rhythmic chewing and swallowing. It was hard getting him to say much, though, and she wondered if he might be a little on the dull side, a man with nerves of wood, until she kissed him on the neck and found out that he had deep reserves of nervous energy. In one second, he distributed the box of popcorn over six rows of seats.

To Lyle, winter was frightening. He woke up cold in the morning. Somehow he and Janice didn't make enough heat together, and then there was the slab of ice on the window that got thicker every day. It was too cold to get out the ladder and put on the storm window, and besides Carl might see him and come over and do it right. As he pulled on his pants (the floor was cold, too), he thought about the plumbing. They kept a trickle dripping out of each faucet at night to prevent frozen pipes, but you never could tell. A good pipe freeze could run a guy a few hundred bucks for new plumbing. Stumbling downstairs, he thought he caught the smell of dead car in the air. He cranked the thermostat up to eighty, and down below the old furnace creaked and throbbed in its bowels and shook like a dog shitting a peach pit. One day it too would die and what would he do then? He was in debt for ten other things already, including his wife's orthodontist, a mealy-mouthed guy she met at a Catholic Action meeting who talked her into getting braces (they were cold, too). He owed money on the Chev (deceased). It'd be a cold day in hell before the bank would give him more, a schoolteacher with four kids and a wife with braces and a chickenfeed salary.

In November, everything starts to go downhill, and you can't stop it, it's going to slide as far as it's going to slide. Lyle's philosophy of winter. Nature out of control. What scared him sometimes was the thought that others might be affected even more than he—

Carl? Maybe not. Maybe an older gent, living alone, "a very quiet nice man" the dumb neighbors would tell police when it was all over, the sudden sniper attack from an upstairs window, the quiet old psychopath picking off children with his .22 as they trudged home in the twilight. A man did that once, maybe North Dakota. He was innocent on grounds of being wacko. There were a number of little houses in town whose windows were dark. Who lived there and what was going through their minds? In the olden days, minds snapped in winter like twigs and the authorities sent wagons out to the small towns and farms to round up cases for the asylum, so what was—And then he heard the kitchen door open. Big boots and a jingle of keys. "Hey!" he yelled. The door slammed. By the time he got to the kitchen, he heard his car start up. Carl revved it a couple times.

"That's hard on the carburetor," Lyle thought. He went upstairs to take a shower so he wouldn't have to thank him.

January, olden days. Jim and I were in the woods by the lake, talking about bears, and I was so scared, I had to pee. I unzipped my pants and took it out—he said, "Don't! It'll freeze! In midair!" just as I made the golden arc, and for one split second, I imagined it freezing and got so scared, I almost crapped. Even now, I sit up straight at the memory.

"Watch out for icicles," my mother said, but she

didn't mean *that* icicle, she meant the fifty- and hundred-pounders that hung from the eaves, that came to a wicked sharp point. "One of those falls down, it could go right through your head." A huge one hung over the back door, and I thought about it when I put my boots on and stood with my hand on the knob. A boy on his way to school! A good boy! Being careful to slam the door shut behind him, he loosens the giant icicle and its point, sharp as an ice pick, slams all the way through his skull and down into his heart, the huge butt of the missile splitting his head like a tomato. "He didn't stand a chance," the sheriff said, standing over the small, still form, one white hand still clutching a bookbag that contained the dead boy's assignments, which were posthumously awarded gold stars.

I left the house fast, escaping that death, but other deaths waited for me. Icicles in the trees: you couldn't watch out for them *and* watch out for holes and bear traps. Holes in the ice on the river: you couldn't see them under the snow, but one misstep and suddenly you'd be in freezing water under the ice, no way to come up for air. Holes in the ice on the lake: we fished in them with a dropline, but what if a giant snapper yanked on the line and pulled you through? It was a small hole, and all your flesh would come off.

Older children told stories about pump handles and kids who put their tongues on them. You put your tongue on a pump handle when it's so bitterly cold, the spit freezes, you're stuck there. Then either they pull you away, ripping your tongue off, or else pitch a tent over you and wait for spring and hope for the best. It scared us little kids, the thought that one day during recess we might forget and put our tongue on the handle—who knows how these things happen? Maybe an older kid would make us do it. Maybe we would just forget—one moment of carelessness, and *glurrp*, you're stuck, and the teacher has to grab your head and, *rrrrrrip*, there's your little red tongue hanging from the handle. When you're little you believe that evil can somehow reach out and suck you in, so maybe you'd be lured toward that pump—maybe it would speak, "Hey kid, c'mere. Stick out your tongue," and put you in a trance.

So we little kids stayed away from behind the school where the pump was, and when we went out for recess, we kept our mouths shut. We did this, knowing also that a person who breathes through his mouth can freeze his lungs. You should always breathe through your nose: the nose warms up the air. You swallow air so cold through your mouth, suddenly there is a little chunk of ice in your chest where your lungs were. There are no last words when a person dies that way. You stand frozen in your tracks, a little blood leaks out your mouth, and you topple over in the snow.

One January morning, Rollie Hochstetter went in to town for a new belt for his woodsaw and got back home to find a couple dozen chickens, ducks, and geese strewn on the snow between the henhouse and the tool shed, their throats ripped open and blood spattered around where they'd been dragged and shaken, and all the other livestock in an uproar, even the Holsteins who looked like they'd been to the horror show. A pack of wild dogs did it. Rollie found dog tracks, and his neighbors said they had seen big dogs roaming in the woods, former pets who went bad, who hit Rollie's because he had no dog to guard the place since Rex died.

It was a caution to all, especially to us children who walk to Sunnyvale School just west of Rollie's, some of us with a half-mile hike each way. A lot crosses your mind when you're eight years old and the light is dim and the road goes through dark woods and there are wild dogs around, even if older children are with you.

In fact, it's worse with older children. They're the ones who say, as you trudge down the hill toward the ravine, "It's breakfast time for those dogs, you know. They're probably real hungry now. You know, they can smell food miles away. And they can tear your flesh off in about two minutes."

"They are more afraid of us than we are of them," you say, but you know it's not possible for a creature to be more afraid than this. "Not when they're hungry, they aren't," they say. "When they're hungry, they can run as fast as forty-three miles per hour, and they go straight for the throat, like this—" and someone screams in your ear and grabs your neck. *Cut it out! Leave me alone!*

You look down the road to the dark ravine, watching for slight branch movement, as if spotting the dogs would make a difference. You are dressed in a heavy snowsuit and boots like two club feet. You couldn't outrun a snow snake. Then they say, "If they do come, I think we should give them one of the little kids and maybe they'll let the rest of us go." And then one of them yells, "Here they come!" and they push you down in the ditch and everyone gallops down the road and through the ravine, girls screaming, lunchboxes banging.

Oh, yes, I remember that very well. I remember who did it, and I'm sure they remember too. I don't get letters from those older children saying, "Sure enjoy your show. Remember me? We went to school together." They know I remember.

Winter is absolute silence, the cold swallows up sound except for your feet crunching and your heart pounding. And sharp cracks in the distance, which could be ice or trees or could be the earth itself. A planet with hot molten rock at the middle, that is frozen solid at the top—something has to give. The earth cracks wide open and people disappear in it. Limbs fall off trees and pin you to the ground. You walk into deep holes full of snow. You step into a bear trap covered with snow. Snap! it breaks your leg. You step into a deep hole, and there's a bear in it, a bear who has eaten nothing but dirt for weeks. He chews your arms off first and then eats your head.

Of course, if the Communists came, there wouldn't be anything you could do. They would line us up in the playground and give us a choice: either say you don't believe in God or else put your tongue on the pump handle. What would you do then? You could say, "I don't believe in God," and cross your fingers, but then how would God feel? Maybe He would turn you into a pillar of salt, like Lot's wife. Or an icicle.

After sixth grade, I left Sunnyvale and rode the bus in to Lake Wobegon High in town, where Mr. Detman was principal, a man who looked as if wild dogs were after him and a giant icicle hung over his head. Worry ate at Mr. Detman. He yelled at us when we ran downstairs, believing we would fall and break our necks and die on the landing. He imagined pupils choking on food and wouldn't allow meat in the lunchroom unless it was ground up. He had his own winter fear—that a blizzard would sweep in and school buses be marooned on the roads and children perish, so, in October, he announced that each pupil who lived in the country would be assigned a Storm House in town. If a blizzard struck during school, we'd go to our Storm Home.

Mine was the Kloeckls', and old couple who lived in a little green cottage by the lake. She kept a rock garden on the lake side, with terraces of alyssum, pansies, petunias, moss roses, rising to a statue of the Blessed Virgin seated, and around her feet a bed of marigolds. It was a magical garden, perfectly arranged; the ivy on the trellis seemed to move up in formation, platoons of asters and irises along the drive, and three cast-iron deer grazed in front: it looked like the home of the kindly old couple that the children lost in the forest suddenly come upon in a clearing and know they are lucky to be in a story with a happy ending. That was how I felt about the Kloeckls, after I got their name on a slip of paper and walked by their house and inspected it, though my family might have wondered about my assignment to a Catholic home, had they known. We were suspicious of Catholics, enough to wonder if perhaps the Pope had ordered them to take in little Protestant children during blizzards and make them say the Rosary for their suppers. But I imagined the Kloeckls had personally chosen me as their storm child because they liked me. "Him!" they had told Mr. Detman. "In the event of a blizzard, we want that boy! The skinny one with the thick glasses!"

No blizzard came during school hours that year, all the snowstorms were convenient evening or weekend ones, and I never got to stay with the Kloeckls, but they were often in my thoughts and they grew large in my imagination. My Storm Home. Blizzards aren't the only storms and not the worst by any means. I could imagine worse things. If the worst should come, I could go to the Kloeckls and knock on their door. "Hello," I'd say. "I'm your storm child."

"Oh, I know," she'd say. "I was wondering when you'd come. Oh, it's good to see you. How would you like a hot chocolate and an oatmeal cookie?"

We'd sit at the table. "Looks like this storm is going to last awhile."

"Yes."

"Terrible storm. They say it's going to get worse before it stops. I just pray for anyone who's out in this."

"Yes."

"But we're glad to have you. I can't tell you. Carl! Come down and see who's here!"

"Is it the storm child??"
"Yes! Himself, in the flesh!"

NEWS

The Lake Wobegon *Herald-Star* (formerly the *Star*, then the *Sun*, then bought by Harold Starr in 1944) is published every Tuesday and mailed second-class to some fifteen hundred subscribers, most of whom don't live there anymore (and wouldn't if you paid them) but who shell out $30 a year to read about it. They're Harold's bread and butter: retirees in Tampa and Tucson and San Diego, who keep track of old chums through the obituaries; and people who ran away from home to escape winter and much more, for whom the paper (a gift subscription from Mother) is fresh evidence of a life worth leaving; and then the ones lured away by the pleasures of school and good money, who can afford to be nostalgic.

This ghostly crowd is fascinating to Harold, even their personal checks are fascinating, he wishes he could afford to hang onto them. Violet checks, emerald checks, russet, puce, buff, robin's-egg blue, charcoal gray, fuchsia, lapis lazuli, saffron, apricot, peach, burgundy, tangerine; some are dappled, flecked, stippled, even scented (lilac, orange, pine), printed on a landscape, pictures of ocean or mountains (one printed on a pine forest so dark he could barely make out the amount); some come with a saying, "Work is love made visible (Gibran)" or "Have a nice day" or "The Lord is my Shepherd; I shall not want," and one arrived with "If a man does not keep pace with his companions, perhaps it is because he hears a different drummer—Thoreau" printed across the bottom in cursive type against a ferny background, it came from a former Leonard halfback now living on Bonnie Brae Drive in Fresno. The *streets!* Harold has readers on Melody Lane, Flamingo Way, Terpsichore Terrace,* West Danube

---

*Terpsichore Terrace is the address of the former Wobegonian who wrote 95 *Theses* 95, a neatly typed manifesto that he brought home in late October 1980, along with a fine woman from Boston whom his parents wanted to meet, since he had married her a few weeks before. His parents live in a little white house on the corner of Branch and Taft, where his old bedroom under the eaves has been lovingly preserved. He left his wife to look at it and snuck away to the Lutheran church, intending to nail the 95 to the door, a dramatic complaint against his upbringing, but

Pass, Ventura Vista, Arcadia Crescent, Alabaster Boulevard—look at the checks, it's as if everyone who left town resolved never to live on a numbered street or an avenue named for a President or a common plant, nor on a Street or Avenue *period*, but on Lanes, Circles, Courts, Alleys, Places, Drives, Roads, Paths, Rows, Trails, with names like Edelweiss, Scherzo, Galaxy, Mylar, Sequoia, Majorca, Cicada, Catalpa, Vitalis, Larva, Ozone, Jasper, Eucalyptus, Fluorine, Acrilan, Andromeda—an atlas of the ideal and fantastic, from Apex, Bliss, and Camelot through Kenilworth, Londonderry, Malibu, Narcissus, to Walden, Xanadu, Yukon, and Zanzibar,

---

then something in his upbringing made him afraid to pound holes in a good piece of wood, and he heard the Luther Leaguers inside at their Halloween pizza party and was afraid he would be seen—also, he was afraid the 95 would blow away since all he had were small carpet tacks. So he took it downtown and slipped it under Harold Starr's door with a note that said, "Probably you won't dare publish this."

Harold considered publication twice—first, when his pipes froze and the office toilet burst, putting the Linotype out of commission and leaving him short of copy, and again when he had three wisdom teeth pulled and sprained his ankle, which he had hooked around the pedestal of the dentist's chair, and had to use crutches for three days during which he heard the same joke about those teeth having long roots more than thirty times—but he held off, and the 95 remains on his desk, in a lower stratum of stuff under council minutes and soil conservation reports.

In the same stack are some letters from the anonymous

plus all the forestry variations, Meadowglade, Mea-
dowdale, Meadowglen, -wood, -grove, -ridge. *Look
at this!* A check from Earl's boy, Arlen, the little turd
who tried to set the woods on fire, now doing well
on Ibis Parkway and writing cream-colored checks
bearing a photo of himself and wife and kiddos.
Arlen has gained a hundred pounds and has a cater-
pillar on his upper lip.

"If they got checks like this, can you imagine what
they got in their homes? I'll bet they got everything
you can thing of. I'll bet they got organs." Harold has
his eye on an organ for himself and Millie, a $1395
Spano spinet with two keyboards and attachments

---

author asking for his manuscript back. Like so many
writers of manifestos, he forgot to keep a copy, and over
the years his letters have descended to a pitiful pleading
tone quite unlike his original style.

I simply can't understand despite repeated re-
quests ... This is very important to me ... The ms. is
mine and I need it *now* for a longer work I'm writing ...
I know you are busy and please forgive me if I seem
impatient but I beg you to *please* attend to this small
matter. I enclose a stamped self-addressed envelope.

Five such envelopes sit in the stack, with five addresses that
show a trend toward the east and south, with one brief long
jump to California. Three are plain manila envelopes, two
are Federal Express. The manuscript of *95* has sustained
some coffee damage but is in good shape, except for three
pages that are missing. "They are around here somewhere,
I remember seeing them," says Harold, "and as soon as I
get this desk straightened around and find the damn things,

including Autochord, which, when you play a note of the melody, gives you a whole rich chord, so an average person can learn to play pretty well in about two hours. The Spano combines the best features of theater and church-style organs. Harold thinks it would help him relax in the evening and not hit the hard stuff so hard. Some nights he goes home and drinks Jim Beam whiskey until he is nineteen years old. An organ would give him something to do. He also has his eye on a better toupee than his current rug, which has a nylon shine and tends to slip forward.

Publishing a paper in a small town, where readers

I'll send it all back to him. I'm just one person, you know, I'm not the U.S. Post Office."

Here, unabridged, is the document as Harold has it.

95 THESES 95

1. You have fed me wretched food, vegetables boiled to extinction, fistfuls of white sugar, slabs of fat, mucousy casseroles made with globs of cream of mushroom, until it's amazing my heart still beats. Food was not fuel but ballast; we ate and then we sank like rocks. Every Sunday, everyone got stoned on dinner except the women who cooked it and thereby lost their appetites — the rest of us did our duty and ate ourselves into a gaseous stupor and sat around in a trance and mumbled like a bunch of beefheads.

2. Every Advent, we entered the purgatory of *lutefisk*, a repulsive gelatinous fishlike dish that tasted of soap and gave off an odor that would gag a goat. We did this in honor of Norwegian ancestors, much as if the survivors of a famine might celebrate their deliverance by feasting on elm bark. I always felt the cold creeps as Advent

know precisely what they want, is a big headache for
Harold. He ran a hardware store in Aitkin before
entering journalism, which he did for love of the
mighty Mergenthaler Linotype—

> O the Linotype is fickle.
> She breaks down twice a day.
> But when she hits the matrice
> She will steal your heart away.

An old printer taught him a few things, such as where
to hit it when the monster eats the hot slugs and spits
lead in your face, but nobody had to teach Harold the
pure pleasure of sitting down to the keyboard and

---

approached, knowing that this dread delicacy would be put
before me and I'd be told, "Just have a little." Eating "a
little" was, like vomiting "a little," as bad as "a lot."

3. You have subjected me to endless boring talk about
weather, regularity, back problems, and whether something happened in 1938 or 1939, insisting that I sit quietly
and listen to every word. "How's it going with you?" you
said. "Oh, about the same," you replied. "Cold enough for
you?" It was always cold, always about the same.

4. You have taught me to worship a god who is like you,
who shares your thinking exactly, who is going to slap me
one if I don't straighten out fast. I am very uneasy every
Sunday, which is cloudy and deathly still and filled with
silent accusing whispers.

5. You have taught me to feel shame and disgust about my
own body, so that I am afraid to clear my throat or blow
my nose. Even now I run water in the sink when I go to the
bathroom. "Go to the bathroom" is a term you taught me

tapping letters, the brass matrices clicking into their carriage, then whirring off to take the molten lead as you peck along, two lines ahead of the slugged lines dropping into the galley tray—and what a puny thing is the smudged scrap of yellow copy paper in the brace above the keys, compared to the immense engine clattering and sighing—those satisfying sounds: *tiptiptiptip, bracabracabraca-cock ... chung! pickapink-hhhhnnnn, shhhhhhhht, fffft— chung ... shhhhhht, plank!*

The headache is the yellow paper. Harold never did well in English, or civics, or writing home from the Navy. "I never claimed to be the world's greatest

---

to use.

6. You have taught me the fear of becoming lost, which has killed the pleasure of curiosity and discovery. In strange cities, I memorize streets and always know exactly where I am. Amid scenes of great splendor, I review the route back to the hotel.

7. You have taught me to fear strangers and their illicit designs, robbing me of easy companionship, making me a very suspicious friend. Even among those I know well, I continue to worry: what do they *really* mean by liking me?

8. You have taught me to value a good night's sleep over all else including adventures of love and friendship, and even when the night is charged with magic, to be sure to get to bed. If God had not meant everyone to be in bed by ten-thirty, He would never have provided the ten o'clock newscast.

9. You taught me to be nice, so that now I am so full of

writer," he has admitted. Even armed with his copy of *The Editor's Source: One Hundred Basic Stories*, he squints at blank paper, bites his lip, kneads the back of his neck.

What the readers want is a good writeup. A Leonards game should be five hundred words long and mention every boy who played, e.g., 'Donnie Olson made a couple good tackles." A sale at Skoglund's, Ralph's new meat counter—those deserve a photo and also a hundred words or so. A girl who makes the Dean's List at college, a boy who finishes basic training—people like to have a nice little article they can send to relatives. A wedding deserves a

---

niceness, I have no sense of right and wrong, no outrage, no passion. "If you can't say something nice, don't say anything at all," you said, so I am very quiet, which most people think is politeness. I call it repression.

10. You taught me to worry about my face. The fear of acne, which will follow me to my grave, began when I was fourteen, a time of life when a person has no skin but is all raw flesh (skin-colored), and grew a crop of zits around my nose and learned various positions, sitting and standing, in which I could keep a hand to my face. They were triggered by fear. You said, "I'd like you to have a nice complexion for Dorothy and Bob's wedding. They'll be taking pictures." So I wound up looking like a three-bean salad. I died inside to see myself in the mirror. Better that those blotches meant nose cancer; at least I could go to the hospital and get flowers. What I had, people don't send flowers for. When I was sixteen, I bought the first ski mask in town. "Why don't you smile more?" you said.

11. You taught me, "When the going gets tough, the tough

379

major literary effort. It has got to have sweep and grandeur to it and a hundred details, all correct. You don't want to put white tulle on someone who was wearing peach taffeta.

Spelling counts about eighty percent when it comes to names. If an Ingqvist sees Ingquist or Engqvist or Ignqvist, it gets under her skin, and pretty soon she is mentioning to her friends how it seems to her the paper is getting *worse*, and how Mr. Starr looks— well, *plastered* half the time, poor Millie, it's such a *pity*; and, all in all, you'd be better off if you had said it was Etaoin Shrdlu who won Garden of the Month and the $10 gift certificate from Buehler's.

---

get going," teaching me to plod forward in the face of certain doom.

12. You taught me to be competitive even in matters of faith, to take pride in the great privilege of having been born Lutheran, even at moments of contrition. Religious intolerance was part of our faith. We believed that Catholics were illiterate peasants, foreign-born, who worshiped idols. In Sunday School, we looked up to see a gory picture of "Christian Infants Martyred at the Hands of Papist Clergy." We believed there was a secret tunnel between rectory and nunnery. We believed they poisoned the pets of Protestants. Whatever they believed, it wasn't right.

13. In place of true contrition, you taught me to be apologetic. I apologize continually. I apologize for my own existence, a fact that I cannot change. For years, you told me I'd be sorry someday. I am.

14. You taught me to trust my own incompetence and

News

The most controversial item this week is:

FLYING SNAKES
Snakes cannot fly, but some can glide
for up to thirty or forty yards.

True or untrue? And—

Contrary to popular belief, pigs can
swim. In a USDA experiment in
1966, a Hampshire boar swam forty
yards, defeating a dog by two
lengths.

Also, a tip from the extension home economist on

---

even now won't let me mash potatoes without your direct
supervision. "Don't run the mixer so fast that you get them
all over," you say, as if in my home, the walls are covered
with big white lumps. I can't mow a lawn or hang tinsel on
a Christmas tree or paint a flat surface in your presence
without you watching, worried, pointing out the uneven-
ness.

15. You taught me an indecent fear of sexuality. I'm not
sure I have any left underneath this baked-on crust of
shame and disgust. For years I worried because my penis
hangs slightly to the left, and finally read in a book that this
is within the realm of the normal, but then wondered, What
sort of person would read books like that?

16. You have provided me with poor male role models,
including the Sons of Knute, the Boosters Club and others
whose petulance, inertia, and ineptitude are legendary. I
was taught to respect them: men who clung to tiny grudges
for decades and were devoted to vanity, horsefeathers,
small potatoes—not travel but the rites of trunk-loading

using salt to remove wine stains from white table-
cloths (should drinking be encouraged by showing
drinkers how to cover their tracks?), but nothing controversial close to home, such as the big stink at the
school board meeting where some taxpayers
demanded that they stop teaching French. One of
them held up a French I text opened to a Renoir
nude and said, "We don't know what these kids are
reading here. We got no idea. It could be anything."
The story in the *Herald-Star* only said, "Textbooks
were also discussed."

"I have to live here, too, you know," is Harold's
first principle in journalism.

---

and map-reading and gas mileage; not faith but the Building Committee; not love but supper.

17. Listening to them, I was taught to keep quiet. Stupidity
had the floor, always. Argument was impolite.

18. You instilled in me a paralyzing nostalgia for a time
before I was born, a time when men were men and women
were saintly, and children were obedient, industrious,
asked no luxuries, entertained themselves, and knew right
from wrong. I, on the other hand, was a symptom of everything going to hell in a handbasket. I was left to wonder
why I bothered to be born.

19. You brought me up to respect fastidiousness as incar-
nate virtue, Christianity made evident. As a tiny child, I
lined up my string beans in a row on the plate, taking
exactly three per bite. I hesitated to eat the mashed
potatoes, lest the little gravy lake spill. I kept useless collec-
tions of stamps, seashells, postcards, rocks, delighting in
their deadly neatness. In our home, all surfaces were meant

News

So the *Herald-Star* didn't say one word about the council meeting where they discussed Bud's use of one stick of dynamite to dig Mrs. Tingvold's grave last February and a motion by Einar to censure him. "*Rest in peace!* That's what it says on my mother's stone! *Rest in peace!* What a joke!" he yelled at Bud. Bud was so mad he tipped his chair over. "You try digging a grave and see how you like it!" he yelled back. People talked about it for weeks. But not a word in the paper.

It wasn't news that Ruthie and Bob got married, marriage was more or less inevitable under the circum-

---

to be bare; emptiness was the ideal. The fear of dust (amathophobia) was endemic. One little book lying on the floor: "The house is a mess. Why can't you ever put things back when you're done with them?" We were passionate about snow-shoveling and made nice even banks. In summer, I edged the lawn, trimmed around trees, attacked dandelions. When Grandpa died, we tended his grave zealously, kneeling at the stone to landscape his resting place. "He was a good man," someone said once in the cemetery. "*Ja,*" you said. "I've been thinking of applying a little Turf-Builder. And maybe a fungicide."

20. In our theology, hard work was its own justification, a guard against corruption. Thus, we never bought an automatic dishwasher or a self-cleaning oven or a self-propelled mower with bag attachment, believing they would lead to degeneracy. We raked the grass clippings into a pile and later burned it. We did not use it for garden mulch because mulching kept weeds down and it was important that children weed the garden, slaving through the long hot

stances; the *news* was the miracle of architecture
Mrs. Mueller worked on Ruthie's dress, making it
look flat in front, and then, six months later, the baby
boy—not *out* of wedlock, but not quite far enough
into wedlock either. Abortion was never considered,
they being cradle Catholics and Father Emil being
himself. As he says, "If you didn't want to go to
Chicago, why did you get on the train?" The poor
kids. Poor Ruthie. Bob got shnockered at the wedding dance, and she drove them to a $50 motel room
in St. Cloud and sat on the bed and watched a
Charlie Chan movie on TV. "The bridal suite featured violet satin bedsheets and a quilted spread with

---

afternoons. It was good for them. It kept them from moral
turpitude.

21. Suffering was its own reward, to be preferred to
pleasure. As Lutherans, we viewed pleasure with suspicion.
Birth control was never an issue with us. Nor was renunci-
ation of pleasures of the flesh. We never enjoyed them in
the first place.

We were born to suffer. Pain was pooh-poohed. If you
broke your leg, walk home and apply ice. Don't complain.
Don't baby yourself. Our mothers ironed sheets, underwear, even in July. Our fathers wore out their backs at
heavy, senseless labor, pulled their own teeth, lived with
massive hemorrhoids. When Grandpa had his heart attack,
he took one aspirin and went to bed early. We children
suffered through dull repetitive schoolwork, under the lash
of sadistic teachers. Punishment was good for you,
deserved or not; if you hadn't done wrong, well, then it was
for last time.

22. A year ago, a friend offered to give me a backrub. I

ironed-on bride & groom appliqués, a heart-shaped mirror over the dresser, a bottle of pink champagne in a plastic ice bucket, a bouquet of funereal red roses, and her husband sick in the john," the *Herald-Star* did not report. "The bride felt queasy herself. Reception was poor, and the picture kept flipping. She adjusted the brightness knob to sheer black and turned up the sound. The man in the next room, with whose flesh hers was now one, dressed in white cotton boxer shorts with blue fleur-de-lis and a yellow 'Keep On Truckin' T-shirt, sounded as if he was almost done. Wave after wave of multicolored wedding food had come out of him, propelled by

---

declined vociferously. You did this to me.

23. Two years ago I carried a box-spring mattress up four flights of stairs, declining offers of help, and did something to my back which still hurts. I didn't see a doctor but did buy a different mattress (orthopedic). Someone helped me carry it up and I felt guilty and kept saying, "No. Really. I got it now," all the way up as my back killed me and my eyes filled with tears.

24. Recently, I dropped my air conditioner on my foot. I think this is related.

25. Despite the bum foot, I kept running four miles per day. I love the misery of running. I love the misery of feeling I should run more, hundreds of miles, and do it on my knees.

26. You taught me to believe in quietness as a sign of good character, that a child who sat silently with hands folded was a child who had overcome temptation. In fact, I was only scared, but being a nice quiet boy, I was offered as an example to other children, many of whom despise me to

vodka sours, and now he was unloading the last of the wedding cake and the cheese dip and the liverwurst snacks. The bride, whose personal feeling about vomiting is that she would much prefer to lie very quietly for three days, tried to occupy her mind with the pleasant memory of being class orator in a blue ankle-length sateen graduation gown with bell sleeves and blue pumps and a mortarboard cap with a yellow tassel and reading five hundred words on the subject 'Every Conclusion Is a New Beginning,' but she wasn't sure she felt so hopeful about the conclusion taking place in the next room. And she needed to pee.''

---

this day. I did not have to be shushed on Sunday afternoon but went about my glum business of cutting out pictures from the rotogravure and pasting them into a scrapbook, being careful not to snip too loud. I learned that quietness could be used to personify not only goodness, but also intelligence and sensitivity, and so I silently earned a small reputation as a boy of superior intellect, a little scholar, a little sunbeam in this dark world, while in fact I was smug and lethargic and dull as a mud turtle.

27. Even now, I go to someone's house and think I am being a good guest if I am very quiet, don't ask for anything, and refuse anything that's offered. This behavior makes other people think of me as a nincompoop.

28. I find it very hard to whoop it up, hail a pal, split a gut, cut a rug, have a ball, or make a joyful noise. I'm your boy, all right.

29. You taught me not to go overboard, lose my head, or make a big deal out of it, but to keep a happy medium, that

News of Mr. Rognes's mother's death was passed on by the paper in four paragraphs, which mentioned "her many contributions to church and community work" and the "long illness" but which failed to convey the great surprise of death to the decedent. Sick as she was, delirious, in and out of her mind, nevertheless she heard Pastor Ingqvist when he asked, "Greta, are you prepared to die?" She opened her eyes wide. "I'm going to San Diego next week!" she snapped. She repeated this several times in the last two days. When Nils took her hand and said, weeping, "Mother, I love you," she said, "Stop blubbering. I'm going to San Diego, and that's final." Death

---

the truth is in the middle. No extremes. Don't exaggerate. Hold your horses. Keep a lid on it. Save it for later. Be careful. Weigh the alternatives. Wear navy blue. Years later, I am constantly adjusting my feelings downward to achieve that fine balance of caution and melancholy.

30. You taught me not to be "unusual" for fear of what the neighbors would say. They were omniscient, able to see through walls. We knew they'd talk, because we always talked about them. We thought they were nuts, but still we shouldn't offend them.

31. Your theology wasn't happy about the idea of mercy and forgiveness, which only gave comfort to enemies, and so, although you recited the Lord's Prayer every Sunday, you remembered your debtors and managed to not speak to certain people—a major feat when you live in a town so small and attend the same church as they, an act of true dedication. In your behalf, I still dislike Bunsens. I have no idea why.

took her unawares. For thirty years, she bossed every church supper with such a sharp tongue that younger women suddenly forgot how to butter bread and boil water. Her own demise was unthinkable; she simple didn't think the world could do without her.

The courtly formality of the *Herald-Star*, its severe discretion, are courtesies that most newspapers once extended to aristocracy, as Clarence Bunsen pointed out to me one day when I complained about it, being fresh out of college. "The dukes and marquises took life at a pretty fast clip, but newspapers back then knew enough to mind their own business," he said.

---

32. Your own mistakes you managed to explain to your own satisfaction. When you hurt people, you explained that you didn't mean to. When you gossiped malicious gossip, you explained that "everyone knows this and besides it's true." You had a good reason for every dumb thing you did which you said I would understand someday. I don't. I don't understand it at all.

33. *Oh, I think you can do without that.* Your words come back to me when I look at a new sportcoat. Good Scottish tweed, it costs $130, and when I try it on, it makes me feel smart and lucky and substantial, but you're right, I can do without it, and so I will. *You can get a perfectly good one at Sears for half the price.* If I bought the $130 one, pride would leak in and rot my heart. Who do I think I am?

34. For fear of what it might do to me, you never paid a compliment, and when other people did, you beat it away from me with a stick. "He certainly is looking nice and grown up." *He'd look a lot nicer if he did something about his skin.* "That's wonderful that he got that job." *Yeah,*

News

"They didn't go to press every time a count spilled soup on himself." (I was eating a bowl of chicken noodle soup right then and was in the process of spilling.) "I don't say it's right, but then I don't know if what you're doing is right either." (I was starting a novel about Lake Wobegon right then and was in the process of gathering information.) "What are you going to do? Tell the world that your grandfather was a cattle thief?"

"Which grandfather?" I said. Then I said, "My grandfathers weren't thieves, either one! What are you talking about?"

"See? You writers are all alike. Ready to believe

---

well, we'll see how long it lasts. You trained me so well, I now perform this service for myself. I deflect every kind word directed to me, and my denials are much more extravagant than the praise. "Good speech." *Oh, it was way too long, I didn't know what I was talking about, I was just blathering on and on, I was glad when it was over.* I do this under the impression that it is humility, a becoming quality in a person. Actually, I am starved for a good word, but after the long drought of my youth, no word is quite good enough. "Good" isn't enough. Under this thin veneer of modesty lies a monster of greed. I drive away faint praise, beating my little chest, waiting to be named Sun-God, King of America, Idol of Millions, Bringer of Fire, The Great Haji, Thun-Dar The Boy Giant. I don't want to say, "Thanks, glad you liked it." I want to say, "Rise, my people. Remove your faces from the carpet, stand, look me in the face."

35. The fear of poverty haunts me. You weren't poor but you anticipated the possibility by believing you were.

389

the worst."

Almost anyone in town who has normal hearing and eats a slow lunch at the Chatterbox is a better source of straight poop than the *Herald-Star*. If you order pie and take your time, Dede will take a swipe around the salt and pepper with a damp cloth and say, "I heard that Miss Bomer might not be coming back to teach English," and you say, "Oh really? What's that all about?"

"Well, I shouldn't be telling you, I suppose," she says, "but you'd hear about it eventually anyway, so—" and she tells about Miss Bomer's romance up

---

36. The fear of illness. You were seldom ill but you were always prepared to be.

37. Your illnesses were the result of exhaustion by good works, mine the result of of having disobeyed you and not worn a scarf, not taking vitamins. I crawl into bed like a dog and feel not only unwell but unworthy. If someone came in to shoot me, I'd turn on the light so he could take better aim.

38. The fear of poverty and illness, brought on by a sudden craving for cheap wine. A flaw in my character, a weak seam, and one day I bend down to tie my shoes and hear a rip in my head, and on the way to work I pick up a gallon of muscatel, and spend my lunch hour in the alley. A month later, I have no job, no house, no car, and my nose is dark purple and swollen to the size of an eggplant. My voice is like sandpaper, I cough up gobs of phlegm, my liver feels like a sandbag. My teeth are rotten stumps. I crap in my pants and lurch toward strangers, mumbling about spare change. The flaw was created by disobeying you. "Someday

north with a younger man, a violinist whom she had met at a roadside spa, and sparks flew and turned into spontaneous combustion, and Miss Bomer is now about to throw away her career and follow the rounder east where he performs in cafes with a jazz combo. She was seen with him in The Starlite Club near Lake Winnibigosh, drinking a sloe gin fizz and looking into his eyes with a moony expression.

I never heard about the violinist. Back when I was in school and we invented romances for Miss Bomer, it was either the new pharmacist Wendell or Carl Krebsbach's cousin Ernie Barfnecht, No-Neck Ernie, who drove a potato truck. Of course, it was wrong to

---

you'll find out," you said, and I probably will.

39. Damn.

40. Damn.

41. Damn.

42. Damn.

[Three pages missing.]

56. In our house, work was a weapon, used as punishment, also to inspire guilt. You waited until I sat in a chair and read the funnies, then you charged in: "How can you *sit* with this mess all around you?" I looked down. One lonely sock on the floor, a Juicy Fruit wrapper on the table. You snatched them up, sighed as if your heart was broken, and stalked out. A great sigh, so loud it could be heard in the back of the balcony. You worked your fingers to the bone, and did anyone lift a finger to help? No, they didn't. When I lifted a finger, you told me it was the wrong finger and I was lifting it the wrong way. When I vacuumed, suddenly

tell lies and besmirch her reputation, but it's also wrong to ignore people and take them for granted: everyone would like to be thought *capable* of sin and maybe even mildly interested. (I once tried to spread a rumor that I had an offer of $15,000 to leave radio and fly out to the coast but when the story came back to me, it was $1200 to go to Seattle.)

Sin, however, was not a staple of my earliest fiction. My first reader was my mother and her taste ran toward goodness, or something as close to goodness as I could get. She saved every scrap of my work in a bureau drawer, every worksheet from school, and I was so impressed when I found this stash one

---

vacuuming became an exact science, a branch of physics, and I was doing it all wrong—you snatched the hose away and said, "Here, I might a well do it myself," which was what you intended all along.

57. You taught me that, no matter what I thought, it was probably wrong. The world is fundamentally deceptive. The better something looks, the more rotten it probably is down deep. Some people were fooled but not you. You could always see the underlying truth, and the truth was ugly. Roosevelt was a drunk and that was that. New Deal? What New Deal? A sham, from beginning to end. There was no Depression, a person could get work if they really tried. There was more to everything than anyone knew. This teaching has led me, against my better judgment, to suspect people of trying to put one over. At the checkout counter, I lean forward to catch the girl if she tries to finesse an extra ten cents on the peaches. That's how Higgledy-Piggledy makes a profit. That's why cashiers ring up the goods so fast, to confuse us.

day—my work collected in a box! maps colored by me! my letters ("AaBbCcDd" etc.) and my correct answers ("The cat *ran* into the house. The cat *jumped* onto the table. The cat *ate* the food")—I got to work producing more. If she thought I could fill in the blanks in Mrs. Meiers's sentences pretty well, wait till she saw some real writing!

I began my career in a lower bunkbed, using soft coloured pencils and a Big Red Indian Chief tablet, which I kept on the slats of the top bunk. I stored the stories in the springs. The colored pencils were for different moods, such as brown for sadness, red for happiness, and blue for when they were outdoors.

---

58. Believing there is always more than meets the eye defeats the sense of sight. Always looking for hidden meanings, a person misses the lovely surface of the world, even in spring. Surely those green leaves are hiding bare branches. If you look hard enough, you will glimpse them: dark, malevolent, and a big trunk that if you ran into it hard enough, it would kill you.

59. Nonetheless you set store by a certain orderly look to things. Dinner was at noon, supper at five-thirty. This is so ingrained in me that I eat whether I'm hungry or not. I eat everything put before me. It is a sign that I am good.

60. Clean clothes made us respectable.

61. A clean house distinguished us from colored people.

62. Bigotry is never a pleasant subject so you didn't bring it up but you stuck by your guns anyway. Indians were drunks, Jews were thieves, and the colored were shiftless. Where you got this, I don't know, because there were none of them around, but you believed it more absolutely for the

Mostly I wrote in red. Animals were the stars of the show and children. Children hung out with animals who often spoke to them.

"Hi, Eddie."

"Puff?"

"Can I get you anything?" Children wished for things and animals brought them. It was better than Christmas, you got what you wanted, and nobody argued since there was plenty for everyone. If you wanted to, you could fly—birds would help you—or you could be invisible. You could walk into the radio and be in shows. Hang out with the masked man between shows, when he and Tonto were relaxing on

---

utter lack of evidence. *Everyone* knew about those people. It was common sense.

63.–67. [Obliterated by beverage stain.]

68. Everything was set in place in your universe, and you knew what everything and everybody was, whether you had ever seen them or not. You could glance at strangers and size them up instantly. An article of clothing, a phrase from their lips, a look in their eye—you knew who they were, and you were seldom generous in your assessments. "She certainly thinks a lot of *her*self." "I'll bet that's not *his* wife." "If that man's not a crook, then today's not Sunday," you said one Sunday. It was something about the shape of his head. You could tell. They couldn't fool you. And now I do this myself. I adopted the mirror-reverse of your prejudices and I apply them viciously. I detest neat-looking people like myself and people who look industrious and respectable. I sneer at them as middle-class. In elections, I vote automatically against Scandinavian names.

the plains. You could become a magnificent person whose body is covered with fine white feathers that give off a radiant light, once you learn to spell *radiant*.

When I say "my mother," I mean the woman who raised me—my real mother was in the carnival, she was the fat lady and the tightrope walker, and I was born during an outdoor show—she thought it was some pancakes she ate, and there she was fifty-seven feet in the air over the Mississippi River, she dropped the balancing pole and she caught me by the ankle as I fell—I still have a mark there—and somehow she made it to the other side and handed me down to the

---

69. In fact, you imbued me with the sensitivity of a goat. I say vicious things about old friends to people I barely know. I say vicious things to people's faces and then explain that I was kidding.

I am truly cavalier toward the suffering of innocent people, including that which I myself cause. The other day, I almost ran down an old man in a crosswalk. I hadn't seen him. My friend grabbed my arm and yelled and I slammed on the brakes. Rather than apologize to the man, I turned and explained to my friend that I hadn't seen him. And I hadn't. I didn't even see him after I stopped and he stood there, dazed and terrified. I don't really see anybody.

70. When I hear about deprivation and injustice in the world, I get up and change the channel.

71. What can I do? It's not my fault. I didn't make them. God did. It's His world, let Him take care of it.

72. Anyway, I was brought up to believe that whatever happens to people is their own fault. There were few if any

man who ran the cotton-candy stand and said, "Here. Take care of this for me, willya?" And went back up and walked the tightrope to the west bank of the Mississippi. Then the rope broke, so she went on to Fargo with the strong man, figuring I'd catch up later, but the cotton-candy man misunderstood—I was an ugly child so he figured that was why she went on, and late that night, driving through a small town, he stopped the pickup and laid me on a doorstep with a note that said, "Sorry about this but it's not mine either," and gave me the pencil to play with.

I still have that pencil. It's my only souvenir of

---

disasters that you couldn't explain by citing the mistakes made by the victims. "She never should have married him." "He never should have been there in the first place." Even if you had to go back thirty years, you could find where they took the wrong fork in the road that led directly to their house burning down, their car being hit by a truck, their hands being eaten by corn pickers.

73. If they had been more like you, they would have been all right. But they weren't paying attention. They lacked your strong sense of the cruelty and hopelessness of the world.

74. You misdirected me as surely as if you had said the world is flat and north is west and two plus two is four; i.e., not utterly wrong, just wrong enough so that when I took the opposite position—the world is mountainous, north is east—I was wrong, too, and your being wrong about the world and north made me spend years trying to come up with the correct sum of two and two, other than four. *You gave me the wrong things to rebel against.* My little boat

where I came from. I write with it, though not so much now as I used to because it's so short.

Mrs. Magendanz, wife of the Leonards coach, was snapping beans on the back step one afternoon when her neighbor, old Mrs. Dahl, leaned across the lilacs and said, "I sure would appreciate it if you wouldn't spend quite so much time at the window staring at us," and stalked away before Mrs. Magendanz could think up a reply. She had to call up Mrs. Dahl. She said, "How would you know I was looking if you weren't looking at us?" Mrs. Dahl said, "The fact that I may sometimes look in your direction doesn't

---

sailed bravely against the wind, straight into the rocks. Your mindless monogamy made me vacillate in love, your compulsive industry made me a prisoner of sloth, your tidiness made me sloppy, your materialism made me wasteful.

75. I wasted years in diametrical opposition, thinking you were completely mistaken, and wound up living a life *based more on yours* than if I'd stayed home.

76. Because you always went to bed at ten, I stayed up half the night, chain-smoking (you were opposed to cigarettes), drinking straight gin (you didn't drink), and, given time, might have cut off my arm, it being yet another thing you would never have done.

77. I wasted some good years thinking proudly that I wasn't anything like you. Having grown up with ugly wallpaper, I painted all my walls off-white and thought I'd finally arrived. Bought a white couch, yours having been purple. My place looks like February.

mean I take the slightest interest." "Likewise, I'm sure," said Mrs. Magendanz.

So she began to pay closer attention to the Dahls, wondering what they had to hide, and soon noticed that the old man visited the garage morning and evening for about two minutes each. A secret drinker, evidently. Poor Mrs. Dahl. No wonder she was afraid. She thought Mrs. Magendanz had seen the old coot staggering around the house and screaming abuse at her. But Mrs. Magendanz watched closely for a few days and saw no signs of it. Did he go out to the garage to smoke? To chew? To look at dirty pictures? One day it dawned on her that he must have

---

78. I resist washing my dishes because it makes me feel obedient: the sink is disgusting.

79. I revolted by becoming a sensitive person, which I am not. I hate folk music. I don't care for most of the sensitive people I feel obligated to hang out with. Many of them play guitars and write songs about their feelings. I have to pack up my Percy Faith records when they come and put the box in the bedroom closet and pile winter coats on it, and despite the mothballs I'm afraid they'll take one sniff and say, "You like light classical, don't you." I pour a round of Lowenbrau, being careful not to pour along the side but straight down so the beer can express itself, and they say, "Did you ever try Dockendorf?" It's made by the Dockendorf family from hand-pumped water in their ancient original family brewery in an unspoiled Pennsylvania village where the barley is hauled in by Amish families who use wagons with oak beds. Those oak beds give Dockendorf its famous flavor. These beer bores, plus the renovators of Victorian houses, the singer-songwriters, the runners, the

an outhouse in the garage. The Dahls had moved off the farm into town only two years before. He had found that his bowels wouldn't budge on a flush toilet, so he dug a pit in the garage and was using it twice a day.

She steeled herself to do her duty, and the next morning when he disappeared into the garage, she walked over and pounded on the door, prepared to give him a talk on sanitation, but when he lifted the door, she saw nothing but an old garage with a lawn-mower and garden tools and a workbench with cans of lacquer and jars full of nails and screws. One thing caught her eye, a calendar above the bench with a

---

connoisseurs of northern Bengali cuisine, the collectors of everything Louis Armstrong recorded between August 1925 and June 1928, his seminal period—they are driving me inexorably toward life as a fat man in a bungalow swooning over sweet-and-sour pork. You drove me toward *them*.

80. This is one I can't say. It's true and it's important, having to do with sexual identity, but if I said it, I'd hear you saying, "How can you *say* that?" and I know I'd feel guilty. So I won't. *You* know what I mean.

81. Another thing of the same sort.

82. Another.

83. Guilt. Guilt as a child, then anger at you for filling me with guilt, then guilt at the anger. Then I tried to relieve *that* guilt by presenting you with a wonderful trip to Los Angeles to see your aunt. You protested that I didn't need to, then you went, and you conspired to make it awful. You cashed in the first-class plane tickets and flew tourist, you

picture of a beautiful girl in a bathing suit holding a wrench. The girl had long brown hair, and she smiled out from July 1943 as if it would never end.

"That's my old calendar," he said, "I've had that since 1943. Used to keep it in the barn, that's how it got banged up a little. The Mrs. wouldn't have it in the house, you know. I always liked it because that looks a lot like her when we was married. Of course, she didn't go around like that, but that picture, I'd swear it was her. I look at it and I think, That's Evy. Sounds crazy, I know, but you know, we didn't take pictures then. No camera. Never thought about getting one. So this is all I got."

---

cancelled the reservation at the Beverly Wilshire and stayed at a cheap motel in Torrance by the freeway, then you came home miserable (but happy) and gave me a refund.

84. I took you to a famous steakhouse on your anniversary. You agonized over the menu and ordered the cheapest thing. I pleaded, I argued. I ordered the prime rib. I felt guilty as I ate it, just as you intended.

85. With the refund from the trip, I bought you a pearl necklace and a pair of gold earrings. You never wore them. "I'm afraid of losing them," you said. "Here? In the house?" I said. "You never can tell," you said.

86. All those birthdays and Christmases, when you turned to me and said, "You shouldn't have," you really meant it. You were the author of the story, not me, and it was supposed to be about generous parents and an ingrate son. Once or twice, dark marital suffering was hinted at, with the clear intimation that you had stuck together for my sake. I felt wretched for months.

News

All I have is the end of a black phone. It sits on the kitchen counter and before I dial the number, I wash all the dishes in the sink, as a sort of token, so this kitchen will look more like theirs, and I turn off the light. Eight digits, a six-second delay, and a clunk, then the hard burr of the country telephone. My call follows a trunk route north to St. Cloud, then north and west, takes a sharp turn alongside a narrow oiled road, and there it enters a system that my late grandfather built, which is where the call clunks. You can tell the weather up there by the sound of it: more metallic in cold weather, like a tire hitting a bump in hot

---

87. A scene, repeated thousands of times:

You (in the easy chair): Dear? As long as you're up, would you mind—
Me (in the doorway): What?
You (rising): Oh, never mind. I'll do it myself.
Me: *What?* I'll do it.
You (sighing): No, that's all right. You'd never find it.
(Or: "You might burn yourself." Or: "I'd just have to do it myself anyway." Or: "It's nothing.")

88. A scene from early childhood: our Sunday School class learned "Joy to the World" for the Christmas program. You asked me to sing it for the aunts and uncles when they came to dinner. I said no. You said yes. I said no. You said, "Someday when I'm dead and in my coffin, maybe you'll look down and remember the times I asked you to do things and you wouldn't." So I sang, terrified of them and terrified about your death. You stopped me halfway through. You said, "Now, come on. You can sing it better than that."

401

weather, and of course static during a thunderstorm.

My grandfather was the leading light of the Lake Wobegon Rural Telephone Cooperative, its first president, the man who signed up investors and walked the fencerows and dug holes for the posts. The first ones stood about eight feet tall, the wire hung on a bent nail. They had telephones in town long before, of course—the Ingqvist twins, who lived for innovation, had the first, a line to their mother's, in 1894—but it took my grandfather to convince the good countrypeople that the phone was more than a toy. He was a tall, handsome, godly man and so

---

89. A few years later, when I sang the part of Curly in *Oklahoma!* and everybody else said it was wonderful, you said, "I told him for years he could sing and he wouldn't listen to me."

90. I did listen to you, that's most of my problem. Everything you said went in one ear and right down my spine. Such as, "You're never going to make anything of yourself." When I was laid off from a job, you couldn't believe it wasn't for something I had done, something so awful that I wouldn't tell you.

91. Everything I said had hidden meaning for you, even, "I'm going to bed." "You can't even spend a *few minutes* talking to your parents?" you said.

92. Every tiny disagreement was an ultimate blow to you. "Is this the thanks we get after all we've done?"

93. My every act was a subject of study: "What are you doing?" you asked a million times. "Why didn't you do it before?" (Or "Can't it wait until later?") "Why do it

admired that when the preacher at his funeral chose the text "For all have sinned and come short of the glory of God," his neighbors considered it an insult. One cold day, his chimney caught on fire and his house burned to the ground, and as he stood raking the coals in the cellar, he thought about telephones. He was not a man to take suffering as God's judgment if a remedy was close at hand. In 1921, he rebuilt the house (without a fireplace), organized the phone company, and drew up a contract between the township and the Lake Wobegon volunteer fire brigade. In the same year, he bought a Model T, his first car, and gave an acre of pasture for a township cemetery.

---

here?" "Why are you so quiet?" *I'm thinking.* "About what?"

94. My posture, facial expression (if any), tone of voice, gait, all were of constant critical interest as you strove to achieve a perfect balance in me.

"Sit up. Don't slouch." Then, "Relax. You make me nervous just to look at you."

"Why such a gloomy look?" Then, "Wipe that smirk off your face."

"Pick up your feet." Then, "Can't you walk without sounding like a herd of elephants?"

"Speak up. Don't mumble." "Keep your voice down."

95. Now you call me on the phone to ask, "Why don't you ever call us? Why do you shut us out of your life?" So I start to tell you about my life, but you don't want to hear it. You want to know why I didn't call.

I didn't call because I don't need to talk to you anymore. Your voice is in my head, talking constantly from morning

The rural co-op merged with the town company in 1933, and a pupil in Grandpa's Sunday School class who worshiped the ground he walked on has been running it from her pantry since 1942, Elizabeth, who was my Sunday School teacher for many years. When she was a child, Grandpa took her along when he walked the phone line in the spring, checking for loose or leaning posts and also watching for hummingbirds and picking purple lilac blossoms and a toad or two. "He never went anywhere without a child in tow," she says. "He had seven of his own, but if those weren't available, he'd shop around until he found another. He might be driving to town for a bag of nails he wanted right away for roofing, but he still needed that child to ride with him—he'd come pull you out of school if he had to."

The pantry off her kitchen holds the old switchboard, still in good condition, and also the steel cabinet with the switching equipment that took over from it when they went to dial telephones in 1960, but she keeps on top of things just the same. If someone doesn't answer their phone by the fifth ring, she does, and usually she knows where they went and when they're expected, so many customers don't bother dialing in-town calls, they just dial o and she puts them through. If you do reach her instead of your party—say, your mother—she may clue you in on things your mom would never tell you, about your

till night. I keep the radio on, but I still hear you and will hear you until I die, when I will hear you say, "I told you," and then something else will happen.

mom's bad back, a little fall on the steps the week before, or the approach of Mother's Day, or the fact that when you were born you were shown off like you were the Prince of Wales. A few customers accuse Elizabeth of listening in and claim they know the click that means she's there; but it isn't a click, it's an echoey sound, as if you and your party had moved into a bigger room. It's a wonder that she keeps track of us so faithfully, what with her age and arthritis and her great weight. She suffers from a glandular condition and is pushing three hundred pounds. Nowadays, five rings is as quick as she can make it to the phone, even from her kitchen table.

When I talk to her, I don't always hear an old fat lady; sometimes I hear the girl who walked the line with Grandpa in the spring of '21. I am a person she bawls out on a regular basis, and when I call home and the phone rings and rings, I brace myself for her "Yes?" and "Oh, it's you," and "I don't know if I care to talk to you or not," and then the lecture. I have disappointed my friend so many times. I live far away but news of my sins travels fast, and she always finds out. She found out when I flunked out of college. And then when I got a divorce—the worst, in her book—for almost a year afterward, she cried on the phone when I called. Many times she has told me, "I just thank God that your grandfather is dead and not around to see you now." And yet, if I ask her about him, she is always ready to change the subject, a sort of forgiveness. I simply say, "Is it true that you used to go with him when he walked the phone line?" and she says, "You *know* I did. Heavens. I've told you that a hundred times," but she's willing to tell it once more, and then it's spring, the sweet song of the rose-breasted grosbeak drifts from the wood tinged with green across the young alfalfa, the bumblebees buzz, the toads sing in the ditch, my tall handsome grandfather with the sharp blue eyes and brush mustache ambles along the bank above the road looking for the first rhubarb, the little girl scrambling to keep up.

"To me, there wasn't a thing he didn't know. Every flower, every tree. Every living thing, he just cared about it all and he expected you to care, and so of course you did. He talked to you like you were smart and would want to know these things, what bird that is and, here, this is a Jack-in-the-pulpit and—the *names* of things, that everything has a name. That isn't a 'bush' over there, those are *choke-cherries*, birds eat them, we make jelly from them. I don't think that man was ever bored in his life unless he was sick in bed. After my father died of diphtheria when I was five years old, I always looked on him as my father, and I used to stay up to his house with your aunts and uncles when my mother would go to Iowa to see her relatives, and once I remember—it was January and *bitter* cold—he woke up all us children in the middle of the night and told us to get dressed. Well, we did. We didn't ask any questions, we just got bundled up, and he led us out through the yard and up the path into the woods, eight children— your Aunt Flo was only four, I believe, and I helped carry her—*in the dark*, no lantern, mind you, just the moon, the coldest night of the year, and none of us was a bit afraid, because he was there. Not even when we came to the edge of the trees and looked up and there on the top of the hill was a wolf. He sat on the snowbank and looked at us. He was pure silver. He didn't move a muscle. In the moonlight he looked like a ghost. Your grandpa knelt down and put his arms around us and said, 'I want you to take a good look and remember this because you may never get to see it again.' So we looked good. I can still remember it like I'm looking at it right now. I can see that wolf and I can feel his arm around me."

When I talk to her, I often feel I'm talking to my grandfather who died before I was born, and I try not to hold back the truth, even when the news is so bad it almost breaks her heart. There is some dignity to this, though the truth is not easy. When her nephew Wesley was replacing some shingles on her roof, he put his foot on the main phone trunk line to steady himself and snapped it off and then figured if he didn't mention it, just tied the line to the gutter, maybe no one would notice, maybe it would get better on its own. So the phones were out for five hours, and when Bud found the break, Wesley said, "Oh, yeah, I saw that—I was sort of wondering what it was."

When I look at the lines I've busted, I don't sort of wonder about them, I know what I did; I know they didn't fall off the side of the house because they were tired. Still, it's hard to say what you've done and not write up a better version.

I can see how I could write a bold account of myself as a passionate man who rose from humble beginnings to cut a wide swath in the world, whose crimes along the way might be written off to extravagance and love and art, and could even almost believe some of it myself on certain days after the sun went down if I'd had a snort or two and was in Los Angeles and it was February and I was twenty-four, but I find a truer account in the *Herald-Star*, where it says:

> Mr. Gary Keillor visited at the home of Al and Florence Crandall on Monday and after lunch returned to St. Paul, where he is currently employed in the radio show business. Mr. Lew Powell also visited, who recently celebrated his ninety-third birthday and is enjoying excellent health. Almost twelve quarts of string beans were picked and some strawberries. Lunch was fried chicken with gravy and creamed peas.

The newspaper's correspondent on the scene was Aunt Flo herself, and the careful reader can see that she still dotes on her wayward nephew, pointing out his gainful and glamorous employment and suggesting that he is no slouch on a bean row, either, giving a little plug for family longevity and complimenting the guests with a good lunch. Aunt Flo does not make her famous fried chicken for any old shirttail relative who comes in off the road.

It's my first appearance in the paper in several years, and though it leaves out so much that one might like to add, about travels, awards, publications, it leaves out even more that one is glad not to see, about pride, gluttony, lust, and leaves me feeling better about home journalism. The story is accurate, as I read it, and everything is there: the sun beating down on us in the bean field, the elderly gent sampling the berry crop, the goodness of creamed peas and of poultry allowed a free and happy life and then rolled in flour and pan-fried, the goodness of Uncle Al, who said, "You remind me so much of your grandfather." He was referring, not to my life or character, but to a similarity of mustache. A small compliment, and it pleased me for days afterward and I read as much into it as I possibly could.

SPRING

The Sons of Knute Ice Melt contest starts on Ground-hog Day, when they tow Mr. Berge's maroon 1949 Ford onto the lake, park it forty yards offshore with a long chain around the rear axle, and wait for spring. It's the car Mr. Berge was driving one warm March day when he hung a right at the dam and headed out to his fish house to check the dropline, forgetting he had hauled in the house three weeks before because the ice was melting. Now, the ice was even thinner, though covered with fresh snow. The car slowed down suddenly a hundred yards out, and when he gunned it she stopped dead and dropped a foot as if all four tires went flat. He couldn't open the door so he cranked down the window and climbed out and crawled up on the roof. His cries for help brought out the Volunteer Fire Department, which sent him one end of a rope tied to his dog Mike and dragged both of them through the slush back to shore. The car sank a few days later in six feet of water. They got a chain on her that summer, though, and winched her out. Mr. Berge, who had made some extravagant promises to God while lying on the roof, donated the car to the lodge, and so every year the Ford has repeated its sinking routine for charity. You guess the day and hour she will go down, at a dollar per guess. The winner gets a boat, and the profits go to the Sons of Knute Shining Star scholarship fund to send kids to college and make them more brilliant than Mr. Berge, who, like anyone who ever did a dumb thing in a small town, was reminded of it ever afterward. "Good night, then," he says when he leaves the Side-track Tap. "Good night, then," they say. "You go right home now, don't stop on the way. And keep off the ice then."

The first week of April is a good guess, though the car has sunk as early as late March and as late as the third week of April. Once it never went down. They parked it over the end of the long sandbar that comes off the point, the one that has ended a few fishing trips before they got to where they were biting, when the sandbar bit the boat and the fishermen pitched out in the mud. The Ford sat there in four inches of water, a sort of buoy, and the scholarship fund earned hundreds of dollars.

In April, giant icicles let go of the eaves and crash to the ground. Bare pavement appears and Duane gets a screech out of his back tires he has waited all winter to hear. Birds arrive: the redwing blackbird ("o-ka-leeeee"), robin ("cheer up, cheer up, cheer-ily"), killdeer ("killdeer, killdeer"), and the Norwegian nuthatch ("I tink so, I tink so, probably"), a brownish-gray bird with a spot of white breast, which lives in barns and feeds on coffee grounds. It has been around all winter. "I tink so" is its spring song. The winter song is "I don't know, I don't know. Who can tell?"

Who can tell? Sometimes we get a good blizzard in late April, even in May. Odd as it is and (like a misplaced parenthetical comment that makes no sense when later he said, 'Don't, darling. Please don't. Please, Marie," but she went ahead and did it anyway) daunting, still—this is Minnesota. "Spring? Don't be nuts," some people say even as the snow begins to melt. The backyards look as if giant bison were camped out there, lounging around. This stuff here—dogs didn't do this, it's too big, this is from a bison. It was a dog, though, who came shopping in the garbage can and spread the items out for inspection. Evidently he didn't care for orange peels, coffee grounds, brown lettuce, old fruitcake, *or* rotten potatoes.

So warm, but still you have to dress warmly. This is the season for colds. My parka was inherited from Mr. Hoglund, who died in 1947—I wear a dead man's jacket. All of us get hot during recess, and soon there is a pile of parkas in the corner of the playground.

Out on the country road, you can see the Norwegian bachelor farmers have hung out their sheets. "When a bachelor farmer begins to smell himself, you know winter's over," says Clarence. Barney bought his sheets for a quarter at the Lutheran rummage sale, which got them from Irene Bunsen because Clint said they gave him headaches at night. Hawaiian sheets with big swashes of tropical colors. If you saw Barney on the streets and wondered what kind of sheets he slept on, Hawaiian would be your last guess. His name is John; he was nicknamed Barney for his aroma. When I first saw his sheets flapping in the wind, I was four years old. I asked if we could stop. I thought it was a carnival and there were rides. In a few weeks, there will be—when the bachelors hitch up their Belgians and head out to the edge of the dry stubble. Drop the blade, cluck at the team, and off they go. The moldboard throws the turf over and releases the aroma of sweet black earth.

The first week of April is darn early to get out in the field to cultivate. Roger Hedlund, who I went to school with and who looks almost exactly the same as then—same flat-top, same calm look as when he missed two free throws with one second remaining that lost the district championship for the Leonards in 1958—got out early the first year after his dad, Ivan, finally turned the farm over to him, got too close to the woods where the snow was melting, and got stuck and worked at it and got the Farmall dug down to the green clay, down to the axle. It took three neighbors with three tractors to haul him out. The ruts are still visible, a decade later, a trench from an ancient battle. Archaeologists could dig down and find the lumber they used for traction.

Embarrassing, to get stuck in your field. You're out in the open, just like in basketball, and the sound of a giant Farmall submerging carries a long way. It's not like a fart that you can pretend was something else. No spiders bark that loud.

So now, as they sit in the Chatterbox and talk about getting in the fields, they stick it to Roger once more. "*Ja*, Roger may be getting out today and do some excavating." "*Ja*, Roger, he plants deep." They stick it to him harder because it's so hard to get a rise out of Roger. He's so calm. He won't give them the satisfaction. He keeps it inside, like Ivan, who years ago blew up his old dairy barn, having built a new one, but Lord, to use as much dynamite as he did—he broke every window in his house and scattered lumber over half the country. People found boards from that barn for years after. And some of them took them back to him. "Here, Ivan, I believe this is yours."

In Lake Wobegon, we don't forget mistakes. I know I remember those free throws like he just missed them. It was March 1958. He didn't cry, didn't swear, didn't even look at the floor. He just went back on defense for that one remaining second. Looked for his man as his man heaved the ball into the crowd. We all sat there stunned, our eyes filled with tears, but Roger looked—well, like Roger. He seemed surprised it was over. He was ready to play four more quarters.

Spring

We were favored to win that game against Bowlus, they were nothing, a joke, so most of us didn't bother to go to the game. We were saving up for the trip to State and a weekend at the Curtis Hotel, which was what should have happened, but the boys stood around, threw the ball away, took dumb shots, and then Roger came to the line for two, the Leonards down 51–50. The first shot hit the front of the rim, the second wasn't even close.

So now, as he pulls his cap on his head, takes a last slug of coffee, stands, turns, and tosses his wadded-up napkin into the garbage can twenty feet away, everybody at the table thinks the same thing. They don't say it, but they think it.

On the first real warm day, you can sit on the back steps in your PJs before church, drink coffee, study the backyard which was such a dump a week ago you wouldn't have wanted to be buried back there, but with the tulips coming on strong and a faint green haze on the lilacs, a person can see that this is not the moon but Earth, a planet named for its finely ground rock containing organic material that, given sunlight and moisture, can produce plant life that may support advanced life forms such as Catholics or Lutherans. School windows open and faint wisps of talk drift out and some choral music. Rototillers start up, and the first *whap* of a ball in a glove is heard. Sometimes the scratch of a match is heard, struck by someone who had vowed to put the Luckies away for Lent. The sulphur flares up, the coffin nail glows, the delicious smoke rushes into the poor man's suffering body, and he sighs with delight, emitting a cloud.

After finishing the cigarette, he calls himself a terrible name.

On the first real warm Sunday, attendance is down at church, people deciding that, God being everywhere, they can worship anywhere—what Fr. Emil calls "the Protestant fallacy"; he strolls around after Mass, surprising some absentees who were busy worshiping with rakes and didn't see him coming.*
"Oh! Father! My gosh! Didn't see you! Good morning."

"Yes. Almost afternoon. Funny how the morning just slips away, don't it?"

"Yeah, that's right, Father. That's for sure."

"Such a beautiful day, it'd be a shame to have to be indoors on a day like this, now wouldn't it?"

"Well, that's true, Father. You got a point there."

Mrs. Schwab is in her yard Sunday morning, working up a show of peonies, the giant double whites she put in last year, but she's not resting on

---

*Blue laws once frowned on Sunday labor, also loud recreation, unseemly dress, and any "deportment inconsistent with proper reverence," and those laws still frown but do it in private, in the book of old ordinances, in a section unread for many years. Still, as recently as last summer, when Corinne Ingqvist, home for the weekend, walked four blocks to the lake in her red bathing suit, people who passed her going the other way, to church, felt that something was definitely *not right*. It bothered them. She is Pastor Ingqvist's cousin, a slim connection, but it made for a disturbing note, a long red honk in the middle of a peaceful Sunday morning. They prayed that she would leave town, and on Monday she did.

her peonies, she's expanding west toward the clotheslines, digging a kidney-shaped bed for her western peony annex where she'll put in yellows and reds. She doesn't care for delicate blooms, she goes for the gorgeous Las Vegas floor-show-type flowers. Tiger lilies, snowballs, asters, and dahlias. Flowers that sag under the weight of their fabulous hats. Big American Beauties and giant mums that when you see them you can almost hear the Casa Loma orchestra. The yard movement in Lake Wobegon has been toward the activity yard, but Mrs. Schwab carries on the old show-yard tradition. You'd no sooner toss a softball around in it than in her living room. Too many ornaments for one thing, and then, too, you wouldn't want to track in on a lawn so carefully edged and pruned and preened and combed. That's Mr. Schwab's job. He's already mowed and raked and dug out the dead spots and resodded. The birdbath has fresh water. The two iron lawn chairs are out, with the molded scallops on the backs that keep you from slouching. The bricks laid diagonally in a trench to make a border around the beds—he's retrenched, relaid them. The B.V.M. sitting on her platform of rocks with the porcelain bandshell overhead—the plastic tent has been removed and the shrine cleaned. And soon Mrs. Schwab's flowers will burst into blossom, and the Mr. and Mrs. will take their seats and enjoy the breeze that brings them steady whiffs of extravagance—she in her yellow peony dress, he in his luau shirt, listening to the ball game, snoozing, a white hanky on his bald head, she with a *Reader's Digest* Condensed Book, snoozing—both of them sitting up suddenly now and then to examine the garden. Is something out of place? Did they detect a brown leaf, a stone in the grass, a dead stick? Was that a deadly garden pest moving around in the flowers—is it time to get the bug bomb, move in on the flanker? No, it's only a butterfly, cruising through the blossoms. It is perfect. It is the paradise yard they worked for, their heart's desire, the garden of love.

Crocuses, tulips, and those little blue and yellow flowers, what they call Norwegian incarnations, up by May 17, *Syttende Mai*, and the incarnation of Elmer, asleep in the canvas hammock. He makes a handsome bulge, a great pendulous form like a fat cocoon about to drop its load and become a butterfly. Other people rake as he snoozes, including Pastor Ingqvist across the alley, who wishes he had let his sleeping lawn lie. Matted down, it looked grasslike, but raking opened it up for analysis and he can see that the crabgrass and quackgrass prospered mightily last year, while the bluegrass and Bermuda fainted and grew weary, and now serious measures are called for, but the Building Committee, which is the steward of the parsonage and its lawn, is made up of farmers who don't take grass seriously, including Mr. Tollerud, who said, "A little spraying, that's the ticket," although a herbicide now would only result in total destruction. Pastor Ingqvist would like to take grass less seriously, but his neighbors are church members whose lawns are clipped, weed-free, dense, dark green, and whom he often sees on their knees fighting off the invasion of false lawn from their minister. They look at him with (he thinks) reproach for not doing more good works with his grass. Meanwhile, Elmer, who hangs in the breeze sawing lumber, has an okay lawn, not the Yard of the Month, but a darned good piece of turf. He throws some seed on it every spring and it jumps right up. Mrs. Elmer tends her shrubs and flowers like she was the Fourth Musketeer: she wields her trowel and clippers and whacks them around a little, and they stand up and grow like crazy for her.

Over a block, on Lilac Street, Ella Anderson cleans out her flower beds, her first venture out of doors since before Thanksgiving. Her bad hip can't navigate on ice, and now after four months cooped up, her arthritis is so bad, she is having to learn a new stand-up style of gardening.

Horrible to imagine: kneeling down, getting stuck, having to wait for someone to walk by, and calling out, *Help, help me.* Horrifying. If Henry were right there, she could say, "Oh, heavens, my legs went to sleep. Give us a hand up, dear," and it'd be a little joke, but Henry's inside and miles and years away. Calling for help from someone she barely knew would be an *emergency,* and Charlotte'd find out and call a family meeting. "This has gone on too long, Mother. It's time we did something about you and Dad. I'm worried sick about you there by yourselves." Ella doesn't want a meeting, though she'd like to have more visitors. Just her and Henry in the house, and his mind comes and goes, not that he's such bad company either way. When his mind goes is when hers gets sharper. At any moment, he's apt to think he's on the Burlington Zephyr from Chicago to

St. Paul and ask, "Where are we now?" and she has to think fast and describe what's going by the window. Not just "Oh, fields. The river. Looks like a town coming up"—he wants to know what crops, what town—he may be gone in the head but he knows the old Zephyr route, and if she skips a stop and says, "We're coming into Pepin, dear," he'll say, "You mean you didn't tell me when we went through Fountain City? You should have woke me up."

"Oh, I'm sorry, dear. *This* is Fountain City."

"Oh, yes. Well, I should have recognized it myself. Fountain City. Lovely town. I have a cousin lives here, I ought to look him up one of these days."

The cousin died at St. Mihiel, south of Verdun, in General Pershing's army. Henry never mentions him in the lucid moments, but during his spells, there's Frank, twenty years old and selling shoes and exciting the women of Fountain City, and so Henry is eighteen, which means that she hasn't met him yet, and the woman riding the train with him is someone else he calls "dear"—who is she? It takes presence of mind to keep things straight—and she looks out the window and says, "We're passing a little farm, dear, a dairy farm it looks like, with Golden Guernseys, and now we're catching up to a truck on the highway, with two boys and a collie riding in back, and now we're coming into a narrow ravine and way up in the sky are two hawks, circling."

Ella is the only one who can give Henry this train trip. If Charlotte were here and he asked what town were they going through, it would be an emergency. Charlotte would have a fit and call a doctor. To Ella,

Charlotte's faith in doctors is made of the same stuff as Henry's trip on the train.

Charlotte is fifty-three and heavy, taking after the women on Henry's side, who became dumplings by middle age, but Charlotte doesn't feel like a dumpling, she's worried sick about her health. She'll drive a hundred miles to see a new specialist she's heard about, practicing all the way her speech about her symptoms, which remain constant, like the route of the Zephyr. Ella knows them like she knows that Pepin comes after Fountain City: feeling tired all the time, dizzy, nauseated, gas pains, backache, headaches, cramps, constipation, white tongue, shortness of breath, poor circulation in the legs, what feels like a lump *here* and *here*. "If I knew everything that was wrong with me, I'd be dead by morning," thinks Ella. Instead, in the morning, she gets up, using a new technique of sitting on the edge of the bed and falling forward and catching the dresser and pulling herself up. Sixty-some years ago she used to climb trees. This is more adventurous.

She wishes more people would come and talk to her and tell her things as she tells Henry what's out the window. His window on 1918 is open, and hers on May 1984 is stuck half-shut and she needs a little help. So she has put out a sign, written on cardboard with big Magic Marker letters and tacked to a picket and stuck in the flower bed. VISITORS WELCOME. FREE COFFEE. COME IN.

When Charlotte heard about it from her friend Mrs. Magnusson, she had a fit. She called up her mother, in tears, and said, "I visit you. I come over there every chance I get. What more can I do? How can you embarrass me like this? You couldn't have told me before you did it? Can't you see how foolish it makes me look? It makes me look terrible! Now please take it down. Please."

Poor Charlotte, she takes everything so personal. She lives in a trailer park near St. Cloud ("It's not a *trailer* park, Mother. They're mobile *homes*. You should try it, you'd like it.") She and her husband, Roy. Charlotte suffered a miscarriage in 1956 and they have no children. Roy fell off a scaffold ten years ago and hasn't worked since. Charlotte is a secretary at a clinic. They don't respect here there, they treat her like dirt and have for almost twenty-five years Some days, when Ella's phone rings at five-thirty, she lets it ring until it stops, knowing Charlotte is calling with news of outrageous things they did to her at work, especially the office manager, Bernetta Grinnell, who is thirty-one, stacked, dumb as dirt, and has been out to get Charlotte for years. Bernetta is sleeping with one of the doctors. Charlotte knows the score and Bernetta knows that she knows, so there you are. Bernetta dumps everything on Charlotte's desk, then takes credit for the work. She gets away with murder. She takes two hours at lunch, and she steals from petty cash. She lies about Charlotte to the doctors, so Charlotte hasn't gotten a decent raise for years. It's terrible.

"You should quit, dear," Ella has told her a couple hundred times. "Oh, sure. Quit. That's easy for you to say," Charlotte says. "Can't you see? That's exactly what she wants me to do. I'm not going to give her the satisfaction."

Everything happens to Charlotte. Boys throw toilet paper on her little yard. Why would they do it? Neighbors' dogs pester her. The manager of the trailer park refuses to do anything. He's a stupid good-for-nothing who sits in his office and drinks beer all day. She's afraid of him. He has threatened her. Then there's Clifford, her hairdresser. She's gone to him for fifteen years, and he's terrible. She tells him how she wants it, and then he goes and does it exactly opposite. She looks a fright. She hates to look in a mirror afterward, for fear she'll have a stroke. She suffers from high blood pressure anyway, and almost any one of these things, the neighbors or Clifford or Bernetta, could finish her off any day. She has talked about her problems to her minister, but he's no use at all. Sits around with his nose in a book, acts like he's better than everyone else, and when she tells him things, he sits there and smirks at her. Smirks! He's supposed to help her and comfort her! Instead he sits and *smirks*! One of these days, she is going to slap his face.

"I'm getting old," she told Ella on the phone. "I'm so old, and what have I done with my life? Nothing." When she was seventeen, Charlotte won the American Legion Auxiliary District Essay Contest with five hundred words on the topic, "America the Beautiful," and got $15. Now, many years later, that success comes back to haunt her. "I should have been a writer," she says. "I don't know why I didn't. I wish I had gotten more encouragement." Charlotte reads two or three novels a week and is sure she could write better ones if she had the time. She has good ideas, but ideas aren't enough. You need an in. She knows that. She wasn't born yesterday.

One night she sat at Ella's kitchen table, cutting up cucumbers, and suddenly dropped the knife and said, "I don't know what I'm going to do when you're gone," and cried bitterly, and Ella tried to comfort her. "Don't worry, I feel just fine," she said. Ella doesn't think about death much herself. Not as much as she did thirty years ago. She thinks about visitors. Loneliness is too dramatic. It makes troubles seem tragic, and hers are quite ordinary old-lady troubles, she thinks, and would seem more ordinary if she had some ordinary visitors. Not like Charlotte. Charlotte is an event.

Spring. I'm twelve and am getting a little tired of Jim's rules playing guns—he gets to be whoever he wants to be and we have to be Custer or FBI or Russians and have to count slow to fifty when we're shot, whereas he gets to say "You just winged me!" and we're supposed to believe it—so I take a walk. Carl Krebsbach and his friends hang out by his garage in the alley down from the school. I sit on a swing and look down the alley and see them, six guys watching Carl sand the rust spots off the fender skirt of his terrific red '48 Chev. It would be nice if they saw me and yelled "C'mere!" but of course they don't, being older, they have their own rules, so I go over there. Sneak down the alley to the garbage cans and listen in—Harold Diener is saying, "That asshole!" and they laugh. I say it to myself a few times, to get the hang of it, and then *slowly* edge around the corner and slip into the garage and stand by the rear bumper as if I've been there for hours. Trying to blend in and be unnoticeable like a tree or a dog, but Harold sees me. "What do *you* want?" he says. I say that I just came to see what they were doing. "So now you saw. Beat it." Actually, I would like to hang around for a while. I say to Carl, "Can I help?" and, miraculously, he hands me a scrap of sandpaper. "You scratch the paint, he'll break your arm," says Harold. I work away at the tiny brown spot, and the spectators go back to what they were talking about, which was a teacher who gave Junior an F on a book report he had copied from the book jacket, which reminds them of all the money they're going to earn when they get out of goddam school, and of Minneapolis, of this guy George knows in Minneapolis who works at the Ford plant and drives a Cadillac ("He don't care what they think!") that has a beer spigot on the dashboard and the front seat tilts all the way back to make a bed, electrically, when you press a switch, which is fascinating indeed but not to Harold. He keeps staring at me. I'm the fly in his ointment. I try to be invisible, a good little worker, but I feel his eyes boring into me. Then he says that he doesn't know how *they* feel about it but *he* feels that you can't have someone in the car club who hasn't gone through *initiation* otherwise every jerk in town is going to be hanging around—he says to me, "You know what a tire run is, dontcha?" Actually, I don't, and am not curious to find out, but he and Junior and

George think it's a great idea. They get a tire and Harold grabs my arm and we head over to school. I could yell for help and probably he'd let go, but I decide to show that I can take it, whatever it is, even when we climb up the toboggan hill behind school and I start to get the idea. And I am right. They hold the tire and I am supposed to sit curled up in it, bracing myself, and roll down the hill. I hate them all. I hate them so much that I say, "This isn't anything. I've done this." I actually make myself believe it, and get in the tire! One mighty push and I start to fall, spinning faster and faster—I close my eyes—I hear them yelling far away—it *bounces* off the ground, it thumps and the ground roars by and sky, I'm so dizzy I feel sick—now it's on grass, hissing, and then it *bounces* so hard my guts hurt, off a tree, and I fall down and *I get right out and sit on the grass as if nothing happened*. Everything is a blur, but I look around as if I am admiring the lovely foliage this time of year. When my head clears so I can make out foliage, I get up and walk away from the tire, back to the garage where Carl is sanding away. He looks up. "Those assholes," I say.

Every spring when the car goes down, the Sons of Knute sing—

> Beat those rugs and clean the biffy.
> Now is the time to make it spiffy.

—and go to work cleaning the Lodge, a sacred service in the ancient rite of Knutedom, but sacred more for the ritual than for the result. They start at noon with the Call to Order and the ceremonial Passing of the Pail, then the Installation of the Ancient Vacuum and the Removal of the Deceased Plants, and a symbolic swipe of the Fraternal Dustrag, and then it's time for the Opening of the Amber Essence of the Blessed Hops. "It smells like somebody's buried in there," says my mother, who's never been in there but has a sense for that sort of thing. Most Knutes smoke, and by April even they are noticing it—even Elmer who smokes three packs a day. Elmer once woke up in the night smelling smoke, and it turned out to be himself. That was when he cut down from four.

Long ago, the Knutes formed a secret service organization called the Nogebow Ekal, whose aim was to perform good deeds secretly for the pure pleasure of helping others and accepting no thanks or recognition,* a principle that all incoming Knutes were secretly sworn to uphold. "Believe me, if they'd ever done anything, we'd have heard about it," says Mother. Her skepticism is shared by others. The secret of Nogebow Ekal, like the secret of the Knutes' pressed coffee, is one that not many care to know.

The Lodge is square, squat, brick with sandstone sills and cornerstone (1907). Under the rear, southwest corner is a jack. The foundation cracked under that corner and was removed in 1948 so a new one

---

*"Do we share our worldly goods? You betcha!
Do we care for all the sick and poor?
Are we kind and generous? I guess so!
Are we Christian gentlemen? *Ja shur*!"
—*Sons of Knute Songbook*, #42

could be put in. The jack is there temporarily until the Knutes decide exactly how they want to go about that.

Storm windows come off in April, screens go on— on a certain day that is not known until it arrives, the first Saturday when people feel they are about to suffocate. The fear of drafts dies hard, and then the massive storms are pried off and the windows opened and a little fresh air blows in which shows a person how dismal and stale the old air was and awakens a person to the dank carpet, the mildew, the dead winter dust on everything, the general corruption of indoors after so much cold weather, like what grows on meat in a closed jar after six months in the fridge, which leads directly to spring cleaning.

One fine Saturday morning, Diane opened her eyes and smelled something bad from under the blanket. Ed had been doing that a lot lately. She threw off the blanket, releasing it into the room like a black cloud, and then saw how grimy the windows were and that it was almost nine o'clock. Nine o'clock! She heard children downstairs rooting around for breakfast. One said, "You little jerk!" Then the smack of a hand, a box of cornflakes fell on the floor, and she smelled hot dogs and something like burning marsh-mallows.

Never known for her housekeeping, Diane none-theless was struck by the feeling that things had gone too far and if they went one inch farther, her family would slip right over the edge and live in a plywood container at the town dump, sleep on old mattresses, and eat out of large plastic bags.

Ordinarily a bather, she showered, out of urgency, and pulled on her jeans and sweatshirt ("One Tough Mother"), yanked the covers off Ed—"Out of the sack," she said; he said, "Huh?"—and hit the kitchen at a fast walk. It was marshmallows all right. Little Eddie was frying them with two wieners. Beth started to explain that it wasn't her fault and that Paul had said mean things to her. Diane stuck a finger in the girl's face. "Upstairs. Sheets off the beds, rugs off the floor, curtains of the windows. Bring it down here, everything. Five minutes. Go." She snatched Paul on his way out the door. "Get a broom, a bucket and the sponge mop. I'm going to show you how to wash floors. Go. Now." The little boy at the stove looked at his wieners; his lower lip curled, and a tear ran down his cheek. She put on water for coffee. She put bread in the toaster. She pried the wieners from the pan, scraped burnt marshmallow off, and made him a wiener sandwich with ketchup and fresh marshmallow, his favorite. "Finish that and then get your butt down to Grandma's," she said. "We got work to do here."

When Ed appeared, she had washed and dried the dishes, put a load of curtains in the washer, and swept the kitchen floor. She poured him a cup of coffee and put a list in front of him, including Storm Windows, Take Out Mattresses & Carpets, Basement & Garage, Rake Lawn—"What's the big rush all of a sudden?" he said.

She was more than ready to tell him. She had a good sharp speech on the subject of Being Tired of Living in a Pig Sty. She was way ahead of him. Racing around the kitchen, slamming stuff into cupboards, scrubbing the floor with short hard declarative strokes, she had been talking to him long before he showed up. She had worked up a head of steam.

—"I'm sick of looking at this mess." *Bang*. "You drop your stuff all over—socks, towels, the paper, dirty dishes, all over the house." *Slam*. "I'm sick of it. I'm not your mother, you know." *Bam*.

—"I'm sick of being ashamed to have people stop in. Not everybody lives like pigs, you know. Not everybody wallows in dirt!" *Swoosh*. "This place isn't fit to live in!"

—"I am through with trying to do it all by myself." *Swoosh*. "Being an unpaid servant around here." *Swoosh*.

—"We're going to clean today! We're going to start living like decent human beings for a change!" *Squeeze*. *Bang*! "Otherwise you can find someone else to keep house for you." *Bam*.

She drove them all morning like a dog drives sheep. He hauled the storms to the garage, washed windows, hosed down the screens, put them up, the two children hauled carpets out and hung them on the clothesline, swept floors, dusted, she washed floors and walls, and when she detected lack of motion in their sectors, she was *there*, in two seconds, to bark at their heels and turn them in the right direction. She clapped her hands like a coach. "Come on! Let's go! Move it!" She fixed peanut butter sandwiches for lunch. They ate standing up. The children looked at her as if she was crazy.

The washer chugged along all day, and the dryer. She did all the scatter rugs, the curtains, living room drapes, dresser scarves, antimacassars, couch coverlet and pillow cases, the lace tablecloth, the sheets and bedspreads, plus regular wash, and between loads, she waxed the floors and cleaned the bathroom. She put Beth to work with furniture polish and sent Paul outdoors to help his father, but the children were starting to slow down, lose orbit, wander off—she caught Beth reading a book, she sent Paul to the basement for a paint scraper and when she noticed he was missing and went down to find him, he leaped up from behind the furnace—he had been lying on a plastic lounge chair, evidently trying to locate the scraper telepathically. "What's the matter with you?" she yelled. The boy looked at her, confused, tired, at the point of tears. "I don't know where it is," he pleaded. "Why are you so mad at me? You yell at me all the time. *I* don't know how to clean floors!"

"Help me beat rugs," she said. He slumped along behind her upstairs and out to the backyard where Ed had dumped the carpets in a heap. They hung them over the clotheslines, and she got a strip of molding out of the garage, snapped it in two across her knee, and handed him one. "Beat," she said.

He gave the carpet two light taps and little puffs of dust came out. "No, like this," she said, and she started to whack it hard. Dust flew. He watched in amazement. Diane is small but she laid into the carpet as if it was the cause of all her trouble. In the carpet was not only filth and squalor but also ignorance, sloth, corruption, lack of ambition, everything that is dull and lifeless and corrosive to the spirit. She beat it senseless and moved on to the next, beating in the name of Christ and the apostles, in memory of generations of women who devoted themselves to scrubbing and scouring and purifying the world—heroic women who took up arms against filth and stagnation and against that dull, slack-jawed, slug-footed, limp-wristed, shiftless, listless, leisurely, lazy, lead-butt, slow-leak attitude of loungers and loafers and laggards and lumps and lie-abouts who were all too ready to accept filth as a way of life—she walloped the carpets with all her might, clobbered them up one side and then the other, and the boy gradually caught on. He swung from the heels, hard—"Hit flat! Not with the tip! Flat!" she hollered—getting a good *thwack* on every swing, amazed at how much dust was in them, carpets that had been faithfully vacuumed and yet ten, twenty, thirty *thwacks* and still more dust, it was endless, almost.

"There," she said. "Good work. You're a good rugbeater." She caught her breath, then they hauled the rugs into the house.

Inside, it smelled of rich lemony polish and floorwax, the top layer of odor, and beneath was the smell of outdoor air, faint blossom and green, and beneath that was another aroma, so plain but so sweet, the smell of *clean*. Not soap or detergent, simply *clean*.

The smell took Diane by surprise, her nostrils full of dust. She stood in the middle of the living room and took deep breaths. Ed was finishing up the raking on the side lawn, which had released the green smell. She called out the window, "Come in and smell the house."

Spring, Mrs Hoglund opens the windows of her little green house, and you hear how her fall crop of piano students is doing these days. She works them hard through the early painful EGBDF—FACE phase and on to the Bach two-part inventions and "To a Wild Rose" and "Gypsy Song" by Ostroushko, which is supposed to evoke the dancing of Romany maidens as they return to the village with their load of kindling. Hard to imagine, dancing with a bundle of firewood on your shoulders, and not easy to play either, with so many quarter-notes in the left hand. "Not so draggy, Curtis. Pick it up. It's meant to be happy. Don't just play notes. Play music. *Now*, one, two, three—four, five, six." And Curtis's music follows you a little way down the street.

In spring, the odometer of our good old Fairlane read 99999.2, the first car that Dad ever bought new so all those miles were ours, our history, including all the wonderful times he said, "Jump in. Let's go for a ride." It was the gadabout Pernell in him speaking. A Pernell great-uncle was among the first to get a car, and he was in such a hurry to go nowhere in particular that he ran it off the road and into the creek, hauling back on the wheel and yelling *whoa*! Dad loved to jump in and go for a ride, one of his few impractical traits. He'd start out, then think of a place to go, usually someone a ways away who we could visit. But we couldn't stay long. "We got to go," he'd say after one cup of coffee. On vacation trips, he'd pretend not to see a Reptile Garden or a Scenic Overlook even though we all pointed it out to him; he wanted to keep going. A vacation day when he didn't put at least six hundred miles on the odometer was mostly wasted for him. So when he got home from the grocery store with the odometer teetering on the brink, about to turn a fresh chapter in our life, he said, "Jump in," and we all jumped in and took off north around the lake, our eyes glued to the dial. A beautiful day, pretty as a postcard: a boat riding on the lake and someone standing up in it, hauling up anchor; two hawks lying on the wind, not moving their wings, two dark specks motionless against the clouds drifting east; and, amazing!—Mr. Hanson aboard his big Belgian, Scout—riding bareback, a deacon of the Lutheran church, digging his heels into Scout's ribs to make him run a little, a horse so trained to the cultivator he is nervous about running and bucks a little—the deacon slips and falls forward, his face in the mane, and grabs onto Scout's neck— Dad slowed down to a crawl for this show, and then (of course) we looked and the odometer read 00000.1 and we had missed what we came for. Dad said he could put the rear wheels up on blocks and run her in reverse until the odometer got back to zero and we could try again, but instead we ate supper. We opened the dining room window and the front door to let a breeze blow through. It was Saturday.

Spring

The room smelled of grass and hamburgers and furniture polish.

Another spring years later, a different Fairlane, same furniture polish (Johnson's Glo-Coat), and similar burgers, the Saturday night of the Junior-Senior Prom, me in a white tuxedo. We believe that dancing is wrong—it leads only to carnal desire, that's the whole purpose of it, to excite lust—but I don't intend to dance, as I've told Mother fifty times, and looking at me, perhaps she can see that I don't and am not likely to excite a girl to the point where she'd want to, so I get the use of the car. I took a hot bath (until carnal desire came over me), inspected my face for horrible blemishes, and put on my clothes, everything new and wrapped in plastic, underwear, black socks, shirt, the rented suit, and stood in the dining room door to be inspected, feeling like the famous host of a panel show. My sister looked up and laughed. Dad glanced up, a little embarrassed by so much display of raw hope. Only Mother took a good look. She stood up and fixed a few stray hairs, adjusted the black bow tie, shot the cuffs, flexed the lapels, and walked around back and pinched off a loose thread. "You look very nice," she said. She pulled out a hanky. "Do you need this?" she asked. I didn't. I had two. An invisible microscopic speck of dust appeared on one shoulder, and she brushed it away with the hanky, and then, noticing something above my left eyebrow—unconsciously, out of habit, she spat a little *ptui* in the hanky and rubbed my forehead. *Mother spit.* Our holy water, the world's most powerful cleansing agent.

That spot burned all night. I kept rubbing it.

I knew that the gymnasium was not going to look like the Donelson mansion in *Last Dance at the Old Plantation*, in which the family goes ahead with the spring cotillion although it is 1861 and the shades of war are settling on Charleston, but I liked that book for its debonaire style and could imagine myself in it. *"Oh, Papa," Emily said, her brown eyes glistening with tears, "don't it seem almost criminal to dance while men are dying?" "Darling," he replied softly, "we must go on with the cotillion so that gentlemen will have something to die for."* The gym was the gym, even with card-tables in it and sprays of lilac, and the watering trough in the middle of the floor, even though decorated to look like a fountain, was a watering trough. Still, the lights were low as they were that night at Swancroft. *He pulled her to him, his handsome features slightly darkened by the cares of army life, and kissed her. "Oh, Randolph," she cried. "I didn't know you cared!" "Miss Emily," he said, softly, "another month may find me mortally wounded on some distant battlefield, and as I die, I shall have only this moment to remember."* I didn't expect to find that depth of feeling at the Prom, but I could feel some sense of fading youth and impending tragedy and wished that Donna would too and know that this shining moment in life was passing quickly and we didn't have much time in which to declare our passion for each other, of which she did not give even a hint, dancing with Roger Hedlund. I watched her from beside the punch bowl, a stainless steel kettle from the cafeteria with blue crepe paper wound around it, and held my Dixie cup high, in an interesting pose.

"Hey, B-B Brain, whatsa matter? Your dog die?" It was John Potvin. He popped me hard on the shoulder.

"You're crude. You know that?"

He said, "Don't be so negative," and pulled from his jacket a small bottle and poured clear fluid into my cup of Parisian punch. "Vodka," he said. "Whatsa matter? You don't drink?" So I did. It heightened my sense of elegance, and then I had another to make the moment shine brighter, and then a little bit spilled on the white jacket and instantly spread, like ripples from a rock in the pond, and then I thought I'd like some fresh air. We went to the parking lot, and I had a little more, and then the shining moment was over and it was time to be alone.

She told me the next day that she wasn't *with* Roger, only dancing with him. She had to dance with somebody, didn't she? I didn't expect her to go to the dance and sit, did I?

Randolph lost a leg at Chickahominy and returned to Charleston too late for the 1862 cotillion. "*I hope it was brilliant and that you were the belle of the ball,*" *he said, leaning against the white pillar.* "*Oh Randolph,*" *she replied softly,* "*the evening was empty without you. I was invited to dance but my heart wasn't in it. I spent the cotillion right here, sitting on the step, watching the road, waiting for you to come.*"

"I always meant to send you to Europe and I never

did," Charlotte said. "I meant to send you on a cruise to romantic places. That was always my dream, to send you and Daddy to Bermuda, Buenos Aires. Or China. China would be nice. Wouldn't it? And now it's too late." Charlotte looked so sad, Ella said that she never had the slightest interest in going, which upset Charlotte. "You mean I was a fool to think that all those years?" she said. "I dreamed and hoped for nothing?"

"It was a nice thought," Ella said, "and that's what counts."

"It's the greatest disappointment of my life that I never sent you anywhere."

"Oh, now. I'm very content. My brother was the traveler in the family. He didn't need to be sent, he was gone before you ever noticed he'd been back."

Her older brother, Spark, was a pioneer in Lake Wobegon aviation. He flew to St. Louis and back when he was nineteen. In 1925, following service in the Army Air Corps, he bought a Curtis-Ingham, flew straight from Lowe Stokes Field near Atlanta to the family farm west of town and crashed in a field of beans and walked to the house and slept for twenty-seven hours while the neighbors came by to admire his uniform. He was tall and slender and strong as a whip, and he sported a full mustache, a white neckerchief, and a scar on his cheek. He had not flown nonstop because he was anxious to be home, he simply had a nonstop nature, and after a day on the ground, he was ready to take off, but the Ingham had busted a strut and his mother burst into tears if he so much as mentioned flying, so he took up farming for a year, which he hated, and the following fall, as soon as the beans were in and the field safe for take-off, he revved up the Ingham and roared away into the sky. He went to Brazil, he went to the Arctic. Five years later, he disappeared on a flight over North Dakota. His mother listened at night for his engine overhead. No trace of him was ever found. Years later, Ella had his name carved on her parents' grave marker.

––––––

The Class of 1960 saved up $322.65 in two years of holding car washes, dances, and a pancake breakfast, and then in our senior year, we doubled our capital with the lucrative popcorn and ice cream concession at football and basketball games. There was talk of giving it to the Junior Red Cross. The spring before, the Red Cross thermometer rose only to $34, a scandal, so in September, at our class meeting, President James Tollefson presiding, our adviser Miss Falconer suggested that we seniors turn our concession money over to good works. The Red Cross, she reminded us, is always there when you need it, providing help to people in floods, fires, earthquakes, famine, and epidemics. Schools smaller than ours raised hundreds of dollars every year. "I have a feeling that you're mature enough to consider helping those less fortunate than ourselves," she said. Donna Andreson, president of the J.R.C., said, "I think this would be the greatest thing we could do with this money and I think it'd be a wonderful example to other kids." We voted it down, 69–7. She was so mad, she stalked out of the room and went and sat in the girls' lavatory.

It was our money, though, and we had the right to spend it however we wanted to, and we didn't want to give it to charity. We wanted to *see* something from it. Russell suggested a big senior class blowout: shoot the wad, buy steak dinners, beer, hire a band, do it in Minneapolis where people know how to party. "Why not?" he said. "It's our money." But we were, as Donna said, "a class with high ideals." Our ideals didn't include the Red Cross but they didn't include an orgy either. Most of us agreed with Donna Bunsen when she said, "I want our money to go for a gift to the school, to buy something that we'll be remembered by."

It was only September, we had eight months left, and yet nostalgia lay heavy on our hearts and the premonition that in real life we would cease to be special. In this quiet little pond, encouraged by doting teachers, we felt successful and shining in *some* way, but once graduated we would disappear into the crowd of faceless adults and be like everyone else, old, a little tired, disappointed, and things not work out. College would be too hard and flunk us; the Army would unmask us as cowards; marriage would turn sour and love would die. One way or another, we would find disgrace, as others had. A man who had quarterbacked the Leonards in 1951 when the team was 10–0 and went to Grand Forks and won the Potato Bowl: he was in St. Cloud Reformatory for stealing $219 from a blind person. A good student and a member of the Student Council, now doing time behind bars. There were others like him. When Donna Bunsen said, "I want our class gift to be something special that we can all be proud of," she was right, and she didn't have to add: "This may be one of the last things we'll ever do right"—we all knew that.

Previous class gifts didn't say much for them. The portrait of Henry Ford from the Class of 1920 honored a man nobody cared about; 1928's trophy case was an embarrassment (half empty), and the marble water fountain, compliments of 1931, was a big waste of money. The gold auditorium curtain from 1951 was ugly, and the globe in the library was all but useless. The gift of the Class of 1917, it was a world that no longer existed. A plaster bust of Shakespeare was the legacy of 1947, a nice idea, but succeeding generations had gone to work on it with crayons and made the Bard look like an old cocktail waitress.

After we voted down the less fortunate, President Tollefson opened the floor for nominations and got (1) a stained-glass window, (2) a piano, (3) sending Clara the cook to cooking school (ha ha), (4) a clock, (5) a student-citizenship trophy, and each had a few supporters and the rest of us groaned. That wasn't what we wanted at all!

When Marjorie stood up, I thought she was going to nominate a gift to the missionaries, she was that sort of person. She focused her big watery green eyes on us and said, "I think we should do something to recognize teachers. We owe so much to them, and someday we'll think back and remember, so I think the money should be spent on a tribute to teachers." I couldn't see Miss Falconer, our adviser, sitting in back, but she was probably beaming at Marjorie like a lighthouse. "I nominate an oil painting of a teacher who has been very important to us, and I nominate Miss Falconer as the teacher."

She sat down to a great studious silence. President Tollefson wrote "Oil Painting, Miss Falconer" on the board. Then Miss Falconer herself rattled her necklace and stood up. "Oh, my dear Marjorie," she said, sniffling. "I don't know when I've ever felt more honored—just the idea is an honor, but I can't let you do this, and I do mean this from the bottom of my heart: there are so *many* teachers, so many fine teachers who are much more deserving of this—for me, just having the *opportunity* to work with so many outstanding young people like yourselves, not only as a teacher but also, I'd like to think, as a friend—this has been reward enough for me."

Donna Andreson then seconded the nomination. Fern Shoenecker said she was ready to vote. She moved that the nominations be closed. James wasn't sure about parliamentary procedure. "Vote!" a bunch of girls said. "It's a democracy." Eva Wirtz said she withdrew her nomination of the piano, she was in favor of the painting. A bunch of girls clapped, a larger bunch now; the tide was moving toward Miss Falconer in oil. She said she'd be glad to leave the room if we wanted. "No! you don't need to leave the room," the girls said. I looked at Lance and he looked at me. We were sick. "Say something," he whispered. I couldn't think of what to say. This was some kind of *joke*. We all had Miss Falconer, we knew who she was. She had it in for boys. In choir, every day she looked around to see who hadn't learned his part—she could smell fear like an animal—and made him stand up and die for a few minutes. To think that we would perpetuate her in a work of art was something we could look back on in later years and get sick all over again. Miss Falconer was the last person I'd want to see in a painting: oil, finger, or any other kind. She had, all by herself, cured me of a longstanding fascination with choirs. She had almost cured me of music.

The first choir I heard was the Lutheran. Aunt Flo's house was across the alley from Lake Wobegon Lutheran, and at ten-thirty Sunday morning, as our little flock of Brethren sat on her kitchen chairs and warbled, the chickens taking the melody, the geese and ducks in the vicinity of it, we heard the Lutherans strike up a processional like powerful oarsmen pulling away from the line. I knew that the Lutherans were on weak ground doctrinally and many of them were wordly and smoked and drank beer and even went to dances, but when I heard them sing, I could imagine the choir marching through the church in their magnificent robes of spun gold, the congregation standing, and I envied them the wealth, the splendor, of their song.

Down the street and over one block was Our Lady of Perpetual Responsibility, and when the Lutherans paused for breath, I heard the strains of mass, Fr Emil's voice rising and falling in Latin—those mysterious Catholics! In the spring, the windows open, birds singing, two blocks apart the two choirs squared off against each other in a wonderful match of sanctity, and I wished I was marching with one of them.

A warm Monday morning in April—the first warm morning, suddenly spring—downstairs, Grandma is whistling under her breath, and Mother comes to the stairs and sings our names. And I sing back, "I don't have any socks. Where's my shirt? She won't get out of the bathroom." But it really is spring and warm out, and today we beg for the luxury of cold cereal instead of oatmeal, Mother's soul food, and I try to leave the house without my scarf, in a spring jacket, and this time I win, though Mother sings, "You'll be sorry. You'll catch cold. Don't blame me." And I burst out the door before she can change her mind, and it is spring. Yesterday was cloudy, dull, cold, quiet (or maybe I had wax in my ears), but this morning the birds are out in force, a kingdom of robins and bobwhites and meadowlarks camped out along the route to school, singing invisibly from the trees and tall weeds thousands of bright notes like reflections of light on water—singing out against this dreary town streaked with mud, the brown grass with the souvenirs of dogs, the last stubborn patches of ice in the woods—and up the street under the bare trees and down from the hill come trios and quartets and duets of children, some of them singing, some of them hitting the singers.

Spring

Mine eyes have seen the glory of the burning of
    the school,
We are torturing the teachers, we are breaking all
    the rules.
We broke into his office and we tickled the
    principool,
And truth goes marching on.
Glory, glory, hallelujah.
Teacher hit me with a ruler.
I knocked her on the bean
With a rotten tangerine
And she ain't gonna teach no more.

And then, in Mrs. Swenson's seventh-grade class, we stand by our desks and sing with all our hearts, "O beautiful for spacious skies, for amber waves of grain. For purple mountains' majesty above the fruited plain." It is then, after we sit down and Mrs. Swenson says, "Take out a clean sheet of paper and number from one to fifteen," that I suddenly remember why I was dreading today in school. Not because of this test—it's current events, my best subject. Monday is choir day, and today we all go down to the lunchroom and Miss Falconer is going to drill us again in three songs she has been drilling us in since January for the all-district choral concert in May, and which we sang last Monday even worse than we did when we started, and the worst of all were us tenors.

Miss Falconer is an elegant lady, almost like a duchess compared to our mothers—she wears real jewelry and tailored suits and spike heels and white blouses with ruffles, and her glasses, studded with precious gems, hang from a pearl chain around her neck. She is so beautiful, like a lady out of a magazine, that when she looks at me, I can't look back at her, I look down. "Look at me!" she barks. "How do you expect to sing in rhythm if you don't look at me? I'm here to direct you."

Rhythm isn't our problem in the tenor section so much as the notes are. We do drag a little but only because each of us is waiting for the boy next to him to sing the note so he can get it. And just in case the note is wrong, we sing very softly. "I can't hear you, tenors," she has said over and over. "Look at me. Watch my hands. And—" And we sing worse, so badly she stops us and sighs a long sigh and says, "This is not that hard, children."

It is hard. She has picked three hard songs by foreign composers with one name. "Serenade" by DesCanzi, "O Tall Papaya Tree" by Del Monte, and "April Is in My Mistress' Face" by Morley "April is in my mistress' face, /And July in her eyes hath place, /Within her bosom lies September, /But in her heart a cold December." When I sing about her bosom, I think of Miss Falconer in her underwear with leaves between her breasts. Some of the tenors cannot sing "Within her bosom lies September" without snorting and gasping, because Bill Swenson once sang it "Within her bosom lies Bill Swenson."

"Perhaps," Mrs. Swenson mentioned once, "perhaps they could do better with something like 'Red River Valley.' "

Miss Falconer gave her a withering look. "I'm not going to baby them," she said. "They are just going to have to learn that music is something you have to work at and apply yourself. You can't sit around singing cowboy songs all your life. Listen to this," she said. She played a record of an English boys choir singing "April Is in My Mistress' Face." "Those boys are the same age as you and younger," she said. She played the record again. We despised them, their fluty voices, the little twerps. But Miss Falconer wouldn't give up. "It's April! April! Not *Aprul!*" she said. "Open your mouths. Look at me. Think about what you're singing. And—"

And—we sang softly, listening to the boy next to us for the note, and we thought about bosoms—and now it is Monday again and "April is in my mistress' face" and I am sitting next to Jerry Swedeen, fourth from the end in the tenor section, looking at the back of Donna Bunsen's neck as Miss Falconer taps her pencil on the music stand. "Tenors," she says. "I want you to sing your part for me so I know you have it. One at a time."

One at a time. Death; we all die inside. My heart has collapsed. No it hasn't—it's pounding like hammers. My face itches. Girls poke each other and whisper and smirk at us: Ha ha ha ha ha ha.

"James," she says. James stands up. He always knows his part. He takes piano, he has an advantage. "That's very good. Thank you. Bill—" Bill has now learned the song from James. "Fine. Jerry?"

I now almost have the song in my mind from James and Bill, and now Jerry destroys it. He sings all over the place. Miss Falconer tells him to sit down. "You girls—I hear whispering. You may sit down, Jerry. Gary?"

"I don't feel very good, Miss Falconer."

"If you're well enough to be in school, you're certainly well enough to sing."

"I don't think I can. I don't feel good." It's true. I fell terrible. We had bread with yellowish gravy on it for lunch—chicken à la king with string beans and green Jell-O with mayonnaise and crushed walnuts— and I honestly think that if I stand up and sing in front of everybody right now that this whole lunch—

"Sing," she says.

I stand. I study the notes for a moment as if—if I look at them hard enough, they will jump into my mouth.

"April is in my mistress's face, /And July in her eyes hath place," I murmur, and then at the thought of what is coming, I begin to suffocate. Girls snicker. Miss Falconer doesn't even look at me. "That's enough!" she barks.

I come home ashamed and stay in the backyard.

I'm not very hungry, thank you. Meat loaf, no thank you.

I do dishes with my older sister. She sings a song we always sing together when we do dishes, but I don't feel like singing it, so she sings it with my mother.

> Tell me why the ivy twines
> Tell me why the stars do shine.
> Tell me why the sky's so blue
> And I will tell you why I love you.

Because God made the stars to shine,
Because God made the ivy twine,
Because God made the sky so blue,
Because God made you, that's why I love you.

I go to my room and fall face-down on the bed and
wonder why God made my life so embarrassing.
What I want most is to sing—to be a famous singer
like Elvis or Ezio Pinza or George Beverly Shea and
stand on stage with light all over me and open my
mouth and out comes my magnificent voice and
people get weak listening to it because my voice tells
them that life is not miserable, it is impossibly beautiful, but instead I open my mouth and out come faint
cries of ducks, awful sounds, a drone, a whine. My
heart is full of feelings, but I can't sing worth beans.

I make myself feel better, as I so often do, by putting a record on the phonograph and pretending I'm
the singer. My Uncle Tommy, who attended the University of Minnesota and made something of himself,
had sent me a souvenir record of "Minnesota, Hail to
Thee," sung by the University chorus and Mr. Roy
Schuessler, baritone. I get out the record, and imagine
that it is Memorial Day and sixty thousand people
have come to Memorial Stadium to honor the dead
and also to hear me, Roy Schuessler, and the chorus
sing our state song. The governor is there, and
mayors and ministers, and five thousand Boy Scouts
in formation holding American flags; my family has
driven down from Lake Wobegon for the occasion,
and after I sing, we'll go to a swank restaurant and
have sirloin steak and french fries.

And now the moment has come. Sixty thousand people rise to their feet, the stadium is hushed, as I put the record on the phonograph and stand, head up, feet apart, at the foot of the bed, arms outstretched, facing the wall, facing the great wall of faces turned up toward me.

And as I mouth the words, "Thy sons and daughters true will proclaim thee near and far," my mother walks in with an armload of laundry—she walks between me and the chorus to the dresser and puts socks in the top drawer. The governor, the sixty thousand fade away—the song goes on.

"What are you doing?" she asks.

"I'm practicing," I say. "For choir."

Miss Falconer's portrait was painted by an art student at the University for $400, and from the looks of it, the two women did not hit it off. The artist seemed to have the same impression that we did: not only does the figure look stern, pointing a pencil viewerward, but her face is flushed and her eyes are ever so slightly crossed. There is a barely visible mustache.

It was unveiled at a school assembly on the last day of school, 1960, though Miss Falconer had already seen it and, though she couldn't very well say so, she hated it. She hated it so much that when she looked at it, she looked exactly like it: ticked.

As a special surprise, we seniors stood and sang "Red River Valley," which we had forgotten was not a favorite of hers. "Come and sit by my side if you love me, do not hasten to bid me adieu," we sang sadly, with foreboding, and got on a bus and rode to

St. Cloud and had a class dinner with the rest of our money, where we promised to keep in touch and be friends forever.

REVIVAL

After a year at St. Cloud State, Johnny Tollefson came home something of a success, having notched a 3.2 grade average and published two poems in the literary magazine *Cumulus* (under the names J. Robert Tollefson and Ryan Tremaine), and promptly smashed the front end of his dad's Fairlane on old Mrs. Mueller's rock garden. It was a fine June afternoon and she was talking on the phone to Mrs. Magendanz about a woman whose house got robbed in St. Cloud in broad daylight, when she heard the screech, a couple loud thumps, the crunch of metal, and finally the hiss. "Jesus, Mary, Joseph! Some-

452

body's hit me!" she said. He had managed to take out her ornamental deer, a plywood Dutch windmill, and the martin house, and left two black ruts across the new sod. He didn't damage the rock garden much, her son Earl having cemented it pretty good. The front of the car was mashed in back to the engine block, and the hood was sprung. Johnny sat with his hands still on the wheel, blood running down his chin. "Dear God in heaven!" she said. "I knew something like this was going to happen!" She braced one skinny arm against the car and put her other hand over her eyes. "Dear Jesus, I'm about to faint," she whispered.

He shouldn't have driven the car home after that. With the radiator smashed and the oil left behind on the grass, the engine overheated and then, seeing the idiot light flash red, he drove faster, thinking the wind would cool the engine off. So, beyond the damage to the front end, the valves had to be reground. It came to $350 all told.

"Byron," his wife said when Mr. Tollefson got home. "By." She held onto his arm, slowing him down, and then routed him into the kitchen and sat him in a chair. "Be patient," she pleaded. "Don't talk to him when you're so angry." But Byron couldn't talk much, he was so disgusted. He skipped supper and went to Mrs. Mueller's. Earl had stood the deer up and the martin house, but the windmill was totaled. And two nests of martin chicks were dead. That was the worst of it. "Mother is taking it pretty hard," Earl said. Byron could see that by the fact she didn't come out and offer him coffee. "She's so nervous to start with, and then this—"

"I don't know," Byron said. "I just don't know."

Earl said, "Well, they all grow up eventually."

"I don't know."

From his wife, Byron got the story that his son "didn't see the curve" and it "happened so fast [he] couldn't do anything," which made no sense. The curve had been there since God was a boy. Was the kid drunk? What the hell?

That night, after hearing a speech he had heard on other occasions,* Johnny went up to his room, took out a yellow legal pad, and wrote:

---

*I. I don't know what's wrong with you.
  A. I never saw a person like you.
    1. I wasn't like that.
    2. Your cousins don't pull stuff like that.
  B. It doesn't make sense.
    1. You have no sense of responsibility at all.
    2. We've given you everything we possibly could,
      a. Food on the table and a roof over your head
      b. Things we never had when we were your age
    3. And you treat us like dirt under your feet.
  C. You act as if
    1. The world owes you a living
    2. You got a chip on your shoulder
    3. The rules don't apply to you
II. Something has got to change and change fast.
  A. You're driving your mother to a nervous breakdown.
    B. I'm not going to put up with this for another minute.
    1. You're crazy if you think I am.
    2. If you think I am, just try me.

Revival

The car swerved and ran off the road
Into the yellow flowers.
Some roads aren't there.

He looked at his nose in the mirror. Dr. DeHaven
said it was broken but not badly so he just put a piece
of tape across it. It looked good with the tape, like
a fighter's, and Johnny hoped it would be a more
distinguished nose with maybe a scar. His face was
too childish. He wished he had a beard like W. Greg
Hatczs. He had tried, but with his blond hair, what
grew out didn't make a big impression. W. Greg, on
the other hand, had a huge multicolored beard, reds

C. You're setting a terrible example for your younger
brothers and sisters.
III. I'm your father and as long as you live in this house,
you'll—
A. Do as you're told, and when I saw "now" I mean
"now."
B. Pull your own weight.
1. Don't expect other people to pick up after you.
2. Don't expect breakfast when you get up at noon.
3. Don't come round asking your mother for spending money.
C. Do something about your disposition.
IV. If you don't change your tune pretty quick, then you're
out of here.
A. I mean it.
B. Is that understood?
1. I can't hear you. Don't mumble.
2. Look at me.
C. I'm not going to tell you this again.

and browns and some whites. You looked at him, you thought, *Writer*.

W. Greg Hatczs was the author of *Fragments of the Piece: A Dream Passage*, which he had read a chapter of to Mr. Davenport's creative writing class at St. Cloud during his week as a writer in residence. He was from Minneapolis. He wore a brown herringbone sportcoat and a gray turtleneck sweater and was as big as a desk. Johnny didn't remember what the chapter was about, it didn't have sentences and paragraphs as such, but he had liked the spirit of it and the boldness of the writer, who made Mr. Davenport look like a dink.

Mr. Davenport, who gave Johnny's story "Song of Larry" a C-minus, and at the part where Larry's parents turn into plastic lawn chairs, Mr. Davenport wrote in the margin: "Where are we? Who is Devereaux DesChampes? Point of view? *Unclear*." Obviously, W. Greg was operating under no such restrictions.

Naomi Swenson, who sat next to him in class and took good notes, had managed to write only one word in her spiral notebook: *surrealistic*. She seemed to be pretty much right about that. W. Greg was not big on structure; the chapter seemed to take place in a Greyhound bus depot where General Custer had gone to sleep off a hangover. Or it might not have been Custer, who knows? And when the writer came to the end, it was hard to tell that it was the end. Some students thought the silence was maybe part of the story, a blank page thrown in for contrast. Then he asked for questions.

The students looked at him thoughtfully for a long time, as if the chapter had made such a profound impression on them and had raised so many questions in their minds that it was hard to narrow them down to just one. Finally Naomi raised her hand. The author nodded.

"This may seem like a dumb question," she said, "but where do you get your ideas?"

He smiled as if she had asked what was his favorite food. *Dumb question*, everyone thought. W. Greg lit a cigarette and blew a cloud of smoke that filled the entire room.

"That's not a dumb question, only an impossible one," he said, and all of the *A* writers smiled at him in an understanding sort of way. "I suppose I *could* say that I get my ideas from writing," he said, "but that begs the question, doesn't it?"

Naomi turned red and bent over her notebook, pretending to study it (surrealism . . . surrealism . . . surrealism), shielding her face from the smirky looks the *A* writers gave her. *Where do you get your ideas?!!* Didn't she know that a serious artist's ideas come out of *himself*, out of his inner life and the struggle to realize his strange and absolutely inescapable *gift*, the dumb broad?

Her question struck John afterward as not dumb, not impossible, but certainly difficult. When *Cumulus* printed his poem "Death Dad," he was so happy to see his name in print he sent a copy to his mother, who called him on the phone two days later and said she had never felt so humiliated in her life.

"Where did you *get* this?" she said. "*We* never talked like that! Our home isn't like that at all! It's so cynical! Where did you get those ideas? You certainly didn't get them from us!"

He explained that the poem was metaphorical and that the dad in the poem, who wore blue pajamas and a red chenille robe (which Byron happened to wear), was purely fictional.

"It's only a poem! It's symbolic!" he said.

"Explain that to your father," she said, and hung up.

To the serious artist in him, the question "Where do you get your ideas?" made writing seem ordinary and so *prosaic*, like a hobby ("Where do you get your Austrian first-issues?"), implying that maybe writers subscribe to an idea service, a newsletter called *Lots o' Plots*, or maybe readers send in ideas ("Dear Mr. Roth: This may be a dumb idea but how about a novel in which a guy turns into a breast? It's just an idea, thought I'd pass it along. Feel free to use it and fill in the details as you see fit. P.S. Love your stuff!").

And yet—It stuck in his mind. His humanities prof, Marvin Voss, in "Hum 100: Undercurrents of American Thought," talked about Hemingway, Fitzgerald, Steinbeck, as if their ideas were simple reflections of their times, like so many iron filings arranged by powerful forces that they could not understand then although he did now.

When John looked at his own writing, he was disturbed by the thought that it came from Mr. Davenport, a fan of Nissan, a Zen master of the three-line *zazu*, whose tiny oblique poems Mr. Davenport recited in a thin, tremulous voice, hands upraised, wiggling his fingers. After hearing a few, John could sit in his room and write a dozen.*

---

*Dorm Songs:

Four layers of brick boxes,
Stacked by the river,
Each one filled with music.

A stranger sits on my bed,
Eating a box of tiny animals.
It is his room, too.

The hot lamp lights the book,
A box full of sentences wiggling
Like earthworms drowning in paper.

Green beans and meatballs
In steel boxes under hot lamps.
A pool of white potato!

I push the empty plastic
Along the steel rails, collecting
Myself from a small assortment.

I find myself in The Rec,
Once again a disaster.
Lights flicker with emergency.

The tiny steel ball
Rings invisible bells,
Gravity descending.

The paper ball bounces

This thought did not lead him to retire from the field of serious writing, however; it made him resolve to try even harder that summer. His work (as he referred to what he had written) was imitative because had never forced himself to look deep enough within, so he would go back home and write things that came directly out of his own life and experience.

He sat at his blonded maple desk every night, trying to write better. His dad had bought the desk for him when he was eight. His legs were cramped in the well. The desk lamp, with Mickey and Goofy dancing on the base, was an old birthday gift. The

---

Between wooden hands on the green table.
Someone is knocking!

A hard diamond of light
In the middle of the dark glass.
Then "Leave It to Beaver"!

Wally, are you crying
There in the dark room in the box?
Wally, are we brothers?

Mr. Davenport suggested revising one verse to "A sharp diamond of light/In the center of the dark glass./Then a boy named for a small-boned creature!" but he gave it an *A* and added, "See me sometime. I'd like to talk." Evidently he had forgotten that John had seen him several times and that he, Mr. Davenport, had talked a lot each of those times— female consciousness and male mythology and the right side of the brain, which, in John, went numb after a few minutes of nodding. He felt he was too much like Nissan already.

shelves above the desk held old Landmark books, *A Boy's Life of Lindbergh*, the Hardy Boys and the Christian adventures of the Minnehaha Creek Gang and the Flambeau Family,* along with his Paul Samuelson Econ text, Commager's *Living Ideas in America*, the *Our Living World* from Bio 101 and *Elements of Public Health*, and Parrington's *Main Currents of American Thought* (abridged), which he had bought thinking that he, an American, might read it and find a current of his own. The bed was his boyhood bed, with a footboard that forced him to invent new sleeping positions, and under the bed was a peach crate full of old train track. A bullfight poster was tacked to one wall, a Leonards pennant to another.

It was hard going. He was nineteen years old, and his experience up to that point consisted of childhood, growing up and going to school, hanging around with friends, and spending a year in St. Cloud. Lake Wobegon was a lot like any small midwestern town. It had no Skid Row or bohemian section, where a writer could meet exotic, desperate, or vicious people and collect impressions and feelings to use in his stuff. Several in Mr. Davenport's class had

---

*Authored by Wm. Dixon Bell, the Flambeau Family Series (Hutton & White) competed head-to-head with the adventures of the Minnehaha Creek Gang (Augustana), a group of seven Luther Leaguers who, in book after book, enjoyed good clean fun, cheerfully helped around the house, and used nonviolent resistance to bring vicious nonbelievers one by one into the faith.

been to Europe and used it as a setting for poems such as "Paris: A Triptych" or "Fourth of July in Florence." He had only been to Canada. Once. Barely.

He made a list of experiences he thought he should have in order to become a better writer. He left No. 1 blank, for fear his mother might see it. No. 2 was Europe; No. 3 was despair. In April, he had thought of writing to Naomi and suggesting they go to France together and kill two birds with one stone, but after five or six drafts, the letter still lacked clarity. Europe was a long way away. It looked as if he'd have to settle for No. 3. Maybe Mrs. Mueller's rock garden was the beginning.

"Why do you stay in your room all the time?" his mother asked him one morning as he stood at the kitchen counter, spreading peanut butter on a hamburger bun.

"I'm not in my room now, am I?"

"No"

"So then I don't stay in my room *all the time*, do I?"

"Well, a lot of the time."

"I sleep in my room. There's a lot of time right there. You want me to sleep on the living room couch?"

"Oh, Johnny."

One reason he stayed in his room was the sheer number of *Oh Johnny*s he heard when he came downstairs, about one every two minutes, plus his dad's *Oh, for pete's sakes*, *Good Lord*s, *Grow up*s, and *I'm talking to you*s. Nothing about him was right in their eyes, not his clothes, his hair, the food he fixed himself or the way he ate it, the way he sat in a chair or got up from a chair, the way he dried dishes or walked across a room or closed a door.*

He literally could say nothing that they agreed with, *nothing*. He had tried to come up with things at the dinner table: "I saw Mr. Berge today, he was so drunk he didn't know where he was or why"—his dad had said that a hundred times, but when John said it, his dad told him to have a little pity, that if he (John) had been through half what Mr. Berge had been through, he might have a weakness, too. He said, "Uncle Jim is sure a hard worker." His dad said, "What would you know about work? You wouldn't know it if it came up and bit you." He said, "I was thinking maybe I'd paint the shutters tomorrow." His dad said, "I remember the last painting job you

---

*"I *iron* you clean shirts, why can't you wear *those*? It wouldn't hurt you to comb your hair once in a while. Beans? What sort of lunch is that? Don't eat so fast, what's the hurry? Sit *up*, it hurts just to look at you. Don't you know how to sit in a chair? Put your feet on the floor, and don't lean back, you'll break it. Speak up, I can't hear a word you're saying. Don't talk to me like that. Don't give me that dirty look. Pick up your feet when you walk. *You* didn't dry these glasses—look at this, you call this *dry*? Why do you always go around slamming doors? How many times do I have to tell you? When are you going to learn? Why can't you get it through your thick head? What's the matter with you?"

did, you got half-done and ran off and left the brushes sit in the paint can."

If he was to say, "I believe in God the Father, God the Son, and God and Holy Ghost," his dad would say, "A person sure wouldn't know it to look at you." Or he would say, "Don't talk with your mouth full," or "It's about time," or maybe he would convert to Unitarianism on the spot ("The Trinity? Don't be ridiculous!").

"Dear Naomi," he wrote one night. She lived in Sauk Center, where she was a carhop at a drive-in.

The summer is passing slowly here. I'm writing quite a bit, nothing worth mentioning. I've thought about starting a novel, but I hate to start something I don't think would turn out to be good. I might join the Army in the fall or else just bum around. Right now, I'm too depressed to think about it. I hate to sound conceited but it's hard to live under the same roof with people who have so little interest in ideas or even just conversation as my parents, especially my father. I think he must resent me for going to college, which he never did, because every time he opens his mouth, he tries to cut me down to size. Well, I don't want to be his size. If I thought I'd be where he is in twenty years, I'd kill myself right now and get it over with. I don't mean that we ought to sit and talk about poetry or anything (though that might be nice), I'd settle for one minute's conversation in which he accepted that I'm not six years old. Instead he can't look at me without coming down with both feet, and then of course the little kids pick it up—I asked my sister to please not come in my room without knocking and she said, "You're not so smart." Which is the general drift of conversation here: "Who do you think *you* are?" I don't know, I'm trying to find out the only way I know how, and it's hard enough to write without people constantly harping at you. Well, enough about my problems. I hope you're doing better. Call me sometime. It'd be nice to get together and talk to someone about something other than what a terrible person I am.

Writing quite a bit? He was writing a ton. Under the influence of *Leaves of Grass*, four months overdue at the college library, he found he could rapidly fill up whole pages of legal pad.

You say I'm not so smart and you're right but
neither are trees or rocks,
White lacy clouds, the glow of early morn, lakes,
clumps of grass, meadowlarks, bullfrogs, clods of
mother earth, corona of moon, cougars, the leaping spermatozoa.
I have walked among them, I have absorbed, I have
remembered them all unto myself.
O unutterable arboreal wisdom!

He woke up early, ten or eleven, read Walt over coffee to prime the pump, and hit the legal pad until he was overwhelmed by how much had come out and how much more there was, and had to go out and hoe the tomatoes to settle himself down.

He wrote a story entitled "The Story Writer," about a young man named Nils Sjogren who holes up in a rooming house to write and becomes weary of his endless egoism.

He sat for a long time looking at the white page filled with words until it became a meaningless blur. Suddenly he realized he was extremely tired of writing about himself, about his view of things. Suddenly it occurred to him that all he had ever done was think about himself. Slowly he reached for the box of matches. He lit one and held it to the corner of the paper and watched it burst into flame and curl up into black ash. He thought it was one of the best things he had ever done.

Then, for want of a better idea, he sent Nils to a bar and got him drunk. Nils drank "more whiskies than he could remember" and stood on a bar stool and delivered a speech explaining that his spirit had been crushed by small minds. "You tell me to be neat! I say neatness is the death of the soul! You tell me to take out the garbage! If I took out the garbage, there wouldn't be much left! You tell me to be on time! What you know about time, you could tell in one second! You tell me to cut the grass! You say it's getting long! Of course it's getting long! That is the beauty of life! Of which you know nothing! *Nada!*" Then Nils left Tinyburg for the oilfields of Venezuela.

The search for No. 3, despair, led him to write "The Story Writer, and then, the same afternoon, to go to the Sidetrack Tap to get drunk himself. It was a Wednesday, he was in the mood for an experience after hours at the desk, he was down to less than three dollars and in a mood to blow it, and besides, his parents would be going to church that night and wouldn't be home to see him stagger in.

The Sidetrack wasn't much as despair goes, but it was convenient, and his mother had told him since he was a child never to go in there, a recommendation in itself. She said it was an evil place and quoted Scripture to prove it: "Men love darkness rather than light because their deeds are evil." And the Sidetrack certainly was dim. When he was twelve, he'd gone in for a glass of water, which Wally gave him, and when his mother found out, she decided maybe Scripture wasn't caution enough. She said, "You drink out of a glass down there, you're asking for diseases I'd rather not even talk about. Filth! It's a filthy place!" And he knew she was right. A child's sense of smell is acute, like a dog's, and the odor of stale beer and smoke from the Sidetrack when the door opened almost knocked him over as a boy.* Once he walked by the door just as Arne Bjornson fell out, and it frightened the boy, how awful the man looked, his face dead, and how he smelled—he stank as bad as Bill Tollerud, who had a bet with another boy in seventh

---

*I felt the same when I was young—the patrons of the Sidetrack seemed unspeakably crude and filthy and degenerate and old. Now they seem about my age.

grade to see who could go longer without taking his gym clothes home to be washed. The bet went on into eighth grade. Bill was the winner.

By that Wednesday, a week after the crash, Mrs. Mueller was recovered from the shock and able to concentrate on what really troubled her, the prospect of sudden violent death. That morning, she unlocked the two deadbolts on her back door and stuck her head out, half expecting someone to chop it off with an axe, perhaps an inmate from Sandstone prison who had escaped in the night. She had not heard of an escape on the Maxwell House News that morning, though there was an item about an old lady taken hostage in Florida that gave her the creeps. A psychopath had jumped out from the flower bed when the old lady went to hang up clothes, and he hauled her indoors and tied her with clothesline to her own kitchen table and kept her there for thirty-six hours until sharpshooters plugged him through the heart. Imagine! she thought. The state of things today.

Mrs. Mueller has lived alone in this one-bedroom stucco house since the late Mr. Mueller died in 1951 of a ruptured blood vessel. He was putting up curtain rods one minute and the next he was dead on the floor. He was forty-seven. Now she was sixty-eight. That was how she wanted to go, too, quick, no trouble, no pain. Certainly not at the hand of a psychopath. Once in Minneapolis she thought a man was going to kill her. He almost crashed into her when she made a left-hand turn into a SuperAmerica, then he made a violent U-turn, squealed up to the pumps, jumped out, and screamed abuse at her. She was in her car, her doors were locked, and she turned on the radio to drown him out, she was so scared. The news was on: an item about a plane crash that killed fourteen people. She has never set foot on a plane,* but it seemed to go right along with the horrible face in the window saying he hoped she rotted in hell. You go up in planes, you go to Minneapolis, you take your life in your hands. You're not even safe in your own backyard.

It was six a.m. of what the radio said would be a perfect day, already warm under a partly cloudy sky and a sweet scent of grass in the air and the dew on her snowball bushes. The Tollefson boy's tire marks were healing over. The tulips were still bright and the peonies were coming right along. She saw one tulip had keeled over, but otherwise the flowers were all present and accounted for. The fallen tulip made her think *inmate* for two seconds—had he put his big foot there and was he now crouched around the corner of the house, a length of garden hose in hand, waiting for her to turn her back? No, he was not.

---

*One of a declining number who say, "You couldn't pay me enough to go up in one of those things," Mrs. Mueller rides the Greyhound to visit Kathy and Danny in Orlando, two days and two nights by land as against three hours by air, but she's in no hurry. She sits behind the driver and eats from a big sack of good things she had made and hopes that whoever sits next to her will not be the hijacker.

Nobody was there. The hose was coiled over the faucet where she left it.

Mrs. Mueller knew him as Don. She had thought of him so often, seen him coming at her, been grabbed and hustled indoors and thrown onto the sofa, and always he said, "Don't scream and you won't get hurt," and once he told her his name. Don. He wore dirty dungarees, sneakers, a black T-shirt, and dark glasses. He smoked cigarettes, which he stamped out on her floor. He pulled the blinds and paced like an animal. He rummaged in her dresser, throwing clothes on the floor. Sometimes he had a gun and other times a butcher knife, and once he had a screwdriver. He made her cook for him. He demanded whiskey. She had none. He got mad and threw a glass at her. He threatened to cut her throat and throw her in a closet. Sometimes he grabbed her by the arm and said "Get in there!" and shoved her toward the next room. Always he said, before he left, "Don't tell anybody or I'll come back and kill you," and she never had told. She knew he was not a real person but she was afraid he would become real. She thought she should tell Earl. The subject, however, never came up. *There is a man and he is going to come and kill me one of these days*: that wouldn't go over so well with Earl. "How do you know, Mother?" *I know*.

Mrs. Mueller's trip out the back door was to put a package of garbage in the garbage can. She had wrapped it the afternoon before, a milk carton full of her slight scraps—dollops of melon pulp, two grapefruit shells, burnt frozen dinner, a stale heel of bread, and a whole box of figs, a year old, a gift from a grandchild—and had thought to take it out then, but the shadows in the yard looked funny, as if they might include one of a man standing beside the house, waiting for the lock to click. One click and he'd spring like a tiger and be inside with her. She left the package on the table in the mud room.

Now she descended the back steps, peering ahead to the dim place alongside the garage, the walk between the lilacs and the garage, and the alley. So thin, her arms and legs like branches of a crab apple tree, her skin like waxed paper, and her small dark eyes darting from bush to bush.

That night, after supper, John put on a clean shirt and hiked down to the Sidetrack, taking his legal pad with him to record his impressions. His first one was of gloom and musty smells and deep darkness, the orange and purple jukebox, beer signs, bright green felt. He stood inside the door, waiting for his eyes to focus, thinking of a cave in which small hairy animals sit and chew each other's ears off. Three figures stood at the pool table and gawked at him.

"Chonny! Chonny my boy! What you doing here?" It was Mr. Berge, sitting on the stool nearest the door. His baggy old-man pants almost dropped off him as he stood up to shake hands, and he hoisted them up a foot. "Lemme buy you a beer! How you been, Chonny! No! Better yet! A beer and a bump!"

Wally set up a glass of beer and a shot of whiskey next to Mr. Berge's. John had been thinking he'd have a vodka sour, it being a drink he knew about first-hand from the Matador Lounge in St. Cloud, but he wasn't going to betray inexperience in front of this bunch. He sat next to Mr. Berge, who had fished two crumpled dollar bills from his pocket, and he put the shotglass to his lips, and tossed the whiskey back—or some of it partly back, until he coughed, and a few drops went up his nose, and his eyes filled with tears. It tasted like acid. He turned away so Mr. Berge wouldn't see. Then the beer. He never had liked beer. Beer parties were big deals at school: twenty carloads of students out at an abandoned granite quarry, a beer keg in every trunk, radios blasting, and beautiful women careening into the bushes to throw up. Beer made him think he was drinking something that had died.

"Oh, it's a helluva deal, ain't it, Chonny. *Ja*, we're having fun now, you betcha," Mr. Berge cried. "*Ja*, I was so surprised you come in, I coulda shit my pants. Wally! Don't let these glasses sit empty like that! Whatsa matter wicha? *Ja*, Chonny, it's good to see ya. Good to see ya. Put her there, buddy. *Ja. Ja*, I always like your dad, thought he was a good guy. Good guy, Chonny. *Ja*, lot of people say those Tollefsons, they walk around with their noses in the air, those Tollefsons they think their shit don't stink, but you know, I never thought that. I always thought, hell, they're people just like anybody else, like to have a good time. *Ja*. So here you are. *Ja*, it's good to see ya."

It occurred to John that it didn't make sense bringing the legal pad along to record impressions, his main one being a hardening behind the eyes. He took microscopic sips of the second whiskey. He wanted a glass of water. He felt like he was coming down with something. Mr. Berge was yammering a mile a minute about something—it was hard to follow—about people all being the same. He hollered to Wally for another round. Wally muttered something but he brought the drinks. "Watch yourself, kid," he said to John. "It's a stormy night for sailors. Don't let the ship go down."

John found a pencil and wrote, "Stormy—sailors—ship." He thought he might use it in the story about Nils, where Nils is in the bar and gives the speech. Have the bartender say it. "Whatcha writing, a letter, Chonny?" Mr. Berge said. He leaned over to see and his breath hit John broadside, the worst breath he'd ever breathed, the breath of a badger who'd been in the dump all day.

He stood up. The stool had cut off the circulation in his legs. They were asleep. He didn't know if he could walk. "Gotta run. Thanks. See you," he said, patting Mr. Berge on the shoulder, and turned toward the door. He leaned on it and in the blaze of hard sunlight he didn't notice the two steps down—he walked into air, staggered and pitched forward toward the gutter, and in one sharp instant as he fell, saw clearly six feet away his Aunt Charlotte and Uncle Val—fell headlong like a tree cut off at the ankles and hit the pavement on his knees and one elbow—and then he stood up too soon and the blood left his head and he got woozy and fell sideways against the hood of a brown pickup.

Charlotte and Val were dressed up with Bibles in hand, on their way to church. They stopped and tried to say something. Val said, "Johnny!" John said, "I tripped and fell." "I'll say you did," Charlotte said. She started to reach for his arm, he took a step forward and a step back, she drew back. "Oh, Johnny," she said. "Just look at you. Your shirt is ripped, you look like a crazy person."

"Why don't you come with us to church? It's going to be good. Bob and Verna are here," Val said. John said he didn't feel well. Val could see that. "Come tomorrow night, then," he said. "Johnny," Charlotte said, "do you ever stop and think what you're doing to your mother? I hope you don't let her see you like this. She'd just die if she saw you right now."

"It isn't what you think. I *fell*."

"It always starts out small, Johnny, and then one thing leads to another. Please don't drink. Please."

"Okay."

They walked away, then Charlotte turned. "I'm praying for you, Johnny."

"Thank you, Aunt Charlotte."

"Are you all right?"

Actually he was. He was starting to think this might be a good story. He'd change some details, of course. In the story, he'd be drunk—gone out drinking to forget a great personal sorrow, a wound, a wound of love—that'd be the title, "The Wound of Love"—and he'd stagger out the front door and be met by two Lutherans, Fran and Vern, who would bawl him out good, and the story would go on to reveal their essential hypocrisy and that of the entire town. He could work in Bob and Verna, the Bible-thumping evangelists, and get Mrs. Mueller in, too, except she'd be twenty-one, his lover, and he would die crashing into her rock garden, and that would be the ending.

He thought of this, making his way home, and sat down at his desk and ripped off the top sheets of the legal pad, which were dirty and torn, and there was a clean sheet. A lovely sight, a clean sheet—and he wrote, bending over the page, gripping the pencil tightly, chewing on his tongue:

James was fourteen years of age when his father was sent to prison for grand larceny, and it left a gap in his life that only he knew about.

Mrs. Mueller was one of two Catholics in town who attended the revival meetings of Brother Bob and Sister Verna of the World-Wide Fields of Harvest Ministry of Lincoln, Nebraska, at Lake Wobegon Lutheran church for five evenings, Tuesday through Saturday. To Bob, Mrs. Mueller was a great prize, a real living Catholic, and he courted her and her friend Mrs. Magendanz, assuring them he had nothing against the members of the Roman church, only the hierarchy. Father Emil thought of revivals as something that Protestants do to each other out of boredom with a theology that lacks substance, and he tucked a warning against it into his homily on the Third Sunday before Bob and the Second and the First, which only proved to Mrs. Mueller that the truth hurt. Even good men refused to see it. "Old Bob hits the nail on the head," she told Mrs. Magendanz.

The Ministry's headquarters is in the basement of

Bob's sister Beatrice's house, who is married to Pastor David Ingqvist's wife Judy's uncle, and from that loose connection comes an event that annually promises to tear the Lutheran church limb from limb. "The meetings were interesting and we praise God for His great love for us, as Bob so wonderfully brought out," Judy wrote to her aunt one year, "but I do wonder if he sometimes gets carried away in his description of death and damnation. And when he predicts that there will be more Lutherans in the lake of fire than there are stones in the fields, I consider that less than edifying." (In response, Beatrice sent her "An Examination of So-Called 'Lutheranism': Fourteen False Doctrines Revealed in the Light of Scripture.")

To see a man get carried away is exactly why so many Lutherans love the Ministry, however, including Val and Charlotte; what Bob revives in them is the memory of swashbuckling preachers of their youth who roved through the old Norwegian Synod putting the fear of God into a generation that was slipping toward relaxation. Children of God-fearing parents were slipping—slipping away in Model-Ts, drifting away in the night, slipping into worldly dress, slipping into St. Cloud and Avon and Little Falls for needled beer at roadhouses and dancing to jungle music and playing slot machines; young men and women brought up to lead a godly life were drifting, drifting, asleep in the boat on the Niagara River drifting toward the cataract and sure death, and someone had to shout to wake them up. Scoffers at spiritual things, drunkards, fornicators, blasphemers, proud, shameless, foolish beyond belief: such persons cannot be gently reminded of the truth, somebody has to grab them and shake them *hard*, as the late Rev. Osterhus did to Bernie Tollefson one hot summer night. Bernie ran with a loose crowd who drank at the Moonlite Bay roadhouse and boasted of having gotten girls in a family way, and Bernie came to church one Sunday night on a dare from his chums and sat in back and *smirked* at Rev Osterhus until the evangelist would stand it no longer—he leaped from the pulpit! Dashed to the back pew! Seized the young man by the neck before he could slither away! Hauled him out and up to the altar! Threw him against the rail! The sinner fell weeping to the floor, and the man of God knelt over him, one knee in the small of his back, and prayed ferociously for light to dawn in his blackened soul. When Bernie stood up, he was reborn, and he yelled, "Thank you, Jesus!" over and over, tears pouring down his cheeks— "Now *there* was what I call *preaching*!" says John's Uncle Val, Bernie's brother, a deacon and Pastor Ingqvist's faithful critic. He says of the pastor's sermons, "He mumbles. He murmurs. It's a lot of on-the-one-hand-this, on-the-other-hand-that. He never comes straight out. He never puts the hay down where the goats can get it. It's a lot of talk, and many a Sunday I've walked away with no idea *what* he said. Can't remember even where he started from. You never had that problem with the old preachers. There was never a moment's doubt. It was Repent or Be Damned. We need that. This guy, he tries to please everybody. Just once I wish he'd raise his voice and pound on the pulpit. That way I'd know he wasn't talking in his sleep."

Bob and Verna drive a white van with hundreds of Scripture verses painted on it, such as "The wages of sin is death," which is one thing that sets them apart from Pastor Ingqvist; his Ford station wagon has only one text, a bumper sticker: "Lake Wobegon, Gateway to Central Minnesota"—is that the mark of a man of God? The white gospel van draws plenty of stares with all that writing, which Verna painted freehand, so it doesn't look slick or professional but it's the Word and, as Bob says, "Once you've seen the van, you can't say you never heard the Gospel. You have no excuse. Anyone who's seen it will have to answer to God someday."

Bob once walked onto the field at a Vikings-Bears game to speak to the players about honoring the Sabbath and was led away by police. He once threw forty pounds of tracts from the Foshay Tower in Minneapolis on a day when the wind was right for carrying them toward the Catholic northeast section and was arrested for littering. ("Littering!" he told the court. "*Littering!* The day that spreading the Word is called littering is the day this country has taken its final step away from God!" He was found guilty.) Val conceded that "Bob loses his head sometimes," but he felt that excessive fervor was better than none at all. Val felt that Pastor Ingqvist never had much of a head to lose. When Bob and Verna came for revival, they stayed at Val's house, whom they met on their first visit to town in 1972 (to visit

478

Judy). Bob went for a stroll after lunch and, seeing a man mowing his lawn, Bob approached and said, "If God so clothe the grass which is today in the field and tomorrow is cast into the oven, how much more will he clothe you, O ye of little faith?" He shouted this, and Val could hear every word clearly over the mower. He shut off the engine and they sat down and had a long talk. Bob said, "I feel called to come and preach." "Then come," Val said, and he got the trustees to agree to it. Pastor Ingqvist said he thought a week of Bible study might be better, and Val said, "Fine. Brother Bob can come for *two* weeks, then." So began the crusade.

The white Scripture van pulled into Val's driveway on the Saturday evening before revival, Bob having preached Friday night in Fargo, and he and Verna were in church Sunday morning, in the second pew, far forward of the congregation, like outposts, Bob in a red plaid jacket that kept you apprised of his whereabouts. During the sermon, Bob often bent down in what appeared to be prayer. He also cleared his throat, "Hragh-*hmhhm!*" at various points. After church, there were rival hand-shakings, Bob at the front and Pastor Ingqvist at the back. And after Sunday dinner, there was a brief dispirited argument at the parsonage.

"Every year I dread this," David said.

Judy said, "I dread it, too."

"All week I feel like I'm eight years old. That Old Testament stare of his, those big black eyebrows. He's got that talent for judgment that makes people freeze in their tracks. And it's not such a great talent, you know, making people feel guilty—just about anyone can do it if they put their mind to it."

"My dear, if you feel so strongly about it, why don't you tell him what you think of him?"

"Your uncle Bob isn't someone a person can converse with."

"He's not my uncle. And you don't have to converse with him—just tell him what you think."

"He'd take it the wrong way."

So?"

"What do you mean, 'so'?"

"So what. Tell him anyway."

For the revival, Bob and Verna hung a thirty-foot-long canvas backdrop behind the pulpit, covering the altar and the painting of the Good Shepherd, which Bob considered a graven image, with a verse: I AM THE WAY, THE TRUTH, AND THE LIFE, in red letters like neon. He drove nails into the walls to hang it from, fresh nail holes every year—like notches on his gun, David thought, who cringed when he heard it, *bam! bam! bam!*—and Verna rounded up the Lutheran hymnals and put out tattered copies of their Singspiration songbooks. Verna played the organ. She played everything quivering with tremolo, as if it were a funeral for your entire family; even "Onward, Christian Soldiers" sounded dirgelike, the soldiers all dead.

Attendance, low on Tuesday and Wednesday nights, picked up for Thursday and Friday. Friday night, the church was almost full. All of Bob and

Verna's regulars, plus the Brethren, plus the Lutherans who don't want to be seen *not* being there, plus some surprising people the regulars have dragged in. Mr. Berge and Elmer and Oscar, the old guys from the Sidetrack, and a couple of bachelor farmers, all in a row toward the back, looking slightly feverish in their winter suits, their only suits. Mr. Berge! In church! He hadn't darkened a pew since God knew when.

In the first pew, Bob sat, bent low in prayer, and when Verna finished "I Love to Tell the Story," he was in no hurry to get up. Often he remained in a prayerful attitude for five or six minutes, and of course a person's mind wanders and you think about your car and whether it's up for a trip to the North Shore, you mentally balance your checkbook, you try to remember the name of the resort in Schroeder with the housekeeping cabins where you and your wife spent three days and made love six or seven times in a saggy bed in a dark room that smelled of mildew and previous couples and you recall one of the six or seven times, then suddenly you are gripped with remorse: My God! A man is pouring out his heart to the Lord, and here I am thinking about copulation! My God! And right then was when Bob stood up, climbed the stairs, put his Bible on the pulpit, and looked at you—at *you*, in a way that you knew he knew and you knew he knew that you knew he knew.

"Let us pray." A pause. Then he thanked God for this, another chance to hear the Gospel, perhaps the last, as we all knew from prophecy that we were in the last days, the world was drawing to a close, the

Lord would soon come, perhaps tonight during this meeting, perhaps now—this moment—before we draw another breath. . . . He prayed that the Spirit would be at work among us, seeking out the hardened heart and bringing it to a conviction of sin. "Lord, there is one soul here tonight who is without Thee, who is struggling in dark waters, without hope of salvation—Lord, we pray that the Spirit will speak to that soul—it may be a stranger, or it may be someone we know quite well, someone who attends church regularly and yet who can find no peace, no satisfaction—Lord, Thou knowest who it is—Speak to that boy, that girl, that man, that woman, so that they will not leave this place still in sin but will come forward and kneel at the altar of mercy and receive Thee tonight as their personal Saviour. Amen. *Let us sing*. . . ."

> Let the lower lights be burning,
> Cast a gleam across the wave.
> Some poor fainting, struggling seaman,
> You may rescue, you may save.

The thought of the struggling seaman makes a strange minor chord with your recollection of the motel in Schroeder, you feel ashamed for having heard this pun, as childish as "Gladly the Cross I'd Bear." Oh, unregenerate heart . . .

> Softly and tenderly, Jesus is calling,
> Calling for you and for me. . . .
> Come home, come home.
> Ye who are weary, come home.

This hymn was almost unbearable for Mr. Berge, for whom it brought a picture of his mother standing late in the evening at the kitchen table, kneading bread. The smell of yeast and Fels-Naphtha. Seven children and a worthless drunken husband, a worthless worn-out farm north of Parker's Prairie, a pile of dirty clothes in the corner, and her ashamed to attend the Norwegian Baptist church because she had nothing to wear, singing hymans late into the night. She knew hundreds of them. Almost any hymn makes Mr. Berge ill with grief, so he can hardly get his breath.

Another long silence, then the reading of the text, usually from the Old Testament. Bob likes to start there, a long way off from the Gospel, with the Old Covenant and the great men God raised up to lead His wavering people, Moses, Joshua, Saul—his voice rises and falls in pulpit cadence, once again your mind drifts from the shore as your eyes settle on the back of Joyce Johnson's neck, the part in her hair and two stout braids, which never interested you before but suddenly your mind slips into dark waters, you and she are by the creek, and she takes off her dress— *just like that*! Says, "Let's go swimming," and takes off her dress—no underwear, naturally, and you can't help but look at her, this fine woman, a pillar of the youth program, now naked in bright sunlight, walking into the water and holding your hand, and now you turn and embrace—and right then, Bob snapped his Bible shut and descended from the pulpit.

"I was planning to speak on discipleship tonight,"

he said, "but the Lord has laid another message on my heart. A hard message. One that many here this evening may not want to hear." He stepped down the three steps like a man entering the water, and to the churchgoing, who were used to clergy staying in their place, penned up between the font and the altar, it was a thrilling moment. As he disappeared from the pulpit microphone, Bob's voice rose, and when he reached the first pew, gripping it, his eyes sweeping the bowed heads, his voice was in full cry and could be heard clearly by those who had sought refuge in the rear.

"You think you live in a Christian community. A town of good Christian people. Well, let me tell you the truth. You don't.

"You go to church on Sunday, you give money, you're active in the women's circle or the men's fellowship, you think that makes you a Christian? Well, it doesn't. The body of Christ is not a club. You don't join it. You are *called* to it!

"Let me tell you, my friend—right now, as I speak, Christ is calling some of you—calling to you from the cross of Calvary, calling on you to give up your so-called 'Christian' life and follow Him—and many of you are saying, 'No, Lord, I can't. It's too hard, Lord. What will the neighbors say? What will my minister say? What will people *think* of me?' My friend, I beg of you: think of the consequences when you reject the Saviour who died for you in favor of leading a 'good Christian life'!"

—This quiet, churchgoing town, on the surface

peaceful and hard-working and decent, is in fact a whited sepulcher, a Sodom and Gomorrah, a sinkhole of sin and corruption and degradation and debauchery, for God looks on the heart, and in our hearts we are guilty of every sin—even adultery and murder. Yes! Adultery and murder! Lust in our eyes, blood on our hands! *Compared to what's in our hearts, Sing-Sing is a Sunday School!* 'For *all* have sinned and come short of the glory of God!' There are no 'little' sins; sin is sin; a 'little' one is the same as lying face down in the gutter. It all leads to the same place. To hell. The Lake of Fire. Eternal damnation. An eternity of torture by fire. A Hiroshima that never ends. An *eternity!* And you, dear friend, are worried what the neighbors will think? Think about eternity: imagine a sparrow coming to Lake Wobegon once a year, sitting at the water's edge, and taking a drink. When he has drunk the lake dry, eternity will have barely begun! But in the everlasting Lake of Fire, there will be no water. You will call out, you will weep, you will tear out the hairs of your head, begging God for *one drop* to soothe your parched mouth, but God will not hear your plea. God will say, "I never knew you. Depart from me, thou unfaithful servant." *If people in this town would spend half the time reading God's Word as they spend watering their lawns, it would make the difference between heaven and hell.*

Now every head is bowed and every mouth tastes of dust. The reference to sprinklers makes them cringe. All too clearly, they see the little arm spinning a tent of water onto the cool green grass as they themselves sit surrounded by fire, their tongues hot and blackened, pleading for water, pleading for death that will not come. Their flesh crackles and burns and melts but they do not die. This will go on forever.

Now Bob is walking up the center aisle, pausing at each pew, and at the back he will turn and say, "I hear many of you saying to yourselves, 'Later. Not now. Not tonight. Later. I'm still young. I'll think of spiritual things when I'm older. On my deathbed.'

> "Almost persuaded, now to believe.
> Almost persuaded, Christ to receive.
> Seems now some soul to say,
> 'Go, Saviour, go thy way.
> Some more convenient day
> On thee I'll call.'

"Friend, your deathbed may be the bed you lie down in tonight. Or you may never reach your deathbed."

This is the part that rings in Mrs. Mueller's ears. Brother Bob tells of the young man who attended a revival service ("a service much like the one you are attending tonight") and who feared for his soul but decided to put off salvation until a later time. Leaving the church, he drove three blocks to the railroad crossing where a fast C & O freight ushered his soul instantly into eternity, there to stand before the Judgment Throne and face God.

Now every mind is tracing the route home, remembering to stop, look, and listen, but Bob cuts off escape—he tells of others he has known ("young people in the very prime of life") whose lives were snuffed out like a birthday candle. A man of twenty-two, an athlete, young, vigorous, healthy: his heart simply stopped one day, and doctors couldn't explain it. Fell over dead. A young woman, on the night before her wedding, who choked to death on a stick of gum. *One stick*. Dead. A small plane, its engine stalled, fell silently through the darkness, crashing into a farmhouse, the family that had gone to bed hours before never saw the morning sun. Another family, sitting down to breakfast, joking, talking, when suddenly a thin figure leaps into the room waving a pistol and commands them to lie face down on the floor and there, one by one, he murders them in cold blood. The oatmeal was still warm when the sheriff arrived, too late. Dead.

Bob circles around the back where people sit for safety's sake, but there is no sanctuary anywhere in the sanctuary; he carries the terrible news to every corner, and now stops on his way down the side aisle where Eric Tollerud, Daryl's boy, has broken under the spell of death and his skinny shoulders shake, he sobs into his hands. His mother puts her hand on his knee; she, too, is close to tears. The other Tollerud children tremble. Every child in the room trembles. You yourself feel shaky, your eyes are hot and your throat is dry and sore. Your body aches. So stiff that when you lift your arm and put it on the back of the pew, you have to think about doing it. Sniffling begins two pews behind you and spreads. Your own head feels full, and now one tear runs boiling hot down your face, followed by another. You clear your throat, which feels like it's bleeding. Your eyes fill with tears and the room swims underwater, everything drowning in sorrow.

You see your own death, your wife dying, the death of your parents, your brothers and sisters, your children one by one. Bob has opened the door of the church and let death in. Mrs. Mueller whispers over and over, "Lord Jesus Christ, have mercy." The unspeakable sadness and misery of this life. The grave yawns before you, a bottomless hole. You are falling. Today, when you mowed the grass and listened to the ball game, was a little bubble in a sea of suffering and loneliness. There is no hope or sense in this dark world, all efforts are doomed to fail, and nobody loves us and we don't love them because we are drenched with sin; a constant terrible mindless evil grips us all and drags us down, down, down, into dark depths we cannot imagine. How weak, foolish, pitiful is everything you have ever done, the little piles of trash you've accumulated with so much effort, the poor little story of such obvious lies that is your life. Your sin, your very great sin sits on your shoulders and digs its claws into your flesh. A smiling man raises a gun and shoots you in the face. An airplane falls like a bomb. A train can be heard in the distance, coming faster and faster, the cone of light waving frantically, you press the accelerator and nothing happens, you sit on the tracks, your body frozen in place. Your children weep, you have failed them utterly. Your wife weeps, Joyce Johnson weeps, Val and Charlotte—and now Mr. Berge falls to his knees and cries, O Jesus, O Jesus.

Mr. Berge has wept before at revival meetings, and so have you, but this time is different because its *now*. Everything has come together at this moment, your life is balanced on it like a man on the high wire, and a flood of sins, your entire wretched history, pours from you as the Christ appears, patient and loving, at his hour of suffering. On the Mount of Olives, he prays for the Father's mercy until sweat falls off him like blood, while his poor disciples, who have been arguing about which one of them might betray him, fall asleep, even Peter, who will in a few short hours deny that he ever knew Jesus—but you will not, you will rise from the sleepers and say, *Lord I believe.*

This, in a way, you do—not the long walk down to the rail—Norwegians don't do that, too dramatic— but in your heart, there is a voiceless prayer. Christ, have mercy. Lord, have mercy. Let your light shine on me. Lord, lift me. Lord, feed me. Mercy, dear Lord, on my soul. And some light does shine—

Verna played "Almost Persuaded" through this agony, and then "Just as I Am"—Bob began to sing, "Just as I am, without one plea, but that Thy blood was shed for me," and everyone stood up. All the verses. The organ quavered and the voices rang out. The old familiar altar hymn, so well used for years that people know the words and sing their parts from memory, they sound like a choir, so sweet, so true, and then the long closing prayer. "We thank Thee, Lord, for Thy great love to us," Bob intones, and shortly your mind drifts one more time. Perhaps to the ceiling and the circles of light from the four globes hanging on chains—perhaps it's time to do a little painting at home. Strip the wallpaper off your dining room ceiling, see if one coat of Sherwin-Williams won't do the job. Your wife deserves a little work from you. Your shoulders touch as the distant voice drones on, and her bare shoulders come to mind, from the motel in Schroeder, but now she is even more beautiful in the pale evening light as she carefully folds her blouse and then leans forward and unhitches her bra, a simple motion you've observed ten thousand times ("When we've made love ten thousand times, bright shining as the sun . . .") but never found so graceful as now, in sweet memory, and Bob says, "In Jesus' name, Amen." And everyone turns for the door, and out you go into the night that is now charged with such tenderness and feeling, you and the others who wept with you, every star in the sky shines on your head, every cricket sings, the air you breathe is like wine, and the spot where you stand, beside the steps, beside your wife, is in the palm of God's hand who knows the number of hairs on your head, each of them alive and tingling, and He will never leave you.

Mrs. Mueller walked Mrs. Magendanz home, then walked the two blocks to her little house. She was not afraid, not even when she reached for the light switch and touched her cat, John, perched on the easy chair, who leaped and crashed into a vase. She simply cleaned it up and went to bed. She woke up twice, hearing noises, but went back to sleep.

It was in the morning that the notion of the inmate hiding in the shadows came back to mind. She had to make herself unlock the back door, and the fifty feet to the garbage can was a long walk. She pried off the lid and chucked the package in and was about to run back in the house when she noticed how quiet it was.

She couldn't hear a voice, not a car, not even a dog bark. No footsteps on gravel, no screen door slapping. Only the lanyard dinging against the flagpole at Our Lady church across the alley. She waited for some other sound and heard nothing. Then it occurred to her that the Second Coming had taken place. Jesus had come during the night to take His loved ones to heaven, they had all risen up from their beds to meet Him in the air. She alone was left on earth to suffer, she and Don who was probably around there someplace, crouching, holding a gun, chuckling to himself. God had forsaken her because her sins were so great, and soon would come the Judgment when she would be found wanting and be cast into the fiery lake.

The back screen door of the rectory squeaked and Father Emil stepped out in his black short-sleeved shirt, carrying a package of garbage and a garden trowel. He let the door slap shut and came down the walk, limping slightly, and a few feet short of his garbage can, he saw her. He said, "Good morning, Mary." She said, "Good morning, Father."

So he had been left behind too. She wondered about Sister Francis. Were all the Sisters sitting in their kitchen eating Grape-Nuts, unaware of what had happened?

Mrs. Magendanz had said last night that she thought there was a Book of Life where the names of the saved were written and she thought it was here on earth. A hardcover book. "I have a feeling," she said. "It came to me the other day when I was ironing. It's some sort of directory, that people think is something else, like a phone book, but it's the Book of Life. I know my name is written in it, I can tell you that for a fact." Mrs. Mueller always thought of Mrs. Magendanz as not quite right in the head, but sometimes those people come to possess wisdom. Mrs. Magendanz once healed a bad burn on her own foot by holding it and praying five hundred times, "Heal this foot," and when she let go, she said, you couldn't tell it ever had been burned, the redness was gone. If Jesus had come during the night, she thought Mrs. Magendanz would know about it even if she hadn't gone herself.

Father picked a few raspberries and ate them, and had a look at the onion row and the tiny cabbages and the shoots of cucumber vines, and he knelt down by his tomatoes and went to work hilling them up.

She called across the alley. "Father, is Sister Francis around?"

"In the church."

"Are you sure?"

"Saw her myself two minutes ago."

"And it was her—you're sure."

"Something wrong?" He stood up and peered across at her.

"No, I guess not."

"How about a tomato?"

The one he held out to her was slightly green, so

she chose a little red one from high on the vine, wiped it on her dress, and bit off half of it. It was so good, and then the bright sunshine made her sneeze.

"God Bless you," said Father.

The smell of warm dirt came up to her and the sweet taste of tomato, and then she knew what she was going to do—she was going to clean out those snowball bushes. She never really had liked them big droopy things. And she was going to water her yard and sit and read the Gospel of John.

That morning, David Ingqvist made his pastoral rounds, starting with Eric Tollerud, who was okay and thought he would be reading more of the Bible now. Mr. Berge didn't want to talk when David got to his house; he felt grippy and he needed a drink. Joyce Johnson said she didn't know what had come over her last night, but she felt okay, though her husband was mad at her. He said she had barked like a dog.

David's fourth stop was Bert Thorvaldson's, John's grandpa. He was sitting on his porch, sick about a tree. His majestic elm, as old as the twentieth century, had taken ill two years before and now was dead. He had treated it with coffee grounds the summer before and it put out some leaves, but now it was dead, and Carl Krebsbach was coming to cut it down. "Maybe there's something I didn't think of, some medicine they got," he said to David sitting next to him on the porch swing. "Once there were two magnificent things here, Eloise and that tree. Now they're both gone." He didn't mention that his eyes were going bad and that one eye shot off sparks. Without Eloise he was lost in the house. Old man with papery skin, sparks in one eye, sleeping in a strange bed, and now his yard was becoming a desert. David had never made a pastoral call in regard to the death of a tree. He recited the Twenty-third Psalm and led Bert inside. He put on water for coffee. The old man sat at the table and when the chainsaw cut into the tree, he went stiff and didn't move until it was over, and then he thanked David for coming. "*Tusen takk, tusen takk.*"

David had another call next door, to see the Tollefson boy, but he decided to let it go until another day. John's mother had read a letter in Dear Abby about a boy who sounded like hers, who sat around in his room and was curt with people and carried a chip on his shoulder and wasn't making something of himself, and Abby recommended seeking help from the family minister, so she called David.

David glanced at Dear Abby now and then, and it alarmed him how often she recommended ministers. "Talk to your minister," she'd say to the fourteen-year-old girl in love with the fifty-one-year-old auto mechanic (married) who is in prison for rape. Why did Abby assume that a minister could deal with this? The poor old guy is in his study, paging through Revelations, when the door flies open and a teenage girl in a tank top bursts in weeping with passion for an older, married felon three times her age—what is the good reverend to do? Try to interest her in two weeks of handicrafts at Camp Tonawanda?

Poor man. Things were fairly clear to him a

moment before, and now, as she pours out her love for Vince, her belief in his innocence, the fact that his wife never loved him, never *really* loved him, not like she, Trish, can love him, and the fact that despite his age and their never having met except in letters there is something indescribably sacred and precious between them, all Pastor can think of is, "You're crazy! Don't be ridiculous!" *Thou shalt not be ridiculous*. Paul says, "See then that ye walk circumspectly, not as fools, but as wise, redeeming the time, because the days are evil." How does this apply specifically to Trish, in love by mail, or to the Tollefson boy sitting in his room and forming a grudge against the world? When Paul wrote that wonderful sentence, he probably was sitting in an upper room in Athens; it was late at night, quiet, and all the fools were asleep. He could write the simple truth, and no fool was around to say, "Huh? What do you mean? Are you saying I *shouldn't* go for the world long-distance walking-backward record? But I know I can *do* it! I'm *good* at it! I can walk backward for *miles!*"

A worse accident than John's collision with the rock garden happened years ago after Greg Diener came home from the Cities, having been dismissed at the frankfurter plant. His boss thought that running the weenie-stuffer wasn't just a job but an opportunity, a calling, and he fired Greg for his bad attitude. Greg didn't mind. He settled back in with his folks. His room had become a sewing room, but he cleared the patterns off the bed and got caught up on sleep, and after three weeks was feeling much better.

"What do you want to do?" his mom asked. He didn't know. He said he was trying to find out.

"When are you going to try harder?"

"Don't you love me?" he said. "Don't you want me here?"

The Dieners set a deadline for Greg to become less relaxed. He wasn't happy about all the pressure they were putting on him. He was on the verge of making maybe the biggest decision of his life up to that point—what do do—and instead of helping him, they were making it harder.

One night, he and a friend of his from Carl, Minnesota, bought four six-packs of Grain Belt at the Sidetrack Tap. Wally thought it was for a party, he didn't know they were going to drink it themselves.

Parked in the friend's pink Olds beside the Great Northern tracks across from the elevator, it took them only three hours to finish off the supply, during which they became as relaxed as two dishrags, but when the friend, whose name Greg had now forgotten, saw Gary and LeRoy drive by, he said, "Cops! Oh, God!" and headed the other way fast, with his headlights off to avoid notice. Greg didn't think it was a good idea to drive so fast in the dark but he didn't know how to phrase this.

They didn't go far. Where the road turns left, they went straight, into the lumberyard. Dark shapes whizzed past like in a bad dream, and then one came straight at them, and when they woke up sometime later, there were two 3 × 8s in the car. Two boards sticking in the windshield and out the rear window, between the two of them.

Revival

Both of them had bad headaches, but not from the lumber. It had slammed into the car in the one exact spot it could've without killing them instantly. They weren't scratched. Not even a sliver. They sat in the front seat staring straight ahead and tears ran down their cheeks. They climbed out and put their arms around each other and tried to walk. They sat down on the ground. The sun was coming up. There were two boats on the lake. Light pastel clouds hung in the sky. The friend said, "I'm going to do something good with my life." Greg didn't know what he was going to do, but he wanted to yell to the fishermen and tell them that he was okay.

On the same spot where those two got a snootful, in May 1942 the middle Olson boy parked under the cottonwood tree in his dad's Ford pickup with a waitress from Mom and Dad's Cafe named Tina, whom he had taken to see James Cagney in *The Fighting 69th* that night at the Alhambra (renamed the Victory) and whom he had admired for weeks for the blouses she wore, which were the lowest-cut in those parts. They talked about her boyfriend for a while—he had been shipped to Hawaii—and then the boy reached for the gold medallion that hung from a long chain around her neck, curious to see what it said. When his fingers touched her skin, he saw a flash and felt a rumble as the four-story grain elevator a hundred yards away across the tracks went up in an explosion that was felt all the way north to Brainerd. The historic elevator, the pride of Wobegon and its prosperity, burst in a pillar of flame five hundred feet in the air, and jagged chunks of timber fell like bombs on the town. She jumped out and dove under the truck, and he sat looking at the shattered windshield, knowing that he was the cause of it all. "I did it," he said. "It was me."

Two days later, the American heroes of Corregidor surrendered and the Philippines fell to the Japanese.

———

"Anything that ever happened to me is happening to other people," says Clarence. "Somewhere in the world right now, a kid is looking at something and thinking, 'I'm going to remember this for the rest of my life.' And it's the same thing that I looked at forty years ago, whatever it was."

If that is true and our lives are being lived over and over by others, I don't know if I should laugh or cry.

If that is true, somewhere a boy rides next to his father in a car, his eyes level with the top of the dashboard, and pulls back slightly on the window crank which lowers the wing flaps and makes the Ford rise toward the clouds. He tests this principle with his right hand out the window, feeling the lift. He sees that the clouds are following this car; so is the sun. The car is under his power and is the center of the world. The button on the glove compartment fires two machine guns mounted over the fenders. There is also a flame thrower. He can wipe out anybody he sees, such as older boys up ahead playing football in Potvin's front yard who recently laughed at him. The plane zooms past them, *zoom!*, and silent

guns fire and that whole gang falls dead, he doesn't
bother to look back, he knows.

———————

Somewhere a boy eats his bran flakes and his dad
says, "I had to get up in the night to get me a blanket.
It was kinda chilly last night."

"*Ja*," says his mother, "I don't know but what we
might get another frost."

"*Ja*, I remember it was '57, wasn't it, or '58, we got
a frost around now."

"Maybe we oughta lay down straw around those
strawberries."

"*Ja*, you never can tell."

He eats his bran flakes in silence, gritting his teeth.
Why do they always talk about weather and say the
same dumb things?

"What's the matter witcha? Cat got your tongue?"

"*Noth*ing."

This boy is a good reader; his parents are proud of
him. ("Watcha reading there?" "*Noth*ing.") He has
now come to the end of the Flambeau Family Series,
all twelve books, some of which he read twice, trying
to hold off on *The Flambeaus and the Case of the
Temple Emeralds*, but at last was forced to finish,
and now faces a life with no further adventures.
Emile and Eileen don't talk about late frost; their
Manhattan penthouse is well above the frost line;
they talk about ideas, about books and music, and,
yes, even sex, because they are intelligent and literate
and treat their son, Tony, as a mature person. "Oh,
Tony darling, while you're up, would you fix me a

martini?" Eileen called from the balcony. "Have it in
a jiff, Eileen," the young man replied. This sort of
thing never happens in his house. "Oh, Tony darling,
I just had the most wonderful idea! Let's go to Paris,
just the three of us—it's so beautiful this time of
year!" Beauty is a big thing to the Flambeaus; they fill
their lives with it, unlike his folks, whose lives are
filled with dread—"*Ja*, you never can tell": their
slogan, they ought to have it chiseled on their tomb-
stone: "You never can tell." *Why can't we be more
like the Flambeaus?* We couldn't be exactly like them,
of course—Emile's Nobel Prize in medicine, Eileen's former career on the Broadway stage—but couldn't we
capture some of their grace and eat breakfast this fine
May morning and talk of something other than frost?

Somewhere a boy has spread a map on the hood of
the old green Ford and is studying it with the help of
his old man. The boy is wearing a white shirt and
new tan corduroys; in the backseat are a suitcase and
two heavy cardboard boxes, their tops folded shut.
He's going to take the back road to the blacktop and
then straight south and pick up Highway 52 and go
through St. Cloud, though the old man thinks he'd be
better off heading east and then south on 10, or
taking 52 to 152 and then South, either way avoiding
St. Cloud, and just north of the Cities get on the Belt
Line, avoiding the Cities, and swing east and south to
12 and then on to Chicago. "You go through the
Cities, you can get hung up for hours," his old man
says. The boy listens, folds the map, walks around
back of the house, and gives the woman who is weed-

ing the radishes a little peck on the cheek. Shakes the
man's hand, gets in the car, backs out, waves, and is
gone. He thinks he has avoided the Cities for much
too long now, and he is going to drive straight
through the center of them. His dad plans trips like
he was crossing enemy lines, skirting the main forces,
looking for gaps to break through into open country.
Outside of the town, on the back road, the boy guns
the Ford down the hill past Hochstetters' and up the
long incline. Stones bang on the floorboard. The car
leaps ahead at the crest and barrels toward Sunnyvale
School, where two small boys sit in the shade on the
west side. "Fifty-six Ford!" one yells. He is now
ahead, four cars to two, on identification. The other
boy waves at the Ford, which does not wave back.
He is behind, two waves to three. As the Ford flies
past trailing a cloud of dust, he stands and squeezes
off an expert burst from his machine gun, hitting the
gas tank, which blows up, enveloping the car in a ball
of orange flame.

Somewhere a man gets into his Buick in a blizzard
even though he can barely see across the yard to the
barn and his wife and child are pleading with him to
please not to go town. On the county road, crashing
into drifts like ocean waves, he realizes how foolish
his trip is but he plows four miles to the Sidetrack
Tap, runs in and buys a carton of Pall Malls. "An
emergency run, huh?" says Wally, the old kidder.
"No," he says, lying, "I was in town anyway so I
thought I might as well stock up." It's quiet in town,
but a mile south of there, the wind comes up and

suddenly he can't see anything. He is damp with sweat. He can't see the ditches, can't see the hood ornament. He drives slower, staring ahead for the slightest clues of road, until there is none—no sky, no horizon, only dazzling white—so he opens his door and leans out and looks for tire tracks: hanging from the steering wheel, leaning way down, his face a couple feet from the ground, hoping that nobody is driving toward him and doing likewise. Then, as the car slips off the road, he realizes that the track he is following is the track of his own left front tire heading into the deep ditch. The car eases down into the snow, and he squeezes out the window and climbs up onto the road. He is not too far from his neighbor's house. He can see it almost, and the woods. A massed army of corn stands in the snowy field. Visibility is not so bad as in the car, where his heavy breathing was fogging the glass. He's about a quarter-mile from home. The cigarettes, however, must be sitting on Wally's counter. They certainly aren't in the car. *A pretty dumb trip*. Town was a long way to go in a blizzard for the pleasure of coming back home. He could have driven his car straight to the ditch and saved everyone the worry. But what a lucky man. Some luck lies in not getting what you thought you wanted but getting what you have, which once you have it you may be smart enough to see is what you would have wanted had you known. He takes deep breaths and the cold air goes to his brain and makes him more sensible. He starts out on the short walk to the house where people love him and will be happy to see his face.